WINDSWEPT

ANNABELLE
MCCORMACK

Published by Annabelle McCormack

www.annabellemccormack.com

For Patrick—the love of my life, my best friend, and my constant source of support. Thanks for making my dreams come true. And remember: if it's ever a book with pictures, you have to read it.

ALSO BY ANNABELLE MCCORMACK

A Zephyr Rising: A Windswept Prequel Novella (Available July 12, 2022: Preorder Now)

Sands of Sirocco: The Windswept Saga Book 2 (Available September 27, 2022: Preorder Now)

To find out the latest about my new releases, please sign up for my newsletter! I love hearing from readers and have some great offers lined up for my subscribers.

PREFACE

1917: World War One. The intense battles on the Western Front in France have reached a stalemate. Russia is in the midst of civil war and about to withdraw from the Allied effort. Meanwhile, the British Army has made progress battling the Ottoman Turks up the northern coast of the Sinai Peninsula, from the Suez Canal in Egypt to Gaza in Palestine. The objective: to capture Jerusalem.

In March 1917, the British offensive is halted at Gaza. Another attempt to take the city in April proves to be a catastrophic failure with huge casualties. The advance stalls.

Elsewhere in Arabia, Captain T.E. Lawrence makes valuable progress for the British working with local Arab leaders who have been promised an independent Arab state after the war.

They have already been betrayed.

Under the Sykes–Picot Agreement, the British and the French have already secretly arranged to divide the Arabian Peninsula between themselves after the war. What's more, Zionist leaders both in London and in the NILI Spy Network in

Jerusalem have been promised British support for the establishment of a Jewish homeland after the war.

Overextended in their promises and on the brink of facing the full weight of the German army on the Western Front, the Allies are on the brink of collapse. Then hope comes in April 1917 when the United States enters the war on the Allied side.

But mobilizing the American troops will take time. The Germans and Ottomans know that they must strike, and strike hard ... and they have only a limited window of time in which to do it.

WINDSWEPT

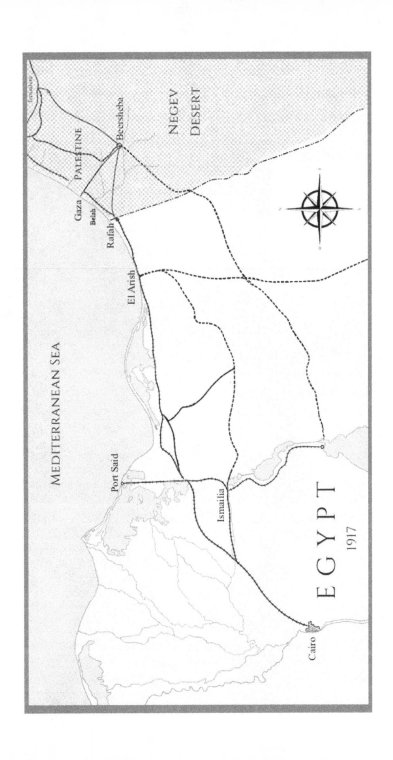

PART I

DEIR EL BELAH, PALESTINE

CHAPTER ONE

MAY, 1917

*W*eary of death, Ginger Whitman couldn't seem to drag herself away from it.

The dim light of dawn shrouded the path winding down the side of the craggy hill. Her boots slid on sand and rock as she loosened the clasp of her short red uniform cape, wiping the sweat on her neck. The stench of decay curdled in her throat.

A half-dozen soldiers worked. Their shovels scraped into sand with a thumping cadence. Each toss of earth devoured the broken bodies in the pits beside them. Some nurses called her foolish for coming here every morning. But who else would come to pay respects? She couldn't recognize the dead faces from her vantage point, but their voices haunted her dreams. Lives cut short by the unending, brutal tide of war.

The chaplain stood nearby, praying. She bowed her head. So many lives she couldn't help save. The bodies of Ottoman Turks fallen on the British line received a similar hasty burial nearby. In death, the heaps of bodies were indistinguishable, save for the remnants of uniforms. Death made equals of cowards and heroes, friend or foe. As the war had progressed, the British government enacted sober policies for burying enemy dead. The government had more hope their enemies would return the favor than she did.

She lifted her hand to her nose, the rotten scent stoking her ire. Her father predicted when she'd joined that she'd learn to hate. He'd called her naïve, claimed when the pleasantries of polite society vanished, she would understand the safety she'd abandoned. He hadn't been entirely wrong—but what he labeled as safety had been innocence cloaked in the privilege of her family's wealth and status. Three years of lost innocence tormented her soul like a festering wound.

She muttered a prayer for the Turkish soldiers too.

As she kept watch, the grey hills transformed to vibrant yellows and baked white stone, dotted with verdant brush. The hillsides lush with vegetation, adjacent to the sea, draped Palestine with unexpected beauty. The now-impenetrable town of Gaza, where the Ottoman Turks held their ground through two costly battles, loomed in the distance. The British advance had stalled. The longer they stayed, Ginger detected an increasing sense of hopelessness in the men she treated.

A sharp sting pricked her forearm. She crushed the mosquito feasting there. She scratched the red welt—one of many. With May's heat growing stronger by the day, pests swarmed in hordes. If her mother knew the state of her skin, she'd faint.

Days before Ginger's debut into society, a blemish had erupted on her chin. Her mother had directed servants to comb the whole of Somerset for a poultice to make it disappear. The days when those things seemed important were laughable now. The world had turned upside down and, along with it, her carefully groomed role. Her mother's letters still brimmed with ideas for Ginger's planned wedding after the war. The thought of a wedding felt like a tether to another life.

Distant gunfire crackled across the ridges of the sand dunes. The troops entrenched a few miles away were starting early. Or some unfortunate soul had risked a cigarette and found a sniper's quick response. She hoped she was wrong. Quiet resumed, and she checked her wristwatch. Dread crept up her esophagus. She'd rather stay around the burial pits than return today.

She climbed the steep hill and stopped to regain her breath, tucking strands of her flame-red hair behind her ears and under her cap. She looked out over the tranquility of the rippling Mediterranean, then turned. Tens of thousands of horses, mules, and camels rested on the plain alongside men waiting for the chance to prove their worth. Or join the mounting piles of bones in the desert.

British blood soaked these lands, and for what? She scowled. Oil fields and the Suez Canal, she'd been told. When she'd been on leave at her family's home in Cairo at Christmas, she'd questioned her father about the rationale behind the British push into Jerusalem. Despite his work at the Foreign Office, he failed to provide her with a satisfactory answer. The British had secured the Canal two years earlier, and she hadn't heard of oil in Jerusalem. The leadership in London had never dressed wounds or held soldiers' hands as they wept over lost limbs. Anger coursed through her.

As pink and yellow hues emerged on the horizon, the railroad tracks and road connecting the troops to the white canvas hospital tents shimmered like a river. She wished she could watch the sunrise. But today she had to answer for her temper and her weak attempt to see justice done.

To think she faced censure because she'd saved a life. The wrong life.

Just one week earlier she'd been ordered by a doctor to leave a soldier to die. *"We can't waste time on him when others are more likely to survive,"* the doctor had said. She'd disagreed and treated the soldier anyway. Now she faced a disciplinary hearing for it.

The rims of her eyes burned. Protocol didn't matter if she forgot her humanity. James wanted her to apologize. A wise, penitent response. But she was tired of pretending the rules always made sense.

"Ginger! On your way back already?" Beatrice ambled toward her, dressed in full uniform.

"I thought you were still sleeping." The sight of her friend set her nerves at ease.

"I heard you slip out. I thought I would come and offer moral support." Beatrice scanned Ginger's face. "Did you not sleep well?"

"I spent the night regurgitating excuses."

"You know you did nothing wrong. Who cares if you have to apologize?" Beatrice squeezed her hand.

A few feet away, a sunbird chirped at their approach and darted from pale-purple flowers dotting the brush. Sunlight caught its black feathers and gave them an iridescent shimmer as it took flight. An unexpected lightness filled Ginger as it soared among the sandy hills. "I suppose so."

"James thinks they won't take any further disciplinary action against you if you apologize. I overheard him discussing it with the matron last night."

Oh James. His inability to help himself was both endearing and irritating. "I rather wish he wouldn't."

Beatrice smiled. "I think it's sweet of him to intercede."

"Yes, but there are enough whispers implying I get away with too much because of his influence. That he's the only reason I'm at the clearing station."

Beatrice lifted her skirt as they started the steep descent toward the railroad tracks. "You do have an advantage between your family and your fiancé. No use denying it. And aren't you here, partially, for him?"

Beatrice's frank honesty wasn't always the easiest to digest, though Ginger appreciated it. She sometimes sensed a hesitation in other nurses to treat her as a peer, despite their equal rank. She'd shared too much about her past with Beatrice to deny the truth, at any rate. And Beatrice still did her the favor of mailing back the unopened letters that arrived each week from the man Ginger's father had wanted her to marry instead of James.

A screech and hiss announced the first train of the day approaching the casualty clearing station. Ginger and Beatrice darted across the tracks. Safely on the other side, they slowed. The empty train cars crawled past them through billowing smoke, about to stop at the railhead. Acrid cinders burned their nostrils.

At the bottom of the next hill, a few crude huts stood beside an enormous stone well, surrounded by a copse of tall palms. Ginger had never understood how vital these wells were until her work in the desert. A soldier she'd treated in Port Said had told her horror stories of entire regiments going half mad with thirst, digging into the sand in their desperation, only to fall victim to the heat.

Fortunately, the British found working wells all over Belah. Despite the abundance, the army insisted upon heavily chlorinating it, ruining their tea. The huts, with their thatched palm-branch roofs, were crumbling structures of stone and mud. The army had little use for them and most of them stood empty.

A strange guttural noise came from one stone hut as they neared it. Ginger and Beatrice stopped, exchanging glances.

"Probably a private in his cups," Beatrice said, her voice dry.

"And if it's not?"

Beatrice tugged at her arm. "If it's not, we still need to hurry along."

Unconvinced, Ginger broke away toward the entrance of the bigger hut, an arch without a door. She stuck her head in, resting one hand on the shoulder strap of her kitbag. Her eyes settled on a man's booted foot.

"What on earth …?"

The foot shifted, then she heard a moan.

Ginger stepped inside.

"What is it?" Beatrice asked.

Ginger's eyes adjusted to the dim light in the hut.

The man curled on the ground was breathing raggedly, and blood soaked his shredded shirtfront. The instinct to rush to his side faded when she saw his uniform.

A Turk.

Panic rose in her chest. His serious injuries didn't mean he couldn't attack her. Even the British soldiers did, occasionally, mad with pain. "It's … an injured soldier."

She approached him, scanning the ground. She didn't see any weapons, but he might have one hidden beneath him. His hands trembled, pressed against his chest. He didn't seem to notice her. His eyes were closed. What was she thinking? He was the enemy. She should report him. She already faced a disciplinary hearing for taking matters into her own hands.

She recognized some wounds on his arms—the unmistakable gouges left by barbed wire. Mud and sand filled his wounds. A nasty scratch was painful, this appeared excruciating. The poor man.

"It's a Turk," Beatrice gasped behind her. "Ginger, get away from him."

Ginger flinched. It would be simple enough, turning him over to the military police and walking away. She had her hearing.

But this man might die any moment.

She sank to her knees beside him, her stomach in knots. Gnats and flies swarmed around him. In this heat, they didn't distinguish between live and dead flesh. If he wasn't cleaned, he'd have maggots under his skin within hours. She pulled away the tatters of his jacket. His arms were heavy and uncooperative. One blood-soaked pant leg revealed a bullet's entry and exit wounds.

Ginger pressed her fingers to his slow, faint pulse. His neck and forehead burned with fever, his skin was slick. His eyes remained closed. Spittle bubbled by his lips. She turned his arms over, where the wounds continued. One, deep and close to his brachial artery, appeared to have a makeshift tourniquet over it, but it needed replacing.

"What are you doing?" Beatrice's voice rose in pitch.

"For Pete's sake, he's not a threat. If we don't help him, he'll die." Precious minutes would determine if he lived. She'd treat him first, then turn him in. She had most of what she needed in her kitbag, but she lacked medicine. Ginger faced Beatrice. "Go to the triage station and get morphine. Quickly."

Beatrice looked horrified. "What about your hearing?"

"His life is at stake, for goodness' sake." She removed cloth strips from her kitbag and met Beatrice's wide blue eyes. "Hurry, please."

Beatrice nodded and whirled around and left. Ginger wrapped a new tourniquet over his arm with the fabric strips. Carefully, she discarded the blood-soaked one. Her hands were sticky with blood by the time she finished.

She elevated his arm over his head and stood, wiping her hands on her apron. The man's eyelids fluttered, his limbs shaking. He was a tall, broad man, easily over six feet.

A satchel lay beside his body. If he had any identifying papers, they'd be in there. A few personal items were inside—a cigarette case, a lighter, and … a Bible? Most Turkish soldiers were Muslim. Further inspection revealed a stamp from the YMCA in Cairo. And the text was in English.

She stared at the Bible.

It made no sense.

His eyes opened, dark irises darting through the slits. He found her gaze and grabbed her by the forearm. "Help me," he rasped. "Help me, please, Sister."

Her jaw dropped. His English was perfect. And he'd even used the British term 'sister' rather than 'nurse.'

The incongruity furthered her unease. She scooted away. "Who are you?"

"Ah … Ahmed." His tongue seemed to stick to the roof of his mouth. "I'm known as Ahmed Bayrak. You must help me."

"I don't understand. Are you British?"

He shook his head. "An ally."

"But your uniform—"

"A d-disguise to spy on the Ottomans. They discovered me." He moistened his lips.

Could it be true? If he was an ally, it was her duty to help him, not just a wish. A knot in her shoulders unwound.

She offered him her canteen. Water poured from his mouth as he drank. "Only a little. If you've been without, it will make you ill." She pulled the canteen back.

"Help me. I have important information for my c-contact."

She wanted to believe him. But it wasn't up to her to discover the truth to his words, much as she wanted it to be so. "I'll treat your wounds." She chose her words carefully. "And give you over to the military police. They'll be able to help you better than I."

He grasped her wrist. "No, you must not."

She stared at his hand, her pulse accelerating. What was taking Beatrice so long?

"Forgive me." He dropped his hand. "You cannot. The enemy h-hunts me. He will find me here."

She dug into her kitbag for the whistle, just in case. "There are no Turks here. You're in a British clearing station in Belah." Her fingertips collided with the cool metal, and her fist closed around it.

His eyes widened. "There's a spy in British intelligence. A traitor. He hunts me." He retrieved a bottle from his pocket with a shaking hand. "Take this. Bury it. Bury it. Please."

She hesitated and released the whistle. She took the bottle and rolled it in her palm. The glass was amber and lightweight. What was in it of such importance? "You want me to bury this now?"

"P-please. I beg you. It must stay safe. It's for Cairo Intelligence."

She wasn't about to dig into the hard, compacted dirt floor with her bare hands. In the corner of the hut a loose stone at the joint of the ground and the wall caught her eye. She pulled it out and tucked the bottle behind it.

She straightened as voices drew closer. Beatrice poked her head through the entrance. "I brought James."

Oh no.

James hunkered down past the entrance. He adjusted his glasses.

Ginger's shoulders hunched with embarrassment. *"I'll instruct Sister Thornton to fetch me if you ever get the idea to do something like this again,"* James had threatened when the news of her censure reached him last time.

"James, I—"

James crossed his arms. "I was waiting in the Mess for you. What are you doing? This is absolute madness."

Ahmed spoke again. "Thevshi. I must find Lieutenant Thevshi."

Beatrice and James both appeared surprised. Ginger hurried to Ahmed. "Where can I find him? Is he here?"

Ahmed shook his head. "No—he's with Cairo Intelligence. Send a wire. He'll come."

His words gave her an odd sense of hope. "Can Lieutenant Thevshi confirm your identity?"

James approached, his gaze fixed on Ahmed. "What's this about?"

Ahmed's shoulders heaved with exhaustion.

"He says he's a British ally, not a Turk," Ginger said.

Despite his obvious exasperation, James's tone was gentle. "The brass will sort him, dearest."

"But he says he'll be exposed to a traitor in British intelligence if we turn him over."

"But of course." James appeared unconvinced.

Ahmed's trembling increased, lines of pain etched on his features. "Did you at least bring the morphine?" Ginger asked Beatrice.

Beatrice cocked an eyebrow. "I did. I'm not useless." She held it out, along with a syringe.

Ginger sat and prepared the medicine. "He's gravely wounded, but he might survive with treatment."

James adjusted his collar. "What about your hearing? You'll be late. And this won't do you any favors. I won't have you sacrificing yourself for this man."

Ginger pinched the flesh of Ahmed's uninjured bicep between her fingers and injected him. "I won't ask permission to treat him. Report me if you like."

"I didn't say I'd report you." A flush came to James's pale cheeks. "I'm not going to."

She'd counted on that. "Good." She put the syringe down and reached for antiseptic. "Are you going to help me or not?"

Ahmed's labored breathing intensified. "You must believe

me." His words came slurred. "The O-ottomans are ..."— another rasped breath—"... shell the railhead. — know their plans ..."

James pulled Ginger away. "Come with me." He tilted his head toward Beatrice. "You too."

They exited into the sunshine. Ginger faced them. "What if he's telling the truth?"

James put a gentle hand on her shoulder. "And what if he's taking advantage of your kindness?"

Beatrice stepped beside Ginger. "He speaks English awfully well for a Turk."

Ginger gave her a thankful glance. Beatrice was too practical not to be fair. "If he's telling the truth, turning him over might get him killed. He's given us a way to verify his identity. Can't we at least treat him until we've found out?"

Beatrice appealed to James. "What if we put him in isolation? He won't be able to leave from there easily. And you could assign Ginger or me to attend to him in the meantime, to limit his contact with anyone else."

"He won't be able to leave. He's too injured." Ginger squeezed James's hand. "It isn't a terrible plan. Please."

James hesitated, then sighed. "Only if you go to your hearing. Now. Beatrice and I will see to his care. If you're late, it will increase your chances of a harsh punishment."

Beatrice nodded encouragingly. "We can do it."

Despite her reluctance, Ginger stepped back. "Start with his right arm. It needs immediate stitching. There's a wound on his torso that also needs debridement. And a gunshot through the left thigh."

James's eyes hinted amusement. "I am a surgeon, you know."

"Oh, and we should take his personal effects into safekeeping. They're beside him."

"I will. My quarters aren't subject to inspection from the

matron like yours are. Now go." James smiled. "Get on with it and make your apologies, Lady Virginia."

Ginger threw her arms around his neck. "I told you never to call me that." She kissed his cheek. "Thank you both. Wish me luck." She hurried toward the main path. The encounter with Ahmed had rattled her confidence about the hearing. An apology would be a bald-faced lie. She wanted to face the surgeon who'd reported her and give him a piece of her mind instead.

The matron of nurses, Miss Walsh, approached the well. "Sister Whitman. I've been searching everywhere for you. The commanding officer is waiting for you."

Ginger stumbled. The matron hadn't seen her leave the hut, had she? Heat crept up her neck. "Ah—yes. I came for the morning burials. Why don't you walk with me?"

The matron hesitated.

What if she had seen? She would never put up with them helping the soldier. At last, the matron fell into step beside her, and Ginger's shoulders relaxed.

They had just reached the officers' quarters, when a faint boom traveled from the Turkish stronghold at Gaza. A whistling sound cut the air followed by a fantastic crash nearby. Ginger grabbed the matron and dove off the path. Another deafening boom shook the earth.

Ginger covered her head with her arms. She rolled over and checked on the matron. "Are you hurt?"

The matron shook her head. "No ... no."

Ginger helped the older woman up. She dusted herself off, her ears ringing.

A black plume of smoke rose a few hundred yards away. The sound came again—an echoing boom, the screeching cry of a shell hurtling through the air, then a thunderous crash.

A medic ran past them. "Run for cover, Sisters! They're shelling the railhead and within range of the hospital tents!"

The matron twisted her hands. "Don't they know we aren't soldiers here?"

Ahmed's warning.

A wave of nausea crested in her as a rumble began on the nearby plain, the stampede of camels, horses, and men trying to escape each intermittent shell.

The wounded in the hospital tents needed immediate evacuation. Ginger ran toward the tents closest to the railhead.

Behind the row of tents, the train raced away, its whistle shrieking.

The matron caught her by the arm. "Sister Whitman, you will get yourself killed!" She pulled her back. "We must find shelter, immediately. Back toward headquarters!"

"But the men—" She wouldn't abandon them.

"Leave the soldiers to it. It won't do anyone any good if you're dead."

A high-pitched wail neared, like the strident cry of a thousand cicadas in the heat of a summer night. Yet it was empty, lifeless. A moment later, a shell tore through a hospital tent. A scream caught in her throat, shock rippling through her limbs as the cries of wounded men filled the air.

CHAPTER TWO

*T*he medical officer standing before her spoke, but Ginger only heard the ringing in her ears. She blinked, her mind unfocused, and tasted the grit of sand in her mouth. Beyond the MO, a pit had replaced the dispensary tent, trapping men in the rubble.

The men. She'd been trying to help the men.

A quick gust of noise rushed her, her ears discerning every decibel they'd blocked before, and the cacophony overwhelmed her. She stood, unsteady.

James.

The horrific scene in front of her seemed calm compared to the nightmarish imaginings pressing into her mind. He'd been within the strike zone. Beatrice too. If anything happened to them, it would be her fault. They wouldn't have been there if she hadn't insisted.

The MO frowned under his thin moustache. He set a firm hand on her shoulder. "You stay on that bench, Sister Whitman. You've had a shock."

He eased her toward it. She pushed through the fog in her

mind. "I have a duty to help these injured men. I'm of no use to anyone sitting on a bench."

A rousing cry came from the debris as rescuers freed another wounded man trapped in rope and canvas and stone. Her stomach dropped. If the hut had collapsed on James and Beatrice, they'd have been crushed.

She extricated herself from the MO's grip. "Please let me go."

The MO scowled. "Take it up with your matron."

Ginger whirled around. Where had Miss Walsh gone? The moments after the shelling remained a blur. "Where is she?"

The MO pointed toward a hospital tent. "Admissions ward. We're being flooded with wounded."

She rushed toward the clearing station wards. She didn't see any other tents missing, but it offered little comfort. The rubble now housed their precious medical supplies.

Ginger neared the admissions tent. The matron would be busy. Maybe she should take the opportunity to check on James and Beatrice.

"Sister! Water, please, Sister, please."

A group of men lay on stretchers on the ground, waiting for admission. Sweat glistened from their skin, the morning sun merciless. One man lifted a bandaged arm. "Sister!"

Ginger found a water station and brought him a cup. Sand caked his face, making the whites of his eyes appear unnatural. He slurped as he drank, his appearance gaunt, haggard. These "men" were younger than her by three or four years, often barely over twenty.

She waved away nagging flies and lowered the cup. He wiped his mouth. "How long they going to keep us out here?"

"I'm certain they'll move you soon, Private. We try not to roast our Tommies."

"Sister, can I have some water too?" the soldier beside him asked.

She gritted her teeth. Her irritation at his request wasn't fair, and she was glad he couldn't read her thoughts. These thirsty, injured men could no more help their needs than she could her growing worry for James and Beatrice.

The soldier took the cup with both hands, his expression grateful. "They're pigs, shelling the hospital."

"It's the clearing station's fault," another soldier said from a few feet away. "They put these tents too close to the dumps and artillery. You think ol' Jacko won't take advantage? They don't care if they hurt women and noncombatants."

The men continued talking and Ginger's mind wandered. She should have heeded Ahmed's words and warned her superiors about the possibility of the bombardment. Now, even more than before, she believed his story might be true.

No matter how much she wanted to tear herself away, each time she turned, another patient called. Wounds needed bandages, shell-shocked men needed attention. Ambulances poured in, both lorries and the camels outfitted with stretchers on either side of their humps.

She lost herself in the grueling work, trying not to imagine nightmarish scenarios. At last, a figure appeared beside her. *James.* She restrained a cry, her throat tightening. He was safe. Her fingers slipped while she sutured a patient's arm. She steadied herself and held the cut together with her left hand.

James bent down beside her. "Those are nice, neat stitches, Sister Whitman."

Her eyes fill with tears at his gentle tone. She blinked rapidly, still focused on her stitching. "I learned from an excellent surgeon." She knotted the thread and cut it, then wiped her hands.

She straightened. Dried blood smeared his disheveled clothes. James folded her into his arms, and she rested her cheek against his chest. "I was so worried."

"As was I. I'm sorry I couldn't find you sooner. Sister Thornton and I finished treating Ahmed and moved him to isolation in the retention ward. But I had to jump into surgery from there."

Her jaw slackened with relief, her mind lighter. Her decision to stay here had been right. The retention ward would be suitable for Ahmed. As the place they kept the most gravely wounded men, it would be quiet, free of disturbance. "Then they're safe—Beatrice and Ahmed?"

James adjusted his glasses and nodded. "The chap has a chance of pulling through. You found him in time. Sister Thornton went to the evacuation ward to prepare patients for transport." He placed his hands on her shoulders. "I feared you'd been in the path of the shells. Were you safe?"

James usually maintained his distance while they were in front of patients and other medical personnel. He must have been truly worried. "I was on my way to the hearing but came this way to help the men."

"Given the circumstances, I'm certain they will postpone your hearing. The higher-ups have more to worry about at the moment." His hands fell to his sides. "I understand they'll be convening the officers and sisters in the Mess this evening."

"Do you think they'll move the CCS further back on the line?"

"I'm uncertain. Doctor Clemens suggested the Royal Army Medical Corps may move the nurses. Perhaps even to the hospital at El Arish." James steered her out of earshot of the patients. "We need to move on confirming Ahmed's identity. I imagine you haven't had time to send that wire?"

If the RAMC moved the nurses to El Arish, neither Beatrice nor Ginger would be available to care for Ahmed. It would expose them. Even with Ahmed's story confirmed, all three of them would face censure—or worse—for having acted without permission. An unsettled feeling gripped her. "I shouldn't have involved us in this."

James's light-blue eyes were pensive. "I wouldn't have agreed to it if I didn't think his claims had merit—more so now with the shelling. But having him here could be a danger to everyone. He's too injured to escape, but we should be cautious. Find that Thevshi fellow, if he exists."

And if Thevshi didn't exist? Or they couldn't locate him? She didn't know how to contact him. She'd have to ask Ahmed for clearer instructions. Ginger bit her lip. "It might be wise to send a wire to my brother. I can ask him to come out here—tell him it's urgent." Henry's work within Cairo Intelligence's Arab Bureau meant he might even know Lieutenant Thevshi.

"I think that's wise." Tenderness shone in his eyes. "I wish I could stay with you longer, but I must return to the operating theater."

They parted, and Ginger returned to her work. The calmer feeling that had first struck her when she'd seen James had diminished with their conversation. She didn't know when she'd get back to Ahmed. Each passing moment prolonged the danger. But involving her brother would be a relief. Henry would know what to do.

The sun had started a deep descent by the time Ginger came off her shift. She'd worked for thirteen hours straight, without a break for tea or meals. As she trudged toward the retention ward, her feet throbbed in her desert boots. Blisters on the tops of her feet ached. The thought of taking the boots off was wonderful.

She found Ahmed in the corner of the hospital tent. She pulled a privacy curtain around him.

Ahmed's eyes were open. His head shifted toward her.

He murmured and pain etched his face as he attempted to sit up.

"No, no." Ginger bent down by his side. "Lie still. You'll hurt yourself." She poured water and offered it. He sipped, and his eyes closed once again.

She pressed her hand to his face. His skin still burned. "How are you feeling?"

His eyes opened, his pupils dilated. "Am I dying?" There was no hint of irony or need for reassurance. The way he asked left the impression he wanted a clear, blunt answer.

Ginger sat by him. "You're very ill. The doctor treating you —Doctor Clark—thinks you may survive, but it's never certain. We can't do much if infection sets in too deeply." She found a thermometer. "Place this in your mouth, under your tongue. Your fever is still high."

The mercury in the tube rose higher and higher. When it leveled off, she checked it in the fading light. 104.6. Dangerous.

She dipped a clean cloth into a water basin by the bed, wrung it, and placed it on his forehead. "I must replace some of your dressings."

He closed his eyes, his eyelids twitching. "Thevshi. Have you sent for him?"

"Not yet. I don't know how to contact him. Where should I send a message?"

His face relaxed under the cool cloth. "A wire ... Cairo Intelligence. D-don't use your name. Use 'Dragonfly.' He'll ... know ... I-I've arrived."

"Dragonfly?" Ginger frowned. "What does that mean? How will he know to find me so I may direct him to you?"

"It's a code ... it means something has gone wrong. Don't speak it." Ahmed licked his chapped lips. "Thevshi will look for me. The less you're involved the safer you'll be."

He mumbled. Ginger listened as she prepared new dressings. Another language? Not Arabic. She knew enough to get by.

"Turkish?" she whispered. "You must use caution. Someone might overhear."

His head shook. "Hebrew." He exhaled. "I was praying."

She concealed her surprise. "You're Jewish?"

He nodded.

Her father had always discussed the politics of the Middle East in front of her, long before the war. She knew of the Yishuv, the group of Jewish Zionists who had settled in Ottoman Syria and Palestine for decades now, to return their people to Jerusalem. But the Yishuv was also pro-Ottoman and had sided with the Turks during the war.

Why would a Jewish man be working for the British? "Are you part of the Yishuv?"

Ahmed met her gaze, his eyes red. "My people are allies to the British. They call us 'the Operation.'" He gripped her wrist. "Sister—if I do die, Lieutenant Thevshi must obtain the bottle I gave you. And my bag. He'll know what to do."

"I assure you, we'll keep it perfectly safe."

His fingers tightened. "No one but Thevshi can know. They are more important than either of us."

Her wrist hurt from his grasp. She placed as calm of a hand on his as she could. "I won't say anything to anyone else." She frowned. "But why me, Ahmed? Surely it's a risk to trust me if it's that important."

He released her wrist. "No more than the risk you've taken with me. You have goodness in you. I trust you."

She glanced away. How many times this morning had she considered turning him in to the proper authorities? Worse still, she planned to send a wire to her brother while contacting Lieutenant Thevshi. If Henry arrived before Thevshi, she would tell him everything about Ahmed.

Ahmed couldn't know how easily lying came to her. Even her life here gave an impression of a person she wasn't. Others would return to difficulties after their time in service, lives forever made harder due to this war. She would return to an estate with servants and never have to lift a finger to do hard labor again.

She was many things, but she wasn't certain *good* was one of them.

CHAPTER THREE

Ginger rushed along the path of the clearing station, raising the long hem of her skirt as she ran. She would be late, blast it. The trip to the telegraph station at HQ took too long. She slowed as she drew closer to the Mess, catching her breath. She smoothed her hands over her torso, straightened her shoulders, and slipped in.

The tent offered the medical officers and sisters a place to eat and convene for indoor recreation. Now, the crowded tables left standing room only. In the center of the tent stood a few officers she didn't recognize. A colonel addressed them.

She edged along the side, avoiding the curious glances leveled in her direction as she joined the other nurses. Miss Walsh scanned her. Ginger offered a polite smile. Wonderful. No doubt she looked disheveled. She hadn't had time to change into a clean uniform after tending to Ahmed, unlike the sisters who had gone to their quarters after their shifts had ended.

Where was James? She spotted him seated at a table of the other RAMC doctors. His eyes flitted to hers and then refocused on the colonel.

"Did I miss anything important?" Ginger asked Sister Hilda Thomas, standing beside her.

Hilda nodded, her expression somber. "A curfew for us sisters, after dark until sunrise. They're also thinking about moving us to El Arish."

Ginger groaned inwardly. The curfew would be problematic. She didn't have much time to spare to dedicate to Ahmed's care, not if they had more days like today. She'd finished tending to him well after dark. It also meant she wouldn't be able to go to pay her respects at burials.

But a move to El Arish would be much worse.

The colonel strode between the rows of wooden tables toward the exit.

Miss Walsh stood. "Sisters, considering the colonel's address, I'd like to offer you a few thoughts." She folded her hands and stared down her thin nose at the noisy departure of other medical personnel.

Ginger wanted to check if James had left, but it was better not to appear unfocused. But would James still have Ahmed's personal effects? She needed to know.

Miss Walsh wrung her hands. "I need to remind everyone to please be careful. We can't afford to take any chances. If anything like this morning happens again, you're under orders to take shelter immediately. Dugouts are being shoveled out beside our quarters."

Ginger had the impression Miss Walsh was addressing her directly. Her fingertips curled into loose fists.

"Happens again?" Sister Sarah Baxter asked from a few feet away. She had a timid, singsong voice. "Matron, they can't possibly think they can get away with bombing our hospitals. Imagine if we treated their injured men that way."

"Maybe we should," Hilda said. She set her hands on her

hips. "Why should we be merciful with their wounded when they're so heartless?"

Ginger didn't have to wonder what Hilda would have done had she been the one to find Ahmed. Irritation prickled her.

"Matron," Ginger said, "what about the move to El Arish? Have you heard anything definitive?"

"Not yet. It's under discussion."

"But what about our patients?" Beatrice asked. "The injured aren't any safer here than we are. Why should we move while they remain here?" Other nurses murmured their agreement.

Ginger hid a smile. Oh Beatrice. It was no wonder they'd hit it off so well from the moment they'd met as fresh-faced nurses in a hospital in Cairo. They'd done every assignment together since then, by request.

"Unfortunately, it matters little what we want in circumstances such as these," Matron said. "But that's enough questions. You've worked hard today, and it will be another long day tomorrow." She cleared her throat. "Sister Whitman, I'd like to see you."

Ginger's cheeks warmed, and she braced herself for a lecture. She approached Miss Walsh as the other sisters filed from the Mess. Beatrice glanced at her sympathetically.

"Miss Walsh, I'm sorry I was late. I—"

Miss Walsh smoothed her black hair under her cap. "Never mind that. I assume you were with a patient." She frowned. "It's about your disciplinary hearing."

Oh yes, that. "Yes, Matron?"

"It's postponed for three days. I'm sorry for the delay, but with the extra load on the surgeons, it isn't possible at the moment."

"I understand."

Weariness creased Miss Walsh's face. "That's it, Sister Whitman." Her tone softened. "You look quite done in. Get some rest."

Her gentleness was unexpected—and a reminder that Ginger hadn't expressed gratitude for the matron's actions during the shelling.

"Thank you for pulling me away from the hospital tents before they shelled the dispensary." She met the older woman's dark-brown eyes. "You saved my life."

Miss Walsh nodded stiffly. "Of course."

Ginger turned away.

"Sister Whitman?" Matron called.

Ginger glanced back.

"I understand your impulse to help. But you must trust the rules exist for good reason, created by those who can see things from a more objective point of view." The matron folded her hands in front of her. "But you're an excellent nurse. No one is questioning that."

Ginger nodded and continued from the tent, her heart heavy. *Rules for good reason.* Rules that, when broken, incurred a father's wrath for dismissing a wealthy 'well-matched' marriage proposal in favor of a doctor who couldn't help bolster her family's estate. Rules that stopped her from entertaining thoughts of the London School of Medicine for Women in favor of a much more 'sensible' nursing education.

Rules that dictated she report Ahmed the instant she saw his Turkish uniform.

The sight of James interrupted her thoughts. He waited between two hospital tents, conversing with an orderly. "I'll leave you two. Let you have some privacy." The orderly grinned at Ginger. "You're marrying the best doc on this side of the Nile, Sister."

Ginger couldn't help but smile as the orderly moved on. "He's right."

"I'm not sure the nineteen-year-old private who died in surgery an hour ago would agree." James massaged the dry skin of his knuckles, a weary strain in his eyes.

She sagged against him, resting her head on his shoulder. "The injuries today were severe. You've saved countless men. You can't save them all."

"It's not that." James's voice grew raw. "I can mend broken bodies well enough. But the cries at night ... These men have so little fight left in them. They don't even understand what we're doing here, in the middle of the godforsaken desert." He sighed. "Sometimes neither do I."

"This offensive into Jerusalem seems as ill-conceived as the ones in France. Thousands of casualties lost for a few inches of ground here and there? And the Germans and Turks always at the advantage."

"They're winning this war." James removed his glasses and cleaned them. "Plain and simple. It's a matter of waiting out the clock. The news from the Western Front grows worse by the day. Almost 100,000 casualties in Arras this past month. Just one battle. We don't have the men. We can't survive and they know it."

She lifted her chin, a surge of patriotic pride provoking her. "The women of our country won't surrender without having their say, if it comes to it."

He beamed. "If all women were as brave as you, I think we'd have a fair fight."

Who was she fooling? Her bravery had serious limits. She linked arms with him, tugging down his jacket sleeve, which always crept up his lanky arms. "Well, thank you. Speaking of fighting"—she lowered her voice—"did you move Ahmed's bag from the hut this morning?"

James stared at her blankly. "His bag ..." His brows furrowed. "Damn. No, I forgot. We rushed from there after the shelling. And with a great deal of trouble. We were fortunate Ian McNeill came along and helped us move him."

Her arm stiffened against his. She couldn't be angry at James for leaving the bag. But involving a third party? "Ian knows about Ahmed also?"

James adjusted his glasses. "He doesn't know the details. We removed Ahmed's uniform and put him in pajamas. And don't worry, Ian's a good lad. Among my favorite orderlies, in fact. I'd put good money on trusting him."

Regardless, she didn't like Ian knowing anything. The more people that knew, the bigger the risk seemed. But the bag was more pressing. "If Ahmed's bag is still there, we should go and get it."

"We? I can get it. There's no need for us both to go."

Yes, but she wouldn't feel at peace until the bag was safely in his possession. If he went without her, she'd spend the night worrying. She threw a teasing smile. "You wouldn't want to leave your fiancée without a chaperone after curfew, would you? Besides, it would be nice to take a walk together. It's been a trying day."

"Ah, well, in that case how can I argue?" He spread a hand before him. "Lead the way."

The star-filled sky was deep, with lights-out enforced after dark except for the brief use of torches and lamps in the operating theaters for emergency surgery. When she'd first come to the desert, it amazed her how on bright moonlit nights like this one she could see nearly as well as in the day. The light illuminated the stones littering the crude path to the well, and they navigated it after a few minutes.

As they neared, Ginger hesitated. The nocturnal snakes and stinging insects inhabiting these spaces would be out by now. "I have my torch." She retrieved it from her kitbag.

She flipped it on and shone the light into the hut. Goose

bumps rose on her arms at the thought of encountering a snake, but, fortunately, she saw nothing.

James moved a few paces ahead toward the bag.

"Wait." She hurried to his side. "Make sure nothing crawled in."

He eased the bag open with the toe of his boot. Squatting, he sifted through it. He jumped back with a cry.

Ginger shrieked. Her torch thudded on the ground and rolled away before settling against a wall, dimming the light.

James caught her by the waist, a deep laugh in his chest. "You goose. I was teasing you."

She chortled. "You … you're lucky I didn't take off screaming." She placed her hands on his chest as her pulse slowed.

James's lips found her temple and lowered to her mouth.

She returned his kiss. At the sound of distant voices, she pulled away. "We should go," she whispered. "The guards posted to the well might have heard me scream."

"Oh, what's a few more moments together? I doubt they'd even look here." James kissed her again.

She cut off his kiss and pushed back. "And if they do? It will do nothing to help my disciplinary hearing."

"I suppose so." James released her. He led her from the hut, the bag over his shoulder, and they walked back in silence, heaviness between them. As the awkwardness grew, she said, "I'm sorry, I— It's been a long day. Be patient."

"You can accuse me of many things, darling, but not impatience."

She cringed. He had been. Their initial plan to marry 'after the war' kept dragging out as the war pushed into its third year. "Nursing—and the patients—are important to me. You know I can't be in the Queen Alexandra's nurses once we're married."

"Yes, but what if the war lasts another five years? Or even two?"

She'd constructed counterpoints to these ideas in the past, but weariness prevented her from easily remembering them. "The war won't go on that long."

"That's what they said the first year. Over by Christmas."

A different tactic, then. "A wedding during the war would be gauche. Not to mention my family is in Cairo. Traveling to England for the wedding would be difficult."

"Then we don't. We marry at the consulate and move on with our lives."

A bubble of irritation pressed on her sternum, as though searching for some valve for release. "I thought you valued my work." Thank goodness they were nearing the nurses' quarters. She stopped as the pathway forked, with the nurses' quarters to the left and the medical officers' quarters to the right.

He squinted. "I value your work. Of course I do." He opened his mouth to add something and seemed to decide against it. "Good night, then."

His figure faded behind a row of conical tents illuminated by the bright moonlight. Ginger reached for her torch and stomped her foot. They had left it in the hut. After the kisses, she hadn't picked it up.

She glanced toward the tent she shared with Beatrice. Her tentmate had a tendency to fall asleep these days as soon as her head touched the pillow. Gone were the nights of shared laughter and stories of their patients. With their grueling workload in the desert, Beatrice showed more signs of exhaustion with each passing day.

She could go after James and ask him to accompany her back to the hut. But he was embarrassed and upset. She didn't want to continue the uncomfortable conversation.

Her father's voice rang in her mind. "But this is what you said you wanted. You knew your mind and heart."

Crushing a few pebbles with the tip of her boot, she

clenched and unclenched her fist, trying to release her frustration. What type of person would it make her to dread the war's end because it meant the start of her marriage? The lie she'd been living had begun to erode. Even James sensed it now.

For a time, she'd even thought herself in love. James was kind, gentle, trustworthy—everything Stephen Fisher hadn't been. She shuddered, remembering Stephen's lurid, smug reactions to her discomfort at his possessive touch, too low on her back, too tight on her wrist. A hungry wolf hid behind the veneer of refined, aristocratic grace. The opposite of the good match her father had seen. But since Stephen had been her brother's closest friend since childhood, escape from the match had seemed impossible. He'd even followed her family to Cairo. She couldn't get away.

Until she'd met James.

No good came from dwelling on this. She didn't have a simple solution. She turned her thoughts to the present dilemma.

Maybe tonight would be the night a beetle or scorpion crawled under her pillow. Sarah Baxter had discovered a family of desert rats nesting in her mattress a week earlier. Ginger shuddered. She needed her torch.

She hurried toward the well. The screech of jackals in the desert filled the night air. A shiver ran up her back. After the second battle to take Gaza, the number of casualties prevented them from bringing all the wounded off the battlefield for days —over 6,000 men. The men who made it to the clearing station told her horror stories of the battlefield: of locals looting the bodies, of unceasing anguished cries. Nothing inspired more nightmares, though, than the accounts of the jackals prowling and feasting through the fields of injured men.

She increased her pace, wishing she'd asked James to come.

The well stood in the distance, the breeze from the nearby

ocean swaying the leaves of the palm trees. Darkness greeted her near the entrance of the hut. Her torch had rolled against the wall and a sliver of light came from it.

No way to check for snakes now. She ducked inside, hoping the light from the doorway would be enough. If James hadn't played that prank on her, none of this would have happened. As her eyes adjusted to the darkness, something scuttled across the ground, and she flinched. The silence amplified her pulse.

A soft footstep made her jump. From the doorway, a torch flared into life. A deep voice came from the darkness. "Stay where you are."

Of all the rotten luck. The torchlight blinded her. "I'm a nurse," she stuttered. "I-I came to look for my torch."

A British officer stepped in from the shadows. "Identify yourself."

Ginger shielded her eyes from the torch's bright glare. "Sister Ginger Whitman."

"Whitman?" A sharp tone entered his voice.

"Yes." She peered through her lashes. "That light is hurting my eyes."

He shone the torch away, giving her a better view of him. Tall and broad-shouldered with dark hair, he wore his uniform well. A major, it appeared. She didn't recognize him, but she didn't have time to fraternize with many officers these days.

He crossed the hut to retrieve her torch. He held it out. "Why did you leave it here in the first place?"

Would he report her? He couldn't know why she was really here. It would be far better to give sensible answers. She took it from him, her fingers tightening around the heavy handle. "I thought I heard a noise here earlier."

A light chuckle escaped his lips. "Somehow I doubt that." He took slow, deliberate steps toward her, too close for her comfort. "Tell me what you're doing here."

Her breath caught at his brashness. Why was he so suspicious? "Can we step outside?"

"No. Answer the question."

His superior tone set her teeth on edge. She'd dealt with her fair share of men who felt the need to put her in her place, but something about his attitude seemed different. "Pardon me, but is there a reason you're questioning me?"

A frown touched his expression. "I saw you enter the hut. I merely followed to be certain all was well."

His response was reasonable. Why did she still feel so nervous? She scrambled for an excuse. "I met my fiancé here earlier."

"Here?" Disbelief showed on his face.

She bit her lip. Now why had she said that? She'd contradicted the reason she'd just given him for being here. Her face warmed. "Yes, sir."

The officer's eyebrow quirked. "I see. You chose quite a spot to meet." He shone the light over the space, pausing over the bloodstains on the dirt floor. He moved toward them and knelt, rubbing the dirt between his thumb and forefinger.

If he was astute, any close observation of those stains could lead to questions she didn't want to answer. But continuing to imply there had been an amorous tryst would get her in trouble also. "You misunderstand. I simply wanted a few minutes alone with him." Ginger glanced toward the entrance, wishing to flee.

He scowled, still staring at the stains. "What I understand is that a wounded man may have been in here. Recently. You wouldn't know anything about that, would you?" He said it in a manner that made it clear he believed she did.

She shifted. "No, I don't. How do you know a wounded man was here?"

He gave her a strange look she couldn't decipher. "Interesting."

She cleared her throat, her impatience growing. "What is?"

He stood and brushed his hands on his jacket. "I find it interesting that a war-time nurse is pretending not to recognize what that is." He pointed to the stains.

She tried to keep her breath even, a tingling feeling enclosing her heart. "I didn't say I didn't recognize blood."

"Then it is blood? You're certain?" He turned, viewing it from her angle. "You haven't examined it, though. And it's quite dark in here."

The brute had twisted her words. "As you said," she let out a slow breath, "I'm a wartime nurse. I see bloodstains daily."

"Then why would you question there was a wounded man in here? Why else would there be blood?"

Her upbringing had given her years of practiced, blank smiles. Hopefully he would simply think she was dull. "Perhaps an animal died in here."

The officer weighed her words, his face tilting. "I'll need to question you."

Ginger retreated against one of the walls. "You're detaining me?"

"If you've done nothing, you have nothing to fear. I'm inclined to believe you're hiding something."

Her cheeks burned. She needed to remain calm. He would only know about Ahmed if she told him. "I'm sure I can clear this up."

"I'm sure you can. Once we speak at length." He directed the torch's light toward the entrance. "Go on."

Who was he? Her fingertips moved over the stone wall behind her and her grip tightened on the torch. "Under what authority do you have the right to detain and question me? I've done nothing wrong."

"I work for Cairo Intelligence."

Her eyes darted back toward the bloodstains. She remembered her telegram to Cairo Intelligence sent an hour earlier:

Lieutenant Thevshi. Urgent. Found something of interest to you, 53rd Clearing Station, Deir el Belah. Please advise immediately. Dragonfly.

Was he Lieutenant Thevshi? How had he arrived so quickly?

She couldn't use the code word, though. She scanned the officer's face, too nervous to feel hopeful. "Are you Thevshi?"

His eyes narrowed. "Get moving."

Would Thevshi respond like this? His anger frightened her. Saying Thevshi's name had been too grave a risk.

She stepped back. "I-I should return to my quarters."

He rubbed his square jawline. "You're hiding something."

Her pulse quickened. "Really, Major. Explaining myself to you is about as important to me as your manners appear to be to you."

"Manners tend to be unnecessary when dealing with traitors."

Unease settled in her chest. Did he think she'd treated an enemy soldier? No—he couldn't. Her anxiety stemmed from her own guilt over the uncertainty of Ahmed's identity rather than logic.

The officer yanked on her arm, without an ounce of gentility. "Let's go."

Ginger pulled free of him. "How dare you put your hands on me?" Raising the torch, she smacked it against the side of his head as hard as she could.

The torch dropped to the ground and the officer cursed.

She blinked at him, horrified at what she'd done. But she didn't want to stay to face his fury, either. Bolting out the doorway, she lifted her long skirt and ran up the path toward the clearing station. Her fingers fumbled at her neck for the whistle she wore. She lifted it to her lips and blew.

The whistle gave one short burst before the officer grabbed her by the shoulder.

She knocked his hand away. "Don't touch me." A drop of blood ran down from his temple.

"You're going to attract unwanted attention this way." He grabbed her wrist.

She pulled her hand back and slammed the heel of her boot onto his toes. "Stay away from me." She kicked him.

The officer's arm tightened around her torso and they tumbled together toward the ground. As he landed on top of her, she gasped for air. A rock dug into her shoulder.

"That's enough. Stop fighting me, Lady Virginia." Unabashed and cold, his eyes locked with hers. His face hovered inches from hers.

She stopped moving. He'd said her proper name.

"That's right. I know who you are—and I know your father and brother. Quite well. Now get up and start walking. We have a lot to discuss."

Only a handful of people at the clearing station knew of her title. But even then she'd made a point of introducing herself by the nickname she preferred, rather than her Christian name. "Then you should know you can't treat me like this." Her voice came in a breathless whisper.

"I'm well within my rights to detain anyone I deem to be acting suspiciously."

"I'm not the one behaving suspiciously." She yanked her wrists up toward his face. Her fingers hooked like claws, digging into his chest. "Get off of me."

"Settle down." He pushed her hands back. "You're making this harder for yourself. I won't hesitate to restrain you if you attack me again."

"You're lying."

"About restraining you or knowing who you are? I meant both."

His weight crushed her. She stopped resisting and her voice came out, choked. "Who are you?"

"Not now. I'm going to stand. Don't even think about trying to run again."

As he pulled her upright, Ginger glared at him. The moonlight glinted in his eyes.

She whirled around to step away from him when the low buzz of aeroplanes stopped them both. Three German bombers approached, heading straight for the clearing station, where the large red crosses on the top of the tents gleamed.

Machine gun fire exploded from the planes, crackling in the night.

"Get down." The officer attempted to grab her by the arm, but Ginger had already started forward. They collided and she sprawled onto the ground. Her forehead smacked into a rock. A cry left her.

"Are you all right?" The officer was at her side.

Spots danced in her vision. She tried to stand, but her knees buckled. His sturdy arms caught her. A clean, soapy scent wafted to her from the fabric of his military jacket. Her head rested on his chest, and he lifted her from the cold desert sand.

CHAPTER FOUR

$\mathcal{G}$inger rolled onto her back. The dim light of dusk came in through the tan canvas above her. She rubbed her eyes, trying to get her bearings as she grew more lucid. Where was she?

A dull ache at her temples overtook her. *Ouch.* She walked her fingertips to a bandage at the top of her forehead.

She startled at the rustle of paper. The officer was seated in a chair beside her. One leg was crossed over the other, he had a book in his hands, but his dark-blue eyes stared at her.

She jerked upright. An acute pain cut at her wrist where she'd been handcuffed to the frame of a cot. "What on earth— what are you doing here?" she asked.

The book snapped shut, and he set it on the bed. "This is my tent," he said with a shrug. His eyes scanned hers, a trace of concern in them. "How do you feel?"

She guessed he was in his late twenties, with a strong, clean-shaven jawline and a firm body filling out his immaculate uniform. Despite his attractiveness, the metal on her wrist was a good reminder of why she should still fear him.

"Why do you have me restrained?" Her skull felt like someone had driven a spike into it. Not giving him a chance to answer, she lifted her free hand, trembling, to her temple. "I can't be here. If I'm found, I'll be thrown out of the nursing service. And if anyone even hears a whisper that I've spent the night here, I'll be ruined. Why did you bring me here?"

He ignored her questions and unlocked the handcuff, freeing her wrist. "I'll return you soon. You hit your head—you'll need to be examined."

She pulled her wrist back and massaged the tender skin where the metal had left an impression. "Am I under arrest?"

He met her eyes. "Should you be?"

Her heart skipped a beat. Did he know she'd treated Ahmed? She sensed he did, however absurd the notion was. Still, he'd removed the restraints.

She glanced around the tent. A large canvas bag stood in the corner, propped against a tent post. A small portable stove and a scratched metal percolator sat on the ground. No personal touches or pictures. "Why did you bring me here instead of the hospital?"

"The Germans took it upon themselves to conduct air raids on the clearing station last night. Under the circumstances, I didn't feel it would be safe to carry you into the gunfire. So I brought you to my quarters instead."

His answer indicated that they must be on the plain where the soldiers were encamped.

"Air raids on the clearing station?" Ginger's stomach felt weak. *James.* "Were there any casualties?"

"Three patients and two field ambulance personnel were killed. A few dental staff sergeants and soldiers wounded."

Thank God. Breathing a sigh of relief didn't feel appropriate. Still, she was comforted no nurses or doctors were on that list. "But why would they attack the hospital?"

"Perhaps they were searching for something specific. Considering the bombardment yesterday, future air raids are a possibility."

Searching for something specific ... or someone? Ahmed? She combed her fingers through her hair, noticing her cap was missing. "Surely they saw the red crosses on the tents?"

He nodded. "I don't see how they could miss them."

His forthrightness shocked her. Officers routinely downplayed this sort of thing. "Are you suggesting the Turks shelled the clearing station on purpose?"

Humor shone in his eyes. "Do you think they closed their eyes while firing and just hoped it would land on our side?"

There was that arrogance from the night before. "But something must be done about it. Can't you share your suspicions with a superior?"

"Yes, I'll be sure to send a message to Foreign Secretary Balfour this morning. Or, better yet, Lloyd George. The prime minister has nothing better to do."

He made her feel like a schoolchild staring at a tutor with a switch. She stiffened. "Major, I don't appreciate being teased. I'm serious."

He cocked an eyebrow. "As am I. What would you like to see happen? For our top men to call their top men and tell them to play war a little more nicely? Shall we threaten them with ... what, exactly? More war?"

She seethed. Changing the subject would be better than dealing with his condescension. "You had no right to handcuff me."

"I needed to be certain you weren't planning on running again. Though I did clear the tent of anything you might hit me with." A large bruise had bloomed on the left side of his face.

As though his behavior hadn't precipitated her reaction. "Was I to assume you wouldn't hurt me?"

"Did I give you any reason to believe I would?" He put the restraints away in the canvas bag.

"You grabbed me. And then attacked me."

"After you ran away." He returned to the chair.

"Your response was uncalled for. Tackling a lady?" He laughed. "Yes, because your behavior was ladylike."

"Given the circumstances, I think my response was justified." She glared. "You've been behaving as though I'm guilty of some misdeed and you don't know anything about me."

"I know that you struggle with telling the truth. And that you've got a strong right arm. At least when you're holding a torch."

Her lips parted. People didn't talk to her like this. Her family's social status ensured her respect in the civilian world. At the front, her role as a nurse came with a rank higher than most of the soldiers she treated.

"What exactly do you think I've done wrong, Major …?"

"Benson." He crossed his arms. "And I'd rather hoped you could tell me the answer to that, Lady Virginia."

She bristled. "Sister Whitman."

He smiled. He leaned forward, setting his elbows on his knees, and clasped his hands. "I already told you I know who you are."

Handsome or not, he was intolerable. Yet, his eyes held sharpness and intelligence. He knew how to be charming while asserting himself—and used it to his advantage. She wished the night before seemed as fuzzy and distant to him as it did to her.

She stood, smoothing her uniform. "I don't know what you're playing at, Major Benson, but if you know my father as you claim—which you've given me no evidence for, by the way —you know he works for the Foreign Office in Cairo. All I have to do is snap my fingers, and he'll deal with your misbehavior. I haven't done anything wrong."

Major Benson's eyes hardened. "That's not true, though, is it? You have something to say. You know something about whomever was wounded in that hut. And I looked into that Lieutenant Thevshi you mentioned."

Her heart beat faster. He stood inches from her, and she felt the urge to flee from him again.

He must have arrived recently. Once out in the desert for any length of time, the scent of sweat and grime became altogether familiar. He smelled too clean. Major Benson pursed his lips at her silence and stepped back. "Would you like a cup of coffee?"

The sociable gesture didn't feel at all comforting. She shook her head and he turned and moved toward the small stove in the corner. Her gaze fell on his book, which remained on the cot. She couldn't recognize the foreign language. Maybe Turkish?

When Major Benson stood, he held a steaming coffee mug. He gestured toward the bed. "Sit." After a moment, he added, "Please."

"Would it matter if I said no?"

He smiled congenially. "Not at all."

Damn his charm. She sat, her posture stiff. He took the chair opposite, relaxed and in control.

"Lady Virginia—"

She gritted her teeth. "Please don't call me that."

He inclined his head, his eyes puzzled. "Is there a reason why you want to distance yourself from your title? Or your family?"

His shrewd observation unnerved her. "I've done my best to avoid the assumption of social privilege in front of my colleagues."

He choked on his coffee and moved it away from his lap to prevent spilling any of it on his trousers. "This from the same woman who boasted minutes ago of her father's connections?"

She narrowed her gaze at him. "My colleagues are an entirely different matter to you." Why did this man elicit such a strong, irritated reaction from her?

"I simply want to ask you a question or two." He stared at her over the rim of his coffee cup.

"Such as?"

"How do you know Lieutenant Thevshi?"

He'd come straight to the point. She fidgeted. "He's a friend of my brother's in Cairo."

He watched her with interest. "So your brother mentioned him? But you've never met him?"

She raised her chin. "It's not any of your business, Major."

"Whose business would it be, Sister Whitman? That name you're tossing around is dangerous. And, from what I under-stand, it means you're involved in something far outside of nursing."

She cursed the moment she'd mentioned Thevshi. She shouldn't have said anything. "I didn't ask you to investigate Lieutenant Thevshi. And I don't need your help."

"And the wounded man that was treated near the well?"

Saying anything could get her into trouble—not to mention James and Beatrice. She pressed her lips together.

He scowled. "Are you always so flippant about matters that threaten the security of our troops, or just when you think you can 'snap your fingers' and have your father save you?" A muscle in his square jaw tightened. "You are not above the law, no matter what your father may have convinced you of."

"This conversation is over." She stood.

Major Benson grasped her wrist. "You know more than you're letting on. You were evasive about those bloodstains in the hut and you weren't honest about why you were at that well. Your story changed while you were speaking." She didn't dare look away from the intensity of his gaze. "I really can't accept your refusal to cooperate."

She had to maintain her silence. Any deviation at this point and she could be endangering both herself and Ahmed. "You've spent too long in the field, Major. Either the sun or threat of danger must be causing your delusions. But I must insist you return me to the clearing station hospital. My presence here could cause me the gravest of scandal and personal ruin."

"And you expect me to believe you know nothing?"

She shrugged. "Honestly, Major, I don't care if you believe me. You have no reason to detain me. If anything, you should consider yourself lucky that I don't report you for the way you've treated me."

"You should care. If I so decide, you'll go to the closest military prison." His voice remained cool and collected, but his eyes burned.

She had the feeling Major Benson was a man accustomed to control—and that extended to his emotions. "I don't believe for one second you'd risk your manhood by claiming a woman could ever best a man of your size and stature." Her voice quivered, despite her show of bravado.

He circled her. Stopping behind her, he leaned down toward her, his lips practically grazing her ear. "I'm not afraid of being bested by a woman. It's how she does it that I concern myself with."

Flutters went up her spine. She turned her face toward his. "I will report you. Not only for keeping me here without cause, but also for the way you manhandled me without remorse. I want your full name and that of your commanding officer." She scanned his uniform for any relevant regimental tabs.

"Go ahead. We both know you're bluffing. My name is Noah Benson." His eyes glittered. "And you're right. I don't feel sorry at all about 'manhandling' you. Maybe a spanking or two as a

child would have taught you not to assault a superior officer."
He leaned closer. "And who I report to is beyond your purview."

She wanted to slap him. But she wouldn't allow him to
humiliate her. "Then go ahead and arrest me. I don't think you
can. You don't have any proof of your ridiculous claims."

Benson sipped his coffee. "I'm going to escort you back to
the clearing station. Only because you should have your injuries
checked. But I'll be monitoring you, Sister Whitman."

Monitoring her? What would that entail? If he followed her
movements too closely, she could unwittingly lead him to
Ahmed. Her throat felt thick as she managed, "Thank you,
Major."

Goose bumps rose on her arms at the inscrutable expression
on his tanned face. He nodded curtly. "Don't wander around at
night. You have a lot more to fear than me in the desert."

CHAPTER FIVE

*G*inger's eyes watered as Doctor Clemens inspected her pupils. He smelled of whisky and tobacco, and she focused on his grey handlebar moustache. He glanced at James and Beatrice, who waited at the foot of the cot. "Sister Whitman was fortunate. I'll discharge her. But it would be wise to reduce her workload. See she rests today. I'll speak to Matron before returning to surgery."

Rest? She had too much to do. Her shift should have started hours ago. And she needed to visit Ahmed and the telegraph station at HQ to see if she'd had any response from Henry or Lieutenant Thevshi.

"I'll take her to her quarters." James gave Doctor Clemens a grateful look. No doubt he had asked the RAMC commander to assess Ginger. The favor wouldn't go unnoticed by others, either.

As the doctor left, Ginger resisted the urge to ask James and Beatrice about Ahmed. With Major Benson on the prowl, speaking here seemed risky. He'd left her rattled.

James approached Ginger as Beatrice closed the privacy

curtain. "I brought you aspirin for that headache." He fished a glass bottle from his pocket.

She sat against the pillows, her head pounding. "Did we get any supplies from Kantara yet? To replace what we lost with the dispensary shelling?"

Beatrice cut in. "Just at the moment you're a patient too."

Ginger met her friend's light-blue eyes. Beatrice had a way of anticipating her arguments well. "I can't take something as precious as aspirin if we scarcely have supplies for the wounded. I'll be fine."

"This isn't the time to argue. You said earlier your headache was unbearable. These are from my personal reserves. And they worked you to the bone yesterday." A red streak colored his face, down toward his neck. "If it's anyone's fault, it's mine. I should have walked you to your tent. I've been furious with myself for failing to. Thank goodness that officer happened upon you."

Ginger stared at her hands, trying to keep guilt from manifesting in her expression. Major Benson had done her the favor of telling the nightshift nurse, Sister Thomas, that he'd found her unconscious by her tent. There hadn't been time to tell James the truth.

But she didn't know what to say. Especially about Major Benson.

James spilled a few tablets into his palm. "I want you to take some. You must take care of yourself."

She closed his fingers over the pills. "I don't want them. Please."

Beatrice cleared her throat. "Why don't we see how you're feeling once you've got dressed?" She patted the foot of the bed. "I brought you a clean uniform. If James wants to meet us outside the ward, I'll bring you to him."

Frustration crossed James's face. He replaced the pills. "I'll be outside."

"Actually—" Ginger hesitated. James could visit the telegraph station for her. Did she have the right to any favors? If she didn't ask, she might not have a chance. "Can you go to HQ and check to see if I've received any telegrams?"

"Of course. I'll meet you at your quarters—if Sister Thornton can walk you there."

As James left, Beatrice scrutinized her. "Something else is amiss, isn't it?"

It wouldn't do much good to hide from Beatrice. "How do you know?"

"You have that look about you." Beatrice sat beside her. "And Hilda enjoyed telling the other girls at Mess about the major who brought you here." Beatrice set a gentle hand on hers. She lowered her voice. "But also—you never came close to our quarters last night. I would have heard you if you had collapsed outside. I was up waiting for you for hours. I only went to sleep because I assumed you'd volunteered to work after the air raids."

Ginger's heart froze. But Beatrice would say nothing.

"The major—" The privacy curtain fluttered as someone walked past. Ginger swallowed. "This isn't the place to discuss it."

"Let's get you dressed and out of here." Beatrice held out the uniform. "The sisters are worried about you. You were the talk of breakfast."

Wonderful. Just when she wanted to draw less attention to herself. "Because of the major?" Ginger dressed, her movements stiff, her head aching.

Beatrice lifted Ginger's boots from the ground and shook them. "No scorpions in these." Beatrice grinned and plopped them beside her. "The major may have added to it. It didn't help that he came in toward the end of breakfast. He's … attractive. The girls noticed him right away. Then Hilda arrived and announced he was one of your many admirers."

Admirers? Ginger chortled humorlessly. "Far from it." She pulled on her stockings, and Beatrice helped her with her boots.

"I wasn't suggesting I believed it." Beatrice smiled mischievously. "Though I wouldn't at all blame you if you took a liking to him." She offered Ginger an arm. "You'd have to be blind not to notice him."

If she only knew. Ginger's cheeks warmed. "I don't know what you're carrying on about."

"I'm only teasing. But do feel free to send him my way, since you're already taken."

They made their way out. Ginger winced at the sun's brightness as a searing jolt shot through her head. Beatrice wrinkled her nose. "Reconsider the aspirin. You won't be a help to anyone if you're in pain."

"I'll think about it." Ginger kept her gaze low, to minimize the light's effect on her head. "Speaking of helping others—I've been eager to ask you about Ahmed. Have you checked on him? His fever was high yesterday evening."

Beatrice grimaced. "It's not good news, I'm afraid. He's delirious, with a fever near 106. James is worried about sepsis."

Ginger's heart fell. "Damn."

Beatrice leaned closer. "I'm worried about another thing. He's been muttering in his delirium. In another language, maybe Arabic. He keeps saying the word *maslukha* over and over. Do you think it could lead someone to suspect he isn't one of our boys?"

Maslukha. She wasn't familiar with the term. "It might be Hebrew. He was praying yesterday—he told me he's Jewish."

"Jewish? With a name like Ahmed?"

Ginger hadn't thought about that, but it was possible he used an alias for protection. "It is unusual." It didn't help that Ahmed was unconscious. She couldn't ask him about Major Benson either. She checked to see that they were out of earshot of other nurses. "What, exactly, did Hilda say about Major Benson this morning?"

Beatrice waved away a few gnats. "She told everyone how he carried you into the ward this morning at a 'scandalous hour' and how he then insisted on coming back and checking on you several times. She claimed he's clearly devoted to you and how outrageous it all was."

Benson had checked in on her already? Ginger puffed out a frustrated breath between her lips. "Hardly. But trust Hilda to make an issue out of it. Why of all sisters did she have to be on the night shift last night? I think I'm cursed."

"Don't let it get to you. Mary Brown will fall in love with another patient soon enough, and then we can all gossip about her. Or maybe one of the Australian nurses will get drunk again. I'll see what I can do to arrange it." Beatrice's eyes twinkled. "But you do need to stay out of trouble. Now, what really happened with that major?"

Feeling sheepish, Ginger summarized her interactions with Major Benson. As she finished, she avoided Beatrice's gaze. "I know—it was foolish for me to go back out on my own. And maybe my own nerves are contributing to it all," she finished. She wished her biggest worry of the day could be something related to her normal nursing duties. "But I just couldn't ignore the oddness of our interactions. I'm afraid he might be the traitor Ahmed mentioned."

Beatrice stopped close to the nurses' quarters. "Let's wait here for James." She shaded her eyes as she scanned the grounds. Worry lined her features. "Why not go to HQ and ask about Major Benson? Surely someone must know him."

"Ask who? I can't ask if he's a spy. Based on what grounds?

I'm helping a patient who might be an enemy but claims to be an ally hunted by a traitorous spy? They'll cart me off to prison or the madhouse." Ginger rubbed her temple.

"What does James think of the major?"

Ginger squirmed. "I haven't told him any details. And I'm not certain that I should."

"And why not?" Beatrice poked her in the ribs. "He's your fiancé, for goodness sake. Of all people, he should be the one you go to first."

The number of things Ginger hadn't told James had begun to overwhelm her. Especially since Ahmed had told her how serious it was. Even telling Beatrice was dangerous. She'd involved her friend too much already. It would be better to change the subject. "Maybe that's the problem. I don't feel comfortable enough with him to tell him."

Beatrice studied Ginger's profile. "Ginger, if you don't want to marry him, don't marry him. But it isn't right to string him along, pretending you're thrilled about getting married."

Beatrice rarely dared to broach the topic, despite their conversations about it in the past. "It's not that simple." Ginger loosened the cape from around her neck. "I gave James my word, and I meant it. I respect him too much to tell him no now, after three years of having him believe—"

"Believe you love him?"

Ginger flinched. "I hope it's not obvious."

"You're living a lie. And you're remarkably good at it. But if you don't think it will catch up with you, you're wrong." Beatrice touched her forearm. "And I don't say that as a parson's daughter, though I'm sounding too much like my father for my comfort." The blue sky brightened her eyes. "When I broke things off with Robert after I met Charles, I thought everyone would think I'd lost my head. But if I hadn't, I'd have missed the only moments that I wish with my entire heart I could return to."

Beatrice's fiancé had been killed at the Somme the year before. The experience had changed her. She had become more cautious, less likely to jump into the silly mischief they'd enjoyed as young, green nurses.

Beatrice's eyes misted. "And honestly, no one said much. In fact, my mother wrote to me to express her relief I hadn't married Robert because of what a bore he was."

If only things could be so easy. Her father would scorn her for breaking off what he'd called a 'rash engagement' after she'd failed to marry his preferred choice. She didn't want to prove him right.

"Speak of the devil." Beatrice nodded toward James, who was approaching. "Talk to him. Even if it's not about the engagement. He loves you and will help you. In the meantime, don't worry about caring for Ahmed—I'll check on him throughout the day. If there's any change, I'll let you know. You should rest."

James drew closer, and Beatrice left for her shift. Frustration rankled within Ginger. It was selfish to think Beatrice could waste time and discuss these issues, but James could never be an objective confidant.

She smiled pleasantly as James reached her. "Anything?"

He shook his head. "Unfortunately not."

She swallowed her disappointment. "Not entirely surprising about Thevshi, but Henry always answers me immediately. It's unlike him not to respond."

"The issue might tragically resolve itself. I'm not encouraged by Ahmed's progress. He seems to have taken a turn for the worse."

She avoided James's eyes. "Ahmed ... was worried he might die. He asked me to search for Lieutenant Thevshi regardless. Said he had important information to transmit to him."

A crease formed in James's forehead. "What information?"

Did she dare tell him about the importance of Ahmed's bag or the bottle she'd hidden? If the information was as sensitive as Ahmed claimed, she could endanger James by involving him more.

"I'm uncertain. But Beatrice said, in his delirium, he's repeating the word *maslukha*. Have you heard of it?"

James's eyes widened. "Are you sure?"

She tensed. "Do you know it?"

James hesitated. "I've heard stories. There's a revolutionary who's been calling himself the Maslukha. He's become practically infamous among the men in the last two months." James frowned. "I'm surprised you haven't heard the term. It's been in the newspapers."

"I haven't had time for the papers." She locked eyes with James. "Are you suggesting Ahmed might be this Maslukha character?"

James rubbed the dark scruff on his jawline. "No ... no, I hope not. He's an enemy. He and his raiders inflict damage wherever they can. The brass is up in arms about him, but no one seems to know who he is."

"I hope not either, but—" Ginger felt ill. "What if Ahmed is? We have no way of knowing." If they'd helped someone so dangerous, the consequences could be horrific.

James set a hand on her shoulder. "Don't panic. Ahmed is gravely ill. He might not make it through the day. I'll look through the papers for reports on the Maslukha's activities. If he's attacked anyone in the last few days, we'll know it's not Ahmed."

His words didn't calm her. "But why would he keep mentioning the Maslukha?"

"Perhaps he's seen what the man does to his enemies and is having nightmares. Supposedly, the Maslukha is ruthless." A weary expression crossed James's features. "You should be resting."

"I won't be able to rest if I'm worried. And it seems the Maslukha is someone to worry about."

James let out a lengthy sigh. "Whoever influences the Arab locals controls their loyalty. British command doesn't want an uprising. It would hurt the campaign into Palestine."

Ginger frowned. "But their worries about the locals never came to fruition. We defeated the Senussi uprising. The Egyptians haven't risen in revolution against us, although we deposed their khedive and installed the sultan. And T. E. Lawrence has rallied many local Arabs against the Turks successfully."

"The men seem to think the Maslukha might be a Senussi tribal leader who refuses to surrender. They think he's building his own army and trying to incite those people you mentioned to join in arms. Egyptians, Senussi, Bedouin, and Arabs joining under a strong banner of leadership against the British could be disastrous."

Ginger shook her head. "Both my father and Henry have told me of how loyal the Arabs working with Lawrence are to us. It would take more than a powerful leader to turn their loyalties. And Captain Lawrence *is* a leader."

James put his thumb and forefinger to her chin. "Even more reason for you to stop worrying about this and get some rest. I'm serious. Have you reconsidered the aspirin?"

Not that argument again.

A few feet from them, a man's voice interrupted, "Ginny!"

Henry? Her heart skipped.

Only a few people called her by that nickname, but it wasn't her brother. She squinted, the sun in her eyes, at the tall officer striding toward her. Dread filled her heart.

CHAPTER SIX

*G*inger steadied herself on James's forearm and attempted composure. "Stephen! What on earth are you doing here?"

Stephen stopped a few feet from her. His icy blue gaze met hers, his fair skin sporting a sunburn. He wiped sweat from under his hat's brim, sweeping a lock of dark-blond hair from his forehead. Even here he looked as though he should be in a white tie, leaning against a bar with a glass of brandy in one hand. "Your brother sent me. He said it was urgent."

Urgent matter. Must discuss in person immediately, her message had read. Why would Henry have sent Stephen in his stead? Henry knew how much Ginger disliked Stephen. Then again, with Henry's recent engagement to Stephen's sister, Angelica, Henry likely felt closer to Stephen than ever.

James cleared his throat. She'd never told James anything about how her father had tried to manipulate her into marrying Stephen. She smiled as pleasantly as possible. "James, this is Stephen Fisher, my brother's friend."

"Just your brother's friend?" Stephen chuckled. "We were almost much more."

James's brows drew together, his eyes reflecting curiosity and surprise.

She flashed a polite warning smile toward Stephen. "Stephen, Doctor Clark is my fiancé." The men assessed each other, and Ginger shifted with discomfort.

"Your fiancé?" Stephen held out his hand. "Captain Stephen Fisher. You may have heard Lady Virginia mention my father, the Earl of Knotley."

James shook Stephen's hand. "I'm afraid I haven't, Lord Fisher."

"Just Captain Fisher." Red spots bloomed in Stephen's cheeks. "Do you have a moment to speak in private, Ginny?"

Her cheeks warmed. James appeared displeased with the turn in the conversation. "Actually, I'm heading to my quarters to rest for a while."

"Rest? It's midday." Stephen crossed his arms. His uniform was perfectly tailored and made from materials far superior to the standard issue. "I'm on CID business at El Arish and must return within a few hours. I came because Henry stressed the urgency."

Her irritation with Henry grew. "I'm surprised Henry didn't tend to my request personally."

"On the contrary. His intention is to come out from Cairo. But I was closer, and you worried him." He peered at the bandage on her head. "Are you ill? You look run down, my dear."

Under his scrutiny, her red hair felt more untamed, her skin more blemished by the environment. Nothing would escape Stephen's notice, and he'd carry tales to her family about the horrible state he'd found her in. The less she told him about her concussion, the better.

She stiffened. "A minor scrape." She hoped James wouldn't

contradict her. "Could you excuse us for a few minutes, Stephen?"

Stephen smiled suavely. "I'll be around the corner."

He sauntered away, though not out of sight. If she kept her voice down he'd be out of earshot. James's voice was low. "Knotley. As in Knotley Diamonds?"

She met his incredulous expression and pressed her hands against her warm cheeks. "Yes, his grandfather moved their family to Kimberley in South Africa at the height of the diamond mining enterprise. They did well." Among the many reasons her father was frustrated when she refused Stephen's proposal.

"You were engaged?" James's mouth set to a thin line.

She tangled her fingers into the loose strands of hair by her shoulders. "No. He believed I would marry him, but I never cared for him."

She gripped James's hands, seeking the kind, intelligent gaze she'd often found a refuge. "I never mentioned him because I've long considered him more akin to a pebble in my shoe than a potential suitor." Still, if James learned that Stephen continued to write her weekly, it could trouble him. "He's among Henry's closest friends. And his sister is Henry's fiancée. If Henry thinks he can help with Ahmed, it may be wise for me to speak to him."

James sighed. "I'm worried about your health. You heard Doctor Clemens. Rest is important."

"The sooner we hand this situation over to someone else, the better." She glanced at Stephen. "What if I speak to him in the recreation tent? We could find a quiet corner to sit." Her head would welcome sitting still. James appeared dubious. "Would it help if I take aspirin?"

"Yes. It would." James removed the bottle from his pocket. "If you trust him, I suppose a brief conversation would be fine."

Ginger swallowed the tablet, her throat dry. She parted with James and made her way toward Stephen.

He smiled. "I see you convinced the good doctor I'm no threat. But, really—that's the sort you chose over me?"

"James has no reason to feel threatened. And he's a brilliant surgeon and a gentleman. I'm proud of his accomplishments."

Stephen pursed his lips and pulled a cigarette case from his pocket, his eyes drifting over the arid landscape. "Nothing more detestable than flies and heat." He wrinkled his nose. "Hard to believe God Almighty would choose this wasteland for his 'chosen people.'"

She kept her voice as neutral as possible, restraining the irritation simmering in her gut. "Your father could help you get a position in England."

He shrugged. "I'd rather not." Acrid smoke wafted from his lips. "I loathe seeing you here, though. You should be in Cairo. This is no place for you. No wonder you so rarely answer my letters. I'd be shocked if the post makes it this far."

He would think that. "This is where I'm needed."

"Well, maybe we can see about getting you away from this maggot-infested inferno." He ran one hand over his jacket front. "Now, what's this Henry was so concerned about?"

She motioned toward the path. "Shall we find a seat in the recreation tent?"

"Lead the way."

She clasped her hands in front of her as she walked. Much as she hadn't wanted the aspirin, she hoped it would work its magic quickly. The sooner the hammering in her skull diminished, the more clearheaded she'd be. As they entered the tent, some nurses at the tail end of elevenses glanced at her with surprise.

She smiled politely. Better not to give them any encouragement to ask about her injury in front of Stephen.

She found a small table in a back corner of the tent and sat. Stephen removed his jacket and set it on a chair. "Tea?" he asked.

"No, thank you. The reason I sent for Henry involves a delicate matter." She lowered her voice, leaning toward him. "I found a wounded man yesterday in ... unusual ...circumstances."

Stephen settled in his chair and lit another cigarette. "How unusual?"

She regretted the decision to come here. Though few injured soldiers milled around, distracted with games of chess or cards, it didn't feel private enough.

She scooted her chair closer to Stephen's. "He was in an abandoned hut near a well. And he wore a Turkish uniform." She couldn't mention James's or Beatrice's involvement, no matter Henry's friendship with Stephen. She didn't want them to suffer repercussions. "I decided to treat him before turning him in, as I feared he wouldn't survive otherwise."

Stephen's eyes narrowed. "You treated a Turkish soldier in an isolated location and alerted no one?"

She cringed at how foolish it sounded. "Well, that's the thing. He said he was a British ally named Ahmed Bayrak." This was already going poorly. "He claimed I could confirm his identity with a British agent at the CID named Lieutenant Thevshi. Afterward, I wired Henry."

Stephen's high cheekbones protruded as he took a drag from his cigarette. "Did the man say anything else?"

Her pulse beat faster. His lack of emotional response made her even more nervous. "H-he said he worked for a Zionist organization with the code name 'the Operation.' That he had crucial information for Thevshi."

Stephen crushed his cigarette against the table, jaw clenching. "This is precisely why women don't belong at the front lines. The idea is noble, but we can't expect women to think rationally about matters such as these."

Ginger recoiled. She blinked, his censure stinging more than she would have expected. "He spoke English perfectly and gave me a reasonable explanation. I sent a wire to Cairo Intelligence as soon as I could, to contact Lieutenant Thevshi, as Ahmed was too injured to be a threat."

"What of the authorities here? There are CID men in Rafah and El Arish."

"He said a traitor in British intelligence would catch him if I did."

"And you believed him." His voice was flat. "Still placing your trust in men you barely know rather than those whom you should, I see."

She wanted to scream in protest. He approached her rationale with the same haughty attitude he did everything. "I still trust my instincts and *feelings*, yes." Her conversation with Beatrice about the engagement with James smarted with irony. How could she ever tell her family she'd been wrong about being in love and impulsive?

Stephen patted her hand, his expression softening. "Don't trouble your pretty head about it, darling—it'll work out. Fortunately, I know Thevshi."

Her fingers curled, her anger at him stronger than her relief. "You know him?"

He caught her hand in his, his thumb brushing over the bare space on her left ring finger. The diamond he'd offered her years earlier had been four carats. She still remembered the anger in his eyes when she'd turned him away. Though she tugged her fingers back, he didn't release them. "Yes, I know Thevshi. I am him. It's an old alias I've used for years. Anyone at the CID could have told you had you bothered to ask."

Stephen? Thevshi? The idea choked her.

She pulled her hand away firmly and straightened. "I asked a local CID officer. Major Benson. He didn't mention you." Then again, Benson hadn't given her much of an answer at all.

Stephen's countenance darkened. "Who did you say?"

"Major Noah Benson. Do you know him?"

Stephen lifted his chin. "What does the man look like?"

"Tall. Dark-haired. Blue eyes." Handsome. Intriguing. She shifted. "Articulate. Why?"

"Until a few moments ago, I believed Noah Benson was dead."

Her stomach tightened. "What?"

"Well"—Stephen cleared his throat—"he went missing several weeks ago on assignment in Aleppo. He's not a local CID officer. He's currently listed as MIA."

She tried to grasp the weight of his words. Why would Benson walk around here freely if he was MIA? It could be grounds for desertion.

Unless Major Benson really was the enemy spy Ahmed had mentioned.

She gripped the sides of her chair, dizzy. "I had the impression he arrived recently."

Stephen leaned toward her. "Are you all right? You're flushed."

Damn her pale skin. "Fine. But"—she blinked—"confused. If you're Thevshi, can you confirm Ahmed's story?"

Stephen smiled grimly. "I wish I could make this easier for you, dearest. Unfortunately, you've been manipulated by devious men. The Ahmed Bayrak I know is a Turkish spy known for infiltrating British camps in disguise—often as a Bedouin. The man lied."

Lied? She stared at Stephen, too angry to form a proper sentence. Her mind raced. "But why would he ask me to have you confirm his identity?"

"Because I've been trying to catch him for months. It's been a long game of cat and mouse—no doubt he thought he could escape again and planned to gloat about it." He set his hands on the table. "But you say you've been treating him? Where is he now?"

The low din of noise in the tent distracted her. The shuffling of cards, the patients at tables with blank game faces, Sister Mary Brown's curious looks toward her and Stephen, the scent of cigar smoke—all of it passed through Ginger's senses at a slow, uneven pace.

Stephen's claims made no sense. If he was Thevshi, wouldn't he have known from her wire Ahmed was here? Perhaps the CID had never sent him the wire. But if everyone knew he was Thevshi, wouldn't they have sent it to him immediately?

"Ginny?"

Stephen's voice grounded her again. She met his gaze. If Ahmed was as close to death as James feared, what harm could come from waiting until she understood Stephen's claims to tell him about Ahmed's location?

Stephen grabbed her hand once again. "You're out of your depth, Ginny. Your father won't be pleased to hear what you're meddling in. You should have left this to others."

Ah, there was something she understood. Stephen didn't care about her knowing the truth. He only cared about her being uninvolved. The tent seemed to shrink, the air in it stifling, her high collar too tight around her neck. If she didn't know any better, she could close her eyes and imagine herself in her family's parlor at Penmore, their country home. He'd proposed to her there.

His touch reminded her of the burning shame she'd felt each time they'd been alone before. Her father and Henry never would have understood the discomfort she felt around Stephen

—even if she'd had the courage to voice it. They would have seen it as her fault.

Her mouth felt parched, her lips sticky and chapped. "He got away," she choked out. "I was wrong about his injuries being too grievous to keep him here."

Now if she could escape too.

CHAPTER SEVEN

"*P*lease remember to be on your best behavior at your hearing tomorrow."

Ginger lifted her gaze from the ledger as Miss Walsh hovered over the desk. Ginger's eyes followed the edges of the general admission tent, where two soldiers waited on benches for admittance. Hopefully, they hadn't heard.

Ginger nodded. Outside the tent's open entrance, heat rose in lines in the air. The temperatures spiked at one hundred degrees each day.

In a lower voice, Miss Walsh added, "Unfortunately, I've heard far too many whispers about you in the last two days. An intelligence officer asked about you yesterday morning, after your injury, and the other nurses seemed to think he's a beau. And I heard of an intimate elevenses tea with yet another officer. That won't help you."

"Yes, of course." A flush broke out on Ginger's face. At least Matron had the courtesy of not appearing to believe the rumors to be true. She hoped James hadn't heard. Would anyone be so impertinent as to tell him? She changed the topic. "Miss Walsh,

I'm assuming there's been no further mention of moving the sisters to El Arish?"

"None." Miss Walsh touched her elbow. "Why don't you take a fifteen-minute break? You appear worn down. I'll handle the desk for now."

Ginger thanked her and stood. She left the tent, grateful to escape. The rumors were the least of her problems. Stephen had been furious with her when she'd told him Ahmed had escaped. He'd left the clearing station in his motorcar immediately. She'd spent the better part of the night tormenting herself, wondering if she'd made the right decision. But by lying to him she'd also ruined the chance Stephen would tell Henry it was necessary for him to come.

What was worse, with each passing moment the idea she could be harboring an enemy spy made her sick.

A scuffle in the distance distracted her.

A huddled group of locals, including women and children, stood on the plain, mere yards from the guard posts. British soldiers blocked them, rifles raised. Her heart lurched. What could they have possibly done to merit weapons pointed at them?

She marched over to the highest-ranking officer, a scrawny sergeant who stood to the side. "What's the meaning of this?"

The sergeant scowled. "This isn't your concern. Return to your work."

Anger flared, her fists clenching. If one more man summarily dismissed her, she might scream. "Lower those weapons, at least. Those are children." She stood between them, arms out. The Bedouin group comprised two men and several women and children. One woman carried an infant. Blood-stained bandages encircled heads and limbs. A man wore a torn, bleeding headscarf and leaned his weight on a makeshift crutch. Nausea rose in her. She'd grown accustomed to seeing locals begging along the roadsides and in cities like Port Said and Cairo, but not like this: injured from war and on the brink of collapse.

The soldiers waited on the sergeant for instructions. He grunted and nodded. They lowered the guns.

"What happened?" Ginger asked the locals. "Who are you?"

The man with the crutch bowed his head. "We were attacked," he answered in Arabic. "Four days ago. The Maslukha and his raiders came into our tribe and killed everyone. We were the only ones to escape."

She gasped. "The Maslukha attacked you?"

Several in the group nodded.

But hadn't James said the Maslukha attacked British troops? Hurting innocent civilians couldn't help the Maslukha's cause. She frowned at the man who had spoken. "How do you know it was the Maslukha?"

"He told my sheik before he killed him."

She put her hand out. "You saw the Maslukha?"

His face appeared wan and tired. "Yes. Many of us did."

If so, the man could describe him to British officials. They needed to assist these poor people, and summon an intelligence officer here immediately.

She addressed the sergeant. "These people were attacked by raiders. They need our help."

"They're Bedouin. May as well be Jacko. We don't treat locals here." The sergeant glared. "They're the raiders anyhow. Bedouin steal from our dead, dig up our graves. They're thieves."

She flinched, hoping the Bedouin man didn't understand English. All the Tommies said similar things, making no attempt to hide the enmity many of them had for the locals and Bedouin. "They walked four days to get here, Sergeant. Give me the time to ask my superiors. I'm certain we can treat wounds and offer them some water." She crossed her arms. "And they may have useful information to report. You wouldn't want them to leave without finding out."

The sergeant huffed. "What's your name, Sister?"

She went closer to the group. The youngest children were barefoot. She smiled at a girl, no older than five, who hid behind her mother's skirt. The girl peeked out, her brown eyes bright, her head framed with black curls tied with a long navy-blue ribbon.

Ginger placed her hand on the forearm of the woman carrying the baby. "May I see the baby?"

The woman hesitated before handing the infant to Ginger. Ginger's heart panged. The threadbare blanket hadn't been enough to protect the child's new skin from the sun. Blistered sunburns dotted his pink face. The infant's eyes were closed, his mouth open. The soft spot on the top of his head felt sunken. He was dehydrated. If he didn't receive immediate care, he wouldn't survive.

She returned him to the woman. "Give me a few minutes. We will see to your care."

The gallop of hoofbeats announced British officers. Ginger shielded her eyes from the sun. The soldiers exchanged looks. She shrank back. One was Major Benson.

His eyes met with hers, and he raised a brow. He dismounted, searching her face before his gaze went to the Bedouin group.

Ginger scanned the officers' jackets. Her stomach dropped. Benson was the ranking officer.

"What is the situation?" Benson strode toward the sergeant.

The sergeant appeared uncomfortable. "These Bedouin came out of nowhere. I tried to take them prisoner, but this sister demanded we take them to the CCS."

"Raiders attacked them." Ginger stepped closer to Major

Benson. "That infant is dehydrated. They all need immediate medical attention."

Benson's jaw tightened. He went over to the Bedouin refugees and spoke to them in flawless, rapid Arabic. The elder man answered his questions with such speed that Ginger couldn't follow the conversation. Regardless of Benson's suspect loyalties, he seemed poised and capable in this situation.

A few minutes later, Benson addressed the sergeant. "You planned to imprison refugee women and infants, Sergeant?"

The sergeant reddened. "Yes, sir."

"Thank goodness this nurse had the excellent sense to intervene. Escort them to the receiving station for food and medicine. Once they have rested, we'll put them on a lorry to Rafah. Tell anyone who asks that Major Noah Benson ordered it. I'll need to speak with them more at length." Without waiting for a response, he returned to his horse.

The sergeant barked orders to the soldiers.

Ginger gaped at Benson. She didn't know what was more confusing—that he'd practically ignored her or that he'd supported her.

"Major." She followed him.

He placed one hand on the saddle of his horse. "Yes, Sister Whitman?"

The Bedouin man must have told Benson the same story he'd relayed to her. It couldn't hurt to ask. "The Bedouin man mentioned the Maslukha."

Major Benson's eyes flashed. "You've heard of him, have you?"

His response intrigued her. "Yes." She crossed her arms. "Why would he attack the Bedouin? Isn't he the enemy of the British?"

Benson watched the women and children. "This tribe is pro-

British." He mounted his horse. "Thank you for stepping in, Sister Whitman."

They must have been helping the British with something important if the Maslukha targeted them. "Thank you for admitting them to the CCS."

He regarded the sergeant with irritation. "The Bedouin offer gracious hospitality to others. Not admitting them would be unconscionable. These are their wells and lands. Some men seem to forget."

His moral compass further confused her feelings toward him. "Major—"

His dark-blue eyes flickered toward hers.

Something about the intensity of his gaze made her nervous, unmoored from the confidence she tried to project. She focused instead on a thatch of grass sprouting between two rocks. "Is it possible for you to request to the matron I be assigned to these refugees?"

A smile touched his lips. "Another favor, Sister Whitman? Haven't I already let you get away with enough?"

She hadn't thought about it that way. She didn't want to be in his debt. And he was right. He could have reported her for sneaking around in a hut with James after dark, which could have been disastrous. "I want to help."

Benson tilted his head. "I'm fascinated at the way you spend your time. Aren't there British men to tend to?"

She jutted her chin out, chastened by his rebuke. "I suppose it's no more unusual than a British officer prowling the clearing station when he's MIA."

He dismounted. "I'm flattered you checked into my work here. I assure you my superiors know where I am. Paperwork can be slow around these parts."

She made no effort to hide sarcasm. "Doing my due diligence, sir. Not unlike you questioning the matron about me."

He leaned toward her. "Where's the matron?"

"The general admission tent." She pointed to it. "That one."

He left her. As she watched him disappear into the tent, an unsettled feeling came over her. He wasn't being unkind. But it was almost as though he treated her without deference *because* he knew who her family was, rather than the other way around.

She followed the refugees into the receiving station. Minutes later, the matron found her there, applying ointment to the infant's sunburn. "Sister, are you sure you're well enough to see to this?"

Ginger gestured to the refugees. "I want to help. Since I'm not at my normal duties today, this seems suitable."

Miss Walsh nodded. "I've granted Major Benson's request, but I wanted to be certain it was also what you wanted."

Though grateful, Ginger mused over Benson's actions long after the matron had left her.

The familiar jiggle of glass jars caught her attention. Beatrice approached, pushing a cart of dressing supplies. "I heard you were here. Matron said I could come and help you. It'll make the work go quicker." She stopped beside Ginger, pity shining in her eyes as she scanned the faces of the women and children in front of Ginger. "How horrible. I can't imagine wandering the desert with children."

"Neither can I." Ginger didn't know much about the Bedouin, and her sources of information were anecdotal and often prejudiced. However, these were not women who feared the desert, even with children. Their presence here spoke to a much more serious issue.

Ginger and Beatrice worked side by side in silence until Ginger spoke. "I meant to ask earlier, is there any change with Ahmed?"

Beatrice's eyes widened. "Actually, that's why I was looking for you. His fever broke an hour ago. He awoke and asked for you."

Oh no. Ginger cringed at her own thoughts. She'd dared to take a terrible risk based on the hope his death would lead to a lack of consequence for her. "I'm a terrible person," she whispered.

Beatrice bit her lip. "You're not. You're just stuck. We all are." She placed a cloth strip on the arm of the woman in front of her. "Though, perhaps it's time to ask your friend Stephen if he would help."

She gritted her teeth. She'd rather eat a sand cake than tell Stephen she'd lied to him. "He might. At least he might spare me from the most serious consequences." She glanced at Beatrice. "If it comes to that, I don't want you or James to confess to helping me. There's no reason we should all face censure."

"No, I couldn't—"

"Promise me, Beatrice. Say nothing."

"But—"

"But nothing. You have a compassionate heart, but you'd never have done this if I hadn't asked. We both know it." She prayed Beatrice would just agree. James would fight her on it also, but she didn't need a battle on two fronts.

"I could have tried to do more to stop you."

Small fingers tapped a jar on the cart between them. Ginger glanced over in time to catch the little girl with the navy ribbon reaching out her hand, embarrassed.

Ginger smiled. She'd been looking at the sphagnum moss they used to pack dressings. "You want a piece?" she asked the girl in Arabic.

The girl nodded.

Ginger fished a small piece of moss from the jar and handed it to her. "It's soft. It comes from a land far, far away."

The girl ran her fingers along it and grinned. She sat, delighted with her prize.

Ginger didn't resume her argument with Beatrice. Minutes later, the girl squirmed. From the looks of it, she needed to relieve herself.

Ginger held her hand out. "I'll help you."

The girl looked hesitantly toward her mother. Her mother nodded, and the girl took Ginger's hand. "I'll return her soon." Ginger led her from the tent toward the latrines nearby. She grimaced at the stench of urine and feces.

The door to the latrine creaked as Ginger opened it. She stepped into the cramped space and avoided looking into the pit dug into the ground below, helping the girl position herself. The rank smell stung her eyes. How horrified her mother or sister would be to go into a privy like this.

Despite it all, the girl smiled at her. The simple innocence of her joy warmed Ginger's heart.

When the girl finished, they left the rickety wooden structure hand in hand. Almost to the receiving station, they rounded the corner and ran headlong into Stephen. He held his arm by the wrist, blood dripping down his elbow from a deep gash in his forearm.

The girl's hand tightened as her gaze focused on Stephen and she screamed. She clung to Ginger's skirt.

Ginger crouched beside her. "It's all right, nothing to fear. Just a little blood."

The girl stared at Stephen, wide-eyed, then fled into the tent.

Ginger stood and winced at him. "What happened to your arm?"

"Minor injury from poking around the debris of the dispensary. I was looking for you."

She inspected his arm. He'd need some stitches. "If you go to the receiving station, I can find someone to patch you up." She would do it herself, but she didn't want to volunteer to spend any more time with him than necessary. "I'm surprised to see you here. I thought you left yesterday."

"I did." Stephen inhaled sharply. "But after sending a message to Henry, he requested I return and do some independent investigation of my own. Both on how Ahmed may have got into this camp and Major Benson's status." His gaze followed the direction the girl had gone. "You treat locals at the clearing station?"

"A group of Bedouin refugees came in, seeking help." She lowered her voice. "They witnessed their tribe's attack by the Maslukha. As for Major Benson, he should be nearby. He intervened to help them receive treatment."

Stephen frowned. "They saw the Maslukha? We need to question them immediately. Are they in a terrible state?"

"Dehydrated and injured. I wish we could do more. Sandwiches and soup don't seem like much to help people who've had everything taken from them. They'll be going on a lorry to Rafah soon. Major Benson is arranging it, if you'd like to discuss it with him."

"Yes, indeed. I'll go find him at once." Stephen removed his hat and turned it in his hands. "Quite a noble pursuit on your part. I fear I was too harsh with you yesterday, my dear. You know how much I've always admired you."

Not an apology, but it was the closest to one she would get. She gave him a tight smile. If she planned to tell him anything, she needed to remain congenial. "Come find me in the receiving station later. We can speak at length then."

She didn't look forward to spending time with him but, fortunately, he didn't find her again. Thoughts of what to do about Stephen haunted her as she worked. Any misgivings she might have were all based off her personal dislike of him. She didn't deem him untrustworthy though, especially not if Henry trusted him. Henry wouldn't have sent him otherwise.

Still, she should talk to Ahmed as soon as she finished with the refugees. She couldn't turn him in without speaking to him. Her conscience wouldn't permit it. Afterwards, she'd confer with James and decide.

Major Benson returned as she and Beatrice finished treating the refugees. He led them outside to a waiting lorry. The scent of petrol piqued Ginger's nostrils as the soldiers helped load the Bedouin.

A tug on her skirt made her look down. The little girl she'd helped stood there, blue ribbon in hand. She pressed it into Ginger's hand and then ran back toward the lorry. Ginger smiled and waved a good-bye once she'd climbed aboard.

The soldiers closed a door on the back and the lorry started and pulled away, leaving a cloud of dust and fumes.

Beatrice put her arm around her. "Why do you look so glum? You did a marvelous thing today."

Ginger swallowed a lump in her throat. Had she been so transparent? "It's best we don't treat children here often. It might do me in."

A boom sounded.

A hollow, aching pressure fell through Ginger's chest. She gripped onto Beatrice, horrified as the lorry burst into flames. Debris burst from it with a second explosion. The lorry teetered on one side and slammed into the ground, consumed with fire.

"No!" Ginger screamed as she raced forward.

The heat from the burning lorry scorched in waves. *Oh God, please, no!* Ginger covered her face with her arms, pushing toward the back door. *Please, let them be alive.* The temperatures drove her back. She pictured the young families, the girl, the infant, trapped inside, trying to get out. But she didn't hear them. She couldn't see anyone, just fire. They couldn't have all perished so quickly, could they?

Someone yanked her backward. She reeled, trying to keep

herself upright, and caught sight of Major Benson as he accelerated past her and grabbed the handle on the door. Cursing, he pulled his fingertips back. Ginger lurched toward the door once more, but his strong arms locked around her.

"Don't touch it." His voice was at her ear as he dragged her away. "You'll get burned."

She struggled. "Let me go." Tears stung her eyes, from the smoke and the heat. She coughed, her throat choking. The lorry crackled, the scene like a mirage wreathed in orange flame. Shouts and voices carried across the desert plain as others came running, some men with buckets of water, not enough to help.

How could this have happened? "Let me go."

By the tents of the clearing station, a small crowd of medical staff and sisters gathered as spectators to the scene. They should do something.

Benson pulled her against his chest, his arms tight. "It's too late. The fire is too hot. We can't save them."

Her body trembled, and she covered her face with her hands. The ground swayed beneath her, nausea and fury sweeping through her. This couldn't be coincidence. Something had gone wrong.

Someone must have done this.

Her eyes drifted to the sand near her boots. Debris from the truck littered the space, too gruesome to behold. Her heart shattered. Not three yards away, her eyes snagged on a singed dark-blue ribbon drifting quietly in the hot desert air.

CHAPTER EIGHT

*M*ajor Benson's voice barely registered as Ginger stood in front of him, wrapping his palm with gauze.

"You're far away, aren't you?"

She startled and met his eyes. He sat on a raised bench, in the hospital unit for patients able to walk. "I-I didn't hear you."

He searched her gaze. "I said, you seem to care about those refugees."

"Of course I care, Major Benson. I didn't become a nurse out of some desire to drive my father to an early grave, no matter what he may have told you." She finished wrapping his hand and released it.

"You can call me Noah."

She ignored him and replaced a roll of gauze on the dressing station. "It's not a terrible burn, but keep it wrapped for at least forty-eight hours. To protect the blistered skin."

Benson examined the job she'd done, then took her hand in his. "You did everything you could for those people."

His touch made her fingers tingle. His thumb grazed the soft skin by her wrist, where she'd tied the Bedouin girl's ribbon, and her eyes locked with his.

She allowed herself to accept the comfort he offered. "I failed to save them." Tears pricked her eyes.

"Henry might be right about you."

She closed her eyes, fighting the tears. "Oh?" She tried to keep her voice casual. Why did he affect her this way? "How so?"

"He told me you were the best of them—your family, that is."

She pulled her hand away and tidied the dressing station. "I'm not." Even now, she was hiding Ahmed in the CCS, perhaps endangering them all.

If only Henry had helped her rather than send Stephen. Telling Stephen the truth seemed even more awful after what had happened with the refugees. Someone treacherous was likely in their midst, as both Stephen and Ahmed had warned. But who? She searched Major Benson's eyes, wishing she could read goodness there.

She looked away. She wasn't in any position to judge goodness.

"Ginger." James stood several feet away. From the way he stared at them, it appeared he'd been watching them for some time. An angry scowl rested on his lips.

Ginger knocked over a jar of cotton and pieces tumbled to the floor. She righted it, hastily. "James."

"I heard from Miss Walsh about that accident." His gaze focused on Noah, who rose from the bench. "I wanted to make certain you were all right."

"Yes—I was tending to Major Benson's wounds. He acted heroically and—"

"Thank you, Major Benson, for assisting my fiancée." James's tone was uncharacteristically biting. "From what I understand, you pulled her away from the burning lorry."

Heat crept up her neck. Benson had wrested her away from

the lorry, holding her against him. Others had seen, no doubt. What had James been told?

"The one who showed true bravery was Sister Whitman." Benson nodded toward Ginger. "Thank you for wrapping my hand. I should return. See if they've determined what happened." He strode from the tent.

Ginger turned toward the dressing table and gathered cotton.

James drew near. "Had you and the major met before now?"

Ginger wound a loose thread from a cloth strip around her forefinger. This would have been so much easier if Henry or her father had mentioned him to her. But she knew it wasn't what James implied.

"No." She brushed past him. "I need to straighten up."

James caught her arm. "Is there something I should know?"

Ginger drew a slow breath. She had done nothing wrong. "No."

"Walk with me." James tugged her. He led her from the tent.

She stopped, ignoring the people and commotion around them. "This isn't the time or the place for this." Her voice dropped. "I have too much on my mind. Beatrice says Ahmed is awake, and Stephen has returned. And I just witnessed children murdered." Her voice broke. "Don't you dare accuse me of anything. I can't help it if Major Benson tried to comfort me."

James didn't appear chastened. "I'm trying to be patient, but in the course of a few days, your former beau appeared at the clearing station, and rumors have reached me about the major's attentions toward you. How am I to feel?"

Anger flared in her. "You could trust me."

James nodded curtly. "It would be a lot easier if I didn't feel you're keeping things from me." He stepped away. "I'll find you tonight after my shift."

She kicked the toe of her boot into the sand, sending a spray of pebbles into the tent's side as he left. The accusation about Major Benson stung. But his failure to provide even the most basic comfort after what she'd endured ... how could he be so insensitive and callous?

She rubbed her eyes. She *had* been less than forthcoming with James the last few days, starting with the bottle she'd buried for Ahmed.

The longer she delayed a decision, the worse it became for her.

She searched the path for Benson. Henry wasn't coming to help her. She could tell Stephen the truth, but she knew how that conversation would go. Benson offered an alternative. If Stephen was Thevshi so openly, Benson could confirm it. Dare she attempt to ask him?

She removed her apron as she hurried away from the tent and toward the scene of the lorry explosion. Drawing closer, her steps faltered. The lorry's remnants were a charred skeleton. The recovered bodies lay on stretchers, covered with sheets.

She swallowed a lump in her throat and scanned the faces of the men working near the site.

Major Benson stood nearby, conversing with a general. Ginger stopped at a distance. Something about seeing him with the general inspired hope. His presence here couldn't be as aberrant and suspicious as Stephen had suggested.

The putrid scent of burning rubber reached her, and she forced herself not to look at the lorry again. She couldn't bear it.

She'd had a lifetime of keeping her emotions tightly under cover. But the death of those innocent people, those children, had shaken her to her core. Even when she worked in Port Said and the refugees had come in boats from Armenia, it hadn't affected her this way. Those refugees had also been women and children, claiming the Turks had treated them barbarously and killed them by the thousands. The British had called it a genocide.

But she hadn't witnessed it the way she'd seen this.

Soft footsteps crunched behind her, and a hand touched her shoulder. "Sister—"

Major Benson stood behind her, a curious expression on his face.

"I—" She lifted a hand to her forehead. The words didn't pass the thickness of her throat.

He took her by the hand. "Come this way." He led her away. Someone might see them together, but she was too weary to care about ridiculous gossip and James's unwarranted jealousy.

She followed him across the railroad tracks, toward the beach. The warm breeze from the ocean enveloped her, the salt spray fragrant and filling her lungs. She stopped, squinting against the sun's bright reflection on the waves.

"Are you all right?"

"No." A choked cry left her throat. She removed her cap and sank onto the sand. She had to compose herself. Despite what he'd done to help the Bedouins, Benson was not her friend. She couldn't allow herself to forget that. "I wanted to ask you about Thevshi."

He sat beside her. "I told you before. You shouldn't be using that name so carelessly."

A seabird played in the surf by the lapping waves. "I'm looking for him. It's imperative I speak with him." It was as close to the truth as she dared to tell him.

"Why not ask your brother? You said Thevshi is his friend."

She'd made everything so difficult with her dishonesty. "I sent a wire to him, but he didn't respond."

He raised his chin. "What is it you need to tell Thevshi? I can pass along a message if that's what you'd like."

Despite his calm responses, her alarm grew. She met his

gaze. "Do you know who Thevshi is? You weren't direct with me before."

He hesitated, then nodded curtly. "I do."

Why hadn't he just said so? Much as she wanted to believe him, the admission troubled her. "Can you arrange a meeting? I'd prefer to speak to him myself."

He stared at the bandage on his hand. "It's too dangerous."

She'd been afraid he might say that. "I can only speak to Thevshi. Please. I know it's another favor, but it must be him and him alone."

"What you're asking is more than a favor, unfortunately. Arranging a meeting with Thevshi could be foolhardy if not done with care. I need more details before taking that risk."

She ran her fingertips across the blazing sand. "Stephen Fisher told me he was Lieutenant Thevshi. Is he?"

Major Benson's face darkened. "You mentioned this situation to Fisher?" He shifted. "I have to be honest—I'm confused by your conflicting stories. I'm still under the impression you're hiding something. You need to tell me what's going on. Your behavior at that hut and when I questioned you was evasive. I know you're lying to me about something. And I'm fairly certain it has to do with those bloodstains."

Acid clawed her throat. "I already told you, I don't know anything about that." He hadn't answered her question about Stephen, either.

"Then why won't you look me in the eye and say it?"

She clenched her teeth. Why couldn't he help her without forcing her into a confession? She should have gone to Ahmed first, as she'd planned. She should have asked James for advice. The incident with the Bedouin had clouded her judgement and made her more sympathetic to the major, when the chance of him being the enemy spy hadn't diminished.

"Why should I trust you? You haven't given me any reason

to. And I don't report to you." She wiped her hand against her skirt and stood. "I won't waste your time any further."

"Wait." He scrambled from the sand. "What you're asking is dangerous. And you're not being upfront. You lied before about how you knew Thevshi, didn't you?"

"And you lied about not knowing Thevshi."

"Not precisely. But you're involved in something you shouldn't be. I can help you." He stepped closer to her. "Tell me about those bloodstains in the hut. I think you know."

Her pulse throbbed at her neck, and it made her feel even more vulnerable. She should have expected this. What had she been thinking?

A part of her wanted to trust him. But it wasn't logical. She didn't know him.

She tasted the brine of sweat on her lips, and a faint buzzing in her ears reminded her of the lingering headache she'd ignored the last few hours.

She needed time.

"Meet me at the general admission tent around"—she checked her wristwatch—"six o'clock. We can talk more then." She flashed a tight-lipped smile. "I must return to my patients."

Benson's eyes clouded. "Very well. Six o'clock."

She left him on the beach. Why couldn't anything be easier? She didn't have many options left. She had to talk to Ahmed. But if he didn't give her clarity, what would she do?

CHAPTER NINE

Ginger found Ahmed sleeping. His skin's pale, sickly pallor had diminished, and his forehead no longer burned with fever.

She set to work checking his dressings, when his eyelids fluttered open. Ahmed's eyes settled on her. He smiled. "Sister. You're here."

His relief at seeing her warmed her heart. "I'm here. But I need to ask you some questions."

"Have you found Thevshi?"

"I sent a wire to the CID, as you instructed. I received no response."

Ahmed shifted, and winced. "He might not respond through the telegram. It's too dangerous for him. If you used the code name Dragonfly, he would have known I was here."

Her stomach dropped. If Thevshi had received the message, would he have shown up at the clearing station instead?

His words bolstered Stephen's claims. He'd arrived the morning after Ginger sent the telegram.

Ginger dropped her voice to a whisper. "Ahmed, does Thevshi go by another name? Do you know what he looks like?" "We used these names alone to protect ourselves. I've never met him."

"Ahmed isn't your name either?"

He coughed and shook his head. "No. But I cannot tell you my name. It would endanger my family." Ahmed propped himself up on his elbows, the veins in his neck and temples protruding with the effort. "If Thevshi knows I am here, he will look for me. I must get to him."

"Ahmed, in Thevshi's absence, I can't confirm your identity. You need to give me more information." She hesitated. "When you were delirious, you mentioned the Maslukha."

Ahmed's eyes darkened. "You must be silent, Sister."

"If you don't tell me more, I must turn you over. Do you work for the Maslukha?"

Ahmed appeared torn. "I will tell you what I must." He swallowed, his voice barely audible. "I won't have you believe I work for that devil. I was working undercover in Ottoman territory when Maslukha had a secret meeting with General Pasha. I learned Maslukha's identity and his plans. That is why I must speak to Lieutenant Thevshi. We are in great danger."

Her heart beat faster. "Who is the Maslukha?"

Ahmed shook his head. "I won't put the burden of that information on you, Sister. Men will kill for that knowledge."

She leaned closer. "Who is in danger?"

"The British. The French. Everyone fighting Germans and Turks." Ahmed rested his hand on his stomach. "If the Maslukha succeeds in his plans, he could change the war's course. Make survival impossible."

She'd thought he may have information affecting the British offensive into Gaza. But intelligence influencing the entire war? "How?"

"He plans to murder someone important to the British. And start a revolution against the British among the Arabs and Egyptians. The effect would be disastrous."

"And you can stop him?"

"I stole documents, correspondence between Maslukha and General Pasha. I was almost caught and buried them. That's why what I gave you is so important. They'll lead Thevshi to the documents and Maslukha."

What he'd given her? *The bottle and his bag.* A sick feeling settled into her stomach. If they would lead Thevshi to the documents, she had to protect them. In the wrong hands, it could be disastrous. "Is there anyone else at Cairo Intelligence you would trust? Anyone you know would help you?"

"I don't know who else the traitor may work with. I only trust Thevshi." He grunted and rested his head. Sweat beaded on his forehead. "Do you have morphine?"

Lifting a syringe from her bag, she steadied her hands. "Bedouin refugees arrived here. The Maslukha attacked their tribe four days ago, and they escaped. We treated them, put them in a lorry ... and the lorry exploded."

Ahmed sucked through his teeth as she injected. "I told you. There's a traitor here. If they escaped the Maslukha, they were a threat to him because they could identify him."

She set the syringe down. The traitor worked for the Maslukha? "You're saying the traitor learned about the refugees and killed them?"

The pain eased from Ahmed's face. "Yes. He'll kill me too. It's a matter of time before he finds me. He's been on my trail for weeks."

Sunlight filtered through the spaces between the tent's canvas panels. She toyed with the ribbon around her wrist. Benson had arrived at the camp shortly after she'd found Ahmed. And he'd known about the refugees.

Could he have plotted the explosion on the lorry while she treated them?

Dizziness smacked her, like a strange dousing of embers burning fire down her nerves. He couldn't be such a monster. He seemed honorable. He'd held her with such gentleness ...

Maybe he hadn't pulled her away to keep her safe—maybe he'd wanted to ensure the refugees were dead.

She shuddered. Ahmed's soft breath told her the morphine was taking effect.

A deep, familiar voice caught her attention. She edged toward the split in the privacy curtain around the bed and peered out. Major Benson stood in the doorway to the hospital ward, speaking to an orderly.

Had he followed her? She was so foolish. So naïve. She couldn't trust the Major.

If Ahmed told the truth, she had to save him. She didn't have time to talk to James and ask his advice—he was in surgery.

She had to get Ahmed out and hide him. Now.

Shaking Ahmed's shoulder, she crouched beside him. "We have to get you to safety if the traitor is so close. Where can I take you?"

He rolled his head toward her. "There's a sheik's tomb, along the road to Rafah. It isn't far." Saliva collected by his lips. "I could shelter there. But we have to go by horse."

A horse wouldn't do. Ahmed wouldn't be able to stay upright. She would have to borrow a camel ambulance, which had stretchers astride the beast's humps.

She drew in a sharp breath.

If she crossed this line, there would be no return.

But she didn't believe Ahmed *was* an enemy. And Ahmed wouldn't be able to walk on his own with his injuries. If he tried to get away, he'd die in the desert. Once she got Ahmed to safety, she'd have the time necessary to figure out her next steps.

"You'll have to help me get there," she told Ahmed. She'd never get him anywhere without help. She needed another set of hands.

Damn it. Beatrice wouldn't be off shift yet.

Then she remembered. James had already involved someone else—the orderly, Ian McNeill. James claimed they could trust him. If she told Ian James had requested he help her, Ian wouldn't have a reason to doubt her.

She grabbed a wheelchair from the ward's end. The wooden wheels creaked as she rolled it closer to Ahmed's bedside. "Ready? You can lean against me as you get in the chair."

Ahmed groaned as he shifted. She slid her arm behind him and placed his arm over her shoulder. "When you're ready, try to stand. It'll hurt. But it won't be for long, I promise. I'll get you to the chair."

Ahmed set his feet on the ground, his weight resting against her as he stood. His face puckered with the strain, his body trembling. She inched him toward the wheelchair and lowered him into the seat, her muscles aching from the strain of supporting him. His chest heaved, and he collapsed back.

Her heart pounded.

There would be no escape if she went out the proper exit. Her eyes darted around the ward. Could she protect Ahmed from Major Benson? She raced to the corner and yanked on the ties holding the panel to the tent pole. When she'd made a large-enough opening, she shoved the wheelchair through the side of the tent.

The day had darkened, the sun a melting ball of yellow wax in a bloodstained sky. If she didn't hurry, she'd be leaving past sundown. No time to tie the tent flap shut. Running would attract unwanted attention. She needed to act with calm.

The chair's wheels bounced on the uneven terrain. It would be painful for Ahmed. "I'm sorry," she said. She glanced over her shoulder at the isolation tent. The panel she'd left open flapped like a sail in the wind. She rubbed away grit and sand blowing into her eyes.

She paused at the evacuation ward, addressing the first orderly she saw. "Do you know where Ian McNeill is?"

The orderly pointed to another tent. "He works in the pre-operation ward." He looked at Ahmed. "You have a patient for transport?"

"No, thank you." Her hands tightened against the handles, and she pressed on.

The unwieldy chair stabilized as she pushed it onto the dirt path cutting between the clearing station tents. Lines showed on the ground behind her from the wheels rolling across it. If Major Benson glanced out the tent, he could follow a direct line to her.

Stay calm. Even if he found her, she could claim the patient in the chair urgently needed surgery. Though, it would be difficult to explain why she'd gone out the tent's side rather than through the front entrance.

She pushed harder. Faster. Her booted footsteps felt heavy. The wheels squealed.

With heaving breaths, she pushed Ahmed into the ward.

"Ian McNeill?"

A young orderly who looked barely old enough to shave lifted his dark head. His thick eyebrows rose in curiosity. Would he even be able to help her? He was rail-thin and short of stature.

Still, he'd be better than no one. Her hand gripped Ahmed's shoulder. "I need your help."

CHAPTER TEN

*G*inger awoke to Beatrice shaking her shoulder. She rolled her head further into her pillow and groaned.

"It's time to get ready for your hearing." Beatrice's voice, normally soft and pleasant, sounded like the harsh squeal of an ungreased hinge, and Ginger squeezed her burning eyelids.

"I think I fell asleep twenty minutes ago."

Beatrice sat on the cot, and the mattress sank with her added weight. "Insomnia?"

Ginger pressed her cool fingertips to her eyelids. "Yes. I couldn't sleep. With every jackal's howl, I pictured Ahmed out there, in that tomb—it was hardly better than the hut we found him in the first day. What if I condemned him to die by taking him there?" She opened her stinging eyes. "And I can't even go to check on him this morning. I have that damned hearing. And my shift."

Ginger set her feet on the ground and yawned. She gripped Beatrice's forearm to keep herself from pitching forward, feeling simultaneously jittery and nauseated. Beatrice chuckled.

"You'll need something stronger than tea to keep you going today."

Ginger eased off the cot, her worries returning. There hadn't been time after she and Ian had returned to the clearing station to talk to James the night before. She'd need to send Stephen a telegram this morning. "Am I making a mistake in not taking the help my brother sent me?"

"That Stephen Fisher fellow?" Beatrice went to Ginger's trunk and pulled out a clean uniform. "Do you trust him? I thought you hated him."

"Hate may be too strong a word." Ginger rolled her stiff shoulders. "My brother trusts him." She hesitated. "I don't know. When I'm around him I remember how awful it was, growing up with the expectation from everyone that someday he would be my husband. I felt trapped. He made me uncomfortable and took liberties with how familiarly he acted toward me—but I think he did it because he never dreamed I'd turn him down."

"And what about Major Benson? You seemed to …" Beatrice's kind, understanding eyes squinted. "He seems honest, Ginger. And I think you feel the same way."

Oh, wonderful. Ginger grunted. "Don't tell me you've bought into the gossip too?"

"I've heard the sisters whispering about him—but I think that's mainly because he's handsome. But I know you. And the way he held you yesterday … It didn't surprise me James was jealous."

Ginger stiffened. "I can't be responsible for what Major Benson did. Anyway, I'd imagine it takes charm to be an imposter and a traitor." Beatrice's implication hurt more than she cared to admit.

Beatrice bit her lip, perhaps sensing she'd said too much. "You should get ready for that hearing."

She stood and dressed, determined to focus on the task at

hand. First, get through the hearing. Second, visit the telegraph station before her shift and send a message to Stephen. She'd done everything possible to keep Ahmed safe. It was time to hand this over to someone else, someone who belonged to the intelligence world like Stephen did. Henry trusted him and she trusted Henry. That would have to be good enough. Too much was at stake to keep delaying just because it happened to be Stephen whom Henry had asked her to trust.

And if Major Benson was the traitor he appeared to be, he'd disappear from her life too.

An unexpected wave of sadness struck her upon thinking he might truly be the traitor. She fastened her shoulder cape into place.

She and Beatrice left their quarters, the sun hidden behind thick clouds that would have offered relief if not for the humidity. Parting with Beatrice at the Mess, Ginger continued forward toward the admission tent, where Matron had told Ginger to meet her, then she startled.

Major Benson stood near the quarters for the medical officers, looking at her. Ginger gritted her teeth and avoided his gaze. Why did he always turn up at the most inopportune moments?

She passed him, and he cleared his throat. "Good morning," he said.

She stopped and sighed. "What do you want?" She winced at her own rudeness.

He lifted a brow. "A word."

"I don't have time just at the moment." *Be a little nicer.* "My apologies," she added with a tight smile.

He fell into step beside her. They passed the mobile cooking stoves. Smoke drifted over from the burning wood fires. She waved it away and glanced at him. "I have an important appointment."

"A disciplinary hearing, I believe? I'm heading in the same direction as you, if you don't mind me joining you." From his tone, he made it clear he asked as a courtesy. "You never appeared at the time we'd agreed to last night."

She didn't look at him. "I had something urgent arise with a patient."

"I assumed. Though, interestingly enough, you seemed to have vanished when I asked around." He gave her a sharper look. "The circumstances being what they are, you've left me no choice but to make some changes."

He put his fingers to his lips and whistled.

A young local boy, no older than eight, appeared. He scampered over. He wore ragged, unkempt clothes and was barefoot.

"Ginger, meet Khalib."

"Khalib?" She frowned.

"Don't worry, he doesn't bite. And even if he does, he's lost a few teeth recently. Give the lady a smile."

Khalib revealed two missing teeth, his eyes bright.

Ginger chuckled. "Hello."

"Khalib understands some English, but rarely speaks it. I've been teaching him." Major Benson spouted off a few phrases in Arabic, too fast for her to understand. The boy listened intently and shot Ginger a new, brighter smile as Benson ruffled his mop of hair. Khalib scrambled off once more.

She clasped her hands, baffled by the exchange. "Why did you want me to meet him?"

"He'll be following you. I thought you might want to know. I told him if he promises to be nice, you'll reward him by giving him biscuits."

She stopped in her tracks. "Following me?"

He smiled. "Precisely."

"Why, exactly, are you having a child follow me?"

His face was a mask. "I'm sure you know the answer

already."

Chills crept down her spine. Had she given herself away? "You can't do that."

"Feel free to take it up with HQ. My guess is you won't." They squared off for several beats, then he tipped his hat. "You should go. I wouldn't want to stop the brass from raking you over the coals. I hear you committed the unforgivable sin of saving a young man's life. The conversation has been delightful, as usual." He strode off.

Ginger blinked at his disappearing form, floored by his comments. In one stroke he'd criticized the officers who wanted to reprimand her but kept her at a distance with his sarcasm. Who was he? What she thought she knew of him seemed at odds with what she felt in her gut.

Khalib peeked around a tent's corner.

And now this.

She clenched her jaw and continued on.

As she neared the admission tent, Miss Walsh exited. She gave Ginger a surprised look. "Sister Whitman—haven't you heard? They canceled your hearing. I assumed you'd be enjoying yourself at breakfast."

Ginger's jaw dropped. "Canceled?"

"Yes, well, after Major Benson's character witness and testimony, the RAMC dropped the charges against you." Miss Walsh appeared thoughtful. "He's a persuasive elocutionist. Spoke highly of you."

What on earth?

She grimaced. And she'd been so horrible toward him. Yet he'd also put a boy to spy on her. His motives were incomprehensible.

Miss Walsh patted Ginger's arm as she walked past, leaving Ginger staring blankly at the field in front of the admission tent. The field where the lorry had exploded.

Ginger pivoted away.

Why would Benson speak on her behalf?

What was worse, James was sure to find out about it. Given their argument the day before, what would he think?

She had to find James, before he heard it from someone else.

As she hurried forward, an officer approached from the direction of HQ. Green eyes, a shade darker than her own, met hers. Ginger's breath caught.

Henry.

He was here. Joy and hope shot through her as he noticed her, his eyes widening in recognition.

Ginger ran to him and flung her arms around Henry's neck, knocking him backward.

"Ginny." Henry squeezed her. "I'm sorry it took me so long to get here."

Ginger wiped tears from her lashes. "I can't tell you how wonderful it is you're here." She held his hands. "Look at me, I'm practically weeping. You'd think it's been years instead of five short months."

Henry placed an affectionate kiss on her cheek. "It's rotten luck that you're the sister who left for the war's duration. Lucy grows more intolerable by the day."

Ginger shook her head, wiping her cheeks again. "She still hasn't taken to Cairo?"

"She groans daily for Mother to take her home to Penmore. Never mind the growing torpedo threat. I think she'd gladly walk through a minefield than face another Egyptian summer."

The talk of home made her feel anchored, at last. "And Mother?"

"Tolerating the circumstances as best she can. Her patience for living abroad is about as thin as Lucy's. And she's worried about the both of us." Henry's expression sobered. "Though, both Father and I were worried by your cryptic telegram."

Ginger glanced down the pathway. "I understand, but I wish you hadn't sent Stephen in your place. He's still as boorish as ever."

Henry gave her a rueful look. "That was father's idea. But for my sake—and Angelica's—maybe you could try to cease your war against him? We'd like our wedding to be happy and peaceful, without the drama of your dislike for Stephen."

"He still writes me letters, you know."

Henry shrugged. "He's still in love with you. Take it as a sign of his good taste. Until you're married, he won't give up on the hope you'll change your mind." He grinned. "And maybe not even after that."

Ginger shook her head, disconcerted by the thought. "By the way, another acquaintance of yours is here—or at least he claims to be. One whose allegiances I'm not as certain about. Major Noah Benson."

Henry broke into a smile. "Noah's here?"

Ginger tilted her head at Henry's unexpected reaction. "You didn't know he was missing?"

"Yes, yes, but it's Noah. He's survived tough scrapes before." Henry wiped a trickle of sweat from his forehead. "It'd be good to see him."

Ginger pointed to Khalib. "He might lead you to him. Noah's assigned him to keep tabs on me."

"Khalib?" Henry nodded. "He always knows where to find Noah."

"You know Khalib?"

"He's been following Noah around for years. But why would he have Khalib keep tabs on you?"

She tugged his elbow. "Walk with me. I'm heading to break-fast." She led him down the path. "I found a wounded man hiding in the camp—a Turk, or so I believed. And I treated him."

Henry's jaw dropped open. "Ginny, do you have any idea how—"

"His name is Ahmed Bayrak. He claims to be an agent for the British and has information on the Maslukha's identity and documents pertaining to his plans to kill someone important to the British cause."

Henry's dark lashes blinked rapidly. "A ... Turkish spy?"

She nodded, knowing how bad it sounded. Hopefully, Henry would trust her to not be gullible. "Of sorts. He's Jewish, actually. Speaks English perfectly. He says he was trying to meet with a Lieutenant Thevshi—have you heard of him?"

"Thevshi?" Henry shook his head. "Can't say I have. Who is supposedly being targeted for assassination?"

"He didn't say. Lloyd George isn't due to travel to Egypt soon, is he?" The British prime minister's death would have a devastating effect on the war effort.

"Not that I'm aware of. But Sir Mark Sykes is in the area. He's among the more important diplomats in Cairo at the moment. He could be a likely target." He frowned. "Where is this man now?"

"I've hidden him in a sheik's tomb between here and Rafah." Her eyes fixed on the scar on Henry's cheek, the one he'd received as a young man in Oxford, when someone had dared to make an unwanted advance at her. The memory made her shudder. Thank God her older brother was here at last.

Henry clasped his hands behind him. "All right. You can take me there. Now, what does Noah have to with this?"

Ginger cringed. Her brother wouldn't be happy to hear her speculations. "Ahmed claimed there's a traitor at the CID. I think it may be him."

Henry's face darkened. "Noah? A traitor? Impossible." Anger flashed in his eyes. "This Ahmed fellow has been entirely reckless. How dare he involve you in this?"

Ginger put a hand on his. "Don't blame him—he had no one else to turn to. And he didn't name the major specifically."

"You know far more than you should." Henry glowered. "You should have trusted Noah. Or Stephen. I take it you've yet to tell either of them you've been hiding this Ahmed?"

"I didn't know if I could trust Benson."

"I'd trust Noah with my life." Henry waved a fly away.

Much as Henry's testimony appealed to her, she remained unsure. Would Henry know if Noah was a traitor? "Your friendship with him hardly allows you objectivity. Besides, there's more. Bedouin refugees arrived here yesterday, after the Maslukha attacked them. Major Benson intervened. Hours later, the refugees were killed. It's suspicious."

Henry frowned. "Is Noah still here? I must speak to him. We'll settle the matter."

A tense feeling pressed her chest. "You won't tell him what I've shared with you, will you?"

"I'll consider what to do. I wouldn't want you to be in trouble for this, and Noah follows the rules closely." They neared the Mess and stopped. "When can you take me to see Ahmed? I'd like to go right away."

She checked her watch. "I'd have to ask the matron. It's possible she may let me start my shift later if I explain you've arrived. But we'd have to go by horseback."

A worried look crossed Henry's face. "And the documents Ahmed claimed to have? Does he carry them still?"

The bottle would be easy enough to retrieve and give to Henry, but James had the bag. She'd ask James for Ahmed's bag and give it to Henry later. She didn't want Henry criticizing James for his involvement.

"Ahmed gave me something to hide in the hut where I first found him."

"Can you retrieve it and bring it before we go out to speak to him?"

Ginger nodded. "I'll go from here. If you'll meet me at the stables in a half hour, we can take a pair of horses out to Ahmed. If Miss Walsh denies my request to start my shift later, I'll let you know."

Henry's eyes focused elsewhere. Ginger followed his gaze. Noah and Khalib were striding toward them side by side. Henry grinned and shook Noah's hand when he reached them. "Well, well, Benson. You're not as dead as they feared. Father will be pleased to hear it."

"I'm surprised he hasn't heard it already." Noah's put a hand on Khalib's shoulder. "It's because of Khalib. He helped me escape."

"I hear you have him following my sister." Henry's brows rose.

"Your sister"—Noah's eyes flickered toward her—"has a penchant for trouble."

Henry placed his arm around Ginger's shoulders. "Always. A regular troublemaker, this one."

Henry's presence made her want to flee from Noah even more. She should have taken comfort in her brother's protective nature. But she didn't want Henry to paint an image of her to anyone. Especially not Noah Benson.

"Excuse me—we'll speak later." This would be the best opportunity to speak to Miss Walsh and retrieve the bottle from the hut. Ginger moved away from Henry. She nodded at Noah. "Major Benson."

She hurried away, chiding herself. She should have thanked Noah for his help with the disciplinary hearing.

She chose not to look back, her heart heavy. Nothing about Noah was uncomplicated. Not even the regret she felt for not trusting him.

CHAPTER ELEVEN

Ginger wound through the hilly terrain, bathed in sweat. A threatening cloudy sky had bloomed since sunrise. As she neared the well, a thunderclap rumbled, eerily reminiscent of gunfire from the front.

"Ginny." Stephen sauntered toward her. "Strange running into you here. Shouldn't you be in a hospital tent?"

Her fingers curled into her palms. She couldn't seem to go anywhere without running into someone. Thunder rumbled again, like a church bell urging haste. "Just came down to request some water for the wards." With Henry here, she no longer felt the need to tell him anything. "I'm surprised to see you. I assumed you'd left."

Stephen fell into step with her. "I spent the night at HQ. It was easier than going back and forth."

"You'll be glad to know Henry has arrived. I left him speaking to Major Benson."

He stopped near a stunted, gnarled fig tree. "Ah, yes. I sent Henry word he should come to help you."

The palm trees swayed in a strong gust of wind. "Do you know Benson well?"

Stephen scowled. "I try to limit what I know to as little as possible."

Naturally, Stephen would be jealous of Noah and Henry's friendship. As a boy, he'd spent a month angry with Henry after losing a chess game. He flattened rivals.

"I heard him speaking Arabic the other day. Is he proficient?" She tapped her foot.

"Quite. He speaks several languages with ease." He wrinkled his nose. "Probably worked around immigrants as a child. He is Irish, after all."

Had the past three years made Stephen more loathsome, or had she not noticed the extent to which his snobbery affected her? Then again, she'd changed. Noah's accomplishments were likely far less pedestrian. Irish, though? She replayed Noah's perfect diction in her mind. "What do you mean by Irish?"

"He fooled you, didn't he? He does everyone. He hides those roots well."

A lightning flash filled the sky. She spotted Khalib hanging back twenty feet.

Stephen followed her gaze. "I see you've met Benson's protégé."

"You know him?" For someone who claimed to have little knowledge of Noah, Stephen seemed to know a lot.

"The boy has been doing jobs for him for years. I think Benson sees himself in the child. Camaraderie through being a fellow orphan."

Orphan? The wind hissed, pushing strands of hair onto her face. She hadn't pictured that. Noah comported himself with polish. "Maybe Major Benson understands what it's like to be in his shoes."

"What shoes?" Stephen laughed.

Unconscionable prig. She scowled. "I don't want to keep you from taking shelter."

"Of course." Stephen must have known his joke had bothered her. Or did he think their perspectives were so similar she'd find him funny?

The damp drizzle gave way to a torrential downpour. Stephen sprinted toward headquarters. Ginger dashed toward the huts.

Khalib followed, and she pulled him inside the hut where she'd found Ahmed. He stared at the rain from the doorway, shivering. He jumped at the crack of thunder.

She squeezed his shoulder. Water gushed through the shabby roof and dripped onto Ginger's neck. She'd learned long ago these spring storms in the desert were unlike anything she'd experienced at home. Did she dare retrieve the bottle with Stephen so close by and Khalib in here with her?

Khalib wouldn't understand her actions. She squatted at the spot where she'd hidden it and fingered the wet stone's edges. Dirt filled her nails. Her knuckles scraped against the rock. She removed her hand and rubbed the torn skin.

Khalib watched her curiously.

Her temples throbbed. She waited for another lightning bolt to distract him. At the next flash, she grasped the stone in both hands and yanked it away. Her fingers closed around the bottle.

"What are you doing in here?"

Ginger jumped. She extracted her hand, the bottle in her palm, and faced Stephen in the doorway.

She hoped the darkness hid her guilty expression. She pocketed the bottle and braced her hands on Khalib's shoulders to steady them. "You scared me. I thought we'd take shelter in here from the rainstorm. The boy was frightened."

Stephen studied the corner where she'd been. "You shouldn't be out. It's unsafe. I can escort you to the CCS."

"It's unnecessary. We'll keep moving." She pushed Khalib out the door before her.

"Wait."

She paused, her heart pounding. What if he tried to take the bottle? She was overreacting. He couldn't know about it.

"I meant to ask—did you witness that lorry explosion? You weren't in danger, were you?"

He wanted to ask her about that now? Her heart ached at the memory. "I did. Major Benson and I tried to save them."

Stephen's eyes glittered. "Strange, wouldn't you say? How the major was around when it happened?"

His words echoed her own uncertain thoughts about Noah. She eyed Stephen suspiciously. What was he implying?

Khalib stood beside her and slipped his hand onto her forearm.

Stephen narrowed his gaze at the young boy. His eyes flicked back to Ginger's. "You should get going."

Never more thankful to flee from Stephen's presence, Ginger ran.

Khalib followed closely. The desert absorbed the rain as quickly as it fell, turning the dusty path to mud. Khalib's toes dug into the mud, and Stephen's joke about his bare feet grew more repugnant.

Upon reaching the hospital tents, Ginger pulled him into the receiving station. Khalib shivered. She grabbed a blanket from a supply cupboard, shook it open, and wrapped it around the boy's thin shoulders. "Better?"

He nodded.

"Do you want some hot tea?"

He smiled. "Coffee?"

"I'll see what I can find. Wait here."

Ginger found some brewed coffee near the entrance. She returned with the warm cup and clean towels. She knelt and wiped Khalib's feet. His eyes were solemn and dark. Why would Noah deem it appropriate to bring him to a place like this?

"You'll stay dry here. I must go out again." Hopefully, he would listen.

"I go with you."

"I'll be working. Nothing to tell Major Benson. You can't go with me, Khalib."

He shook his head. He was extremely stubborn or loyal. Maybe both.

Leaving Khalib seated in the corner, Ginger dried her face with a towel. She dabbed at her wet clothing. It would get soaked on the ride to Ahmed. She fished out the bottle from her pocket and peered through the glass.

Something was preventing light from passing through.

She unscrewed the lid. A roll of paper was curled inside.

Goose bumps rose on her arms, and she expelled the contents with a shake, then unfolded the smooth paper.

A coded message was written in a few neat rows.

She couldn't know what it meant—no doubt intentionally. She tucked the message back.

She exited again, not waiting for Khalib, who scrambled after her.

The rain came down in sheets, increasing Ginger's awareness of her own filth. Mud caked her boot heels and several inches of her skirt. She passed the operating theater.

"Ginger!"

She turned in time to see James duck out from the pre-operation ward.

"What are you doing?" James motioned toward the tent. "Get under cover. This rainstorm is terrible."

Despite her frustration with him from the day before, her anger vanished as she stared at him. Ignoring her sopping wet clothing she hugged him and pressed a quick kiss to his lips, her mouth feeling cold against his warmth. She pulled back, a smile on her face. "Henry's here. There's no time to explain. I'll need Ahmed's bag from your tent later. I have to go."

James held on to her hand as she turned away. "Go where?"

She met his gaze, and he pulled off his glasses as rain soaked the lenses. She wished she had told him more. As it was, he didn't even know she'd moved Ahmed. "I promise I'll explain as soon as possible."

"Wait." James placed a hand on her forearm. "Before you do, I have something to say." James straightened. "I'm sorry I've been difficult lately. I meant to find you and apologize yesterday. And I had an idea." He drew her closer, rain dripping from his face. "I think we should request a pass and get married. Right away."

She hadn't expected this, especially given their conversation days ago. Her lips parted in shock. "I—"

"I don't see the point of waiting until after the war anymore. We may as well do it now. We care for each other. My reaction to Major Benson was unfounded. I want you to feel you can trust me with anything. Being married will help."

She stared at her feet. A black caterpillar crawled on the ground near her boot, racing to get away from the rain. "But they'll dismiss me from the Queen Alexandra's."

He slid his hands behind the backs of her arms. "We don't have to tell anyone. We'll marry in secret." An earnest expression shone in his gaze. "I've decided I don't want to wait any longer for you to be mine."

She stepped back, surprised at his possessiveness. If someone had stuffed her mouth full of dry biscuits and asked her to sing 'God Save the King' before His Majesty himself, she would have felt less suffocated.

His face reddened. "I'm sorry. I didn't mean to embarrass you."

At least he mistook her hesitation for embarrassment. She stammered, "I'm not certain I'm comfortable with a secret marriage."

"There are many couples who are getting married at the consulate with the war."

She touched his cheek. "It's a … lovely idea. But for now I have to go. Henry is waiting for me."

His shoulders sagged as he nodded.

Despite her unease, she kissed him. "We will talk about it. I promise."

She left him. Her heart felt as though a cavity had opened over her ribcage, the pain dull and her guilt overwhelming. He expected her to marry him. Beatrice was right. She was stringing him along.

She pushed the encounter from her mind. They'd have time to sort it out later. For the time being what mattered was taking Henry to Ahmed.

As she neared the stables, Ginger lifted her face to the sky. The rain struck her skin, jumping from her forehead and cheeks.

She startled when Henry touched her shoulder. He led two horses. "You ready?"

Ginger took the horse's reins. Khalib watched them closely. "Did you tell Major Benson about Ahmed?"

Henry shook his head. "No. I decided it was better to wait until I questioned the fellow myself."

Thank goodness. She tilted her head toward Khalib. "What about the child?"

"He'll tell Noah we've gone, but he won't be able to follow."

Henry held his hand out to help Ginger onto her horse, then mounted his own. "Let's go."

Guilt gnawed at her as her eyes locked with Khalib. She didn't want to leave the boy in the rain like this, even if he knew how to take care of himself. But he wasn't her responsibility.

She snapped the reins and rode away.

CHAPTER TWELVE

*G*inger's boots sank into the mud as she dismounted. The storm continued, but riding in a rainstorm with her brother had been calming, reminiscent of their childhood.

The tomb's placement off the main road to Rafah made it ideal. She even remembered seeing it from the train when the nurses journeyed from the hospital at El Arish to Belah. It was a shabby stone structure on a flat plain, surrounded by a grove of orange and pomegranate trees.

"Stay here," Ginger told Henry. Rain pooled beside the entrance. "I should talk to him first."

Henry took her horse's reins from her outstretched hand. "I'll tie up the horses."

A lightning bolt and thunder crack parted the sky and the horses whinnied with unease, stomping backward.

Ginger stepped inside. Ahmed lay on a sheet, sleeping. She touched his shoulder.

He shifted. A smile lit his eyes. "Sister."

Seeing him alive made her want to hug him. "I brought help. My brother, Henry. He works for the Arab Bureau."

Ahmed's face darkened. "Sister—"

"I know what you asked. But I can't find Thevshi. I trust my brother implicitly."

Ahmed searched her gaze, his breath labored. At last, he nodded. "If you trust him, I will."

A weight lifted from her shoulders. "I promise he'll help you."

Ginger retreated out into the rain. Henry waited by the horses. "He's willing to talk to you."

Henry touched her cheek. "All will be well. I hate to ask, but please wait here."

"In the rain?"

Henry nodded. "I want him to speak freely, without your further involvement."

Ginger hugged her arms to her chest. Despite the reasonable nature of his request, staying outside was a miserable prospect. She sheltered under a palm tree as he entered.

She patted her palomino stallion's head. Rain ran in rivulets down its neck. The dark eyes blinked at her, and she smiled. She missed riding in the forests around Penmore.

She shivered. She wished a hot bath and a cup of tea awaited her. Few things cleared the rain's chill.

A crash sounded from inside the structure.

What was that?

She rushed to the entrance.

Ahmed's back was to the wall, his collar gathered in Henry's fist. Ahmed groaned, his hands clutching his stomach. Henry struck Ahmed in the face with a fierce punch. Cartilage crunched, and blood poured from Ahmed's nose.

"Henry! What are you doing?" Ginger grabbed his arm.

"He's a liar." Henry swung, but Ahmed caught his fist and

threw Henry. Henry knocked Ginger in the cheek with his elbow.

Disoriented, Ginger cried out and clutched her face.

Henry held a hand toward her. "You hurt?"

Ahmed tackled Henry to the ground. He squeezed Henry's throat.

No!

Henry flailed. Ahmed's knuckles tightened.

Horrified, Ginger's scream pierced the space. "Ahmed, please. Stop!"

Both men's eyes locked on her. Henry grabbed Ahmed's wrists and bent his knees, trying to push on Ahmed's chest, but to no avail. Henry's focus shifted to the ground by Ginger's feet.

She followed his gaze. A pistol lay in the dirt.

"Help me," Henry rasped.

Ginger lunged for the gun. The cold metal wobbled as her hands tightened around the handle. "Ahmed, please let him go!" She ran up behind Ahmed, trying to pull him off and strike him with the butt of the gun, but Ahmed's arm swung out, knocking her toward the door.

She couldn't shoot anyone. But if she didn't do something, Ahmed would kill her brother.

Henry's face purpled. "Shh—oo—"

Rain pounded against the stone of the tomb, like drumbeats in a frenzied ancient sacrifice. Ginger slumped against the wall, her knees weak.

Ahmed's yellowed teeth were bared. He pushed harder against Henry's throat.

Maybe a warning shot would help.

She thumbed the hammer, hands shaking. It didn't move. With the pistol between her knees, barrel down, she used both thumbs to push the heavy hammer back and lifted the gun once more. Her forefinger hooked around the trigger, her aim wavering.

"Ahmed, please!"

Ahmed jerked upright and turned toward her, one hand outstretched.

The shot splintered the humid air, the gun recoiling. Ahmed grabbed his chest and fell.

Ginger gasped. The pistol hung limp.

Henry coughed and sputtered, collapsing against a wall. The dark color in his face faded.

Ginger choked out, "My God, my God ..." What had she done?

Blood spurted from under Ahmed's fingers. He writhed. Her hands grew clammy at his agonized cries, his eyes squeezed shut. *She'd shot him.*

Henry crawled toward Ginger, wheezing. He held his hand out for the gun.

Ginger threw it to him.

Henry dragged one knee up, then the other. He hunched over, hands on his thighs. Crimson bruises were forming on his neck. "Who the bloody hell taught you to shoot?" His eyes widened, the blood vessels near his irises broken. "You could have shot me."

His words barely registered. "I-I'm sorry."

"Leave." Henry coughed. "Get out of here." He lifted the gun, pointing it toward Ahmed.

Ahmed's face contorted in anguish. He was close to death.

Ginger grabbed Henry's arm. Her throat thickened. "Don't. He's dying."

"He would have killed me." Henry's shoulders heaved.

Ginger's hands shook. No. This wasn't ..." She tried to catch her breath, dizzy. "What happened?"

"He attacked me," Ahmed managed before gurgling. Blood dripped from the corners of his blueish lips.

Ginger dashed to Ahmed's side. "Ahmed—" She grabbed his shoulders.

His eyes turned toward hers. They held a look of betrayal.

"I'm so sorry," she said. Apologizing for shooting him wasn't sufficient. She peeled his hands from his wound to inspect it, and he gripped her wrist.

The torment in his features faded. His hand, wet with blood, slipped from her wrist, limp. He released one low, rattling breath.

"Please don't die." Ginger grabbed his chin. His death was her fault. "No."

Spittle formed on Ahmed's lips, his chest still.

Tears blurred her vision. She gripped the lapel of his pajamas. "No—please."

Bile rose in her throat. She pushed past Henry, who reached out a hand. A buzz filled her ears, a whiff of gunpowder wafting past her.

She'd barely stepped outside when she vomited. Henry approached behind her and placed a hand on her back.

She whirled around toward him, wiping her mouth with the back of her hand. "Why?"

"You don't understand." A haunted look filled Henry's eyes.

"What don't I understand? I know ..." She covered her mouth and gagged again. "I shot him. I killed him."

Henry embraced her. "It wasn't your fault."

That couldn't console her. She'd fought so hard to save Ahmed's life.

Only to shoot him. It *was* her fault.

She could hardly breathe.

They jerked their heads up at hoofbeats far in the distance.

Henry pulled out binoculars from his bag, looked through them, then cursed.

Ginger reached for the binoculars. Noah approached, on horseback. A few paces away from him rode Ian McNeill on another horse. She took a faltering step backward, supporting herself on the stone wall.

Henry untied the lead for his horse. "Tell him it was me." His expression appeared half crazed. "Tell him I did it. Save yourself."

"What?" Ginger reached out a hand. "Where are you going? Don't leave me. Tell me what happened."

"There's no time." Henry mounted and turned his horse. "Tell him as little as possible. Tell him nothing Ahmed told you. But if someone must take the blame for his death, tell him it was me."

"But Noah is your friend—"

Henry didn't answer. Noah drew closer.

"I must learn the truth. For all our sakes." Henry bolted into the desert.

The truth? She glanced into the entrance at Ahmed's prone body.

The world faded to a dull blur as she rushed over and untied her horse's rope.

Noah eyes were as hard as flint as he arrived. "Don't even think of leaving." He hopped from the saddle and disappeared into the stone structure, leaving his horse in Ian's hands.

Ginger gripped her horse.

Her fingers trembled, and she swung into the saddle. She'd rather incur Noah's wrath than face this alone. Henry must explain to her what had happened. She couldn't allow her brother to take the blame for a death she didn't fully understand.

"Ginger—" Noah's shout came from the entrance.

She kicked her heels into the stallion's side. It whinnied and bolted forward.

The thick fabric of Ginger's uniform clung to her legs. She headed in Henry's direction, further inland. He galloped far in front of her, a speck of a figure, and hard to see as rain pelted her face. As their horses moved further from the flat coastal plain near Belah, the terrain grew more rugged, filled with craggy rocks and steep sloped hills, the vegetation more sparse. Rain made the ground slippery and, within several minutes, the horse's feet seemed to slide. If something happened to the horse, the reprimand would be severe.

As the minutes raced past, sharp ringing intensified in her ears. She gagged again, acid burning her throat. She shouldn't have touched the gun. A better shot wouldn't have accidentally killed a man.

What could he have possibly told Henry to provoke him?

He's a liar.

Had Ahmed preyed upon her goodwill?

She dug her fingernails into her palms. She deserved punishment for her crimes.

But Henry didn't. Henry hadn't asked for this.

Henry was right—Ahmed would have killed him. And yet, it didn't soothe her heart's heaviness or the fire scorching her conscience.

She came to a valley. Henry had put more distance between them, and she could barely see him.

She slowed. Should she head back?

She squinted as a rider crested the hill behind her. He'd either removed his hat or lost it, but she recognized Noah's tall, dark-haired figure in his drenched khaki uniform.

If she kept going after Henry, Noah would catch them both.

Her mind withdrew to a time long ago when she'd climbed a

tall tree at Penmore, Henry at her side. Upon reaching the top, fear overcame her, and she couldn't climb down.

Henry had tried to coax her down. When his patient attempts to convince her failed, he led her one step at a time. At the last thick bough, before the ground, she'd gripped the tree, refusing to jump. Until she slipped—and Henry caught her.

He always caught her.

She wiped tears from her cold cheeks. Her brother had come out here to help her. And now her actions had placed him in danger. It was her turn to protect him.

Ginger veered away from Henry, galloping across the desert. Eventually, she'd allow Noah to catch her. For now, leading Noah away from Henry mattered most.

She'd lost track of time when the sun peeked out from the clouds, sparking hope the rain might end. Wet hair clung to her face and neck.

The distance between her and Noah grew.

A hawk passed overhead, its mournful cry echoing in the canyons. Noah fell further and further behind.

Moving the horse toward a path cut between two rocky hills, she slowed to a trot.

Noah had disappeared. Had he relented? The sun broke free from the clouds, its warm rays enveloping her. Her shadow elongated before her. She went rigid.

She'd ridden east. Straight into lands held by the Turks.

Could enemy troops see her? The choice between confronting Noah or the Turks was simple.

Ginger turned the horse around. She brought it to a gallop again, hoofbeats echoing loudly around her.

A gunshot cracked through the air, sending a spray of pebbles and dirt toward her.

The horse whinnied and reared. She clung to it as panic

filled her. She whirled her head around, looking for the shooter's location in the hills above her.

Then three more gunshots. At the fourth, her horse tumbled, throwing Ginger off the saddle and onto the ground. She landed on her side, the wind knocked from her. An excruciating pang moved down her hip. She scrambled onto her elbows, heart pounding.

The horse attempted weakly to stand before it stretched onto its side, exhaling one last time.

A cry choked her throat as she stared into the gentle eyes, now lifeless and still. No! *No, no, no.* The stallion was her means to get home. Would there be more shots? Tears stung her eyes, and she attempted to scramble to her hands and knees. She cried out painfully as the blow to her hip throbbed.

Exhausted and distraught, Ginger could hardly think straight. She lay flat on the ground and rested her cheek against the earth. She placed a trembling hand on the horse's warm body.

A soft crunch of footsteps drew closer. She raised her head, the sun in her eyes. A handful of men were clambering down the side of a rocky hill. Their khaki uniforms were not British. They raised their guns at her.

Terror filled her. Turkish soldiers surrounded her, their bronzed faces unsmiling.

CHAPTER THIRTEEN

*G*inger jerked her chin, startling. She'd begun to fall asleep, but she mustn't. Not here. Exhaustion made her bones ache, and her eyes hurt from the effort of keeping them open. She blinked blearily, leaning forward from the concrete wall of the crude stone building holding her. Only the stars indicated the hour. The Turkish soldiers had taken her wristwatch.

Ropes on her wrists and ankles dug into the tender skin beneath them. A jagged rock dug into her backside, the dirt floor uneven. She didn't dare move—during the forced march through the desert canyons, the pain in her hip had flared. The sun had set when they'd arrived at this outpost, but she imagined they'd walked for hours.

Tilting her head back, she closed her burning lids and she tried to swallow, her tongue feeling like a dry sponge against the roof of her mouth. She fought for composure. If they didn't kill her, dehydration would soon enough.

Six soldiers sat beyond the open door by a fire. Occasionally their conversation paused, and one would glance at her. They wore tan tunics over bloused trousers and the traditional Turkish *kabalak*, or sun hat. They appeared several years older than the Tommies she treated. Each had a carefully trimmed moustache.

She trembled, terrified. They'd left her alone since they'd arrived but had searched her for weapons, unapologetic in their roughness. They'd found Ahmed's bottle in her pocket and taken it. The morning's events felt a lifetime ago.

Damn Henry. And damn Ahmed.

How could Henry have left her alone to deal with the consequences of Ahmed's murder? He'd abandoned her when she'd needed him the most. He'd known her fears about Noah's loyalties, and yet he'd downplayed them as though she was a stupid child.

Tell him nothing Ahmed told you.

Her jaw ached from clenching it. Ahmed was dead. Who cared what Ahmed had told her? She should have left him in the hut the day she'd found him. Should have let him die.

She loosened her aching jaw. His blood was on her hands.

The gunshot still echoed in her ears, etched deep inside her soul.

An owl's hoot offered a welcome distraction. The fire outside beckoned. The night was chilly, the desert unforgiving with its sharp dip in temperature. Her clothes remained damp from the rainstorm, and the dampness deepened her shaking. She wiggled her stiff fingers and toes, hoping the circulation would warm them. Did the men hear her teeth chattering? She uncurled her fingers one by one, concentrating on the rush of blood back to each finger.

What would they do with her? In Port Said, after the Armenian refugees from Musa Dagh had arrived seeking shelter, accounts filled the papers of women and girls defiled and crucified at the Ottoman troops' hands. She wanted to believe the best in all people, that the Turkish soldiers didn't differ from the British Tommies—weary men caught in the orders of distant leaders.

Here, her cowardice surfaced, as it had when she'd killed Ahmed.

Her throat seized in desperation. She was a murderer.

She should have done more to save both Ahmed and Henry. Thrown something. Or kicked Ahmed's wounds. That would have been better than killing him.

Her eyes longed to close. Falling asleep around these men was unthinkable. The rest wouldn't be worth the risk.

Something scuttled beside her leg. Ginger squinted and drew a sharp breath.

A deathstalker scorpion.

She didn't dare move.

She'd treated many soldiers for its painful stings. The venom could kill children. Its segmented tail curled over the back, and it approached her calf's exposed skin. She stiffened.

The scorpion began a cautious ascent on her thigh. Her skin crawled at the movement of the eight legs, and she took slow, steady breaths. When it stopped in her lap, inches from her bound hands, its pincers moved curiously.

James had chuckled the first time she'd recounted finding a scorpion in her boots. "They're more frightened of you. How would you like to be woken from your cozy nap by a giant? It'll sting if it's angry."

This one didn't seem angry. Still, the unpredictability of desert creatures frightened her.

Think of James. Of better times.

It was a poor choice. She pictured him in the rain, asking her to run away. Her mind had screamed *no* but if she could return and undo everything, she'd answer differently. Maybe this was God's way of punishing her for being so ungrateful.

She deserved punishment for many things.

A few minutes passed in which the scorpion crossed from one thigh to the other and climbed onto the dusty ground once more. It stopped close to the wall, a few inches away. Ginger let out a nervous sigh.

Her relief lasted a moment. Voices approached, speaking in hushed Ottoman Turkish, incomprehensible to her. One voice stood out.

In time, the owner of the loudest voice crossed into the structure where she sat. An officer, she assumed, from the different markings on his uniform. She hadn't seen him on the march—had he just arrived?

He sniffed, and his mouth twitched under a thin black moustache. He struck a match and held it to the wick of an oil lamp, revealing eyes as green as her own. The room's unlit spaces illuminated with the orange lamplight. The officer sank into a wooden chair by a rickety table in the corner. A small cot lined a wall. A basin sat by the cot, filled with water.

The officer propped his elbows on the arms of the chair. "Who are you?" Despite his accent, she understood him.

Should she give her name? Her father was an important government figure and an earl. It might be better not to. "A nurse."

"English?" His eyes rested on the red cross of her uniform, briefly.

She nodded.

"A spy?"

His logic wasn't terrible. There was little justification for her presence so far outside the clearing station. "A nurse."

The officer frowned. He pulled Ahmed's bottle from his pocket. "What is this?"

A tide of emotion came over her. How could she know? Everything she'd believed had been shaken. But whatever information that message contained, she doubted it was anything the British wanted in the hands of the Turks, regardless of Ahmed's loyalties.

The officer rose. He called out the doorway.

A soldier entered, a thick man with enormous bold eyebrows and curly hair. The officer stepped toward Ginger, then grabbed her by the jaw. "Answer me."

She jerked away. Her hands fisted. What could she say?

The officer spat. His spittle dripped off her cheek.

"Stay away from me." Her chest heaved. "I'm an English nurse. A noncombatant. I was separated from my unit while traveling. You must allow me to return."

"You lie. Nurses do not carry codes. You tell us the truth, English." The officer nodded at the other soldier.

The soldier approached. He placed his boot's heel into her chest, pushing her torso into the wall. Her eyes focused on a long silvery scar down the left side of his face.

Ginger screamed. "Stay away." She grabbed him by the calf. She dug her fingernails into his leg, and he edged the toe of his boot toward her throat. He pressed on the soft spot right above her clavicle. Her legs flailed uselessly, the air squeezed from her chest.

The scene spun. Her ears popped with crushing pressure. She couldn't move his foot away. He pressed more firmly. The fire of the lamplight beyond him swayed and grew more distant.

He would kill her.

At last he pulled away. Ginger threw her hands to her throat, choking. Her shoulders and head sagged.

The soldier ripped her skirt. She jerked back, a shock of fear and humiliation going through her as she weakly tried to cover her bared thighs.

"Enough." The officer appeared beside the soldier.

He showed Ginger the cipher again. "What is this?"

"I … don't … know," she sputtered, her eyes barely open.

The officer's hat wavered into focus. She coughed.

"Try to remember." The officer moved away. The soldier followed him, leaving her shivering in a heap on the floor.

CHAPTER FOURTEEN

*G*inger roused, dimly aware of someone's presence beside her. A blanket lay draped over her. Her bound arms flailed in self-defense. A man's voice hushed her, and a hand covered her mouth.

Her heart beat erratically. She met an unfamiliar soldier's gaze. He crouched before her, concern in his deep-set eyes.

Startled by his kindness, Ginger stopped fighting. He smiled and pulled his hand from her mouth. He draped the blanket that stank of smoke and tobacco over her once again, and it warded off the chill.

The soldier gestured toward himself. "Haluk."

His name? She let out a sob. *"Shukraan,"* she said, thanking him.

He unwrapped a compact package, then pulled something from it and broke it in pieces. He held it out.

Food? Would it be safe? Refusing the soldier's kindness might anger him. She chewed. It tasted like shortbread.

He handed her another piece. Her stomach growled.

Laughter trickled in from outside. The soldier gave her the

remaining shortbread. He slipped out the door. Too tired to sit, Ginger leaned her head against the floor.

Every morning and every evening, the sisters gathered to pray. The words and actions had grown rote to Ginger. Not that she didn't believe. But faith felt distant, as did God. The bleak horror of her work had numbed her to the idea of a merciful God. Why would he listen to prayers for the mundane and ignore the cries of humanity slaughtering itself?

Still, prayers came to her lips. The blood on her hands soaked deep, unwashable. Would God listen to a murderer?

Voices filtered through the stillness while she fought off sleep. As dawn's first light crossed the doorway, the officer returned, another soldier behind him. Ginger straightened, fists clenched at her side, her every sense alert. She inspected the officer's companion and held back a gasp.

Noah.

His gaze held a warning. She lowered her eyes so the Turk wouldn't see her recognition. How had he found her?

Noah appeared as much at ease in a Turkish uniform as he had in a British one. He spoke in Turkish. His ability to blend so seamlessly startled her, tempering the hope he'd come to help her.

He could truly be the traitor serving the Maslukha.

The officer spoke to Noah, and they both laughed. With a grin, the officer motioned Noah outside. They disappeared from view.

Chills rose up her spine.

If he was here to negotiate her release, why wear a Turkish uniform? Henry had seemed so confident in Noah's loyalties— yet after Ahmed's death he'd told her not to share anything with Noah. Why wouldn't Henry want her to trust Noah?

Time dragged on, the shadows from the doorway traveling across the floor as the sun climbed higher.

Noah didn't return.

Ahmed had claimed Henry attacked him, and Henry hadn't corrected him. Something Ahmed said must have deeply rattled Henry. He'd run away, rather than confer with Noah. *I must learn the truth.*

What truth?

Had Ahmed named Noah as a traitor? It was possible. If Henry valued Noah's friendship as much as he'd appeared to, perhaps the revelation of Noah's treachery could have upset Henry.

But upset him enough to attack Ahmed?

She tucked her legs to the side, covering the cold, bare skin of her legs with her torn skirt. Whatever the Turks intentions for her, they'd dragged it out enough. Could Noah be trying to have her released?

Her thirst had grown to a point of distraction. If Noah wanted them to return her alive, she'd think he'd at least argue for her to have water.

But Noah might not be here for that purpose. A rescue mission would have involved more British men. The Turks seemed to know him, even welcome him. Fear snaked its way through her.

Quick footsteps approached, the hard boot strikes thudding against the desert. The soldier who had attacked her came in, followed by the officer.

Noah wasn't with them. Disappointment pierced her heart.

The officer went to the table. "Ready to talk, English?"

Ginger lifted her chin. "I already told you. I'm a nurse, separated from my companions."

The officer pursed his lips and displayed Ahmed's bottle. He set it on the table. "And the secret message?"

"It's not a secret message." She shrugged. "Just a medical

formula. Chemist notes. The bottle keeps them safe from the elements."

The officer appeared skeptical and gestured toward his thug. The soldier shoved her into the wall, pinning her.

The officer approached, his steps slow, his posture menacing. "Now tell me the truth."

The soldier released the pressure. "I have nothing else to say," she managed.

Barking a quick order to the soldier, the officer stepped aside. The soldier dragged her across the room toward the water basin. He thrust her head under the surface.

Warm, algae-tinted water filled her nostrils and mouth. She fought the urge to drink, thirstily, her throat burning. She kicked and thrashed. She screamed, her words bubbles.

At last, the soldier released her. Air hit her lungs and her body went slack, her head dizzy. Each staggered wheeze felt like pinpricks in her throat.

How could Noah allow them to do this to her if he wasn't a traitor? She pictured his taunting treatment at the CCS. Had he enjoyed the gossip he'd provoked—no doubt it had been on purpose. Everything he'd done seemed like a calculated lie.

Noah may not have even put as much effort into the horse chase as she'd imagined. He would have welcomed her folly in riding right toward the enemy he served.

The soldier tossed her against the ground. Her eyes opened, her gaze falling to a crevice by the wall, an arm's reach away. A segmented tail caught her attention there, another deathstalker scorpion. Or the one from the night before.

The officer leaned beside her. "Tell me what you know."

Her words slurred. "There's nothing to tell you."

Her head hit the water once again.

Immersed, Ginger fought the panic coursing through her system. Everything dulled, Keep focus.

One ...

She opened her eyes. The basin's red clay greeted her.

Two ...

The hands against her neck pushed harder, her torso crushed.

Three ...

Water burned like a hot knife against her open eyes. She squeezed them shut again. *Focus. Focus.* Stay alive.

Four ...

Her lungs burned. She needed air. Her legs kicked. Firm pressure held her. Where was Noah?

Five ...

Her pulse pounded in her ears and neck. Air pushed its way from her eardrums. Her head screamed with pressure.

Six ...

Dizziness overtook her. If she breathed, the pain might go away.Noah wasn't coming.

Seven ...

Bubbles rippled from her nostrils and lips. She sucked in a mouthful of water, searing pain ripping into her throat and lungs.

She coughed and sputtered. More water filled her nose and mouth.

The red clay melted from her sight. Her mind grew hazy. Light brightened in her mind's eye. The brightness drew closer. Ahmed's image swam in her mind. A single drop of blood formed in the corner of Ahmed's mouth and dripped to his chin.

Air broke across her face. Her head hit hard dirt. A solid thump on her back made water and bile spew from her mouth.

The officer hovered over her, his thug nearby. Her breaths came in spasms that rippled to her diaphragm.

"Please ..."

The officer poured the basin of water over her and bent beside her. "Yes?"

She tried forming words. The quivering of her jaw prevented her.

"What do you have to tell me?" the officer demanded.

She clamped her teeth, stopping their chatter. A mixture of drool and water slipped from her mouth. She turned her face toward the officer, and sand scraped her chin. "Go"—she sucked in—"to hell."

A gunshot cracked through the air. The soldier fell to the ground.

Before she understood what had happened, the officer shielded himself with her body, his hand sliding around her neck. A knife pressed into her throat.

Noah stood in the doorway, his pistol raised. A sob escaped her.

The officer shouted. The knife dug deeper, blistering pain cutting into her flesh as the blade scratched against her skin.

Noah placed his hands in the air. He spoke in Turkish, his voice calm. He lowered the pistol to the floor.

Ginger's fingers clawed at the dirt. The knife pricked her skin. If she didn't act, she might die anyway.

Her hands found the scorpion in the crevice, her bound hands clumsy.

She lifted the creature by the tail, right below the stinger, and threw it at the officer's face. He leapt up from her, trying to wrench it from his face. The scorpion repeatedly struck at the thrashing man before he knocked it away. It scurried into the wall and from sight.

Noah bolted toward them and tackled the officer.

"Noah, watch out!" Ginger yelled as the officer raised the knife. She drew her knees into her chest. The two men tumbled.

Noah's elbow smashed into the Turk's face, and there came

the gruesome snap of bone. Noah wrestled the knife from the man and slashed at him.

Blood gushed from the Turk's throat. He gasped and gargled. Noah punched him in the face, sending the dying man onto the floor.

Ginger froze.

The knife dripped with blood. It clattered onto the ground.

Noah's chest heaved. He shook out his hand, his gaze focused on the dead officer.

A gash on Noah's forearm oozed. He stood over Ginger, sunlight gleaming on his face. He bent and pulled her into a seated position. "Are you all right?"

Water droplets dripped down her face, her mind in a daze.

He'd killed the officer.

She focused on the cut on his forearm. "You're hurt." She grasped the cuff of his sleeve.

"A flesh wound." He grazed her jaw with a light touch. "Are you injured?"

She'd forgotten about the pain in her hip until then. He'd spared her from far worse. "Yes. My hip."

Running steps interrupted them. Noah dove for his pistol. The kind soldier, the one who had called himself Haluk, came through the doorway. Haluk stared at Ginger.

"Noah, wait!" She held her hands out.

Too late. Three shots followed. Haluk slumped to the ground.

She lowered her hands slowly.

She stared at Haluk. All she saw was Ahmed's face.

"Four more men brought me here," she told him. Were they still outside? They might come running soon too.

Noah collected the guns from the dead men. "They're on patrol. Hopefully far enough away that we have some time before they return. But they may have heard the gunshots. We need to hurry."

Noah cut the rope away from her hands and ankles, then helped her stand. Pain shot through her hip.

"Thank you," she mumbled. "I-I need water."

"I have some in my saddlebag. We must leave. If the others return, we'll be outnumbered. It's why I had to wait so long to get you."

"Wait. The officer. He has something ... of importance." Ginger grabbed the bottle from the table.

The unsaid hung between them, thick and uncomfortable. Noah took the bottle from her and frowned. "Can you walk?"

She rested some weight on her leg and winced. "I don't know."

Leaning down, Noah slid an arm under her knees.

She pulled away. "You don't need to—"

He swung her into his arms. "I'm carrying you."

Too weary to protest, her arms slipped around his neck. She pressed her forehead against his shoulder, not wanting to see the bodies of the Turkish soldiers he'd killed. They would haunt her nightmares.

He carried her from the outpost into the sunlight. She squinted as they passed the remains of the fire that had taunted her overnight, now nothing more than charred, smoking log and ash. The stubs of smoked cigarettes littered the sand around the fire. Noah smelled strongly of tobacco. Had he sat here, smoking cigarettes while she languished?

She glanced over his shoulder toward the outpost, a weatherbeaten stone and concrete structure surrounded by rock and sand and sun. The canyons the Ottomans had brought her through rose in the distance, a few anemic trees and prickly bushes scattered in the landscape.

Noah's horse stood beside a post and water trough. Nothing but open, flat desert met her eyes in that direction.

Noah set her down by his horse. She swayed. "Are you ill?" he asked.

She tried to meet his gaze, tears in her eyes.

"Why did you come?" she managed. Stubble covered his jawline, and she noticed a scar on his temple she hadn't seen before. "Who are you?"

He gave her an odd look. "I came for you." He removed the *kabalak* from his head and let it fall to the ground. "I'd think that would be obvious."

"Yes, but—" Ginger breathed out, weakly. "How did you find me?"

Noah pulled a canteen from his horse's pack and handed it to her. "You should drink some water." He unscrewed the top and held it out. "I followed you, remember? Not the wisest thing I've ever done—riding into Ottoman territory with only my sidearm—but I knew if I lost sight of you, you'd be much more difficult to track."

She sipped at the metallic warm water and had to restrain herself from gulping it down. She handed it back and drooped against the horse. "But why? And how did you get that uniform?" She ignored the buzzing flies, some circling the horse and landing on its soft mane.

He looked down at the khaki tunic and shrugged out of it, leaving his undershirt. "My uniform is in my pack." He tossed the tunic alongside the *kabalak*. "I had to kill a scout for this. Which is another reason we should go. There's a chance the men on patrol could find him."

Noah leaned on the saddle, his dark-blue eyes alertly searching the horizon. "You have a lot to answer for, Ginger, but if you're worried I'll hurt you, you have nothing to fear. I'm returning you to the clearing station, and we can sort out what you're involved in there."

The clearing station? "You're taking me back?" A traitor wouldn't return her, would he?

His brows drew together, his expression suspicious. "Do you not want to?"

"No—of course ..." A cry broke from her. "Of course I want to." She wiped tears from her eyes.

Noah pulled her into his strong arms once more. This time the gesture wasn't merely functional. His embrace held comfort and kindness. A kindness she wasn't sure she deserved.

She'd put them both in danger. "I—" She tried to find any suitable words. Questions burned in her mind. Her tears stained his shirtfront, her shoulders shaking.

His arms tightened. He stroked her back. "You were brave. You fought like a wildcat." He set his hands on her shoulders. "We must go. It's dangerous to waste even a minute."

He brushed her tears away with his knuckles. The horse stomped and whinnied, the clopping sound echoing out into the void of the dry rocky desert that shimmered like a fish's scales in the midday sun.

Noah helped her onto the saddle. The hard leather pushed against her hip, and a throbbing pain shot through her leg. Despite the pain, she felt hope. Climbing behind her, Noah rested her against him. He flicked the reins and they bolted into the wilderness.

CHAPTER FIFTEEN

*T*he horse's hooves pounded the earth with rhythmic steadiness, a pulse that carried over the vast terrain. Despite the heat, Ginger trembled. The near-drowning had chilled her to the bone. She longed for a change.

Though they'd ridden for hours, the sun remained high. She scanned the horizon for the British clearing station, but flat sand and rock stretched as far as the eye could see. The landscape was unfamiliar. They'd ridden away from the canyons that had brought her to the Turkish outpost, seemingly deeper into the desert. "Are we getting close to the clearing station?" she asked.

"The trek to Gaza is too dangerous to return the way you came. We have to ride southwest and head north again. We'll have to stop before then." Noah shifted, his arms shiny with sweat. "You haven't stopped shivering."

She shifted at his voice's soft rumble against her neck. "The night was bitter in wet clothes." She twisted the saddle blanket's fringe in her fingertips. "Will this route take a long time?"

"Much longer than it took you to ride out. I'm not sure how you made it that far without someone shooting you."

But they had. And killed her horse. She choked, thinking of the gentle beast, now decaying in the desert. "Where are we stopping?"

"A Bedouin camp, ahead."

"Is it safe?"

"As safe as we'll encounter out here. Some of Khalib's relatives are there. I've taken advantage of their hospitality before." The horse slowed. He leaned forward and patted the steed's neck. "I know you want to return. But she's tired. And needs water. Carrying two people is a lot to ask of any horse in the desert. We'll rest there for the night."

It made sense. And offered more evidence affirming his moral character.

They continued in silence, her thoughts as confused as ever. If she told Noah the truth now, she would lose everything. Her confession would ruin her life. Even Henry seemed to have understood when he'd pleaded with her to tell Noah he'd shot Ahmed.

Did she deserve freedom, though? She'd done everything to forfeit it, not least killing Ahmed. "Will the Bedouin take us in for certain?"

"They won't ask questions. They pride themselves on their hospitality. They may not speak directly to you. But visitors need to behave with decorum. Keep yourself covered up at all times."

A flush came over her face. "Anything else I should know?"

"I'll guide you through it. They have specific rituals for their guests. When you come into their camps, they offer you the protection of their household."

"You know a lot about them." She wished it was easier to look at him. "How is that?" Everything about him was an enigma. Stephen had said he was an Irish orphan, but he spoke with a flawless English accent that could have fooled the Court of St James's. And he'd convinced the Ottoman soldiers at the outpost he was Turkish.

"It's part of my job." The horse slowed further. "I've spent almost the entire war in the Arabian peninsula, making contacts amongst the leaders of Ottoman dissidents in the Arab community."

"As T. E. Lawrence has done?"

"Similarly. Our roles have been different in the long term, mine more to embed myself in the cities and seek out pro-British parties." He adjusted the reins in his hands. "There are many Arabians from here to Syria who want to see these lands free from their Ottoman oppressors. The Turks made many enemies among the Arabs in the years preceding the war."

She'd known about the Egyptian discontent with Turks before the war—it had been part of the reason the Ottomans had been so easily ousted in Egypt, their khedive deposed and the entire region declared a British 'protectorate.' Many Egyptians had believed the British would help them with their nationalist goals. But she knew little about the Arab nationalists. "Have the Ottomans been fighting insurrection amongst the Arabians as much as we have against the Egyptians?"

"More so than us." Noah rode into a dry gully, where the compacted earth made the ride easier. "Most of the officers in the Iraqi-Ottoman army are nationalists. The Turks execute Syrians, the Hashemites of the Holy Cities—anyone who raises a voice against the Ottoman Empire. It's why Lawrence and others were successful in brokering the help of some Arabian leaders."

"But if they're nationalists, they must believe the British will grant them their lands and freedom after the war." She squinted at him. "Have we made such promises?"

Noah didn't answer for a few moments. At last, he said, "Are all British nurses this curious about political maneuvers as you?"

She stiffened. "If you're trying to tell me it's not a woman's place to ask questions—"

"Calm yourself. I'm not concerned with something as undeniable as the equality of female intellect. What concerns me is *you*. And whatever you're involved in. If the man I found you and Henry with is who I believe, you're in a world of trouble."

Goose bumps rose on her arms. Had he recognized Ahmed? Before she could ask, Noah pointed toward the horizon. "You can see the Bedouin encampment ahead."

Dark square tents stood out from the landscape, the world otherwise swimming in waves of heat rising from the sands, like ripples in a pond.

They rode into the camp, and three men approached. Noah addressed them in Arabic. The men stared at her bared legs, and she tucked them in. They would think her torn skirt immodest.

One man disappeared into the tented camp, leaving the other two there. Their hands rested against the rifle barrels across their torsos.

"What now?" she asked Noah.

"They're asking the sheik if we can stay."

"What if we can't?"

"We'll be fine."

The man returned shortly, accompanied by a woman in long flowing robes. She approached them, a black scarf in her hands. Noah dismounted. She greeted him warmly but kept her distance. "Ginger, this is Hafia."

Hafia unfolded the scarf and gave it to Ginger. Noah helped her from the horse and tied the scarf onto her head. "The women here cover their heads. And you don't want to make the other women too uncomfortable. Even if you weren't beautiful, your fair skin would make you a prize."

The compliment surprised her. It was hardly the adjective she would use for herself at the moment.

Ginger gripped Noah's forearm. "My hip still hurts."

"Lean on me." Noah handed the horse's reins to a man and grabbed the saddlebag. Hafia started forward.

Hafia's form was shrouded by dark robes and head coverings. "Do you know her?"

"She's Khalib's aunt." He didn't offer any further explanation as they followed her.

Khalib's aunt? Why would the boy be wandering with Noah if he had such close relatives? "Why doesn't she take care of him?"

"She has ten children."

"Ten?" She barely imagined any child growing up here, let alone ten.

They didn't go far. At a tent, Hafia stopped. The entrance opened, revealing a short man with a beaklike nose and a dark triangular beard on his chin. Lines by the corners of his eyes revealed years of squinting. He wore a long *aba* tied with a red sash and a *keffiyeh* on his head. He held his hands out. Noah released Ginger. The man placed his hands on Noah's shoulders and pressed his nose to Noah's.

Ginger startled at the intimacy of the movement, which Noah took in stride.

"Take off your shoes," Noah instructed Ginger.

After they'd removed their shoes, they followed the man into the tent.

"Meet Saleh." Noah introduced them in Arabic.

"*Marhaba.*" Ginger bowed her head as she said hello. He must be the sheik for Noah to show him deference.

Saleh smiled. He led them to a low table in the middle of the tent. Noah helped Ginger sit on the pillows surrounding it. As Saleh spoke to Hafia, Noah leaned toward her. "Before they take us to our tent, they'll offer us three cups of coffee."

"Coffee?" Ginger's brows rose.

Hafia placed two cups in front of them. As she poured the steaming drink, the scent of dark-roasted beans and cardamom filled the air.

Ginger reached out, but Noah held her hand back. "Wait."

Another young woman placed a water bowl before Noah. He dipped his hands and rubbed the water over his hands and wrists then dried them with the cloth she handed him.

They set the bowl before her. "What is it?"

"Rosewater," Noah said.

She followed Noah's lead. The water was refreshing.

Noah lifted the coffee cup with both hands at the same time as Saleh. "The first cup is for the guest, the second for the sword, and the third is for a good mood."

Ginger sipped at each refill of coffee, her stomach turning. Despite their kind offerings, she didn't want ritual coffee and formality. She wanted a glass of water and food. Sleep.

At last, Hafia ushered them from the tent. "Saleh would like for us to join them this evening." Noah glanced at her. "But I told him you're ill and you need to rest first. You look like you need it."

"I need water." She kept her tone low. "And I'm not interested in amusing anyone." She sounded positively churlish. Or, worse, like her sister, Lucy. She could practically picture Lucy sitting in a wagon holding a parasol the time they'd ridden out to visit an esteemed dignitary in Egypt with her father. Her father had threatened to cut off her dress allowance to get her to disembark.

"Hafia said she would get us goat's milk. Water is a precious resource."

Lucy's memory wasn't enough to move her. "Yet they waste it with rituals and roses." Noah shot her a look and she winced.

She didn't want to add crankiness to the list of things she owed him apologies for.

Hafia stopped at a tent and handed Noah an oil lamp. She left them.

Noah pushed aside a tent panel, and they entered the cooler space. A low and long structure with braided rugs hanging at the sides, the tent itself appeared constructed of coarse animal hair. Blankets and cushions lined the sleeping area. The tent smelled of spices.

Noah set the saddlebag down and guided her to the blankets. "You can lie here. We're welcome for dinner, but Hafia promised to bring bread before." He glowered at her. "This may not be what you're accustomed to, but consider yourself lucky. And please try not to insult our hosts."

She sank wearily in the blankets. "I'm not trying to insult anyone. But between being nearly drowned this morning and not sleeping for days, I'm exhausted."

Noah squatted beside her. "That's understandable. But these people are saving our lives. Give them the respect they deserve." His gaze held with hers, his mouth setting to a firm line. "This isn't the time to throw a tantrum."

She caught sight of his arm. The wound from the Turkish officer still oozed. "I need to treat that now." She placed her hand on his wrist.

He shook his head. "You said it yourself—you need rest."

"Don't be stubborn. Let me help you. When Hafia returns, ask her for a needle and thread. And spirits."

A soft call outside the tent stopped their argument. Noah moved to the opening, and Hafia handed him a cup and a plate with bread.

Ginger came up beside him. "Thank you." She looked at Noah sternly. "Ask her."

Noah spoke to Hafia in hushed tones, and she left.

"Did you ask?"

"Yes."

Good. At least he wouldn't fight her. She lowered herself to the blankets.

Noah sat beside her and offered her the milk. She sipped it. It was warm but better than the tinned milk she'd had in recent months. Despite her hunger and thirst, nausea curbed her appetite. She handed it back. "I can't eat right now."

He didn't comment, thankfully. Minutes passed, and Hafia returned with the supplies. Once she'd gone, Ginger sat beside the oil lamp. She removed the cover and heated the needle in the flame. Rolling up her sleeves, she approached him. "Lie down and give me your arm."

He complied without protest. She laid his arm across her lap. A sniff to the bottle of spirits stung her nostrils. The alcohol should help clean the wound. She poured it on the cut. His hand tightened to a fist.

"You're lucky the knife didn't go any deeper." She started stitching. He didn't move, save for a flinch as the needle pierced his skin. "Doesn't it hurt?"

Noah grimaced. "Of course."

He would be the type to be stoic about pain. "You don't have to hold it in. I've been around plenty of grown men who've cried for their mothers while I tended their wounds."

He relaxed a fist. "You don't give yourself enough credit. You're exceedingly gentle."

She held the wound together with one hand, stitching with the other. "This will leave a nasty scar, I'm afraid. You'll have to watch for infection over the next few days."

Only their soft breathing was audible.

He glanced at his arm. "Who taught you to stitch so well?"

Her breath caught. *James.* She'd barely thought of him this morning, given the circumstances. He must be beside himself with worry. Given her disappearance, who knew what he might think?

"What's wrong?" Noah searched her eyes.

His genuine concern startled her. How did he seem to intuit her emotions so well? But she couldn't possibly speak to him about James. "Nothing." She finished the stitching. "I'd wrap it if I could, but we'll have to wait until camp." She inspected her work. Under the circumstances, it would do.

He glanced at it and pulled his arm away. "Thank you."

She wrapped her arms around her torso. "I wish I could do more. It's my fault they injured you."

Noah stood and went over to his pack, his face unreadable. "Take my uniform shirt to wear while you sleep. It'll be more comfortable than that ruined dress." He held the olive-green shirt out toward her.

She took it from him and stared at it as he left the tent. Fumbling with her buttons, she peeled the dress away from her body. Her skin felt waxen after having been in wet clothing for so long. She unfolded Noah's shirt, and sadness came over her. Pressing her face into the soft cloth, she fought for composure.

She wanted desperately to trust him.

And yet.

Here they were, far away from the British encampment, with no one to affirm his loyalty. He could have brought her here to coax her into trusting him, to make her more dependent upon him. And he had Ahmed's bottle.

She slipped the shirt over her shoulders. As she finished buttoning it, Noah cleared his throat from the outside. "May I come in?"

"Yes." She arranged a blanket over her bare legs, curling her dress into a ball.

He didn't comment on her appearance and pulled his uniform trousers from the bag. "If you don't mind, I'm going to change out of these Turkish trousers. They're snug. I don't want to ask you to leave the tent—"

She turned away from him. "Of course." Her cheeks warmed as she lay on the blankets. His belt clinked and she shut her eyes. Her imagination, on the other hand, was a few steps out of her control.

Her thoughts jumped to that moment after the lorry explosion, when he'd held her hand in the clearing station tent, and the way her skin had tingled at his touch.

Don't be ridiculous. She gritted her teeth at her mind's odd betrayal.

The sound of him opening his saddlebag once more told her he'd finished changing.

She glanced around the tent. Would he sit on the saddlebag? "Are you going to sleep?"

Though he'd pulled on the British uniform trousers, he hadn't replaced the jacket and wore the undershirt. "I don't need to yet. And I can sleep sitting."

She didn't know him. She didn't trust him. But she said it anyway. "You can lie next to me if you'd like."

He hesitated.

She gave him a wry glance. "We both need rest."

The corners of his lips turned up. He didn't argue further.

He lay beside her but maintained a few inches between them. Her heart pounded. She imagined pushing closer to him, her back against him the way it had been during the ride.

Noah's unbridled fury with the Turk flashed in her mind. She startled, her hand settling on her throat. She found the comforting glow of sunlight peeking through the tent's fabric.

Noah's hand cupped her shoulder. "It's all right."

He propped himself up beside her. She shifted onto her back and studied his face.

"You're safe," Noah said. "I'll keep watch. I don't need sleep."

Turning away, she swallowed a lump in her throat. At his side existed danger, alluring and unnerving.

CHAPTER SIXTEEN

*G*inger's mind slogged, her eyes opening. In the darkness, she struggled to remember where she was.

The Bedouin camp. With Noah.

She rolled toward him and found him sitting at the other end of the tent, beside the lit oil lamp, a book in his hands.

"Noah, what time is it?" How long had she been sleeping?

He adjusted the oil lamp and checked his watch. "Past nine. We missed dinner, but I'm sure I can get us something."

She swung her legs out from under the blankets, overly warm. As the cooler air hit them, she remembered she wore his shirt and stayed seated.

He tucked the book into his bag. "Did you sleep well?"

She combed her fingers through her long hair, feeling disheveled. She'd slept soundly and deeply, but a sleepy fog hung over her. Still, for the first time in days, her eyes didn't burn. As anxious as she'd been to return to the clearing station, she was grateful they'd stopped.

He donned his uniform jacket and straightened the collar. "I won't be long."

Fear rose in her. "Is it safe here?"

"You won't be disturbed."

Despite his assurances, she preferred he stay with her. "Are you certain?"

"Yes. But stay. It's best you don't wander alone, regardless. Hafia brought water shortly after you fell asleep." He pointed to a pitcher and water basin in the corner and strode out.

Her thirst almost made her bolt from her spot. With a feather-light touch, she ran her palm over her throat. She felt bruises there and winced at the fine raised cut on her neck where the officer had pressed a knife blade.

At once, she wanted to rid herself of any remnants of their touch.

She scrambled from the blankets and crossed the tent on her hands and knees toward the water basin. Piercing, needlelike pain tore through her hip. An enormous bruise covered the side of her hip to mid-thigh. No wonder.

She knelt beside the basin and poured some water. She drank, relief coursing through her.

After she'd drunk her fill, she dipped her hands into the cool water, washing her arms. Dirt and blood encrusted her fingernails. Her fingers stumbled against the edge of the basin. Ahmed's blood. Or Noah's.

She peeled away the curled remains of the bandage on her forehead from a few nights earlier, when a mild concussion had been enough for doctors and nurses to fuss over her. She swallowed a lump in her throat. Crying would do no good. It wouldn't help undo everything she'd done.

She unbuttoned the shirt and washed herself as best she could. When she'd finished, she found her dress still balled in the corner of the tent.

She didn't want to wear it ever again. She buttoned the shirt once more.

Male voices neared. She stiffened. Would they come into her tent?

The tension in her shoulders didn't ease as they faded away.

Why hadn't Noah returned?

She'd drunk too much water, especially after dehydration. Discomfort in her lower belly grew. Would there be a privy outside?

Grimacing, she put her boots on, careful with the rope burns around her ankles. She wrapped a blanket around her waist to cover her legs, limped her way toward the entrance, and stepped out. Several other tents stood nearby. Smoke from torches filled the air, along with the musk of livestock. She squinted in the darkness.

As though he'd been watching for her, Noah exited a nearby tent, a package wrapped in brown paper under his arm, a platter of food in his hand. Their eyes locked.

Noah strode toward Ginger, scowling. He pulled her inside by the elbow. "Going somewhere?"

Embarrassed, she folded her arms defensively.

He shut the tent. "I told you to stay here."

"I didn't go anywhere." He didn't need to make her feel like a child.

"But you were about to." Noah's eyes flashed. "Wearing nothing but a shirt and a blanket. Are you incapable of listening? If you wander around looking like that, you'll attract unwanted attention." He set the food by the bedding. It steamed, some type of browned meat over rice, yogurt, and dates. Her stomach growled but she hesitated, still uncomfortable.

His eyes narrowed. "It's goat. Consider yourself lucky. The other option is usually camel."

"I'm not being picky." She added stiffly, "I need to relieve myself."

Noah's look softened. His gaze traversed the tent, and he

crossed the floor to fetch her a clay pot with a lid. "I'll step outside again. Let me know when you're done and I can go empty it."

Ugh. Her lips tightened. Once the episode was behind her, she sat and shooed a fly away from the food. Noah didn't produce any utensils. She lifted a piece of meat to her lips and chewed. She hadn't realized how hungry she was. She avoided shoving a fistful of rice in her mouth, aware of Noah's gaze.

Noah sat on the cushions beside her. He rubbed his eyes and released a slow sigh. "I'm sorry. The customs—they're important to the people who live here."

She avoided looking at him. "I know you think I'm nothing more than a spoiled heiress, but I've been in this area of the world for years. I won't embarrass you if I can avoid it."

"Embarrassment is the least of my concerns." He helped himself to the food. "Have you heard of the white slave trade?"

She cocked an eyebrow at him. "Slave trade?"

"White women, primarily, kidnapped and exploited by their captors as prostitutes. Turkish harems filled with European concubines." He swallowed a bite. "But women with your... qualities ... could fetch a pretty price, Ginger. It's not every day people in these regions encounter a redhead with green eyes. You may not have the foresight to know what some men might imagine when seeing a woman wearing nothing but a blanket around her bare legs and a man's shirt."

A blush burned at her face. She tightened the blanket around her waist.

They finished eating in silence. "We'd better get going." Noah cleaned the platter.

Going? Were they returning to the clearing station? "And where, exactly, are we going?" What was she supposed to wear?

"Saleh would like us to join him for festivities, as his

honored guests. Please be gracious. We'll leave here at dawn and return to camp." He set the platter near the entrance to the tent and lifted the brown paper package he'd brought inside with him.

"You haven't even asked me anything. Don't you want to know what happened?" The words came out strained.

Noah's eyes narrowed. "Would you tell me the truth if I asked? You haven't."

"I didn't think I could trust you." A goat's bleating reverberated outside, a further reminder of their surroundings. Ginger stared at the fabric of the shirt she wore. "I thought you may have been responsible for the lorry explosion."

"You're implying I killed the refugees? What makes you believe what happened to them wasn't accidental?"

Her heart beat faster. "An accidental explosion that killed a group of people who could bear witness to the Maslukha?"

Noah sat. "Why do you think the Maslukha has anything to do with this?"

She looked away. Four stories conflicted—Ahmed's, Henry's, Stephen's, and Noah's. Yet she'd never given Noah the benefit of explaining himself. She'd made assumptions.

But Henry told her not to tell him anything Ahmed had said.

Noah tapped his thumb against his knee, an exasperated look on his face. "If you think I would murder infants and children, it'd make me more than just dangerous. It would make me utterly depraved."

His mouth twisted. He held out the package. "This is for you. The woman I bought it from had been saving it for her wedding, but I found a price she'd take for it."

The paper crinkled as Ginger took it. She couldn't meet his eyes. That was the problem she'd had from the start—she didn't truly believe he was a depraved man. "What is it?"

"Something for you to wear."

She removed a dark-blue silk dress, hand-embroidered with delicate white beads and cross-stitches. "It's beautiful. But I'd have to return it to the woman you bought it from."

Noah shook his head. "It's unnecessary. You'll need something to wear on the ride. And I paid enough that she can buy herself twenty more dresses if she would like."

"I'll give you the money for it when we return." She ran her fingers over the beads. "I don't want to owe you more than I already do."

"Fine." Noah crossed his arms, the muscles taut. "Get dressed. They're waiting for us."

A child laughed while running past their tent. She thought of Khalib and closed her eyes. That's the sort of man he was. The type who rescued Bedouin orphans. Who helped the refugees. Who offered her his shirt and bought her a dress.

"Wait." She grabbed his forearm as he neared the exit. "I don't believe you hurt the refugees. I'm sorry it took my capture and endangering the both of us for me to realize it."

Anger simmered in his eyes before he stifled it, tightening his jaw. "If you wanted to thank me, you would tell me everything you've been hiding from me."

She wanted to trust him. But confessing to Ahmed's murder and implicating Henry terrified her.

Noah put his hands on her shoulders, searching her face. Her skin tingled again at his touch.

"Damn it, what's it going to take for you to trust me? What do you want from me, Ginger?"

"How could I trust you after the way you treated me the night we met?"

"I'll admit it wasn't my best moment. But can you honestly say you gave me any reason not to suspect you?"

When she didn't answer, he huffed and pushed her away. "Get dressed."

A few minutes later, Ginger joined Noah outside. He stared at her then tore his gaze away. "Glad to see it fits."

She lifted her chin. It wasn't much of a compliment, but something in his reaction seemed more appreciative of her appearance. "Thank you."

He offered his arm and led her through the camp. Stars twinkled from corner to corner, a deep band of white swirls pulsating with breathtaking brilliance.

A group was gathered before a fire in the distance. Drums echoed in the stillness and wind instruments whistled. She smiled at the peacefulness of it. "What do they expect of us?"

Noah shook his head. "Nothing. They want to share time with us. They'll sing, dance, chant, recite poetry—whatever suits them. And there's coffee and camel's milk."

Ginger smirked. "Of course."

"If you don't want coffee, shake your cup."

They arrived at the bonfire, and Saleh met them. He brought them to a carpet near his and they sat, bathed in the fire's warmth. Wood smoke drifted past them, and Ginger leaned into Noah, avoiding the smoke trail. A man stood and spoke. The others in the tribe listened with rapt attention. Ginger's Arabic failed her. "Do you understand?"

"He's telling stories." Noah face was near hers.

Goose bumps rose on her arms. "What about?"

Noah listened. "This one is about a beautiful woman. It came time for her to marry, and her father chose three suitors."

After a few beats, he added, "The first was rich. The second was admired. The third was poor."

A story she could relate to. Ginger smiled. "Which did she choose?"

"She knew the first man would have many wives, and she

said no. The second would have many lovers, and, likewise, she said no. The third could only offer her his love. That was the man she chose."

"Fortunately for her, her father gave her a choice."

"She probably wasn't a British heiress. Though it seems your father gave you a choice, didn't he?" Noah's posture relaxed. A woman offered him tea. "Would you like some?"

She nodded. The sweet, fragrant spices calmed her as she sipped it. "My father made his wishes clear. He hasn't forgiven me for choosing an engagement to my fiancé rather than Stephen Fisher. But I'm sure it will all be well when James and I marry after the war."

Noah stared into the fire. "And, yet, you don't seem happy or excited about that prospect."

Pressure settled against her heart. Once again, he pried too deeply. She pasted a tight smile to her face. "I'm thrilled. It's hard to think of marriage during war."

Noah gave her a sidelong glance. He seemed on the verge of saying something and stopped with a shake of his head.

Defensiveness rose in her. "What?"

Noah drew his legs up. He set his forearms on his knees. "I find it hard to believe. You're quite a contradiction."

She frowned as another drumbeat started and a man chanted an unfamiliar tune. "You don't know me."

"True." He lifted his chin. "But I know you're passionate. You ran into fire to save those refugees. I know you don't care about breaking the rules or lying when it suits your purposes. That entire disciplinary hearing was meant to put you in your place. And let's not forget how we met." A smile lit his eyes. "A woman as headstrong and spirited as you—it seems to me if you met a man you truly loved, you wouldn't wait to marry him. War or not."

Her smile faltered. She drained her teacup. "You're mistaken in your impression of me, Major Benson."

He laughed. "And we're back to that again? I must have spoken a bit too accurately for your comfort if we've returned to more formal ways of addressing each other."

She glared. "Maybe it's because you pretend to know so much about me, but don't. And I know nothing about you. Unlike you, I won't try to guess who you are."

Noah lay against the carpet, facing the stars. "You're a terrible liar."

His boldness didn't shock as much as it had before, but it still irritated her with unnatural force. "Something you would know based on your skills in deception?"

"Yes." Noah slipped one hand under his head. "But also because you've been attempting to guess who I am since you met me—and keep arriving at the wrong conclusion. I told you who I was, Ginger. It was you who chose not to believe me."

"It's not so simple when others have warned me about you."

"Then you should check your sources."

The drums resounded, tolling with a deep melodic rhythm that echoed her heartbeat. She looked away from him. The possibility he might be everything she hoped—honest, a patriot, trustworthy—tantalized her. But it was too late now. An honest man would have no choice but to turn her over for the murderer she was.

And here she was talking about the future and marriage as though it was a possibility. Noah may not have proof she'd murdered or hidden Ahmed, but could she live with herself if she didn't confess?

A dance began as one musician played solo on what looked like a large lute. She settled back, fascinated, as one man stood in the center of a group of men who formed a semicircle and held hands, their movements synchronized. Two women began singing and Ginger asked, "What's this?"

"The Dabke. It's a traditional dance."

A group of women came toward her and held out their hands. She winced, knowing her hip would scream. But she didn't dare ignore their request. She wasn't about to allow Noah to label her a snob once again. She smiled through the flaring pain and pushed forward, determined.

They grabbed her arms, showing her some simple steps, crossing their right feet over their left. A few men had pulled Noah up similarly.

He looked as if he belonged.

The manner of the dance saved her from the worst of the pain—they gripped each other's arms tightly. She held on, avoiding too much weight on her injured hip. She couldn't follow the steps, regardless. Laughing at herself, she thought of the Queen Charlotte's Ball, where she'd been presented to the sovereign as a debutante. If someone had told her she'd be dancing in the desert with Bedouin women six years later, she wouldn't have believed them. Yet the company was much more enjoyable now than it had been then.

Here she felt free.

The men and women danced across from one another. Ginger's eyes met Noah's. He smiled as she tripped through the dance steps. Despite their distance from each other, they shared a laugh. The warmth in his eyes pushed a flare of excitement through her.

She broke away at last and limped toward the carpet, then dropped beside Saleh. Within a few moments, a spry elderly man crouched before her. He smoked a long pipe, his lips curled over the bit. He lolled his head toward her a few times and offered her the pipe.

Ginger hesitated and glanced at Noah, who continued dancing. He had asked her to be gracious.

She accepted the pipe and took a drag. She coughed, the smoke filling her lungs. The elderly man grinned. He furrowed his brow. Not wanting to offend him, she sucked on the pipe once more, this time holding the smoke in her mouth.

Noah arrived beside her. He pulled the pipe from her hands and handed it to the man. "Tell me you didn't smoke that."

She shrugged. "You told me to be an agreeable guest."

"Ginger, it's hashish." Noah waved the man away.

She froze. "Why would he give that to me?"

"He's an old man with dim faculties—probably from spending his days smoking." Noah held her hand. "Let me think of something to get us out of our duties here. We should get you back."

He spoke to Saleh. Ginger watched the fire, the orange flames licking the atmosphere. Time slowed, her senses dulling. Noah pulled her upright. "Let's go."

"We've only just arrived." She waved toward the women who had pulled her into a dance.

Noah wrapped his arm around her and led her away.

She stopped him about halfway back. "Dance with me."

He lifted his brows. "Here?"

She nodded and wrapped her arms around his neck. "Under the stars. With the drums as our music." Her heart slammed against her ribs, despite the calm she felt. She traced his jaw with her fingertips. "Please."

He took her hand. "We don't want to upset our hosts by behaving inappropriately."

She laughed. "Then why did they put us in the same tent?"

"Because I told them you were my wife."

Something in his words made her knees feel weak. His wife?

The term had such a fierce sound to it when he said it. She gave him a sidelong glance.

She had promised to marry James. And yet—she didn't want to be his wife. Not in the way Noah made her envision the term when he'd said it. A wife in every sense. Her thoughts felt clearer than ever before. It had to be the hashish.

Noah's grip on her tightened as they approached the tent. "You should rest. I'll wait outside."

"Nonsense." Ginger unbuttoned her dress. "You slept perfectly well next to me before. We're both capable of handling ourselves. And James won't know if you don't tell him. I won't."

Noah led her inside. "First, don't disrobe outside." He buttoned her dress once more. "And, second, you don't have a nightgown here."

She laughed. "I forgot."

Noah helped her over toward the blankets. "Go to sleep. The hashish will wear off by morning."

She stretched. "I feel delicious." She pulled his hand. "Sit."

Noah lowered himself beside her.

She loosened her hair from her braid, letting it cascade over her back. She should kiss him. She stared at him. "Noah?"

He glanced over.

She moved her mouth toward his.

Noah turned his face away, and her lips grazed his cheek. "Go to bed. It's not a request."

Embarrassment doused her like water. "You don't think I'm pretty enough?"

Noah pushed her hair behind her ear. "You're the most beautiful woman I've ever seen." He dropped his hand. "But we shouldn't complicate this any further than it is."

Ginger lay onto the blankets, curling her knees. "Because you found me and Henry with a dead man."

Noah rubbed her back. "That's a gigantic obstacle."

"Because of Ahmed. When what I wanted to do was save his life." Ginger shook her head, the words flowing freely from her. But it was true. She'd wanted him to live. She would never forgive herself for the irony of his death. "Ahmed told me he'd learned the Maslukha's identity. Do you think that's what the cipher in that bottle contains? The name of the Maslukha?"

"Ahmed told you too much." Noah lay beside Ginger. He put one arm behind his head. "I think it's better we save this discussion for later. I don't want you to wake up feeling like I took advantage."

She rolled toward him and propped herself on an elbow. "Oh, I nearly forgot how much my hip hurts." In the dim light from the oil lamp, she could barely see his eyes. "Have you ever been with a woman, Noah?"

He covered his face with his hand. "This isn't the type of conversation we should be having, either."

"Just answer the question." She walked her fingers up his bicep, feeling the hardened muscle underneath her fingertips. "I'm sure you're the sort of man who can have his pick amongst the pretty faces."

"But not the sort of man who would discuss it with a lady."

She scooted closer, her lips brushing his earlobe. "If you start treating me like a lady now, I'll be furious with you. I've never met a man who seemed to dismiss me for it as much as you do." She'd never felt this bold. "Answer me."

He stared at the ceiling of the tent. "Yes."

The answer made her stomach flop. "How many?"

He shook his head. "That's enough questions for one night. Trust me. You'll be glad I stopped you, in the morning."

His words didn't seem to sink through her mind. "And you think I'm prettier than those women you were with?"

He turned his face toward her. "You just want to hear it again, don't you?"

She gave a carefree smile. For the first time in days, her worries seemed so distant. She closed her eyes, the tent feeling cavernous. "Still, you think I'm beautiful."

His voice sounded hoarse. "You are. Now go to sleep."

She slipped her hand into his. Her mind already swirled with dreams.

CHAPTER SEVENTEEN

*G*ood God. What had she done?

A rooster crowed nearby.

Ginger peeked through her lashes. The spot beside her was vacant.

Thank goodness.

She covered her face with both hands. She'd tried kissing Noah. And he'd turned her away. She didn't know what was more mortifying.

She sat bolt upright. And she'd told him about Ahmed. She tried to recount her exact words, but they seemed distant and hazy. Whatever she'd said, it was probably enough to expose her, regardless of his loyalties.

Her hip wasn't any better and the insides of her thighs ached, the muscles painful from riding a horse astride. She massaged them.

Noah cleared his throat and she froze. He sat at the other side again, one knee drawn up, the other leg stretched in front of him. "Good morning."

"My legs are aching from horseback riding." She straightened her skirt. Should she say anything about her behavior the previous night? Would he?

"I'm sure they are." Noah stood. "They might get worse sooner rather than later. We should make an early start—we have a long day ahead. We'll have to stop to water and rest the horse a few more times before we reach the clearing station tonight."

She rose with as much grace as she could muster.

Noah studied her. "I'll meet you outside." He left, and she blinked at the space he'd vacated.

"You're a stupid, stupid woman," she muttered. He probably thought so too.

They met outside and departed from the Bedouin encampment, saying their good-byes to Hafia and Saleh. She pushed herself away from him on the saddle, reliving the embarrassment of her attempted kiss. She fought the temptation to jump from the horse.

Managing centimeters between them, her bruised hip ached. Long after the Bedouin tent disappeared, she relaxed and settled back.

His fingertips curled on the reins.

Years of careful instruction taught her never to lower her inhibitions as drastically as she had the night before. She'd made a complete fool of herself. What was worse, she'd enjoyed it.

Noah's arms were too comfortable. Images of James haunted her. She couldn't imagine riding in James's arms like this. She'd worried about incurring James's anger at her recklessness. She could never explain the past few days. Not with honesty.

The morning's golden radiance distracted her. She stretched her shoulders, her neck stiff.

On the horizon, white airy clouds took shape. With her father's assignment to Egypt three years earlier, she'd been eager to rush into the Sahara—a vastly different desert than this, but startlingly beautiful. That was all she'd seen back then. The golden sand, shimmering like a vast sea of jewels, and the clear blue skies. All of it exotic and wild, the gossamer dreams of her inexperience.

Even her first terrible sunburn hadn't dampened her enthusiasm.

Now, the desert landscape had changed for her. Death showed its face everywhere. In the dry, cracked earth, the skeletons of creatures. The lack of trees reminded her of the dearth of water but also the limited ability to build something as basic as a fire.

Lost in thought, she'd settled still closer to Noah. She should say something. Talking would be easier than over-analyzing her every movement. The silence made it even more obvious.

"May I ask you something?"

Noah shrugged. "It depends on the question."

"Where did you learn to speak Turkish?"

"When I first joined the Ottoman Army."

She laughed sarcastically. "Hilarious." Still, the laughter did her good, and the tension between them dissolved somewhat.

He smiled. "I first came out in 1910, for archeological purposes. As it turned out, my aptitude for languages ended up being more useful than a mild interest in mummies." He paused. "Wouldn't it be easier if we stop pretending?"

She tensed. "Pretending what?"

His forearm grazed hers as he flicked his wrist. "That we're not attracted to each other. However complicated and unfortunate it may be."

This was precisely what she wanted to avoid. "That's a bold assumption on your part." She grew conscious of their closeness. Still, he hadn't said the attraction was one-sided.

Her stomach flip-flopped.

Noah handed her the reins. "Hold this." He rolled his jacket's sleeves. The tanned, golden skin of his forearms glistened.

She frowned at the stitches on his left arm. "If you expose it to the sun, the scar will be worse." Her fingertips lingered on his skin. He jerked his arm away.

She murmured an apology. Noah stiffened. He unholstered his pistol.

Vultures circled in the sky ahead. Ginger shaded her face. "What is that?"

Noah took the horse to a gallop. The buzzards didn't move as they drew closer, flapping their black wings at the disturbance.

Three crude crucifixes protruded from the earth.

Noah slowed to a stop. Ginger gagged, covering her mouth. Men hung from the crosses, half naked and flayed. Flies and other insects crawled from their decaying flesh, and the smell of death was putrid.

A burnt Union Jack hung around one man's shoulders.

Ginger shielded her face, her cheek pressing into Noah's chest. These were the horrors she'd heard the men speak of but never seen.

Noah went rigid. "These were British scouts."

A long loose black feather rolled over the sand in a breeze. "Why would the Turks do this?"

"They didn't. Look at them."

A symbol had been carved into each of their chests. "A.R.M. What's that?"

"I've seen him do this before. Abu Rigl *Maslukha*." Noah's eyes darkened with anger. "He stole the name from a folklore tale about children who don't listen to their parents. A monster kidnaps them and cooks them alive."

Ginger's nausea rose. She covered her nose. "I'm going to be sick."

A vulture landed on a crucifix again and stared boldly.

Ginger pushed herself down from the saddle. She winced and grabbed a rock. "Shoo!" She threw it at the vulture. It flapped and hopped down the wooden beam.

She grabbed another rock and threw it. Then one more. The last one hit the bird, and it flew away to join its brethren.

Noah's boots hit the ground. "I know you're angry. I am too. But we can't stay here."

"No one deserves this. This is beyond inhumane!" She hugged her arms to her chest. "How could—"

"I don't know." The outline of the muscles in his neck and arms were tightly corded. His right hand fisted. "I have to put a stop to it. But we're in danger here. These men haven't been dead long. A pack of vultures as large as this would make quick work of their bodies."

Ginger's eyes traversed the sparse terrain. Hills rose in the distance, which could mean they were getting closer to the area she'd ridden from. But hills also hid enemies. "We should bury them."

"It's not safe."

"They're our countrymen. We can't let vultures eat them." She drew a shallow breath, the pungent decay overpowering.

Noah's eyes flashed and he nodded. He removed a folding trench shovel from his saddlebag. "Wait on the horse or a few feet away, if you'd like. The work may sicken you."

"I'm helping."

Noah removed his jacket and dug quickly. When he finished, his soaked undershirt clung to him. Ginger felt a twinge of guilt. Despite her conviction, she shouldn't have insisted he do this. The stitches in his forearm could rip. And who knew when they would reach a well or oasis?

Noah cut the men from the crucifixes, and Ginger helped

him lower the bodies. "God forgive our inhumanity." They lowered the last man into the grave, on top of the other two.

Noah shoveled the sand on the grave. "God has nothing to do with this. This falls on the Maslukha alone."

They tiptoed around the topic of Ahmed, and it weighed between them. She expected him to say something, but when he didn't, she asked, "Do you think the Maslukha can rally the Egyptians to an uprising?"

Noah wiped his brow with the back of his hand. "There's certainly enough anger toward us in Egypt. No amount of time will ease the tensions in the Egyptian patriots who see us as oppressors."

He roused her curiosity. "Anger that's justified?"

"War will always be a game of justifying the interests of the many over the few. We needed the Suez Canal and a stable country to provide us with a base of operations for Gallipoli, supporting our Eastern allies and this current offensive. But the Egyptians have benefitted financially and militarily from our presence, and there are many who welcome us there." He paused, his hands on the shovel's handle. "I suppose it comes down to whether the Maslukha can motivate them sufficiently."

"And if the Maslukha succeeds in an uprising?"

"The Palestinian offensive could become another catastrophe, like Gallipoli. It could mean our defeat by Germany." Noah tossed dirt toward a buzzard stalking the grave. It flew off. "More men will die, but the moral blow will be enormous. Britain needs good news. These past months have been disastrous. The Russians have nearly abandoned us, and the Western Front of France moves no further from a stalemate."

Ginger blinked, suddenly understanding. Either an uprising in Egypt or a larger Palestinian front would mean England would have to divert troops away from the Western Front and send them to the Middle East, which was a much smaller front by comparison. Fighting two large-scale fronts could be devastating for war-weary troops. "And with the talk of Russia pulling out of the war …"

An impressed look came to his eyes. "Precisely. If Russia pulls out of the war, Germany will be at liberty to concentrate its forces on the Western Front. If the Ottomans engage us here and force us to spread our troops thin—"

"Germany could crush us on the Western Front." Ginger bit her lip. The Germans had every reason to want Palestine to become a larger conflict. "But the Americans are coming, aren't they?" The troops and nurses had celebrated a month earlier when the United States had at long last declared war.

"The Americans are hardly ready to help. It'll be many months before they'll be capable. Maybe longer." Noah finished covering the bodies. He checked the sun's position. "We should go. We need water"—he lifted his chin toward the buzzards— "before we become their next meal."

He helped her mount the horse and climbed behind her. An unusual tightness closed in on her heart. The smell of death stayed with them, clinging to their hands as they rode. Was it so far from the truth? She was guilty of murder. And even if the lives he'd taken in the past few days had been to save her, did it lessen the stain of blood?

By the time they reached an oasis, Ginger felt ill. Noah watered the horse in a stone trough that served Bedouin camels, goats, and horses, and she searched for a place to wash the stench from her hands. The palm trees around the well provided shade and shelter and she knelt by one of them, using Noah's canteen to rinse her hands.

She froze at a slithering movement.

Brown and black scales flashed as a snake emerged from under a rock from the bath she'd given it. The triangular head raised, eyes in slits.

A crack splintered the silence. Ginger jumped, then stared at the bloodied spot where the viper had been.

Noah approached from behind her, gun still in hand. "It didn't bite you, did it?"

She backed away, ears ringing, the smell of gunpowder in the air. Blood trickled down the rocks. "You killed it."

He holstered the gun. "Of course I killed it. It was about to strike." He kicked the body into the brush.

She should thank him. But the blood and death agitated her. Ginger straightened, narrowing her eyes. "How can you be so callous about killing? Doesn't it eat at your soul? How do their faces not haunt your every moment?" She scowled at the canteen she'd dropped. Glaring, she walked back toward the horse. She wasn't sure whom she was angrier with: him for his ruthless indifference to death or herself for being attracted to him.

"Ginger, it was a deadly viper."

"But you don't care. Man or viper—it makes no difference. You kill without a second thought."

An impatient look came across Noah's face. "I know what I am. I'm not pretending to be a priest." He retrieved his canteen.

"But how can you live with yourself?"

"Some of us serve by healing. Some of us through our capacity for destruction. But everyone has murder in their heart. It just takes the right circumstance to reveal it." He swigged from the canteen. "In your case, maybe helping to protect a brother? Or was it the other way around?" His gaze pierced hers.

A knifelike pain gouged her heart. She thought about the night before. She hadn't told him about the events surrounding Ahmed's death—had she? She didn't dare tear her eyes away. "Did you pry information from me last night?"

"I did nothing of the sort." He stepped closer. "Though I should have. But I didn't want you regretting anything else."

"How noble." She set her hands on her hips. "No doubt you asked the Bedouin man to give me that pipe." Her words, and the possibility, increased the tension in her shoulders. "You probably wanted me to spill my secrets. And then you could stand back and play innocent."

"You're not doing yourself any favors," Noah snapped. "Only confirming your own guilt."

"My guilt?" Ginger's voice fell flat into the surrounding void. He'd avoided the accusation. "You've done nothing to show me you're trustworthy."

He frowned at her. "Nothing?"

She regretted the words. She owed him too much to be ungrateful. She stared at her feet. "I didn't mean it that way—"

"Too late." Noah crossed his arms. "We've been dancing around this for a while. You want to accuse me? Go ahead, accuse me."

She raised her chin. "I was told there was a traitor in British intelligence. And I think you're him."

"Based on what? Did Ahmed tell you I was the traitor?" Noah stepped closer, his eyes dark. "I don't think he did. Ahmed Bayrak knew me, but by one name: Lieutenant Thevshi. And he never would have accused me of being a traitor."

Her gaze stayed fixed on his. The leaves of the palm tree swayed above her. "You're Thevshi? If you truly are, you could have told me long before this."

His expression softened. "I'm not accustomed to revealing dangerous aliases to nurses in clearing stations—and one I never expected would ask me. I regretted not being able to tell you, but I couldn't."

"And you can now?" Her anger bubbled over. "Now that it's too late?"

"What choice do I have now? Ahmed is dead. I know you and Henry talked to him. I know one of you killed him. And I found you with part of his intelligence for me in a goddamned Turkish outpost." Noah tore his cap from his head. "You could have avoided it. Those British scouts who died back there"—he pointed behind them—"died because the Maslukha continues to wander freely, and no one knows who he is. No one but Ahmed did. Those scouts died because Ahmed wasn't able to reach me."

She slapped him before she could think twice. "How dare you put their deaths on my shoulders?" She lifted her hand to slap him again, and he caught her by the wrist.

She yanked her wrist away, her shoulders heaving. "Ahmed told me there was a traitor hunting him—and who should appear at the CCS right away? You. Then when I asked Captain Stephen Fisher about Thevshi, he told me *he* was Thevshi and you were missing in action. And then the lorry exploded—and you—*you* were one of the few who spoke to those refugees."

Noah gaped at her. "Stephen Fisher? And he's the one whose word poisoned you so much against me?"

She curled her hands into fists. "No—you did it yourself. Even now, how am I supposed to believe you're Thevshi? What proof can you give me you're him?"

A red mark showed on his face where she'd slapped him. "You would have to trust me."

She swallowed stinging tears, her gaze traveling to the dead, limp body of the snake. "But that's the problem, isn't it? I don't trust you." She stepped further from him. "My own brother chose not to trust you."

He jerked his head in surprise at her words.

"And you think I trust you?" Noah tucked his canteen into the saddlebag. "Isn't it highly convenient that the Earl of Braddock's daughter was the one who found Ahmed in Belah? Not to mention the lies you've told me."

"Convenient!" She stamped her foot. "Convenient? Finding Ahmed is the worst thing that's ever happened to me. I should have turned him in. I should have walked away from him, but he was dying and I knew if I didn't save him, he wouldn't make it. And what has it got me?" She motioned toward the oasis. "I'm in the middle of the desert, after I was attacked, beaten, almost killed. Nothing about what happened was convenient. And I don't care if you don't trust me."

"Good. I'm glad that's settled. Now get back on the horse." He mounted.

Smug, arrogant bastard.

"I'm not riding with you for another second." She limped away, her shoulders thrown back with as much confidence as she could muster in her disheveled state.

The ground crunched as he trotted beside her. "You're going the wrong way."

She drew herself straighter. "Then point me in the right direction."

He lifted a hand and pointed to his right side. "That way."

"Thank you." Stepping forward, she swallowed her pain. She sped up, gritting her teeth.

The horse's shadow fell over her once again.

"You're planning on walking the whole way?"

"If that's what it takes. I'm not in any particular hurry to be taken to HQ and thrown out of the nursing service or good-ness-knows-what."

Noah blocked her path with the horse. She stopped short. Flies landed on the horse's mane. "You're being ridiculous. Get on the horse."

Ginger shook her head. She needed him, even if he destroyed her life afterward. But, blast it, he didn't have to know it.

"So help me God, I will tie you and throw you over this

horse if I need to. I'm not in a mood to argue. And, believe it or not, I'm not eager to throw my life away to humor you."

"Then return without me."

He cracked his knuckles. "Damn it, Ginger, don't make this harder on us both."

She sped around the front of the horse, escaping him. "How is this hard on you?"

Noah landed on the ground behind her. He grabbed her arm.

"Enough. You are absolutely the most infuriating woman I've ever met."

She pulled her arm back. "Last night you used a different adjective."

He smirked. "Maybe I wanted to make you feel better after you tried to kiss me. Oh, that's right—you aren't attracted to me."

She stiffened, his words biting and painful. Despite everything she'd hidden from him, his instincts about her attraction to him had been correct. "Well, I'm glad you've found the correct term now. I'd much rather we be honest."

He stepped closer. "And maybe I didn't want a beautiful woman kissing me because of hashish." His eyes narrowed. "Maybe I wanted it to be something more."

It seemed harder to breathe.

"Now get on the horse." He grabbed her by both wrists, pulling her closer.

"Or what? You'll shoot me too?" She raised her chin in a dare.

"No—" He held her chin with his thumb and forefinger. "But I might change my mind about that kiss. And if you don't get on that horse, I'll assume you want me to."

Heart beating wildly, her gaze moved to his mouth. She wanted him to. No use denying it. He seemed to know it as well.

Pulling her closer still, he dug one hand into the back of her

hair, the other encircling her waist. On the precipice of something she didn't understand, a strange, unrelenting desire blos-
somed within her. James's face flashed through her mind, and
she forced the image out. There would be no stepping back
from this betrayal. And yet she wanted more than anything to
feel his kiss, to step into the unknown with him.

He kissed her, his lips brushing against hers. She drew her
face back. Her lips tingled, the moment electrified. Tilting her
mouth toward him, she drew his head down. His mouth
descended on hers with unrestrained passion.

His hand splayed against the small of her back, holding her
closely. The kiss was raw and sensual, unlike any kiss she'd ever
experienced. As abruptly as he'd begun, he dragged his mouth
away from hers. He pulled her cheek against his chest. His heart
pounded through his shirt. She closed her eyes, her thoughts
unclear.

Taking a deep breath, he pushed her away.

Her mouth fell open, her lips still throbbing from the sensation of his kiss.

Her pulse raced. She wanted to scream at him. She wanted
to ask him why he kissed her. She wanted him to kiss her again.

She locked her gaze with his. His heart had pounded too.

He hid his expressions and thoughts from her, with skill. But
this? He had no more mastery over it than she did.

Admit it. For God's sake, be honest. She'd known she was falling
for him. Every tease, every look set her pulse ablaze. She'd never
met someone who challenged her the way he did and yet treated
her like an equal. Frustrating and fascinating and maddening
and wonderful …

She closed the space between them, and he caught her waist.
His lips parted against hers, and she slid her arms around his
neck. Off balance, she closed her eyes and pushed her body
against his. His arms tightened as they kissed each other.

The nature of the kiss spoke of something deeper. Not only urgency and desire but something else—an unknown promise they could find in the other.

His hand cradled the nape of her neck, the other pulling her closer still. His lips were demanding, insistent, his tongue colliding with hers in a manner that would have seemed strange were it not for how natural it felt. They shared one breath, and she hungered for more.

If ever she'd experienced a moment close to perfection, this was it.

He cupped her face with his hands and pulled back, her lips feeling bruised and pulsing.

She waited, hoping he'd say something. What would he think? How could she share something so passionate with someone she barely knew?

"Please get on the horse?" Noah asked.

Ginger nodded. They reached for the saddle at the same time. Their hands touched, and Ginger stared at their fingertips.

"You first." Noah cleared his throat.

She mounted. "I-I thought I might ride behind you this time."

"Sorry, but no." Noah swung up behind her. His forearm brushed against hers as he took the reins.

"Why not?"

"Because I don't trust you." With a flick of his hand, they started forward.

"I won't do anything foolish."

His chuckle rumbled in his chest. "This coming from the same woman who rode into Ottoman territory to evade me."

He had a point. She wouldn't concede it, though.

"What if I give you my word?" Ginger glanced over her shoulder at him.

"Darling, your word has to be worth something in the first place for me to take it."

The endearment reminded her of James, and panic struck her. He could never know about this. She twisted her mouth. "Don't call me that."

"Don't get carried away. I mean nothing by it."

"Well, don't say it. I have a fiancé. Which you seem to have forgotten."

"I'm not the only one who seems to have forgotten him."

A fresh wave of guilt passed through her. She sucked in her lower lip, running the tip of her tongue against it. She stopped, determined to push the kiss from her mind. She couldn't let it matter to her, even if she wanted it to.

They'd crossed a line from which she doubted they could return. He'd called their mutual attraction complicated and unfortunate. It was so much more. Even if they could have been allies, they'd complicated the process so much, she didn't know if it was even possible anymore. She'd given James her word—and betrayed him. Her mind was too clouded with the exhaustion and troubles of the past few days to know what to do.

But, for the first time in her life, her heart felt alive.

CHAPTER EIGHTEEN

*I*n view of the British camp, the ragged slopes of the hills jutted into the night's black sky. The sight normally made her happy, but now Ginger dreaded it. The warm scents from the nearby date farms mixed with the aromatic, salty sea air.

Her stomach churned. She wasn't sure if she was ready to face Miss Walsh and the RAMC and explain her disappearance —or see anyone in the chain of command. Worst of all, she didn't know what to say to James.

Close to the tents and horses of HQ, Noah slowed.

A figure approached them. When he was a few feet away, the moonlight revealed his face.

Stephen.

He'd been waiting for them? How could he have known when they would return? This couldn't be good. His claim of being Thevshi nagged her. Despite Noah's inability to prove the fact, her gut told her Stephen had lied about it.

"Major Benson. A word." Stephen barely glanced at Ginger.

Noah sat straighter. "I need to escort Ginger to the clearing station first."

"That would be 'Lady Virginia' to you. Don't forget your place."

"Don't forget yours, Captain," Noah said.

Ginger restrained a smile. She enjoyed seeing someone put Stephen in his place. Especially someone Stephen considered himself so superior to socially.

Stephen sniffed. "It's imperative we speak. My orders are from above." His voice was smug.

Noah dismounted. He stretched his shoulders and tied the horse, then held his hand out for her. She slid in front of him, her hip stiff. She braced against the horse.

"Stay here." Noah strode off with Stephen. They stopped out of earshot but in view. One of the larger airplane hangars stood in the distance behind them. The moon's light outlined their figures.

The wind carried Noah's voice. "Absolutely not."

Stephen's answer was incomprehensible.

They argued for a few minutes, then Noah returned to Ginger. He jerked her forward by the wrist. "Follow me."

The lack of gentility startled her. Was he angry with her?

They hurried toward the officers' quarters at HQ. Stephen trailed behind. Once there, Noah directed them toward a tent. He opened it and ducked inside. "Sit." He guided Ginger to a chair in the tent's corner.

"Whose tent is this?" Ginger glanced around the darkened space, seeing no signs of personalization.

"A spare one I've been using." Noah peeled off his jacket and laid it across the desk.

Stephen followed them in.

Noah glowered at Stephen then glanced back at Ginger. "Captain Fisher contacted your father about your disappearance. Lord Braddock has made arrangements for your discharge from the nursing service, effective immediately, and return to your family's home in Cairo."

Ginger gaped at Stephen, trying to comprehend what Noah had said. It didn't surprise her that Stephen had contacted her father—it would have been a logical next step after her disappearance. But a preemptive removal from the nursing service?

She kept her voice level. "On what grounds am I to be discharged? What 'arrangements?'"

"You're to travel back with me to Port Said, where your father will meet us and take you to Cairo," Stephen said. "Unfortunately, since you went missing, I had to provide a cover to your superiors. The official story is that you and Major Benson ran away for a romantic tryst—"

"What—?" Ginger bolted from the chair. Noah stopped her with a firm hand to her elbow. He dropped his hand.

Stephen continued speaking over her. "—but I've asked for their discretion. You're being discharged accordingly. You'll be removed from the nursing service for the war's duration."

Ginger glared at Stephen. "You odious little man. Is this because I wounded your fragile ego by refusing to marry you?" She clenched her hands into such tight fists that her fingernails dug into her palms.

"I told you she wouldn't go quietly." Noah pulled a flask from his personal belongings and sipped it.

Stephen shrugged. "It's done. She doesn't have an option."

"I refuse to cooperate." Ginger's hands shook. "I have a fiancé. What will I tell him?"

"You should have considered that before you disappeared," Stephen said. "You had every opportunity to tell me the truth before you left. You lied to my face. Henry went to Cairo, told your father how you led him right to Ahmed Bayrak. How you'd hidden him. You're lucky I intervened."

Ginger eased herself into the chair, feeling lightheaded. Henry was in Cairo? While she'd almost died trying to protect him, he'd betrayed her. She narrowed her gaze at Stephen then Noah, incensed. "You both share in the blame of that, considering that you both claimed to be the one person who could have settled this issue from the start. Now, which one of you is actually Lieutenant Thevshi?"

A tense silence settled between the two men as they squared off, eyes dead-locked. Stephen looked away first, toward Ginger. "You're making the assumption Ahmed didn't mislead you."

Neither of them were going to answer? She wanted to scream. "You're the one who lied about Ahmed."

"Not another word about that spy. You're under strict orders not to discuss the affair with anyone." Stephen glanced at Noah. "Including Major Benson. Benson answers directly to your father. He isn't to question you. Your father will handle all aspects of your debriefing."

"My father works for the Foreign Office, not Cairo Intelligence."

"He works in intelligence," Stephen said.

Noah leaned against the desk. "Is Lord Helton aware Lord Braddock is breaking the law for his daughter? Regardless of his position, Sister Whitman should be questioned for her involvement with a foreign spy."

"Going over Lord Braddock's head may not be in your best interest." Stephen's eyes glinted. "But make no mistake, you're being investigated also, Benson. You have much to answer for by going rogue and disappearing into the desert with Lady Virginia."

"He didn't go rogue, he saved my life." Why wasn't Noah saying more to defend himself? The floor was caving in, and the world she had worked so hard to create was vanishing into the abyss. "I need to talk to James."

"I informed him personally. Be thankful you're going home. Now, if you'll come with me—"

"I'll be escorting her to Port Said. And while here at Belah." Noah's tone left no room for argument. "You may accompany us tomorrow if you wish. You're dismissed."

"Lord Braddock explicitly ordered me—" Stephen began.

Noah stepped closer to Stephen, his posture menacing. "Then find the orders. Or, better yet, have him send them directly to me. I'm not about to release Sister Whitman to you."

An ugly scowl twisted Stephen's features. "But—"

"Don't you have anything better to do than hang around Belah? What of your assignments at El Arish? I'd say you're on the verge of neglecting your duties," Noah snapped.

Stephen straightened. "My other tasks were reassigned while I investigated Lady Virginia's disappearance. She's practically family, after all."

"Well, she's reappeared. You're dismissed, *Captain*." Noah's tone was a low growl.

Anger simmered in her stomach as Stephen left. She should have prepared for something like this. She'd been naïve, lured into believing she commanded her own destiny. Nursing had felt secure—something she could rely on, something that was hers.

Her father had snatched it away.

What was worse, her discharge would generate gossip. The other nurses would have a field day speculating why she left the clearing station.

Noah stood within arm's reach, lost in thought. He may as well have been on the other side of the globe. His detached posture offered no familiarity. He lifted the flask again, then held it out to her. "Whisky?"

She shook her head. "I need more control of my life, not less."

He chuckled without humor and recapped the flask. He glanced at the tent flap, which Stephen had left open. He tied it and turned toward her. "I need to know what Ahmed told you. Everything. Right now."

Hadn't her father ordered her not to discuss Ahmed with Noah? "Why didn't you say you were Thevshi in front of Stephen?"

"That's more complicated than I can go into." Noah squatted before her. "I know you don't trust me. But I need the information Ahmed left for me. It's what I'm here for. It's why I came. Ahmed gave you some understanding as to its importance. But I looked at Ahmed's message you recovered. There has to be more. Did he give you anything else? The key to solve the cipher, perhaps?"

"Key?" Even if she trusted him enough to tell him the truth, James still had Ahmed's bag. She couldn't say as much without implicating James.

She'd already betrayed James enough.

She folded her hands in her lap. "Why didn't you tell me you worked for my father?"

"Would it have made a difference?" Noah sat on his heels.

"You're right. I may have trusted you less." Ginger crossed her arms. It wasn't entirely true. Besides, Noah had told her he knew her father and brother and she'd barely believed that.

Noah was an enigma, his loyalties seemingly so complex she couldn't guess who he was. He worked for her father, which would seem to make him an ally, but he said he was Thevshi, which made him Ahmed's ally and ... in opposition to Henry? Henry and her father couldn't be in opposition. Did that make both Ahmed and Noah traitors? And that didn't even factor in Stephen's claims.

But when she was with him she felt safe. Happy. She longed for his teasing smiles and was amazed at the way he seemed to read her mind with a knowing glance.

How she felt was illogical and ridiculous.

But it had been enough to motivate her to betray James. "I need to talk to my fiancé."

Noah's jaw tightened. "I have to know what Ahmed told you."

His insistence unsettled her. Regardless of what she thought of Stephen, her father would be the best, most neutral person to entrust with the information Ahmed had given her. Surely Noah must know that. And if Noah was Thevshi, any information Ahmed had for Noah must also be intended for her father.

She met his eyes. Even if she had to push him away, it would be the safest course of action for now. "I'm grateful for everything you've done for me, Noah—I am. But whatever happened between us in the desert and especially at the oasis— they were confidences we shouldn't have taken. My father will know best what to do about Ahmed"—the words tasted as bitter as they felt—"and I'm going to marry James. I gave my word."

Noah's look was a mixture of anger and amusement. "And yet you had no problem torpedoing your word hours ago."

She raised her chin. "Prove to me you're Thevshi."

His hands fisted. "I can't." He rubbed his forehead, exasperated. "I don't carry papers around to prove it. It would defeat the purpose of the alias."

"How would you have proved it to him? How would he have known he was speaking to the right person?"

"I would have been able to prove it to him."

She searched her memory, feeling like she'd forgotten something important. She imagined him cupping her face in his hands. His lips against hers, soft, coaxing. Her pulse raced, and she shoved the thoughts away and stood. Her attraction to him clouded her judgement and made her want to believe him.

"I need to talk to James." At the least to ask him for Ahmed's bag. But also to explain what had happened.

He loosened the top button of his collar as he stood. "I'll take you to speak to your fiancé. Because I believe you deserve the chance to say good-bye to him and your friends here." He checked his watch. "It's eight. Where should I take you?"

She twisted her hair over one shoulder. "He might be in his quarters. Or in the recreation tent or the Mess. Can you take me to my quarters so I can change?"

They left the tent. She put some space between them as they walked. During their ride, she'd become used to his proximity. The distance between them felt awkward.

Most everything had closed—the tents housing the telegraph station, the post, the officers' store. A few men lingered near the chapel, where a chaplain held a late-night Bible study. The warm winds of the Arabian peninsula whipped around them, stirring the tent's panels and reminding her how everything she'd worked for had been swept away.

She imagined what her father expected of her in Cairo. Stephen arranging her discharge in the manner he had meant she would never work again. An accusation of promiscuity would leave a black mark on her record. Her heart ached. Her time in the desert had been arduous but valuable. Necessary.

While the war continued, she might find another way to occupy her time meaningfully ... but after? She couldn't imagine going back to the life her family had in England before the war. Facing her father now would be bad enough. Continuing under his control would be worse.

Marriage could free her from home, but to whom? James? She dreaded the prospect. Now more than ever. She snuck a glance at Noah.

As they drew closer to the officers' and sisters' compounds, where the sleeping quarters and ablution facilities were, Ginger slowed. An outdoor recreation area off the principal route to the hospital tents provided the officers and nurses with a place to gather around fire pits and benches. With the moon in a gibbous phase, the threat of nighttime air raids faded. A group of nurses and medical officers mingled there, smoking and chatting in low tones.

Ginger froze. There would be no way for her to get into the clearing station without being seen. She was already close enough to be spotted. Her appearance would raise questions, as would Noah's company.

Seeing her hesitation, Noah stopped. "What is it?"

"This wasn't a good idea." Three days away, and she was already an outsider. "Let's return to HQ."

Her alarm grew as a man rose from one bench, staring directly at her. Even from where she stood, she recognized James. "Oh … damn it," she muttered. She'd wanted to explain herself—but she'd hoped to appeal to him without Noah beside her. And from the way James stalked across the sand toward them, he was more than annoyed she'd arrived with Noah. He was furious.

He must have heard the rumors.

She rushed toward him. "James—wait. Let me explain."

James brushed her off as she reached for him. Her eyes widened. What had Stephen told him? "James—no, no, no, you don't—"

"You utter bastard." James stormed toward Noah. He swung, punching Noah in the face. Noah reeled back, holding his cheek.

James attempted another punch, but Noah blocked and trapped James's arm behind his back. With a swift twist, Noah brought James to his knees.

James rolled over onto his side. He grabbed Noah's shirt, but his rage was no match for Noah's skill as he lay pinned. Ginger ran toward the men, voices approaching behind her as a crowd gathered. "Let him go. Please, Noah."

"So it's Noah now?" James's eyes bulged.

"James. Please, be calm. You don't understand."

Ginger placed her hands over Noah's. "Please let him go."

Noah pulled away. He rubbed his jaw. "I've about had it with doing favors for you, Ginger."

She ignored Noah. This was worse than she could have ever imagined. She had to make things right with an audience. She bent down beside James and helped him stand. "Whatever Stephen told you—"

"Do you think I'm so naïve as to believe that narcissist without question?" James's face was red, even in the darkness. "You've been gone for three days! I was half mad with worry. I tried contacting everyone I knew in your family. It was your father who made clear to me what happened."

Ginger's mouth opened as she stared at him, stunned. *Her father?*

And then it made sense. Her father had never wanted her to marry James anyway. He had every reason to drive him away now. To poison the well. Without James, she had no recourse but to return home, fully dependent on her family. Especially with her career as a nurse wrested away.

"My father lied."

"Why would your father lie about something of such magnitude?"

This would all be so much easier if she'd explained about Stephen years ago. "Please. Let's go somewhere to discuss this. Not out here." She put her hand on his forearm. He pulled his arm away.

James eyed her. "Nothing happened between you and the major?"

The kiss. The memory of Noah's arms around her resurfaced. His lips against hers, her response. Other thoughts crept their way into her mind too. The way he'd lain beside her in the Bedouin tent, his body pressed against hers, his nearness on the ride.

"James, please." Curious bystanders gathered closer. They watched James with pitying expressions.

Her non-answer was answer enough. "No." James backed away from her. "Did you ever love me? Or was it all a farce?" His features contorted, as though he struggled to maintain composure himself. "I would have done anything for you." He pointed to Noah. "What does he have that I couldn't have given you?"

Everything.

Her heart answered before her head. She avoided looking at Noah, guilt flushing her. "I barely even know him. You must hear what I have to tell you."

"Not now. It's over."

Over? It was one thing to end the engagement on her terms, quite another to be unceremoniously released from it before all these people. She held in a sob. "But you don't understand."

"I don't want a wife surrounded by scandal." His voice had a broken, tired tone. "Even that I could have managed if I believed it wasn't true. But all I have to do is look in your face ... and you had the gall to come in his company tonight. Leave me be."

James stepped away and Noah blocked his path, grabbing him by the shirtfront. "You're making a mistake. You owe her the opportunity to defend herself."

James looked disgusted. "Get your hands off me."

Noah allowed James past. Tears clouded Ginger's vision as gravel crunched beside her. Beatrice touched Ginger's elbow.

As Ginger folded into Beatrice's embrace, Beatrice whispered in her ear, "James is not worth your tears."

Ginger's gaze moved over Beatrice's shoulder. James parted the crowd as he retreated to the recreation area. She didn't want to see the faces of judgement and disapproval. She didn't even want their sympathy. She wouldn't cry.

James had tossed her aside like a dirty rag. This, after she'd spent years trying to love him. Being worried about hurting him. "I'm being sent home."

"I know." Beatrice grasped her hands. "What can I do?"

"Nothing, for now." She still needed to get Ahmed's bag, and Beatrice might be the only one who could help. But it was too risky to say anything here. "I'll write to you." Ginger dropped her voice. "I didn't do what they're saying."

Beatrice nodded. "They haven't told us details. But I look at you, and I can't help but think you've escaped a Robert and found a Charles." With a soft smirk, Beatrice released her hands and whispered, "If I could have one more day, one more hour with Charles, I wouldn't waste it."

Beatrice returned to the group, and Ginger's heart fell. She'd miss some nurses and their kinship, but she'd never have another friend like Beatrice.

With a clenched jaw, she turned away from the prying eyes. She winced as she marched past Noah, away from the clearing station, her hip hating every step. She headed toward the sea.

Noah caught her by the railroad track and grabbed her arm. "And where, exactly, are you going?"

"What do you care?" She threw him a withering stare.

Noah's fingers tightened around her forearm. "I care more than I should. We should go back to HQ."

"I don't want sleep." Anger coursed through her, uncontrollable. She wanted to scream, to break something, to transfer her rage to something calm and still. She shook, her emotions spiraling.

"I'll take you somewhere else."

"I don't want to go somewhere else. I want to look out at the water." She stopped at the top of the sand dunes. The empty sea stretched before them, a glossy eternal pool of solitude and tranquility. She yanked off her boots and carried them in her hands as she headed down the dune.

She didn't care who followed her now. Not the entire clearing station, not Stephen, not James, not anyone. She started for the water and went right into the waves. The cold shocked her senses, and goose bumps rose on her skin, feeling like a million pinpricks, but she pushed further still. The water invigorated her, the grime of the last few days floating away with the sea foam. She pinched her nose to lower herself under.

When she resurfaced, Noah startled her by encircling her waist with his arms. "What are you doing?" He pulled her back.

"Let me go." Water dripped down her face. There was the taste of brine on her lips. She tried to escape his embrace, but his arms locked tight.

A wave tipped her. He wrested her back several feet.

He worried about her.

I care more than I should.

She turned toward him. "Tell me the truth. If I told you more about Ahmed, would you still even be here? Or would you vanish from my life?" They shifted as the waves sank them further into the sand. He may have already destroyed the one document he'd taken from her.

"I have to stay away from you, Ginger." He didn't release her. "Vanishing would be a favor to us both. I can't see you again after I return you to your father."

His words struck her with unexpected sadness. He didn't pretend to offer her anything. A lesser man would have taken advantage of her with the hashish. Knowing her attraction, he could have whispered sweetly in her ear, used that to manipulate her. But he hadn't.

Trembling, her fingertips grazed his lips. She traced his jawline and pulled him toward her, kissing his mouth.

He didn't respond, his body taut. "We aren't in the middle of the desert. Someone could see."

She'd already gone too far to turn away. "I don't care. What are they going to do? I've already been discharged. My fiancé has broken off our engagement and humiliated me." She coaxed her lips against his. Something wild and unrestrained captivated her. She gently bit his lower lip. "Kiss me."

He groaned. His hands tightened around her waist. He drew her closer, and her eyes closed. He returned the kiss as she clung to him. Her entire body awakened with yearning and desire. His hands moved away from the safety of her back, cupping her breasts, pushing against her.

She wanted this. She wanted *him*.

Forget James.

His tongue dipped into her mouth, and her control slipped. She wrapped her arms around him, digging her fingers into the short hair at the nape of his neck.

Noah's hands worked their way around her and smoothed over her curves to her hips. He lifted her weightlessly in the water and pulled her into his arms. He carried her out and set her down against the sand, the water lapping against their feet.

After dragging a kiss to her forehead, he stepped back. "I don't think we want to make any more mistakes tonight."

She swallowed. "Who says it would be a mistake? Maybe it's the only good thing to come from this."

"Nothing has changed about our circumstances." Noah's voice was tight.

Her shoulders dropped. There he was wrong. Everything

had changed. But she was too weary, too confused to understand what it meant. She walked further from the water and sat. "In some ways, I feel more at home here than I ever have anywhere else." She dug her toes into the sand. "I don't want to leave."

"The beach or Belah?" Noah sat and leaned back onto his hands. "I've found home has little to do with location."

"That's easy enough for you to say."

"What do you mean?"

She cringed, her offhanded remark sounding overly priggish even to her own ears. "I'm sorry. I didn't mean it rudely. Stephen told me about your family."

Noah's eyes flashed. "I'm not sure what he told you. My parents died when I was seven. My younger brother and I went to go live with an aunt. She died eight years ago. My brother died in Gallipoli and was thrown into a mass grave. Is that a thorough enough summary for you?"

Ginger's cheeks heated. When Stephen had told her Noah was an orphan, she'd pictured him barefoot and running in the streets of London, like Oliver Twist. Probably because of Khalib. "Noah, I'm sorry. I didn't realize—"

"I might know what it's like to have a home."

Instead of an ill-formed apology, she slipped her hand into his.

They sat in silence, the waves rumbling, rolling like thick ropes against the beach. The storm had left a calmer sea in its wake.

Despite the peace it offered, regret clung to her. Over Ahmed, over James. She also hadn't said good-bye to the other nurses or her patients. She'd never see them again. She'd wanted so badly to save one life, to prove her worth. In the process, she'd destroyed so much.

CHAPTER NINETEEN

$\mathcal{T}$he train pulled away from the clearing station, rocking Ginger in her seat. The movements grew smoother with speed as the blurred tans and greys melded with the vast blue sky. When she'd come to Belah feeling accomplished and confident, pitying the men who left here broken shells, never had she imagined she would leave here as frail as the men she treated.

She leaned her head against the window. A jostle highlighted the locomotive's shaking. The cars further down held rows of patients on tiered bunk beds lining each side of the aisle. The train also had an operating theater and a ward for the nurses who were assigned to work there. This car was for officers, the wooden benches accommodating two occupants on either side. A handful of officers sat in the coach. Most kept to themselves. Khalib lay on the bench beside them, asleep.

During the last twenty minutes, Noah had ignored both Stephen and Ginger by reading a book. Much as his cool detachment made her wish they were alone, the situation was already uncomfortable enough with Stephen staring at her.

Ginger had always made the journey with other nurses, and she imagined their laughter or stories as they traveled. She was the sole woman in this coach. The other nurses on the train were with the wounded, tending to them throughout the journey. *I should be with them.*

Noah shut the book. He stood, and a flash of pain moved across his face.

"Are you all right?" Ginger asked. A bruise had surfaced on his cheek overnight, from where James had punched him.

"Fine." He checked his watch. "General Darrow asked me to visit him in his train car. I'll return soon." He woke Khalib and they left the coach.

Stephen moved into the seat beside her. She stiffened and examined her fingernails. "Return to your side, Stephen. I have nothing to say to you." All her finishing school rules no longer seemed to matter. Stephen had destroyed her work. She had no desire to be gracious to him again.

Stephen chortled. "You'll be in for a great deal of frustration if you throw your lot in with Benson. He's not who you think."

"You don't know what I think." She twisted her mouth. "And I could say the same about you."

"I haven't changed. You have, though."

"One thing hasn't changed"—she met his eyes—"I still have no interest in you. And ripping away my profession and fiancé won't change that."

"Your refusal to trust me has a cost." Stephen crossed his ankle over his knee. "I could tell you stories about Benson that would make your toes curl. He hasn't been unusually friendly with you, has he? Perhaps even romantic?"

The train's sway mimicked the unsteadiness she felt.

Her throat dried. "Don't be ridiculous. Until last night, I had a fiancé."

"I'm surprised. Benson has a reputation with women. He's

especially known for how well he can manipulate them." Stephen's gaze clouded and he leaned closer. "I shouldn't be telling you this, and your father would be furious if he knew, but you seem to think I'm your enemy."

He kept his eyes fixed in the direction where Noah had gone. "The reason I believed Benson was dead was that I was with him in Aleppo in March. I received the news he intended to betray me to the Turks. I barely got away. I didn't think he had escaped. He vanished, and everyone assumed the Turks had got him."

Ginger searched his eyes. "You think he's a traitor?"

"I'm not suggesting anything. I'm telling you. I've been watching Noah for a long time. He's deeply involved in the region's politics. I think there's a chance he works for the Maslukha himself."

She steadied her hands. Much as she didn't want to believe anything Stephen said, she couldn't afford to completely discount his words. Especially after Henry had told her not to tell Noah anything. "You said Ahmed was a spy that had been thwarting you. That you were Lieutenant Thevshi."

Stephen touched her arm. "Ginger, I said what I thought I needed to say to discourage you from getting further involved with Ahmed. No, I'm not Thevshi. I hoped you would trust me. I care for you. We've known each other our whole lives."

Had Noah told the truth, then? Ginger tried to make sense of Stephen's confession, angry with his lies. His dishonesty made everything so much more complicated. The train's wheels screeched and thumped as they tumbled down the tracks.

Stephen clasped his hands together. "You haven't fallen for Benson, have you? Did he tell you he—"

"Don't be ridiculous. I hardly know him."

"That's my point." Stephen lit a cigarette. "You don't know him."

"I know he saved my life when Henry abandoned me in the desert." She snatched the cigarette from his fingers. She tossed it on the floor of the car, then crushed it with the toe of her boot. "Why don't you return to your seat?"

Stephen laughed. "Sometimes you act as though we're strangers." He pulled out yet another cigarette and lifted it toward her, asking her permission to smoke it.

She nodded stiffly.

"You're the girl who used to sneak off with Henry and me to go riding. Wearing boys' trousers, no less. The one who shared her first sip of whisky with me—and a few kisses that night too."

She glared. Damn those foolish kisses she'd given him. She hated the memory. The effects of alcohol. "I was young and—"

"Spirited. Which I appreciate." Stephen's eyes lingered for a moment on her mouth. His face grew solemn. "And while I wish things had turned out differently between us, you don't have to forget the moments when we were practically friends."

"You were Henry's friend. That's all."

"I'm the best friend you have right now. If it weren't for me, you'd be at the law's mercy. You hid an enemy soldier," he whispered through clenched teeth. "Do you have any idea what it would do to my family's reputation if Angelica's future sister-in-law was convicted for treason? And now you're protecting Benson. Which interests me, given what I've told you about him."

"I'm not protecting anyone. Except myself. And apparently you don't seem to mind having your sister be related to a disgraced woman?"

Stephen tilted his head toward her. "What if I told you there may yet be a way for you to resume nursing?"

Resume nursing? She swallowed a lump in her throat. "And how's that? You saw to it I wouldn't. With the story you concocted, the QAs and Red Cross will both reject me once they see my record."

"I did what I had to do to keep you safe. But I may persuade the right people to wipe your record clean if you help us learn what Benson knows. You'd be amazed at what I can buy you. And you're right. I have no interest in staining Angelica by way of your behavior. Allow me to help you."

She'd had a lifetime of seeing the way Stephen's family used their wealth to buy whatever they desired—Stephen in particular. It was one reason he'd been so stunned when she'd turned down his marriage proposal.

But she would have to help prove Noah was part of something nefarious. With her father taking over, she doubted her importance. "I don't see what makes you think Major Benson would trust me."

"You can be charming when you choose. And he enjoys the attentions of extraordinarily beautiful women. Consider the idea. We all stand to gain with Benson exposed."

She scowled. "So you'd like me to seduce him and betray him? Isn't that what you suggested he's tried to do with me?"

"Turn the tables. You're capable."

"I thought you said you wanted me safe? If he's the murderous traitor you believe, why would you allow me to go anywhere near him?"

Stephen opened his mouth to answer, then stiffened. "Benson is back."

Noah returned with Khalib in tow. Noah caught her eyes before looking away. For his part, he didn't appear the least bit interested in their discussion. He sat on the bench without so much as another glance at them, then lifted his book once more.

Ginger's heart lurched. Everything Stephen said was so hard to believe, but he hadn't been wrong about Noah's romantic advances either. The possibility of Noah's reputation as a philanderer agitated her. He'd told her clearly enough he had no interest in a future with her.

What did she know of men? Pressure rose in her chest, mounting until it seemed her lungs would burst.

In Noah's arms she'd felt safety. But she was a fool if she didn't admit the danger to her heart … and possibly her life.

The kisses she'd shared with Noah seemed so far away and brief. The train ride to Port Said, on the other hand, continued to stretch out, interminably.

CHAPTER TWENTY

*S*tanding at the window in her hotel room the next morning, Ginger watched the streets of Port Said with a heavy feeling in her heart. She'd come here as a nurse two years earlier. Had her father picked it as a meeting place to spite her? She steeled herself to calm, watching the waters of the Mediterranean Sea lapping against the flat shore and golden sand. Green palm trees dotted the streets, and white minarets rose against the blue sky.

She'd arrived at sundown with Noah and Stephen and checked into the Savoy Hotel. She'd bathed and collapsed into the soft bed, where she'd slept more soundly than she'd done in weeks.

Ginger braced herself against the window frame, the scent of lavender lingering on her hair. She limped to the bed, her hip throbbing.

The room was ornate, Egyptian motifs artfully displayed throughout. A cream-and-gold plush chaise lounge with lion's feet sat opposite the four-poster bed. Wallpaper glinted with gold foil lotus blossoms and palm frond designs. Despite his displeasure, her father hadn't skimped on luxury when he'd reserved the room.

She smirked. Perhaps it was an effort to show her what she'd missed. The beauty of the space was difficult not to appreciate.

She slipped into a dressing gown. A breakfast tray on the table near the balcony displayed a tea service, and she helped herself to a cup. There was a knock on the balcony door, and it opened a crack. She yelped and her cup clattered. "May I come in?" Noah asked.

"Come in?" She repeated in confusion.

Noah rested his hand against the doorknob, a warm breeze floating inside. "Were you expecting someone else?"

"I wasn't expecting anyone." She mopped up the spilled tea with a serviette. "How did you get into my room?"

"Key." He shut the door and came up beside her. "Don't worry, I'll be a perfect gentleman. I'm under strict orders to keep you out of trouble." He poured another cup of tea and handed it to her. "I couldn't do that from across the hall, now, could I?"

"Or you missed me." Ginger smiled and sipped her tea. Despite her curiosity at the liberty he'd taken in coming into her room, she didn't mind the company. She lifted a piece of toast. "Khalib could guard my door."

"He did. But I let him take a break." Humor flashed in his eyes. "You're quite the sound sleeper. You didn't even stir when they brought your breakfast." He leaned forward. "Which, coincidentally, is why I came in. I thought it best to keep an eye out."

The wicker chair crackled as she sat. She drew her legs to one side and opened a jar of orange marmalade. "I've needed the sleep." She leaned into her chair.

"Probably much easier to do in your element." Noah sat beside her.

She nibbled the toast. "I'm not sure I'd call this my element. Though you look rested too."

He'd shaven and his uniform was spotless and pressed. "It's a comfortable hotel."

Not wanting to be caught staring, Ginger lifted the silver lids on the containers. Settling on a boiled egg, she sprinkled some salt on it. "Where's Stephen this morning?"

"I sent him to deliver some reports. Unlike you, we're not on holiday. And I'd rather not have him skulking about."

She covered herself more tightly with the dressing gown and leaned toward him. "Well, that makes two of us."

He took a coconut macaroon from a plate. "Strange. Fisher seems to be under the impression since you're no longer engaged, you'll be his future wife."

"He's wrong." She frowned at a smudge of black ink on his hands.

Her gaze darted to the vanity in the room, where she'd left writing utensils and paper. She'd sat to write a letter to Beatrice last night, but the barrel in the fountain pen had burst, forcing her to abandon her pursuit.

"Did you snoop through my things while I slept?" She rose and went over to the vanity. After lifting the pen, she examined her fingers, which revealed a smudge.

Noah sat back. "You're quite observant."

She wrapped her arms over her chest, feeling exposed. "What did you go through? My personals?" The trunk in the corner appeared undisturbed, but who knew how long he'd been in here? The idea made her shiver.

He sighed. "I'm sorry. I had no choice. I needed to be certain you weren't carrying any other messages from Ahmed."

Her heart lurched. "Then you went through my trunk." She gaped at him. "Is that why you're in my room? You wanted to search my things?"

"No, I went through your trunk yesterday, on the train."

It must have been when he'd left to visit some general. Anger flushed her cheeks. "You're admitting you lied about seeing that general? And since you found nothing, you went through my handbag this morning?"

He nodded. "I had to. I wouldn't have been doing my job if I didn't."

"Yes, you would have. Because my father told you to leave it to him, didn't he?" She set her hands on her hips. "Unless you're working for someone else. Like the enemy."

"You'd be in danger if so."

His calm demeanor frustrated her. "Maybe I've been in danger all along."

Noah laughed and approached. "Let me guess. Stephen filled your head with doubts about my allegiance?"

She stepped away. The pain in her leg reminded her of what he spared her from. "He implied ..." She broke off, thinking of the kisses they'd shared. But he'd violated her trust by going through her belongings. "Please leave."

"Why? Don't you want answers?" Noah put his hands on her shoulders, in a move that was both calming and gentle. "This is a game that's hard to play when you're emotionally involved."

She swallowed. "I want to know the truth."

"You want the truth to be convenient." His hands dropped from her shoulders. "If it makes you feel better to not help me because you think I'm a traitor, so be it."

He walked toward the room door.

"I don't know what I believe about you." The admission floated in the air like a bubble, ready to burst no matter his response.

Noah smirked over his shoulder. "Don't worry, I'm not hurt. You'll change your mind anyway. You do that frequently enough."

She glared and threw the rest of her egg at him.

"And your plan to attack a dangerous traitor like me is to come at me with a boiled egg?"

His smugness made her want to scream. "You're intolerable."

He continued toward the door.

She stormed up behind him, hands clenched at her sides. "You're a fraud. You're not even English, like you pretend. And you tried to kill Stephen in Aleppo."

Noah hesitated. "I— What?"

"Stephen told me. You betrayed him."

He slid the lock into place. Walking toward the chaise, he unbuttoned his jacket, his movements collected. She'd struck a nerve. She shrank against the wall, alarmed.

He peeled off the jacket and faced her. His face unreadable, he unbuttoned his shirt.

What on earth was he doing?

She braced her fingertips against the wall. She was closer to the door than he was, fortunately, in case she needed a quick escape. Or to scream for help.

He paused. "Relax. I have no bad intentions." He pulled his shirt away from his shoulders. A wince left him as he removed his undershirt, leaving him naked from the waist up. "This is what happened in Aleppo."

She'd assumed by the way he filled out his uniform that he had a muscular physique under his shirt. He wasn't like most young Tommies, barely out of school and with boy-like bodies that made their uniforms so ill-fitting. What she hadn't expected was for the toned muscles of his torso to be covered in fading bruises and cuts. The abrasions were several weeks old, now tinged with yellows and greens, but it was clear they had been deep.

Noah had been beaten, badly.

He gestured for her to examine him, and she approached.

His wounds hadn't been tended in some time. Some cuts on his torso were healing, but a few were red at the edges and puffy.

This whole time he'd been in pain, probably excruciatingly so, and he'd never once let on. Every insult she'd hurled at him, everything she'd put him through, flashed through her mind. "What happened to you?"

"A few weeks before I met you, my cover was blown. The Turks captured me. I escaped—but not before they did this." She touched a cut, and he grimaced. "Stephen planned to rendezvous with me, but he didn't show. The Turks did."

She pulled her hand away. Stephen's story almost matched his. In reverse. "Why would Stephen betray you to the Turks?"

Noah searched her gaze. "You don't know, do you?"

She shook her head. What did he think she knew?

He hadn't answered her question. "How did you escape?"

"Khalib followed and helped me."

When she'd first met him, she'd believed he was fresh out in the field due to how nicely he smelled. But that couldn't have been the case. "You were in hospital before you came to Gaza."

"Yes."

She should tend to his cuts. "You need medical attention."

"I wasn't cleared to return to duty."

"I can see why." Her fingertips skimmed his hardened muscles, feeling for deeper contusions under the skin's surface. She watched his chest rise and fall. "What did they use to do this?"

"Boots."

She grimaced at the mental image of this strong man being kicked. Something about him made her certain he wouldn't want pity, though.

She traced her fingers over a cut. Goose bumps rose on his forearm and she paused, her fingers catching his. She couldn't meet his gaze but shifted closer to him and pressed her forehead against the taut, lean muscles of his upper arm.

She'd seen injured men, even naked men. They hadn't affected her like this. A tingle swept up the back of her neck and across her face. "I'm sorry they did this to you."

"It's not your fault."

"But I haven't exactly made your life easier."

"Would you have acted any differently if you knew?" Noah reached for his shirt.

She put a hand on his wrist. "Wait. Let me tend to these."

She fetched her haversack from her trunk and set it on the chaise. She worked in silence, carefully cleaning each wound and applying gauze to a few.

Her gaze shifted to a regimental tattoo on his upper back. Many soldiers had them—tattoos increased the chances of their bodies' return home for burial. But she hadn't expected him to have one, since he worked for Intelligence. Many men she'd met through her father and brother didn't have any regimental assignment.

She inspected it. The emblem of the Egyptian sphinx graced the top of a laurel leaf branch. Both the names 'Egypt' and 'Gloucestershire' were inscribed. She'd seen it on the men from the Gloucestershire Regiment before, but she noted something more unusual in his marking. Where the laurel leaves gathered below the sphinx, they took on the appearance of wings and a slender, thin body … like a dragonfly.

She froze.

Dragonfly.

The code word. Ahmed had told her not to speak it. But what if all this time, she'd had a key to knowing if Noah told the truth and she'd overlooked it.

It couldn't be coincidental. Ahmed had told her Thevshi would understand what the code word *dragonfly* would mean.

Was this the confirmation she'd been looking for? She stepped back, not wanting to show him the change in her demeanor. Noah would notice in an instant. "I didn't realize you were from Gloucester." She turned away, cleaning her tools.

"My aunt and uncle lived near there. I joined with the regiment after the war broke out but was plucked from them when they learned I spoke Arabic." Noah buttoned his shirt. "Thank you for your help."

Ginger smiled tautly as she put away her supplies. "It's my job." She had to know the truth. Clarity felt within her grasp, for the first time in a long time. "Why would Stephen do this to you?"

Noah's look grew colder. "He wanted me dead. A better question to ask is why Stephen would lie to you about it."

"Why don't you tell me?"

"I can't. But think. You're clever."

Why would Stephen want her trust? So she would freely tell him what she knew of Ahmed, of course. She startled. "Does Stephen know what information Ahmed was carrying?"

Noah didn't answer her question.

Ahmed mentioned two people who knew what he carried: Thevshi and the traitor hunting him. And Noah claimed to be Thevshi. Which left ...

Her every sense was alert. "How did you know to come? How did you know Ahmed was in Belah?"

"A colleague in Cairo intercepted a telegram to the CID using the code Ahmed and I had agreed to and contacted me where I was in Rafah."

"What code? Don't throw the question back at me. I have to know."

He searched her eyes. "Dragonfly."

She felt sick. Stephen was the traitor? And yet ... Did it surprise her?

She closed her eyes, thinking of every interaction she'd had with him since he arrived in Belah.

The little girl. The trip to the latrine. They'd run into Stephen.

And the girl had screamed.

Ginger covered her mouth. She recognized him.

Stephen worked for the Maslukha.

Ginger fought the urge to step back from Noah. But that wouldn't give her answers. "Tell me what you know."

He turned her wrist toward his mouth and kissed the soft skin right below the palm. "Thank you for your attentions, Sister Whitman. I should go."

"Don't." Her knees almost buckled, her pulse unsteady.

She wasn't used to a man who knew how to charm his way out of these situations like Noah did. "I'm tired of being underestimated. Don't treat me like another stupid woman who doesn't know exactly what you're doing."

The corners of his mouth tipped in a smile. He encircled her waist with one arm, the palm of his hand against the small of her back, strong and purposeful. His words were a fierce whisper. "I wish you *were* any other woman. Then I could force myself to stay away."

"Tell me what I want to know." Their proximity allowed her to feel his heart hammering against her chest. She struggled for calm, his effect dizzying.

He chuckled. "Not on your life." Before she responded, his mouth dipped to hers and he caught her in a kiss. His mouth, soft but demanding, stole her breath. She yielded to his kiss, her eyes closing as it deepened, and she kissed him.

The kiss shocked her senses. A sense of joy swept through her heart as her arms slid around his neck. He wasn't the traitor. He was the honest man her heart had believed. She pushed herself against the length of him, her entire body at once feeling intensely alive. She wanted him the way she'd wanted him in the desert and by the ocean. This time, she wouldn't deny herself.

He edged her to the bed and laid her down with equal control and passion. His hands caressed her. She yearned for his touch on her bare skin. She was losing control, and he was much more experienced at this than she was. But she wanted more. Raw desire moved them both.

With a shattered, ragged gasp, she made a weak attempt at pulling away from him. Their eyes locked mere inches from each other's.

One more moment and they might both come to their senses. She read it in his eyes. She pulled his head toward hers again, kissing him earnestly. She didn't want him to leave. She didn't want to do the proper thing this time.

She'd fought against her feelings, but she was drawn to him more than to anyone she'd ever known.

Was this what love felt like?

Tears threatened her again, thoughts of her abominable treatment of him in the desert rising like ghosts. She needed more than his forgiveness and his good opinion. She longed for a chance to be away from the war, the deceit, and the loneliness. To be with him. She pulled away from a kiss and murmured, "I want you to stay here with me."

He searched her gaze. "Are you certain?"

She'd never been more certain. "Yes."

"I shouldn't. I want to." He kissed her temple. "But it would be a mistake."

"I seem to make mistakes whether or not I follow the rules. But this is real. You know it as well as I. Please stay." She pushed the dressing gown away and untied the top of her nightgown. The warm air hit her naked breast, and she shivered and pulled him down for a kiss.

"You are a temptress. You're making it impossible to say no." Her heart raced as he unbuttoned his trousers.

She traced a finger along the smooth skin of his chest. "Then tell me you'll stay."

"I'll stay." He stood and pushed the clothes from his waist. She tried not to stare, failing. The well-sculpted muscles of his body were more than attractive. Terrified and eager, she didn't have the slightest idea what to do.

Noah caught her gaze. He climbed onto the bed beside her and kissed her mouth. She trembled in his arms as his hands cupped her breasts, her nipples hardening at his touch. His thumbs and forefingers rolled them in his fingers, his hands caressing her. As his kiss grew more insistent, so did the strength of his touch. His kisses trailed lower, and she gasped.

His hand smoothed over her abdomen and she relaxed the tightness of her thighs, allowing his hand to slide between her legs. "Noah—"

His lips returned to hers. "If you want me to stop, I can stop."

"No—" She tried to catch her breath. "I want you to. I've … never done this before."

"I assumed." A smile warmed his eyes.

Her cheeks grew hotter. Had it been the wrong thing to say? Or was it a fault in technique? "I don't know what I'm doing—"

Noah trailed his fingertips over her, feather-soft. "That's not what I meant. I want you. More than I've ever wanted anything."

She'd never imagined anything could feel like this. A cry of passion and pleasure left her, her body aching for his, her hips arching against him.

Their fingertips interlaced, and her breath grew uneven as he guided his body over hers and pushed himself inside her.

She hadn't known what to expect of love making, but it was astonishing and wonderful, all at once.

His lips returned to hers and she met his eyes. Despite how

little they knew about each other, she sensed something in his gaze. Something that echoed her own feelings. A vulnerability, one that he wouldn't verbalize.

Could it be that, like her, he hadn't allowed himself to surrender to reckless emotions like this before? A jumble of thoughts welled in her mind. She couldn't make any assumptions about *what* he felt or thought about her.

She wrapped her arms around his neck, her body entwined with his, her lips against his shoulder as his lips brushed the curve of her neck.

A feeling built within her, something deep and primeval, a thrill that gradually crested higher until she cried out, forfeit to the dizzying pleasure, a shock of bliss rocking her.

With a moan, he pulled away sharply and lay against her with ragged breath. She felt his heart pounding wildly through his chest.

Her heartbeat slowly returned to normal. When he rolled away from her, her legs and thighs shook uncontrollably. She dragged a sheet over her body, embarrassed to let him see her continued response. He slid his arm under her back, pulling her to rest against his chest.

She nestled against him, wanting to still be lost with him. Nervously, she glanced at his profile. "I hope it wasn't disappointing."

Noah kissed her temple. "You were wonderful. And, no. I'm not disappointed. Quite the opposite. I don't know how I'll ever get you out of my head now."

She laughed lightly. "I enjoyed it too." Good gracious, was this what she had been missing this whole time? She wished she'd attempted to seduce him sooner. As crazy as it seemed, she wanted to do it again.

A gentle look came to Noah's face. "You're stunningly beautiful, by the way."

A warm feeling spread through her. "You don't have to woo me now, Major. I'm more than a willing participant in this affair of ours." She cocked her head at him. "Are you really Irish?"

He smiled. *"Tá mé."*

She raised a brow.

He wrapped his arm around her more tightly. "I am."

"But how is it you sound so English? And how many languages do you speak? In the desert you used both Arabic and Turkish—"

Noah held her hand. "I don't want to talk about anything from the desert now."

She pulled her head back. "But there's so much we need to talk about."

Releasing her, Noah pressed two fingertips against her mouth. "Later. For now, let's not."

Ginger gave him a solemn expression. "You would prefer for me to be quiet?"

He ran his fingertips over her lips before leaning to kiss her. "Not ... quiet."

Her cheeks grew warm. "Oh."

"We both know we shouldn't be here. But since we are, it'd be a shame to waste this time with talking."

Her jaw fell open at his boldness. She smiled. It was scandalous and careless. Maybe even dangerous. But a risk she was more than willing to take.

CHAPTER TWENTY-ONE

*G*inger waited for Noah by the lobby door as he left a note for Stephen with the hotel staff. A smile played at her lips. In the room, everything else had seemed to fade away. All the fear, the uncertainty. They'd made love and slept, speaking of nothing of real importance, and it had been wonderful.

Now, he'd caught the attention of some women in the lobby, but when he lifted his head, he looked only at her.

Guilt stabbed her. She didn't have a right to be this happy. Not after everything she'd done. It had also been barely a day since James had broken things off. While her time with Noah made it so easy to forget James, Noah also offered her nothing. As much as her heart wanted a future with him, there was a simplicity in just enjoying the moment.

Noah ambled toward her and led her out into the warm sunshine. The wind carried the sea's aromatic, salty scent. Ginger fought against a breeze and pulled a scarf over her hair, tidying it.

They stepped onto the street, and Noah led her through the

throng of people toward the hotel's café around the corner. She'd had tea here with James. Did moving on with another man with such speed make her a terrible person?

"The last time we were in Port Said"—Ginger eyed the locals —"we nurses needed escorting. The locals would throw stones or spit on us otherwise."

Noah waved off an old beggar holding out his hands. "They won't attack you here. Too many peddlers."

At the café, a red velvet cord sectioned off wicker tables and chairs from the street. A busy Egyptian waiter bustled around the mostly British customers. Noah and Ginger blended well with the other soldiers and nurses taking their leave or working in the city, though Ginger had donned a modest beige suit. It had been so long since she wore something other than an approved uniform that she felt out of place. The waiter scurried them toward a table, then pulled out a chair for Ginger.

The chaos spilled beyond the velvet cord. Ginger tucked her feet in as two young boys ducked by her legs, polishing her boots with rags. The waiter slapped a towel at their backsides, shooing them. He handed Noah a menu and offered a toothy apologetic smile. The two bootblacks returned, crawling on their knees. They grabbed Noah's boots, demanding *baksheesh* for services rendered.

Noah gave the boys a stern rebuke and they scampered off, hurrying over to the people beside them. Ginger's heart broke, but she forced her gaze away. If they helped one person, harassment from the many others around them would follow.

They ordered tea. Ginger leaned toward Noah. "People from home don't understand how a clearing station can be more appealing than the 'civilization' of Port Said."

Noah spread his serviette on his lap. "Our Bedouin dinner seems like luxury dining, doesn't it?"

Her heart fluttered at the memory. "Indeed."

The waiter put a teapot between them, steam rising from the spout. The waiter flashed them a showy smile as he poured them each a cup. When he left, Noah met her gaze. "I take it Cairo isn't any more tempting?"

She frowned at a man selling postcards. "Cairo is as bad as Port Said."

"I'd hope Port Said would hold some better memories from now on."

She laughed, stirring sugar into her tea. "You're awfully self-assured."

Noah caught her fingers, an intimate gesture that both warmed and gave her shivers. "Call it the effect of a beautiful woman." He kissed her hand and released it. "Should we discuss the matter of this afternoon?"

"My father?" She quirked an eyebrow. "Or what happens after this?"

"Let's start with your father. He can't know about this morning."

The idea was so absurd, she threw her head back and laughed. "Why do you think I would tell my father about this?"

His expression sobered. "More specifically, he can't sense we've ever had anything other than a brief, meaningless acquaintance."

She twisted her lips wryly. "You mean you don't think of me as a brief, meaningless acquaintance?"

He looked away. "How I think of you doesn't matter, does it?"

She flinched. If she wanted any further proof he didn't intend for the morning's events to become something more long-term, there it was. "Of course it matters."

Noah focused on the dark tea in his cup. "Ginger, I—"

"Don't. All I was saying is it matters. Not that it changes our circumstances." Her family's objections would be insurmountable. More importantly, the unspoken issue of Ahmed wouldn't dissipate. He deserved the truth from her. Especially now.

"We should also keep it from Stephen."

"Because he'll tell my father?"

"More than that. Stephen"—Noah's eyes followed the waiter —"is a dangerous man whose obsession with you concerns me. And he despises me."

She tensed. She'd never considered Stephen's behavior toward her abnormal. He'd been persistent, yes, despite knowing her disinterest. It had taken her engagement to James to drive him away. But the circumstances of the war had also intervened.

A fly hovered over her tea, and she knocked it away. "I know you didn't want to discuss it before, but we should discuss Ahmed. And I have questions for you."

Noah gave her a hard look. "I didn't ask about Ahmed because I don't want you to think what happened between us had anything to do with that. I felt bad enough for going through your things. The last thing I want you to think is I was trying to influence you into a confession."

She exhaled and swirled the tea in her cup. While she appreciated his forthrightness, she wished she had told him before. "If you know Stephen is so dangerous, can't you arrest him?"

"I don't have concrete proof of his betrayal in Aleppo. I can't arrest him based on my suspicion."

"Maybe this will help. Before the lorry exploded, I told Stephen about the refugees. I was taking a child to the latrines, and we ran into him." She tapped her thumb against the cup, amazed she could speak about it so calmly despite her fury with herself for having trusted Stephen. "The girl started screaming at the sight of him. Couldn't I testify to that?"

Noah shook his head at another peddler who held out an

arm of necklaces. "Testify that the girl screamed? What would it prove?"

"That he's trying to protect the Maslukha's identity. You and I both know that lorry didn't explode accidentally. Stephen is connected to that villain."

Noah squeezed her hand firmly. "Lower your voice, please." He glanced toward the Egyptian waiter. "You have no idea who is being paid to listen."

She leaned in. "Who could hear us with this pandemonium? I'm right, aren't I?"

"It's more complicated than that." Noah remained stone-faced, but his eyes held warmth. "It's one thing to suspect—quite another to make an accusation that can hold its weight in front of magistrates. Especially against someone with as much money and influence as Stephen. Your own father vouches for him. As difficult as it may be, I have to wait until I can bring irrefutable evidence."

"We should tell my father what we've learned," Ginger said eagerly. "My father may not be fair with me, but he does it out of a deep sense of tradition and duty. He loves the Crown and his work for the government. And he's the perfect person to talk to. He must know about Ahmed and the Zionist Operation he worked for. Does he know what Ahmed planned to deliver to you?"

Noah cut her off with a sharp look. "I can't discuss any of that here."

"But my father will want to help destroy the Maslukha as—"

Noah leaned across the table and cut her off with a quick kiss. "We cannot talk about that here." He settled back. "I know he's your father, but I'd prefer he know as little as possible about the extent of your involvement. Granted, it depends on what you already told Henry. It's too dangerous for you to help further."

Her gaze retreated to the serene blue horizon. "But I feel horrible about those refugees. And Ahmed. If their lives were lost because of my actions, I deserve imprisonment—or worse. I want and need to help. Please."

"Believe it or not, you have helped. But now that I'm turning you over to your father, it's safer for both of us if your involvement ends."

He offered a fragile truce.

"But you were right. Ahmed left more information. He said that, together with the message in the bottle, the two pieces could be used to find the documents he buried about the Masl—"

"Ginger. Please." Noah's gaze flickered away. "I need to tell you something now, before you learn about it from someone else."

Her heart skipped a beat.

He crossed one ankle over the other knee and removed his hat. He ran his hand through his dark hair, then set the cap on his knee. His expression was guarded. "This is hard to explain because I can't give you the answers you want. But I don't want to hurt you, given what's transpired between us."

If he knew what she'd hidden from him … "What is it?" The way he dragged on struck fear in her heart.

"There you are." Stephen sauntered up to them.

How had he found them? Ginger pushed down her disgust. She glanced at Noah's impassive expression that gave nothing away.

Stephen sat in a vacant chair. "They said you'd gone out, gave me your note. You might have at least told me where you were going."

His amicability seemed so false now. Whatever Noah had been on the verge of telling her must be important, and she resented Stephen's awful timing.

Noah replaced his cap, the expression in his eyes shaded. "It seems you didn't have any trouble finding us."

The refugee girl's face flashed in her mind, and she had the urge to attack with the rage coursing through her. How could she ever treat him with civility again? But it would do nothing to give away how much she knew. If Noah could act with decorum after Stephen had left him for dead, she would have to manage. She fixed a fake smile on her face. "Join us."

Stephen regarded her. "You certainly look better. I never liked those nurse's rags on you. I'd say a good night's rest and a morning amidst civilization has you glowing."

She avoided looking at Noah and sipped her tea. "I haven't had a proper meal in months."

"Of course not. But you're the one who went to live amongst the savages." Stephen frowned. "I can't say I'm surprised. I remember that god-awful Zulu mission you and your mother insisted on visiting in Cape Town. Why your father allowed it is beyond me." His eyes fixed on Noah. "Though, hopefully the time will soon come when our families can take holidays together."

She narrowed her gaze. The comment didn't even deserve a response.

The waiter returned with Noah and Ginger's food. In contrast to her anemic sandwich, made to please the British palate, Noah ordered more local fare: *koushari*. His plate steamed with the aromatic mixture of rice, lentils, and chickpeas. A generous serving of flatbread sat in a basket beside him.

She bit into her sandwich. "What time is my father arriving?"

"Soon." Stephen spread jam on his scone. "He should arrive by train from Cairo within the hour."

Her eyes darted toward the boats docked in the harbor. Being a stowaway appealed to her. At least, compared to facing her father. The train ride from Port Said to Cairo was five hours long, but delays frequently beset the trip during the day. Maybe he'd be late.

"After lunch, I can return you to your room. Your father requested Major Benson meet him at the train station," Stephen said.

"Should I go with you?" she asked Noah, hoping for another moment alone with him.

Noah shook his head. "No. I'll need a few minutes to speak to your father alone."

She tried to hide her annoyance. Their time together in the room had raced by. What had Noah been on the verge of telling her?

Stephen mistook her anxiety and patted her hand. "All will be well. Your father will see to it."

Her skin crawled at his touch.

"It won't be." Ginger turned her face away. "Nursing meant everything to me. And you took it away rather than giving me the chance to explain myself."

Stephen clamped his jaw shut.

Silence ensued until Noah stood. "I need to get ready to collect Lord Braddock." He left money beside his plate and walked away without a good-bye.

She stared at Noah's fading figure. He'd left her with Stephen, despite everything. She knew nothing of Noah's plans now that this was over except she wasn't to be part of them.

Noah's stoicism was useful for his line of work, no doubt. But, in a lover, she was certain it would lead to absolute heartbreak. He could walk away from her, too, without glancing back.

CHAPTER TWENTY-TWO

Ginger paced in her hotel room. The reds and yellows of the sky tinted the deep shadows in the room. She strode to the window, pulling the curtain closed to prevent anyone from being able to see in from the street.

Something must have happened. Her father's arrival must have been delayed. But why hadn't Noah returned? Stephen might know, but she'd told him plainly enough when he dropped her off in her room after lunch she didn't want his company.

She couldn't stay in her room waiting. Maybe Noah had sent a message to the front desk. She gathered the note she'd written to Beatrice during the afternoon and slipped it in her handbag. The faster she sent the wire, the sooner Beatrice could ask James for Ahmed's bag and have it sent to Cairo.

A knock sounded at the door. Her heart lurched.

Her father?

She hurried over and opened it.

Noah stood in the hallway.

The sight of him calmed her. She slipped her hand into his. "Thank goodness. I was worried."

"Your father sent a wire—he's delayed. Train breakdown in Ismailia. He's staying there overnight and arriving in the morning." Noah scanned her face. "I waited at the station for hours until Stephen came with the message. He didn't tell you?"

"I told him not to disturb me." Ginger peeked at his watch. "You've been at the train station the whole time?"

He shook his head, his eyes dark. "No. I walked through the city. Trying to clear my head."

Whatever troubled him must be serious. A ripple of nervous energy moved through her as she tugged at the lapel of his jacket. "Care to come inside?"

He hesitated, then nodded.

She took his hand and led him in. She locked the door and his fingertips tightened on hers.

They came together in an instant and kissed without restraint, his arms wrapping around her. "I thought of you all day," he said.

"I thought of you too." She pushed him toward the bed. "I'm glad to know I've left a good impression." Unbuttoning his shirt, she offered a teasing smile.

"More than that. Branded my soul." They lost themselves in another passionate kiss and lowered themselves onto the bed. He rolled her onto her back, and propped his head up with his hand.

Despite the intimacy of their kisses, she frowned. He'd wanted to tell her something at lunch. And he appeared troubled. "What is it?"

He kissed her again. Lifting his head, he searched her eyes. "Come away with me. Tonight."

It wasn't what she had expected he'd say. She blinked at him. "But my father—"

"Don't go to Cairo. It's too dangerous. I can't offer you much, but I'll protect you with every resource I have available."

She stared at the ceiling. For a moment, she envisioned running away with him, and joy wound its way around her heart. But she had to be rational. Swallowing, she met his gaze. "Why is it too dangerous?"

"I can't explain it all. I'm not at liberty to. But I'm worried. And I don't want Stephen anywhere near you."

She bit her lip. Why couldn't he tell her more? "But where would we go?"

"I have a friend who runs a network of safehouses. I could take you there for now, until things are safer and I can join you."

"Then we wouldn't be together?"

"Not now but—"

The idea instantly lost most of its appeal. "I would want to be with you. Noah, if I run away from my father with a man, he will never accept me. The scandal will be a blight on my family. There won't be a place for me in society."

He cupped her face with his hands. "I don't care about society, Ginger. I care about you. I want to protect you."

His kiss was urgent and fervent. She wrapped her arms around his neck, her body responding to his touch as his hand slid up her thigh, warm and possessive. She wanted more than anything to go with him, recklessly and without delay, as she'd done this morning when they'd made love.

A key scraped the lock on the door, and they froze.

Horrified, she watched the opening door.

The situation would have been bad enough if it was just her father at the door. But beside him also stood the Egyptian manager from the front desk, with the key in his hand. Behind them in the hallway, Stephen's smug, hard blue eyes met hers.

Ginger sprang away from Noah, her face burning as her father hurried in and sharply slammed the door on the other men in the hall. He clenched his hat in his fist as Noah stood, buttoning his shirt.

Her father's short silver-streaked hair had once been a dark-chocolate brown, like his eyes. A man of medium build, he carried himself with an air of distinguished pride. A short, trim moustache resided above his upper lip, which held a scowl. His gaze was furious.

He said nothing.

Her father wouldn't have brought Stephen and the manager with him had he known. He wouldn't have risked scandal like this. But Stephen? He must have manipulated the timeline. His triumphant, cruel smile seemed to confirm it.

Humiliation oozed from every pore in her body. How could she ever look her father in the eye after this? Though she desperately wanted to, she couldn't look to Noah for comfort.

She stood, barefooted, on the rug. "Father, I—"

He held up one hand to silence her. "And this is the greeting I am to receive? You knew I was arriving tonight, and you still did this?"

Arriving tonight? Fury burned like acid in her esophagus. *Stephen.* "I-I didn't—"

Her father's eyes swung toward Noah. "You filthy scoundrel. How dare you?"

Noah gathered himself. "Lord Braddock."

Her father pointed at him. "I'll have you suspended."

Noah lifted his chin, his jaw squarely set. "I expect you planned on doing that, regardless."

"Nothing happened." Ginger moved toward her father. "Father, if you'll let me—"

"Don't lie to me!" Her father struck her across the cheek. The room spun. She clutched her cheek as her father grabbed her by the hair, his voice a menacing whisper. "You've caused immeasurable damage to our family. If you persist in behaving like a common whore, I'll—"

Behind her immediately, Noah's fist flew at her father's face, knocking him backward. Her father's hat tumbled. Noah grabbed her father's shirtfront and slammed him into a wall. "Strike her again, and I'll do far more."

Lord Braddock's face purpled.

Ginger scrambled up behind Noah. Her father would destroy Noah for this. She put her hand on his back. "Noah, please ..." Her cheek throbbed. "Let him go."

Noah threw him to the floor and glowered.

Her father held his jaw and pulled out a handkerchief. Bloody spittle leaked from the corner of his mouth as he wiped it and drew himself off the floor, dusting his jacket. "Out of my way. She's *my* daughter."

Noah used his body as a shield in front of Ginger. "You won't touch her again."

Her father's eyes remained fixed on Noah. "As though you could ever deserve her. You think she won't come when I call? What other choice does she have? She has no money of her own, and no one will ever want her after this fiasco with you. She's been jilted—and you have a fiancée of your own. Your advantageous engagement to Lord Helton's daughter is the only thing stopping me from demanding your head on a platter."

Her eyes widened, and she stepped back from Noah. The air in the room seemed thinner.

Engaged?

"You're to blame for everything." Her father moved within inches of Noah. "And I'll see you punished accordingly. My orders to eliminate Ahmed Bayrak were clear."

Ginger clutched her hands to her stomach. Her father wanted Noah to kill Ahmed? It didn't make sense. It went against everything Ahmed had told her.

Her father's eyes burrowed into hers. "Get dressed. I'll need to convince the hotel manager to keep his mouth shut. I expect you outside at the motorcar in ten minutes. This nonsense is over."

Her father stalked toward the door, his figure wavy through her tears.

The door closed. Noah reached out for her, and she shrank back. "Don't! Don't touch me." She whirled around, looking for an exit, but she didn't want to follow her father. She went to the fireplace and grabbed the poker, tempted to throw it at him like a javelin.

Her grip tightened until the metal hurt her hand.

Noah came to her side. Cautiously, he put a steady hand on hers. She squeezed her eyes shut.

She'd never imagined a fiancée. She'd been naïve, thinking his mild attempts to stop their romance had to do with propriety or morality or something noble. It was his guilty conscience, and he'd ignored it, anyway.

The poker fell to the floor with a clatter, and she tore her hand away.

She sat, numb, on the bed. Her lungs burned as she gulped down air, unsure of which accusation to confront first. She met his eyes.

"You're engaged?"

A muscle near his jaw tightened. "I should have told you. I tried to tell you. At the café."

"You could have told me before that." She'd imagined he wasn't the type of man who would marry during the war. That he didn't have time for romance. Instead, he'd played her for a fool. He offered nothing because he'd already offered it to someone else.

Noah sank beside her. He touched her burning cheek. "I didn't tell you about the engagement before because—"

"Because you wouldn't have been able to get me into bed if you had." She wiped the tears from the corners of her eyes. "What was your plan? Make love to me and return to your fiancée?"

"No—" His jaw clenched. "There was no plan. I didn't expect any of it. I was swept away by ... you. By everything you are. But I should have stopped it."

That made it worse. She could bear it more if it hadn't been real.

Before her anxious thought spilled into more tears, she drew a sharp breath. "Could I get pregnant?"

He cradled her shoulder with the palm of his hand. "I tried to be careful. I withdrew."

"But there's still a risk, isn't there? I should know, I'm a nurse, for goodness' sake."

He met her gaze and nodded.

"But if there's a child—"

"It's not likely. But if there's a child, I won't leave you to deal with the consequences on your own. I promise."

Even then he didn't promise to marry her. A sob broke from her chest. "I'm such a fool."

"It's complicated, Ginger. But I care about you."

"You care about me, but you'll marry someone else."

A pained look crossed his eyes. "It's not as simple as that. I never planned on falling in love with you."

How could he say that to her now? If he'd said it even a few minutes earlier, she would have melted like butter in his hands. It couldn't be true. He'd planned to walk away from her.

"Just stop. Please don't say things like that to me." She scanned his face. "Unless you're not planning on getting married anymore." She shouldn't say it. It made little difference, and his answer could hurt her more. But she couldn't help herself.

Noah sighed. "I can't break off the engagement. But there are many things I can't tell you. Not because I don't want to, but because I'm not able to."

His words hit her like a punch to the gut.

"Or because you were planning on parting ways with me today, without a backward glance." She moved away from him. "You don't love me. You're nothing but a liar. You begged me to run away with you just minutes ago. And now—you won't break off your engagement? Why? Why even pretend you wanted something more to come of this? Just another opportunity to satisfy your lust?"

"No, I meant it when I asked you to go away with me. Please, let me explain what I can."

"There's nothing you can say that will help." Her tears fell on the bedspread as she struggled for composure. Her eyes burned. Her lips were sticky and chapped. Yet she faced a lengthy train ride with her father. Unsteadily, she rose to her feet. "What about Ahmed? Was it all a lie? What were you going to do with the documents Ahmed carried?"

Thank God she hadn't had the chance to tell him about Ahmed's bag or its location.

Noah stood in front of her. "I want nothing more than to tell you everything. But I can't discuss my work." He put his hands on the backs of her arms and pulled her closer. "Ginger—I never should have ..." He sighed. "My job depends on my discretion, and I've compromised it by allowing myself to care for you."

She yanked herself free of his grip. "Tell me yes or no. Are you nothing more than my father's lackey? He said he ordered you to kill Ahmed. Were you going to follow his orders?"

The conflict on Noah's face was clear.

"Yes or no?" Her voice grew stronger.

"Ginger, the less you know, the safer you are. I got carried away, but I won't endanger you further."

Carried away. Each time he used that phrase it made her want to slap him. As though he'd had no control, no choice. "Answer the question. You owe me that much. I need to know what sort of man you truly are."

Noah brushed her tears away. "There's nothing to answer. I'm bound to my orders."

She shook her head. "I don't believe you. I know you wanted Ahmed to live. I know it with every fiber of my being. You're lying to me now, and I don't understand it. Your evasiveness is proof. I saw you with the refugees and the men in the desert. I know what I saw."

Noah looked away. "You saw what I wanted you to see."

She put her hands on the sides of his face. "Look at me in the eyes. I won't believe it until I hear it from your lips. Would you have killed Ahmed? Tell me the truth."

Noah's hands dropped to his sides, his eyes flat. "Believe the worst about me. That's the truth."

"You're lying." She backed away from him. It was Henry who had tried to kill Ahmed. Henry who refused to trust Noah once Ahmed died. It wasn't possible Noah wanted Ahmed dead if Henry had run away like he had. "Ahmed told me. He told me the Maslukha's plans were far worse than an uprising. He told of plans to murder someone important to the British. You would never let that happen."

Noah's eyes flickered with surprise. "You should forget all Ahmed told you."

The comment stung. "You want to push me away, don't you? Because you don't love me. You haven't chosen me. You think it will make it easier if I pretend you're the villain." She pointed toward the doorway. "I know who the villain is. It's the same man who planned for us to be found in this compromising situation. Stephen stood there, like a rat, smiling at my destruction. I don't know what game he's playing, but you're letting him win by pushing me away like this."

A resigned expression crossed his features, and he pulled her into his arms. "Forgive me," he whispered. "I'll never forgive myself for hurting you."

She pressed her cheek against his shirt collar.

She had to discover the truth. She stepped away. "My father is waiting. He's not a patient man. I have no choice but to go with him."

He put his hands on her shoulders. "You always have a choice." He searched her eyes. "I'll do anything to keep you safe."

"You can't have two women. Please leave."

Everything seemed a dizzy blur as she straightened her appearance and collected her things. When she walked out, Noah was waiting by the lift.

Noah walked her to the motorcar outside. He kept his distance, staring straight ahead as he opened the door for her. She glanced up at the hotel and the wrought-iron balconies facing the sea. In a room up there, she'd given Noah her heart. Yet he'd handed it back to her, battered and bleeding. She climbed into the seat beside her father. Stephen, who sat in the front seat, made no attempt to hide the enmity in his eyes.

Noah closed the door. He disappeared into the hotel, and Ginger's heart constricted.

She couldn't stop the tears. She held her bruised cheek, using it as an excuse for her sniffles. The car pulled away from the curb.

Whom could she trust now? Every man in her life had lied to her and betrayed her. Her father was right—she had no means of survival on her own, not if she played by the rules.

She scowled. To hell with the rules.

PART II

CAIRO, EGYPT

CHAPTER TWENTY-THREE

Of all the sounds Ginger had grown up with, the tinkling of a bell now felt the most foreign, the most disruptive. A bell had woken her, an instant reminder of where she was and the role she was to take: lady, heiress, mute. She dug her toes into the soft Oriental rug in her bedroom as she stood from the bed. No scorpions here. Or, at least, unlikely.

She rubbed her arms, blinking in the darkened bedroom. It was before dawn, around the time she was accustomed to waking in the desert, which meant it was probably one of her parents who had rung the bell for a servant. Only her father rose this early. Outside, the call of the *muezzin* echoed through the streets, beckoning the faithful to prayer.

She grabbed onto the bedpost as she moved forward, her legs sore. A lump rose in her throat. Her body still felt the effects of lovemaking the day before. Noah's image hovered in her mind. The memory was too fresh. His hands caressing her, their bodies intertwined. She placed a hand over her heart. "Noah ..." Her chest tightened.

Could she have been so wrong about him?

Stupid fool. He was a liar, dishonorable.

And she was in love with him.

She rubbed her eyes, the pain bearable once she kept moving. A strange secret, an odd mark of womanhood.

She smoothed her nightgown, running a hand over her bruised hip. Why go to all the trouble with her? Once Noah learned of her connection with Ahmed, he could have been forceful and demanding. If all he wanted were the documents to destroy them, if he cared nothing about her, he wouldn't have gone to the lengths he had to win her trust or make her feel desired.

Then again, she'd practically thrown herself at him. Even when he'd tried to walk away in the hotel room, she asked him to stay, disrobed herself. She cringed, embarrassed.

She hated his fiancée. Had he returned to her by now? Was he in her arms?

Liar. *Liar.* She dug her nails into her palms.

All the whispers between them, the sensual caresses. "It was an act," she murmured, and the pain in her chest nearly overtook her. She rushed toward the window, hoping the morning light would help clear him from her mind. She wouldn't ring for a servant. No matter what higher standard her family expected, she didn't need a servant fussing around or dressing her.

As she opened the curtains, soft sunbeams streamed in, swirls of dust dancing in the light. She pushed open the door to the balcony, facing the lush garden of the Whitmans' Cairo home. Her mother's roses had bloomed, their fragrance intermingling with the dust and sunbaked clay of the ancient city.

Much as she hadn't wanted to return, something about Cairo still thrilled her—a pulse of civilization that beat slowly, uninterrupted by the comings and goings of thousands of years. The European quarter offered unique sights and sounds compared to that inhabited by the Egyptian citizens: well-manicured homes with careful landscaping, cleaner streets, less foot traffic. Horses' hooves clopped as they pulled carriages as opposed to wagons loaded with goods. At this hour, the sweet scent of baking bread drifted from the kitchens. The servants had been awake for a while.

She chose a white silk blouse and a high-waisted blue skirt from her wardrobe, then dressed and sat at her vanity.

The green eyes staring back at her were haunted. She'd gone off to war hoping a new life waited around the corner. And it had. Yet she could never return to who she'd been.

She must be resolute.

Whatever her father's alliance with Stephen was, he needed to know what sort of man he had in his employ. All of it grew in complexity with Henry's undefined role. She would give him a piece of her mind. She gripped the silver handle of the hairbrush and tied her hair swiftly with a ribbon, then sat bolt upright.

Why should Henry be sleeping peacefully when he'd abandoned her so recklessly in the desert?

She slipped on a pair of shoes and left the room, doing her best to keep her simmering anger from bubbling over and turning into loud movements.

She hurried down the hallway and stopped in front of Henry's room. The cool metal of the doorknob helped ground her, and she turned it and tiptoed into the darkness beyond.

A soft snore cut through the silence. Her anger grew as she narrowed her eyes at the bed. How dare he?

She strode to the washbasin and lifted the pitcher of water from beside it. She'd almost been drowned. *Coward.*

She stopped at the foot of the enormous canopy bed. The future Earl of Braddock. How fortunate for him that his father could arrange for him to sleep comfortably in his four-poster bed while other, better men died on the battlefield. The war had hit the aristocracy with particular ferocity, with the odds of dying in battle being so much higher for the genteel officers. Yet her brother had never set foot in the field. He'd been shielded from it all.

Holding the pitcher with both hands, she tossed water on him. He gasped, scrambling from his covers. His foot caught in the sheets, and he sprawled face-first on the wood floor with a thud.

Ginger set her hands on her hips, fixing a glare on him. Henry looked around wildly in confusion before his eyes settled on hers. He grunted and peeled his cheek off the floor. "Is this supposed to be a joke?"

"A joke?" Ginger took slow, deliberate steps toward him. "I don't know." She squatted beside him. "Do you think it's funny? Maybe I should have held your head under a water basin." She grabbed him by his hair above the nape of his neck and leaned down toward his ear. "That's what the Turks did to me, Brother. They caught me as I chased after you. Shot and killed my horse out from under me. Interrogated me. Would have killed me if Major Benson hadn't followed and rescued me."

Her fingers gradually tightened on his hair, and he winced. "Ginny, I'm sorry. I'm so sorry," he managed. "Please let go of my hair."

She released him and sank onto the cold floor. "You left me, Henry." She struggled to keep her voice from shaking. "I sent for you because I was desperate and frightened. And when everything got so much worse, you ran away without explanation."

"It's unforgivable, I know. I know." Henry wiped his face with the sheet.

"Why did you do it?" She couldn't imagine any satisfying explanation.

"I—" Henry sat up and rubbed his eyelids. "I never imagined you'd chase after me." He squinted at her. "Noah rescued you?"

"Yes."

"Did the Turks ..." Henry searched her face. "Did they touch you?"

Her stomach tightened. *That's* what he cared about? She was tempted to break the pitcher over his head. "No, they didn't defile me. I'm perfectly ..." Well, not undefiled. "It doesn't matter. That's insignificant. I want to know why. Now. You owe me."

Henry held her hand. "I owe you that much. And more." His gaze fixed on the floor. "But I can't tell you. I'm sorry. Father forbade it. Has he debriefed you?"

She pulled her hand away. "No. There wasn't time." She couldn't mention to him the circumstances under which their father had found her the night before. "And Stephen came back on the train with us last night, so we weren't at liberty to speak freely." She stood. "But I don't accept your apology. I deserve to know *exactly* why my father and brother appear to be cooperating with a traitor that supports the Maslukha. Because that's who Stephen is."

"For God's sake, Ginny." Henry sat bolt upright, gripping her forearm. "You must forget everything that Zionist told you. He was the enemy. I don't know how you had the misfortune of happening upon him, but you must be silent. You don't understand what could happen if you don't."

"Help me understand," she said through gritted teeth. "Don't you think I've earned the privilege of knowing why my life has been destroyed?"

"Your life? If you persist on the path you've started, you're going to destroy much more than that. Did you even once stop to think about what Angelica's parents might think if they hear stories about you? You're threatening my engagement. To the woman I love. I could lose everything."

Before she could answer, a floorboard creaked in the hall

and the door opened. Their father traipsed in, still in his dressing robe. "You two will wake the whole household. What was that crash?"

"I fell out of bed." Henry glanced at the soaked sheets.

"Really, Henry, if you don't get ahold of that liquor intake, your mother will join a temperance society." Her father looked at Ginger. "And what's your excuse for being here?"

"Oh, now you're interested in my answers? It didn't seem so important to you twelve hours ago." She crossed her arms. "Let the whole household wake. Maybe you'll both be forced to answer me."

"Yes, but you wouldn't want everyone to know every detail, would you? Drawing your mother and sister into this madness is unnecessary." Her father jutted his chin toward Henry. "Get dressed and meet us in my office downstairs. Virginia, come with me."

Much as she didn't want to talk to her father yet, perhaps she should get this over with. She'd hoped Henry would offer her the truth, but he seemed under her father's thumb more than ever. She filed past her father into the hallway.

She passed the tall dark-framed doorways lining the upstairs hall until she reached the main staircase gracing the center of the house. The house was opulent and outfitted with the most gorgeous exotic woods and marble Egyptian craftsmen could offer. She slid her hand down the smoothly curved banister. Her eyes fell on an empty space on the wall that had once featured an ancient stone slab inscribed with hieroglyphics—a palette, as her father had called it proudly, when he'd paid thousands of pounds for it.

"Where did the palette go?" she asked.

"I sold it. Made the house feel like a funeral parlor with so much death in the papers." Her father caught up to her and went down the opposite side of the staircase. "You look well for having slept so little."

"Don't you think we're beyond pleasantries? All things considered, I highly suspect neither of us is too fond of the other at the moment."

"You're still my daughter," he said gruffly. He held the door open to his office.

She guffawed. "Which is why you ignored my tears yesterday on the train? You had more to say to that traitor Stephen Fisher than to me."

Her father strode toward the mahogany desk positioned in front of a wall of leather books. He gestured to a wing-backed chair in front of it. "Have a seat."

She did as he asked, tucking her feet to the side.

Her father sat behind the desk. "I'll have you know, whatever you might think of him, Stephen has always cared for you. By the time I found my way down to the hotel lobby after that fiasco last night, he'd already paid the manager handsomely for his silence. He protects you fiercely, my dear."

Her jaw dropped. What was Stephen playing at? "Protects me?" She gave him an incredulous look. "You understand in order to arrange my disgraceful discharge from the nursing service, he told the brass I had run away for an adulterous affair with Major Benson. Or didn't he tell you?"

Her father's eyes narrowed. "Was he wrong?"

She gathered a fistful of her skirt in her hand. "Yes, yes, he was wrong. I didn't run away to have an affair with Noah! I followed Henry on horseback after he abandoned me in a hut with a dead spy—a man I had killed in defending Henry."

Her father remained stone-faced, unresponsive. It meant one thing: Henry had already told him this. Her face grew hotter, and she leaned forward. "If it hadn't been for Major Benson, I wouldn't be here, Father. That's the truth. You want to suspend him? You want to be angry at him for whatever deceit he may have committed, fine. But Noah's the reason I'm alive. He protected me. Stephen is an agent of the Maslukha, a traitor who tried to have Noah killed."

Silence followed. Her father's lip twitched under his moustache, and he leaned into his chair. "Who told you that? Benson?"

Telling him about Noah's wounds wouldn't help her case. She averted her gaze. "I figured most of it out myself. Stephen has been less careful than he believes." Her throat tightened, thinking of the Bedouin girl. "It is enraging that you already seem to know this. And yet … you haven't turned Stephen over to the authorities."

Her father filled a pipe with tobacco, then held a match to it, puffing his cheeks as it lit. As he clamped it between his teeth, he scanned her face. "Of course I know. That's not what's important. Whom have you told? Benson?"

His response confused her. Why didn't it seem to matter to him? "Does Noah know?" she asked. "About Stephen's connection to the Maslukha?"

"Yes." The sweet familiar smell of his pipe tobacco filled the air. "I need to know everything you discussed with Benson. About Stephen. And Ahmed Bayrak."

"Noah didn't tell me anything, Father." A hinge on the office door squeaked as Henry came in, then closed the door behind him. "In fact, he told me so little that I believed for a long time he was the traitor. Ask Henry. It was Henry who first vouched for Benson. Stephen accused him of betrayal and deceit."

"Of which he's guilty," her father said sharply. "It's the extent of that guilt that I'm trying to establish."

Henry sat in the chair beside her, his dark hair slicked to the side. He barely met her gaze. "I wasn't aware of Noah's treachery until I spoke to that Jewish spy."

She shook her head in disbelief. "No. None of this makes sense. If Ahmed made you aware of Noah's treachery, why on earth would you leave me with him? Ahmed told me the Maslukha is planning to destroy the British cause in Palestine. The documents he carried were meant to help unmask the Maslukha and expose those plans. If Noah was the British intelligence agent he wanted to contact—"

"It's not true," Henry said in a low voice.

"I know what Ahmed said. And if the Maslukha can win the Arab support and lead them against the British, the British will be forced to commit more troops to this area at the same time the Russians are pulling out of the war. The Turkish troops will be free to come at us with full force here while the Germans concentrate their forces on the Western Front in France. We will lose this war if we don't stop him!"

Henry stared at her, a hint of astonishment in his eyes.

"Ahmed Bayrak lied to you, Virginia," her father snapped. "The Zionists have seen the tide turning toward the British. Now they want to disrupt the deals we've already made with our Arab allies in hopes we'll support their cause for a homeland after we've won the war." He drew on his pipe and stood. "You're a gullible woman. You were taken in by a pair of accomplished deceivers working together to destroy a carefully made CID operation."

"CID operation?" She blinked at her father. "What does that mean? That the CID is aware of the Maslukha's identity? That Stephen is working undercover? He works for the Maslukha!"

"If she says much more, you may have to convince the CID to let her join the intelligence community, Father." Henry smiled sarcastically.

He implied her theories about Stephen were true. A sick feeling gripped her.

"Virginia." Her father came around to the other side of the

desk. "I don't know if Ahmed and Benson targeted you deliberately or if you were in the wrong place at the wrong time. But, either way, you are the victim here. We're watching Benson closely, trying to determine his next move. He's cunning, and the evidence of his deceit is thin. But whatever it is you think you know, you must not contact him. He's dangerous and won't hesitate to hurt you if it helps him."

Her desperation grew. "Then why did he rescue me? Why would he save my life from the Turks? What you're saying makes no sense."

"You shouldn't be involved." Her father pounded his fist on the desk. "And you cannot be. If Benson approaches you again, you must tell me. And you can trust I'll be keeping a close watch on you."

"Noah won't rest until he's accomplished his goal, Father." Henry's face looked gaunt, weary. He stared stonily at his hands and then grimaced with a chuckle. "We could always get rid of him."

Ginger stiffened. Henry wanted to kill Noah? She stifled her reaction, her pulse throbbing.

Her father drew himself straighter. "Don't joke like that in front of your sister." Her father frowned at her. "And what of the items you said Ahmed Bayrak gave you for safekeeping? Do you have them?"

Ginger barely heard him, her thoughts racing. Henry wanted Noah murdered. Was she being an alarmist?

"Virginia?"

She lifted her chin abruptly. "What?"

"The documents Ahmed gave you." Her father sat on the edge of the desk, in front of her.

Neither her father nor Henry had given her satisfactory answers. And none of their veiled implications justified what Henry had done to her. She needed to remember the dead men in the desert. The Bedouin refugees. Men on the side of good did not cooperate with such atrocities. The devil take her if Stephen was anything other than a traitor. Stephen might have her father fooled. Or, more chillingly, her father may be choosing to look away for some other, more frightening reason.

"I don't have any documents. I wasn't able to recover anything before I went on a wild goose chase through the desert." She stood and set her hands on the arm of the chair. "And I have no desire to see or talk to Noah again. Thanks to Stephen, Noah's name has ruined my chances to ever work in the profession I love. Now, if you'll excuse me, I think I'll have breakfast."

She turned away before they could see her chin quivering. Even if her father and Henry kept her in the dark, she was sure of one thing: Noah could be in danger. He may have lied to her, but he'd also saved her life. She would be damned if she didn't return the favor.

CHAPTER TWENTY-FOUR

*G*inger made it a few feet out of her father's office before she stopped and supported her weight against a table near the wall of the vestibule. She gripped the smooth marble top.

In a few days, her emotions had crested and dipped in every imaginable way. The main door to the house was twenty feet away. What would happen if she walked through it, without looking back? Would her father or Henry come after her?

Where would she go?

She couldn't expect to survive with nothing but the clothes on her back.

Still, the door beckoned her. She imagined running through it, onto the street. She'd lose herself in Old Cairo, wander the citadel, watch the sunset over the Nile. And she'd wait for Noah to join her. He'd hear through social channels that Lady Virginia Whitman had gone missing, and he'd search for her.

She might have done it, if she believed Noah would find her, as he'd done in the desert.

She laughed scornfully. Her eyes fixed on the newspaper on

the table. The butler had left it for her father. The temptation to throw it into a fireplace crossed her mind. Disrupt even the slightest routine in her father's perfectly ordered life. Make him realize she wasn't worth the trouble. Maybe he'd let her go free.

She straightened.

No, Noah wouldn't come for her. Here she was, wanting to save his life, and she didn't even know how to find him. Was he still in Port Said? She didn't know. He worked for her father, but unlike Henry, who occupied a desk in a cramped suite at the Savoy Hotel in Cairo, Noah worked in the field. His assignments were covert, based on specific intelligence-gathering needs, and he answered only to his superiors. He could be anywhere.

If her father hadn't suspended him.

There had to be some way to warn him.

She needed to be rational and calm. Henry had just been joking. She'd seen the way he acted around Noah. They were friends.

But what if he meant it?

Her fingertips wrinkled the top page of the paper, the ink smudging her hands. She stared at it, unblinking, solutions escaping her. A headline caught her eye. 'Nighttime Air Raids in Gaza Prove Successful for RAF.'

She scanned the article. Nothing about the dispensary's destruction. Nothing about the threats of the German airplanes on the clearing station, or the raids at Rafah.

The article claimed the Royal Air Force had taken out targets in Gaza, which hadn't happened.

Ginger stepped back, the distinct newspaper smell clinging to her fingertips. Tension rose in her shoulders. It was a pile of lies.

But why? Why would the local paper downplay British losses and setbacks and instead claim progress?

"Ginger, darling." Her mother's voice broke her train of thought. Ginger followed its direction to the staircase. The sight of her was achingly familiar, an unexpected relief. An older version of Ginger, Lady Elizabeth Whitman looked tall and graceful as she reached the bottom step, a joyful smile on her face. Abandoning her place by the table, Ginger rushed toward her.

Her mother pulled her into a fierce hug. "I can't think of a more wonderful sight to wake up to. When did you arrive? I waited for hours last night."

"I'm not sure of the exact time—I lost my watch in Belah." Ginger held her mother's hands. She couldn't mention the Turkish soldier who had ripped the watch from her wrist. She flinched. "It's good to see you, Mother."

Her mother linked arms with her. "I can't tell you how relieved we are to have you home. Lucy is thrilled. She thinks your presence means I'll let her go to more social gatherings without me."

Ginger laughed with surprise. She and Lucy had never been close, given their six-year age gap. "If she thinks I'll be going to parties with her, I may disappoint."

Her mother winked. "Don't tell her yet."

"I heard that," Lucy said from the top of the stairs. Lucy glided down the wide wooden staircase. During their time apart, Lucy had grown in poise and beauty. What nature hadn't done, Lucy cultivated with careful attention. Her stylish dress swished above her ankles, her dark-brown hair was fashionably pinned. "Goodness, everyone is up so early this morning. It's a lucky thing I heard you." She wagged a finger at Ginger. "Don't let Mother fool you—they aren't parties. They're charity events for the troops. Mostly."

Ginger lifted a brow. "No doubt with plenty of opportunities to flirt with officers."

Lucy grinned. "Of course." She scanned Ginger's face and figure with a critical eye. "Look at you. You're so brown."

Ginger laughed and planted a kiss on her cheek. "I don't know how you're not. This sun will tan anyone. Have you grown taller since I last saw you?"

"Yes, but I can't seem to get rid of this baby fat." Lucy pouted. "Was it dreadful out there? I've heard absolute horror stories. The girls and I get together at Ezbekieh Gardens every day for tea. They tell me the news they've heard about the front. How did the latest campaign go?"

The door to her father's office opened and her father ambled out, as though he'd been listening by the door.

Odd that Lucy seemed so blithely unaware. "The casualties were high after the battles in Gaza. Terrible losses."

Her mother frowned. "The newspapers say it's going well out there."

"It's not. We've made no progress on the campaign since March. The men are sitting in trenches." How did neither of them seem to know the extent to which the Palestine campaign had proven unsuccessful as of late? She gave her father a quizzical look. "Why is it, exactly, the *Egyptian Gazette* isn't covering this?"

Her father shrugged dismissively. "You must know how it is, Virginia. The troops at the front exaggerate their casualties after battle. Men in the thick of it are the worst source of information. A hundred casualties quickly becomes the story of an entire regiment lost. I'm sure it's similar amongst the nurses. Unfortunately, I wish I had more time to chat, but I'm needed early at the office this morning. And here I am, still in my robe." He nodded at his wife and went up the stairs.

Ginger watched him, frustration building. This was how it always was. He'd downplay her expertise in any matter, make her seem like she was overstating things, negating her opinion.

The battles in Gaza *had* been losses, and while the men may have exaggerated casualties, the medical staff was well aware of the numbers passing through their stations. Surely, as a senior officer in the CID, he knew the truth. It was an odd thing to make light of.

The three Whitman women headed toward the breakfast room. Her mother glanced at Ginger as they entered. "Now what about that fiancé of yours? Is he going to be coming to visit us soon too? I've made more progress on the details for your wedding. Not a simple task, with having to wait on my mother to answer my letters."

The wedding that she had dreaded. It would have been a relief to be released from it if any of it had been on her terms. But she'd been humiliated. Being with Noah had softened the blow, but her pain had changed now. Thoughts of James brought anger and guilt. Thoughts of Noah made her heart ache.

She set her hands on the back of a chair, avoiding her mother's gaze. "James—ah, no, he won't be coming." She sat. How would she explain this to her mother? One of the few things her father had said to her the night before was that she wasn't to mention the events of Belah to anyone.

Her mother bit her lip. "Lucy, would you be an angel and fetch that stack of letters from your grandmother for Ginger from my room?"

Lucy seemed to understand something was amiss. She fidgeted, glancing between her mother and Ginger. "Right now?"

Her mother nodded. "That would be lovely, thank you."

Lucy hesitated before turning and leaving.

Sunlight bathed the room in a glow, the lace curtains throwing patterns onto the newly brushed Oriental rugs and polish of the wooden floors. Large vases filled with roses from the gardens adorned the table. Ginger smiled tightly, a tense knot in her stomach. "Such lovely comforts everywhere."

Her mother sat. "The details of life make all the difference in the world." She settled her elbow against an armrest. "But I've always been one to notice details." She frowned. "Are you going to tell me what's troubling you?"

What would her mother believe? "I called it off with James. We'd grown apart. But as a result, I decided not to reenlist after my leave."

Her mother tilted her head to the side. "But you love nursing."

A servant entered with a tray and set plates and food on the table in front of them.

"I do. But I'm tired, Mother. And it was time for me to set my sights on new goals."

A few cubes of sugar clinked against a porcelain teacup as her mother dropped them in. She poured them each a cup and reclined, the handle of her cup between her fingers. "Why don't you tell me what happened with Doctor Clark?"

Her mother hadn't lost her intuitiveness. Ginger didn't enjoy lying to her, but she couldn't put her in jeopardy. Ginger shrugged, casually. "I suppose I realized to be a doctor's wife I needed a certain domestic quality I lacked." She even kept a straight face.

"Living in the wilderness for a few months will give you an appreciable amount of perspective. I worried when you transferred to that clearing station from the hospital." Her mother paused and swirled the amber tea in her cup. "Then again, I supposed you'd be even more determined to continue on the path you'd chosen. You're headstrong."

Ginger avoided a quick reaction and grabbed a pastry from the tray. The flaky crust melted in her mouth. The opposite of the cold, tasteless porridge Beatrice and the other sisters would be eating at this time of day. Either her family didn't appear too observant of food rations on flour and sugar, or they'd paid the steep costs for the ability to ignore them. The food—and her presence here—felt like a betrayal of all she'd worked for.

She shouldn't be enjoying any comfort. She'd killed a man, and her father had made the entire matter disappear. But he couldn't take the stain away from her hands.

"I can't disappoint you and Father forever." If her mother knew what awaited on the horizon, if hints of the scandal at Belah returned to society life in Cairo, it would absolutely ruin her.

Her mother patted her hand. "You never disappointed me. I'm proud of all you did. But I'm happy you're here. Too much time has gone by without seeing my children every day."

"I'm glad to be here. Though I'm surprised you've lasted in Cairo so long. I know how much both you and Lucy wanted to go home last year."

"They still aren't allowing many wives or officers' families to return to England. The risk of torpedoes from those U-boats is too great." Her mother's gaze fixed on a statue of the Egyptian god Horus on a pedestal beside the fireplace. "Your father loves serving the people. I could never have denied him that. And he's done a fine job. Besides, he's always wanted the best for us. Even if that meant living abroad. You'll see when you marry. Men have different needs from women. Their way of expressing affection for their family often takes them far outside the household."

Ginger held her tongue. Everything her mother said about marriage made it feel cold. Clinical. In Noah's arms, she'd experienced passion. Perhaps Noah *had* ruined her. She didn't know if she could ever marry a man without passion. *Damn him.* She didn't want any other man but Noah. "Marriage isn't something I want to think of just at the moment."

Her mother frowned. Her fingers, warm from holding the teacup, encircled Ginger's wrist. "It's not important. But if anything is troubling you, darling, I want you to feel you can come to me."

"Thank you, Mother. I'm glad I'm able to confide in you." She felt like a fraud.

"You can confide in me about a great deal of things. You'll find me a steel trap."

Ginger kissed her mother's hand. Now that she knew the genuine nature of her father's work, her mother's trustworthiness made sense. Did her mother know more than she let on?

"If you think for one minute I won't ask what you were talking about, you're sorely mistaken." Lucy's entrance broke the quiet moment. She sauntered over, her gauzy, floral dress swishing. Lucy sat beside them and plopped a stack of letters onto the table. "Here, Grandmama's letters. Now, tell me everything. I won't be left out of the family gossip."

Ginger choked on the pastry she was eating. She didn't remember Lucy being so brazen.

"Your sister called off her engagement with James," her mother said. "I doubt she considers it family gossip."

A sympathetic look crossed Lucy's face. "I'm sorry." Her brown eyes took on a solemn expression. "I know how much you loved him. What happened?"

Ginger blinked at her teacup. Had she given such an impression of being in love with James? Those early days of their engagement seemed so distant, such a whirlwind. Her happiness had been equally relief. James was everything Stephen was not, and that had been enough.

She sipped the tea and set it down. "My feelings for him weren't as deep as I believed." Saying something truthful felt good. "It turns out feeling trapped and bound to your word does not a happy engagement make. I wanted something more fulfilling."

Lucy frowned. "But you wanted to be engaged to him, didn't you?" She squinted and then her face brightened. "Did you meet someone else? Who is he?"

She hadn't counted on Lucy's shrewd nosiness to land so close to another truth. "No, there's no one else." The door opened, and Henry came into the breakfast room.

"So many beautiful women in one room." Henry smiled widely. He paused by Ginger's chair and kissed the top of her head. "Glad to have you home, Ginny. Did you get in late?"

"Very." Ginger stabbed at a piece of ham on her plate with a fork, not looking at him. He had to pretend he hadn't seen her yet. But barely an hour into this morning, she was sick of pretending. It had been a mistake to rise so early. Tomorrow she'd stay in her room well past sunrise. She glanced at Henry, knowing her mother would find her displeasure with him odd. "But I was too excited to be home to sleep."

Henry's smile faltered, as though to say, *"Good girl, but try to be more convincing."* He turned to his mother. "Forgive me for interrupting your conversation."

"You should be sorry." Lucy laughed. "Ginny was about to tell us about her latest beau."

This was not a conversation she wanted to have in front of Henry. Ginger's heart skipped a beat as Henry raised an eyebrow. "Beau?"

"Lucy's mistaken. I broke it off with James, and that's that."

"I'd put money on there being someone else who caught your fancy." Lucy leaned closer to Ginger. "Otherwise you wouldn't have said you wanted something else. So who is he?"

"There isn't anyone." Ginger kept eating calmly, aware of her mother and Henry's gazes. She might shake Lucy off. Her mother and Henry knew her well enough to sense her nervousness. It wouldn't take much for either of them to learn the truth from her father. Would he humiliate her by telling them? She smiled at Lucy. "So feel free to introduce me to a suitable match."

Lucy took the bait immediately. "Actually, you could come with me to Ezbekieh this afternoon. We go to the YMCA to help the ladies in the Red Cross hand out sandwiches and entertain the convalescing troops. And you could meet my friends. They're eager to get to know you—I've told them all about you."

The thought of spending time with Lucy's friends didn't appeal. Ginger hadn't made much time for socialization after the start of the war, and the few girls from her circle of friends at home had drifted apart as they married and she went to nursing school. She'd been close with other sisters in the Queen Alexandra's after she'd joined. But with assignments taking taken them to different hospitals or clearing stations, only Beatrice had remained. Most of the other sisters she'd been close to had traveled to France after Gallipoli.

At least with the nurses in the clearing station in Belah, Ginger felt a sense of kinship. The society ladies of Cairo were similar in their pursuits to the society women of London.

Not wanting to ignore Lucy's invitation, Ginger managed, "Not today. I hurt my hip, and I need to stay off my feet."

Lucy pouted. "Fine. But you'd better heal quickly." She snuck a glance at her mother. "Did you tell her?"

Her mother shook her head. "I didn't want to spoil your surprise."

Ginger suppressed a groan.

"You haven't been out on the town in ages, and, fortunately, I've made friends for the both of us. Lady Victoria Everill is throwing a charity dinner and ball at Shepheard's Hotel five days from now, and it will be the social event of the season." Lucy squeaked, waving her hands with excitement.

"Ball?" Ginger cringed. "Lucy, I don't think I'm up for parties."

"Why not? Shepheard's Hotel is the most important gathering spot, and I want to show you off."

"I don't know." Ginger fidgeted with her teacup.

"Oh, lighten up, Ginny. No one likes a bore." Henry winked at her. "You're acting like a dowdy old maid."

"Well, we wouldn't want that." Ginger didn't bother to remove the sarcasm from her voice.

Lucy pressed on, undeterred. "Please? I already told Victoria you'd come. It's difficult to get on her personal guest list. We'll be at her table. I can't disappoint her."

Few things appealed less than dinner with gossipy women who enjoyed flirting and laughing with British officers. Ginger shot her mother a pleading look.

Her mother cleared her throat. "I think we need to let Ginger have some time to rest. There will be plenty of time to socialize in the coming weeks. Ginger says she isn't planning on returning to the nursing service."

Lucy twisted her serviette in her lap, struggling against tears. "If you'll excuse me, please." She hurried from the room.

"Really, Ginny, did you have to be so dismissive?" Henry's face darkened.

Ginger tucked her hair back, feeling badly. Was she being unreasonable? "That's quite a reaction."

Her mother shrugged. "Be easy on her. I know you still see her as a silly girl, but Lucy's grown up as a daughter of this war. She's thrown fund-raising balls, participated in charity drives, and organized Christmas parcel parties. She'll never have a stomach of steel like you. That doesn't make her efforts unworthy."

"I'm not claiming it does." It bothered her that even her mother seemed to paint her as insensitive. What about her own needs? She may not have been in love with James, but a broken engagement should have given her some excuse to nurse her wounds. Time she could have used to try to forget Noah. If possible.

"We're dealing with the sorrows in our lives in our own ways. She's not happy to be in Cairo, but she's attempting to put her best foot forward. You're a woman of compassion. Maybe you can extend some to your sister?" The gentleness of her mother's voice reminded Ginger of why she hated disappointing her so much.

Ginger sighed. "You're suggesting I go to a charity ball with her?"

"Maybe not this one. But think about it. You should have seen how excited she was when she received that invitation. Lord Helton's daughter is the toast of the town, and Lucy has made it her mission to be friends with her," her mother said.

Ginger stiffened. "Lord Helton's daughter?" That was who Lucy wanted her to be friends with? Noah's fiancée?

Henry shifted in his chair, observing her.

Her mother nodded. "Yes, Lady Victoria Everill. She's quite the charmer."

"*Charmer* is putting it mildly. She's practically the social queen of Cairo. And beautiful. Angelica talks about her incessantly." Henry drummed his fingers on the tabletop.

"Isn't she engaged to that friend of yours? Major Benson?" Her mother asked.

Ginger gripped the handle of the butter knife, not focusing on her mother's exchange with Henry. Lady Victoria would be in touch with Noah. It would give her the perfect opportunity to send Noah a message. She couldn't seem too eager to go now, especially in front of Henry. "Oh for goodness' sake, you speak of her as though she were Nefertiti reincarnated."

"You sound jealous, Ginny." Henry gave her a pointed look.

Maybe her father had said something to him about her relationship with Noah. Ginger rolled her eyes. "I'm not the least bit interested in competing with Victoria."

His eyes locked with hers, his expression perplexed. "You've let this war turn you into someone I'm not sure I recognize anymore."

Henry goaded her, but he also made it easy for her to accept Lucy's invitation. She didn't take her eyes off him. "I think after breakfast I'll tell Lucy I'd love to go to that ball."

Her mother blinked. "Really?"

"Well, I don't want to disappoint Lucy. Or convince my brother I'm anything less than ready to resume my place within the Whitman home and society."

Henry leaned against the back of his seat. "I hope you mean that, Ginny."

Did he know how easy he'd made it for her to reach Noah? The invitation was still days away, though. What if her father and Henry tried to hurt Noah before then? But with her father watching her, few opportunities like this would present themselves.

The idea of running into Noah's fiancée made her stomach turn. She could handle the humiliation, though. If he died because she did nothing, she'd never forgive herself.

CHAPTER TWENTY-FIVE

*G*inger entered the main dining room of Shepheard's Hotel and pushed her nerves to the side. The room, designed to transport its guests into exotic opulence, helped her escape thoughts of the task before her. Brocade drapes shimmered in the light of the many crystal chandeliers and Oriental lamps. The head waiter, dressed in long flowing robes and wearing a turban, greeted guests with a solemn smile.

The ballroom itself was grand and decorated in Moorish style. Lofty ceilings gave the impression of an Egyptian temple, complete with towering pillars lining each side of the room. Soft hues of gold, silver, burgundy, and cream covered the wall's hand-painted designs and moldings. Lush palms were artfully arranged throughout the space. Silverware and crystal stemware clinked lyrically amid the orchestra's noise in the back of the room, where couples danced.

Despite Cairo's mid-May heat, Ginger shivered as she followed her mother and Lucy through the crowd to their table. Stephen sat there, along with his sister, Angelica. Her heart fell at the sight of him. No one had said anything about Stephen coming to dinner.

Stephen spotted them and rose. Her mother greeted him warmly.

Angelica embraced Ginger. "I was so excited when Henry told me you were going to be here," she said to Ginger. Willowy and fair, she looked like a female version of her older brother. "Now you can help me plan the wedding."

Lucy pulled Ginger by the arm toward the other side of the table, where a man stood beside a brunette whose back was toward them. "Victoria! Ginny, this is Lady Victoria Everill, Lord Helton's daughter. He's one of the top men at the Cairo Intelligence Department."

No wonder Noah's engagement protected him. Her father wouldn't want to risk his relationship with a superior officer.

Ginger grabbed on to the back of a chair as Victoria turned. Henry hadn't exaggerated her looks. She was striking and elegant with her dark hair perfectly coiffed. Her shimmering dark-blue gown made the other women at the table look unfashionable. She flashed Ginger a smile as she held Lucy by the elbows and pressed a kiss to each of her cheeks. "It's lovely to see you." She tilted her head at Ginger, her expression polite but reserved. "Your sister has raved about you, Lady Virginia."

Ginger offered a self-conscious smile. She should have taken more interest in her appearance. The tiered ankle-length skirt and V-neck seemed good enough when Lucy had lent it to her. "It's a pleasure."

"Victoria is fascinated by women who join the war effort as nurses." Lucy grinned. She sat beside Angelica. The way Lucy said it made it sound as though she considered Ginger an odd specimen to examine.

Her mother allowed a waiter to pull out a chair next to Lucy for her. "I didn't know I'd be the matriarch at the table."

"You elevate the party," Stephen said. "It's a pity Henry couldn't join us. He's not still slogging at the office, is he? I keep telling him to join me out in the field. Get some sun on his skin."

Angelica frowned at her brother. "Don't you know? He's in Alexandria. I would have given anything to attend a ball with Henry. He didn't tell me he was going to be leaving town so suddenly."

Ginger pressed her lips together. Unlike Angelica, she was glad Henry wasn't here. Over the last few days, her resentment with Henry had grown. His trip to Alexandria had helped avoid confrontations, but his absence was also a painful reminder of how casually he'd mentioned killing Noah. She'd tortured herself for days, wondering if she wasn't over-reacting. The last thing she wanted was for Noah to view her as even more gullible.

The only open seat for Ginger remained between her mother and an unfamiliar man. She hesitated, unsure if she wanted to spend the evening conversing with one of Stephen's friends.

Victoria noticed. "Lady Virginia, this is Lieutenant Jack Darby."

The tall, handsome man offered a handshake. "Nice to meet you."

Ginger shook his hand and sat. "You're American."

He winked. "Yes, ma'am."

His easygoing demeanor relaxed her. "What brings you to Cairo, Lieutenant Darby?" She sipped her water.

"Helping a friend."

Stephen leaned forward. "Lieutenant Darby is a lifelong friend of Major Benson's."

The glass in Ginger's hand nearly slipped. Water splashed from the rim and landed on her lap. She grabbed a serviette and wiped it, heat rising on her cheeks. If Lieutenant Darby really was a friend of Noah's, maybe she should tell him about her concerns for Noah's safety. But it wouldn't be possible with Stephen so close.

Stephen pulled a handkerchief from his pocket. "Water can be such a difficult thing to keep in a glass."

Victoria eyed Ginger. "Do you know Noah? Didn't you arrive recently from the front?"

Good gracious, now she really knew Noah was a liar. How could he have told her she was the most beautiful woman he'd met when his fiancée was Victoria? Her mother and Lucy watched her. "Yes, I've just returned from Palestine. I met Major Benson there briefly."

"And he escorted you safely home from Gaza," Stephen inserted with a leer.

"Yes, he was quite a gentleman. It was a stroke of luck he was in Belah as I began my leave."

Victoria looked at her curiously. "Odd, he never mentioned meeting you."

When had Victoria seen him? Victoria adjusted an enormous diamond on her ring finger. An engagement ring, perhaps? If so, Noah's taste in jewels was exquisite—and expensive. Ginger tore her gaze from it, her nerves tingling. She watched the couples on the dance floor, wishing she could keep herself from blushing. "I'm afraid I was a dull travel companion."

Stephen chortled. "I doubt anyone would say that of you." He waved a hand for some wine and leaned toward Victoria in a manner that spoke of an intimate friendship. "She even got him to pull his nose out of a book long enough for tea at the Savoy in Port Said."

Victoria's dark gaze was analytical. "A mighty feat. Noah does enjoy reading." She pulled out a fan. "But I never know where he goes. He pops into Cairo without notice and is gone again before I can blink. For all I know, he's traipsing around with T. E. Lawrence. He certainly seems to prefer the company of the locals."

A waiter with flowing white robes tied with a sash and wearing a red fez poured wine for the table. Ginger accepted a glass. Thank goodness.

"Ah, but you and the major enjoyed the past week together, no?" Stephen tapped his fingers on the table. "From what I heard, you were the toast of gatherings."

Noah was in Cairo? Darker thoughts extinguished the spark of joy lit by the news. He'd spent the week with Victoria.

Oh, God, she was a stupid fool. While she'd been busy pining for him, he'd been socializing with his fiancée. She'd allowed herself to daydream he might appear and whisk her away. A crushing feeling grew in her lungs.

Victoria unfolded a serviette in her lap. "It's been a brief respite. Without an end in sight to this war, I don't know that we'll have many such opportunities in the coming year."

"He's a fool if he doesn't marry you soon." Stephen winked at Victoria. "I hear you may move up the wedding date?"

"We'll see." A tiny smile curved the corners of Victoria's lips.

A single drop of wine made its way down the side of Ginger's glass. Each beat of her heart pained.

"What were you doing out in Palestine?" Lieutenant Darby broke into her thoughts.

Palestine? She stared at him as though he'd asked her how much she enjoyed seeing the penguins of Antarctica. She attempted to string a sentence together. "I-I was with the Queen Alexandra's." At his questioning look, Ginger added, "Nursing."

"Ah." Lieutenant Darby's expression held a note of amusement. "Are you on a pass now?"

Why couldn't she remember his question? "What was that?" Wonderful. She was making a fool of herself in front of Noah's fiancée and his close friend. Ginger twisted in her seat.

Lucy rolled her eyes. "No, thank goodness, she's given it up. I don't see why anyone would want to be out there, but that's Ginny." Lucy turned toward Victoria and continued, "Angelica and I were talking yesterday about you. You must take us shopping next time you go."

Victoria replied, but as the conversation at the table turned, Ginger couldn't register her words. No wonder Noah had no intention of breaking his engagement. Her father was a man of influence, and she was a gorgeous socialite.

Sick to her stomach, Ginger finished her wine in a few gulps. Did Victoria even suspect Noah's infidelity? A waiter quickly refilled her glass and she lifted it again, the contents sloshing. She placed the glass on the table, and a red circle appeared on the white tablecloth under the base of the crystal stem.

She felt as graceful as a cow.

Her mother placed a gentle hand on Ginger's under the table. Her mother must wonder why she'd lost her composure.

Lieutenant Darby's voice came from beside her. "Not as interested in shopping?" He nodded toward Angelica and Lucy, who conversed with Victoria.

Ginger sipped her wine again. "I'm not sure I can separate myself from being a nurse as easily as my sister seems to think."

"I wouldn't think so." He leaned back. "You work on both the Gaza battles? I went to a hospital in Kantara after the first battle. The nurses worked fourteen-hour shifts."

The hospitals in Kantara and El Arish had received most of the wounded men she'd seen come through the clearing station after the battles. They must have faced an onslaught. "Yes, I was on the front for both battles. It was exhausting."

"That's putting it lightly." Darby shook his head. "I didn't fully appreciate what you nurses were doing until then."

Who was Lieutenant Darby? Noah had never mentioned

him. Then again, he hadn't mentioned Victoria either. Or much of anything.

Stephen interrupted their conversation. "Ginny, why don't we take a turn on the dance floor while we wait for dinner?"

The last thing she wanted was to dance with Stephen. "I'm not sure I'm the best dance partner."

"Oh, go on, darling." Her mother nudged her. "You and Stephen always made a splendid match."

Ginger didn't answer, and Stephen stood. He held his hand out to her.

She didn't want to make a scene. Reluctantly, she followed him to the dance floor.

"You're looking better than the last time I saw you." Stephen placed his hand at her waist. She nearly pulled away, thinking of all she knew of him. Everything about him disgusted her.

"I should hope so. The last time you saw me, I was crying." She avoided his gaze, keenly aware of the discomfort of their proximity. "I wasn't expecting your company tonight."

He led her in a waltz. "Victoria's a close acquaintance of mine. I introduced Benson to her. I heard Angelica speaking of her plans, and I knew I had to come."

Ginger clenched her teeth. "To continue to spy on me?"

"I've been hoping we'd have another chance to speak." Stephen cleared his throat. "I'm worried about you. You were much more involved in this whole situation with that Turk than you cared to trust me with, and I understand. But if someday you feel you need someone to trust, please know I'm here. I want to help."

Ginger narrowed her gaze at him. "Help me like you helped those Bedouins in Belah? Or Noah in Aleppo? He showed me what really happened."

Stephen's hand slid firmly, possessively down her back, pulling her against him. "Careful, darling, you don't want to give yourself away as Benson's whore in this crowd." His voice menaced, his grip so tight she couldn't pull free. "Or make me say something I shouldn't. Especially after that scene in your hotel room. One word to my father about it and I promise you the engagement between Henry and Angelica will be finished."

She used every ounce of willpower not to slam her heel on his foot. "Are you threatening me?" A dull ache of fear pressed into her heart. Much as she didn't want to admit it, the threat of ruining Henry's engagement did worry her. For all his recent mistakes, Henry loved Angelica. He would be crushed if he wasn't permitted to marry her.

His lips grazed her ear. "Quite the opposite. Other men might not be willing to forgive what they witnessed, but they don't want you like I do. You'll learn soon enough how much you need me, Ginny. And I'm certain you'll be willing to come to an arrangement that will be mutually … satisfying."

She dug her nails into his side. "That's where you're wrong. I'd rather be known as Noah Benson's whore than give you anything you want." With a smirk, she added, "As though you ever would be man enough to satisfy me."

"You think Benson gives a damn about you?" Stephen's eyes blazed at her. "You're nothing but another notch on his belt. And there have been many notches."

The end of the song saved her from answering. She ripped herself free from his grasp. An angry red tone crept up Stephen's neck. "Stay away from me," she said in a low growl. She spun away from him and hurried through the crowd, Stephen at her heels. Not that she could find much comfort at the table. No matter how friendly Victoria was, being around her made Ginger feel sick.

She arrived as the waiter approached the table with escargots and caviar. Stephen didn't sit. "It's your turn," he told Victoria. He led her away, Victoria's figure swishing beautifully.

Victoria waved at a few tables before she arrived at the dance floor.

"I'm sure Stephen would prefer to dance with you," her mother whispered.

Did her mother think she was so vapid? Ginger stared at her hands, still seething over Stephen's comments on the dance floor. "I'd rather he dance with her."

Lieutenant Darby swirled his red wine in its glass, watching as it ran down the sides. "You looked about as happy out there as a jackrabbit around a coyote."

She ignored his statement, desperate to change the subject to something mundane. "Are you finding Cairo to your liking, Lieutenant?"

"It's a fascinating city." He sipped his drink. "But it's not my first time here. And, please—call me Jack. I know you British love your formality, but I don't recognize my own name when someone calls me 'Lieutenant.'"

She smiled. "I know how you feel. It took me ages to adjust to the title of 'sister.' I felt as though I'd joined a convent."

"They do a good job of making sure you dress the part." Jack grinned. "Someone shows an ankle, and heads start rolling. I don't know that I've ever stared at any woman's ankles thinking how pretty she is."

"Are you suggesting our friends across the pond have forgotten their manners?" Her mother's expression revealed she enjoyed Jack's observations.

"I'm fairly certain we Yankees never had them in the first place." Jack reclined comfortably. "Although, from what I've seen of the world, there's a whole lot of pretending going on everywhere."

Ginger smoothed her dress. "Are you well-traveled? Or just involved with the war effort for a while?"

"Well-traveled. My father was an archeologist and adventurer." Jack loosened his collar. "I spent my childhood combing temple ruins like the ones at Karnak and then shuttling off the next year to explore the ancient civilization of the Incas in South America."

"That sounds fascinating." No wonder he was friends with Noah. They had unusual upbringings.

"*Fascinating* is one word for it." Jack shrugged.

Lucy cut in. "Ginny. What do you think of Lady Victoria? Isn't she a dear? I adore her gown tonight. They say her fiancé is as handsome as she is. I didn't know you knew him. How is he?" Her energy amplified as she spoke. "I hoped he'd be here tonight."

Which one of those questions should she bother to answer? She couldn't let her emotions rule. "Major Benson is handsome. Wouldn't you agree, Lieutenant?"

Jack chuckled. "Oh, I don't know. Women seem to think so. He was never my type."

"Do you think they'll move up the date of their wedding now that he's back?" Angelica asked.

"We should ask her. We can help her with the wedding plans." Lucy giggled. "And we'll assure our invitation."

Ginger frowned at her food. If she received an invitation to Noah's wedding, she'd find a way to escape to England. "Excuse me. I'm going to the ladies' lounge." She rose and gathered her handbag.

Victoria arrived at the table ... and Noah followed directly behind her.

Her heart slammed against her ribs.

Good God, he was handsome. She'd pretended when she met him his looks didn't affect her, but seeing him now, she couldn't deny it.

Did he notice her? His hand was on Victoria's lower back and he scanned the table.

His eyes moved toward her and continued right past.

As if she wasn't there.

She stiffened, hurt budding. She'd hoped to talk to Victoria and pass along a note to Noah—but she'd never expected to see him here.

She couldn't help but stare, her senses alert. How could it have only been a week since Port Said? Their separation had been a quiet torture, one in which she convinced herself how in love with him she was. And now that he was here ... *ugh*. She *was* in love with him.

Her ears rang while Victoria introduced Noah to the group.

Victoria slipped her arm into Noah's. They were the stunning couple she imagined they would be. Noah appeared every bit the polished military officer at her side. Her heart fell. They looked happy together. Victoria's face practically shone as she watched him.

Noah's eyes met hers as Victoria said, "I believe you know Lady Virginia Whitman."

He nodded politely and moved his gaze toward her mother as Victoria introduced them.

A pang went through her.

"I'm so pleased to meet you, Major Benson." Her mother beamed at him. "Stephen tells us we have you to thank for escorting our daughter home safely from Palestine. I appreciate you going out of your way for her."

Ginger bit the inside of her cheek. Her mother didn't know the irony of her statement.

Noah's gaze flicked toward her. "Ah—that's right. The nurse from Gaza. My apologies, I hardly recognized you without the nursing uniform."

Without the uniform? Her face stung, the heat on her cheeks spreading to her ears. She wished Stephen could have heard it.

He would have taken Noah to task for the lie. The one time Stephen would be useful, and he wasn't around.

A waiter came by with a tray of champagne glasses. He stopped near Lady Braddock and Ginger. "For the lovely ladies."

Ginger accepted the glass and sat. She finished it in a few quick swallows.

Jack watched her. "Thirsty?"

"Parched." She fidgeted with the stem of the glass. Trust Noah's friend to notice her distress.

"Let me get you another." Jack fetched one from the waiter.

"Major Benson, you don't disappoint." Lucy's eyes shone. "We've been so eager to meet you."

Noah pulled out a chair for Victoria. A waiter hurried over with a chair for him. Stephen arrived at the table as Noah displaced him from Victoria's side. Stephen sat without greeting Noah, his expression dark.

"And in what capacity do you work for the army, Major Benson?" Angelica asked eagerly.

"For the CID." Noah accepted a glass of red wine. "Though I've spent most of my time out in the field."

"It sounds like fascinating work. Do you enjoy it?" her mother asked.

Victoria laughed and touched his cheek before pursing her lips at him. She leaned closer to him, settling against his arm. "He had better enjoy it. Otherwise his eagerness to accept every assignment outside of Cairo would feel suspiciously like he was avoiding me."

Noah exchanged a smile with her and lifted the back of her gloved hand to his lips. "Never, my darling." He kissed her hand.

Ginger thought she might vomit.

"I would think a week spent in the company of your spectacular fiancée would be enough to shake you of desert attachments." Stephen shifted in his seat.

Ginger gave Stephen a faltering glance. Her serviette slid from her lap, and she jerked her hand toward it. Her head spun from the amount of alcohol she'd consumed.

Would anyone notice if she crawled under the table?

She straightened and turned to Jack. "How are Americans at dancing?"

Jack offered a gracious smile and held out his hand. "Far superior to our British counterparts, like everything else."

She couldn't help but return his smile. Thank God for him. She practically bolted to the dance floor.

"You know," Jack said as they danced, "if you don't want anyone to know you have feelings for Noah, you may want to conceal your reactions to him."

She winced, her head fuzzy. "Is it obvious?"

"I don't think your sister and her friend noticed." Jack twirled her. He hadn't lied about his dance skills.

"And Victoria?" She met his dark-brown eyes. "Be honest. I value it."

Jack twitched his head in a subtle nod. "She's used to women staring at him. Play your cards right, and she may not think it's outside the norm."

Especially when Noah did such a convincing job appearing indifferent to her. Maybe he was.

Pulling her close to him again, Jack said, "I'll do my best to keep Stephen busy. Leave you alone."

"If you hadn't been here tonight, I think I would have left by now. Thank you, Jack."

His laugh was a low rumble in his chest. "I'm here because Noah asked me to be. He told me about you and was concerned about this dinner."

Her ire rose. So Noah wanted to use Jack to keep her in line, did he?

Jack's presence saved her from one more thing—she could

avoid talking to Victoria. She could tell Jack about Noah being in danger—but what about Ahmed's bag? That was something she could only tell Noah himself. "I came because I need to talk to Noah, urgently. Can you arrange it?"

Jack frowned. "Here?"

"No, I suppose not." That might undo what little poise she had left.

Jack scanned her face. "Can I give you some unsolicited and probably unwelcome advice?"

"With phrasing like that, I'm not sure I want to hear it."

"Well, you should." Jack glanced toward their table. "It's none of my business, but he warned me you might try to talk to him. He cares about you, but you have to let it go. It's better for you both."

Of all the nerve. Her fingertips tightened against Jack's hand. "I'm perfectly capable of restraining myself from being inappropriate." She let out a huff. "I'm not here to wrest him away from his fiancée, if that's what you think. I didn't even know he would be here. I planned to send a message through Lady Victoria. But Noah is in danger, and I need to speak to him."

Jack stiffened. "What do you mean?"

"I think someone might try to kill him." It amazed her how calmly she could say that.

Jack appeared flustered for a response. His eyebrows furrowed. "You're not hoping—"

"For goodness' sake. I'm here humiliating myself because I want to warn him. I wouldn't put myself through this otherwise. Now, can you arrange a meeting or not?"

An odd expression crossed his features. "Meet me tomorrow at noon at the Khan. Go to Fishawy's. You know it?"

Everyone knew of the famous souk. "I'll bring my sister with me. My father won't let me out of the house otherwise."

The song ended, and Jack linked arms with her. "Now, look

at me and smile. And laugh, like I'm treating you to a hilarious joke."

"And what joke would that be?"

Jack grinned. "Stephen's a good joke."

"You are rotten." The genuineness of her laughter relaxed her shoulders.

They made their way toward the table. Passing through the narrow spaces between seats, they found themselves face-to-face with Noah and Victoria, who headed out to dance. Victoria stopped and pressed against Noah, scooting off to the side to allow Jack and Ginger space.

As Jack moved by Noah, Noah whispered to him. Jack nodded.

Noah's proximity made him difficult to avoid. Ginger met his gaze. For a flash, the warm, passionate man she'd known stood there. Her heart thudded, her arm brushing against Noah's as Jack pulled her past.

Noah followed Victoria onto the dance floor. The way he stared at Victoria—as though she was the only woman in the room—shattered Ginger's heart. He'd looked at her that way in Port Said. The chill of being in the shadows now was more than she could bear.

Jack gave her a keen look as they arrived at the table. Ginger sat and lifted her champagne.

Jack pushed water toward her. "You might want this."

She raised a brow and met his gaze. No doubt Noah requested he stop her from drinking. She emptied her champagne glass.

Jack turned away wordlessly. She'd had about enough of this evening. She needed fresh air. Ginger grabbed another glass of champagne from a waiter and bumped her way past the row of chairs.

Her eyes fell on the dance floor where Noah and Victoria swayed. Noah bent his head and kissed Victoria.

Doing everything to keep the tears from her eyes, Ginger fled from the ballroom. The cooler air of the lobby did nothing to assuage the flush of grief and shame. "Enough," she whispered to herself. "Enough."

CHAPTER TWENTY-SIX

*G*inger held her throbbing head and leaned against the dust-covered stone wall between two stalls at the Khan el Kahlili. She pulled the brim of her hat over her eyes, shielding them from the intense midday sun.

"Look at this necklace. Think it's genuine gold? It can't be at that price, can it? The man said it was real." Lucy's voice broke through Ginger's thoughts, sounding shrill. She stepped out from a stall.

Ginger eyed the necklace in question. "I don't know."

"I think I'll buy it." Lucy's face brightened.

"Don't buy it without haggling. Whatever price he names is too high."

Lucy disappeared without listening.

Tobacco smoke billowed from a nearby café, hanging like a cloud in the alleyway of the famous bazaar where sun mixed with shadow, filtering between the buildings but never quite reaching the ground. Her stomach turned at the mixture of scents in the market. She never wanted to touch a glass of wine again. She squeezed her eyes shut as a group of British soldiers playing tourists drifted past the stall where she stood.

"Are you certain you don't want to go home?" Lucy appeared beside her again.

Ginger forced a smile. "It's the crowdedness of these narrow streets. Makes it feel more like a labyrinth than a market."

Lucy smirked. "Is that what it is?" She tucked her purchase into her bag. "You woke up looking green, you know."

With a flash of horror, she considered she might be pregnant. She still had two weeks left until her monthly cycle. But, no. It couldn't be. It'd be too early for morning sickness, and she'd had more than her fair share of alcohol the night before.

Lucy peeled Ginger from the wall. "We don't have to do this today. We can go home."

Ginger sidestepped a soldier who was arguing with a vendor over the price of a leather hat. The scent of cooking meat reached her nose, kebabs of greyish dripping meat turning her stomach more. "I'll be perfectly fine. I want to enjoy a day with you." She glanced at her watch. "Though, some mint tea would help settle my stomach. There's a café around here—Fishawy's. It's one of the oldest and best known in the souk."

"Lead the way." Lucy shook her hand at a fortune-teller who approached her. "But there's a man selling scarves back there— I'd like to return and look at them later."

"Henry used to lead me through here when we first arrived in Cairo." Ginger's eyes fixed on a stall filled with fake antiquities, *ushabtis* of Egyptian pharaohs and gods.

Lucy laughed, her arm tightening on Ginger's. "With your wonderful sense of direction, I'm sure we'll get there past midnight." They turned a corner, and Lucy recoiled at a snake charmer. The snake rose from its basket, a group of Australian soldiers watching it with fascination. Her last encounter with a snake, she'd been the one watching it, unable to move. Noah had killed it and kissed her...

No. She couldn't let herself think of these things anymore.

Ginger helped Lucy edge past. "Don't worry. The snakes they use have their venom glands removed."

"I loathe them." Lucy shuddered. "The way you hate rats."

"There are plenty of those around here too."

They found Fishawy's and ventured inside. Ginger scanned the space, searching for Jack. She glanced at her watch again. Nearly noon. Where was he?

They sat at a rickety aluminum table. The marble top, cracked and battered, resembled most of the décor. Dingy yellow paint peeled from the walls decorated with gilded arabesque mirrors.

Ginger ordered mint tea. Lucy rocked back and forth on the uneven legs of her chair. "I feel like I am going to fall off this seat."

"Here, take mine." Ginger stood and held out a hand toward the chair.

"I suppose I should accustom myself to discomfort." Lucy took the seat Ginger vacated.

Despite Lucy's flair for the dramatic, it was an odd, mournful thing for her to say. Ginger cocked her head to the side and sat. "How so?"

Lucy clutched her handbag on her lap. "With Father selling so much and dismissing so many servants. He sold the house in London, you know."

Ginger's mouth dropped open. "What?" When had this happened?

"You mean Mother didn't tell you?"

She stiffened. "No."

"She probably didn't want to upset you." Lucy pushed a

strand of damp hair from her forehead. "Mother said it was because of the war, but the real reason is Father has driven us into financial straits. Everyone assumes I notice nothing." She smirked. "But about a year ago some of Mother's jewelry started disappearing. Artworks too."

Ginger's mind reeled. She thought of the missing palette from their home in Cairo. Why hadn't her mother said anything?

Lucy teared up. "That's the reason I've been so upset to be in Cairo. I think Father may sell Penmore. I don't think they can afford it anymore. I don't want to stay stuck in Egypt forever. I want to go home."

Ginger dug into her handbag for a handkerchief and handed it to Lucy. "I'm sure Mother wouldn't let Father sell Penmore without telling us." The news of their family's ruined finances troubled her. Her father was a proud man. One who would do anything to keep the family from losing their status.

Lucy wiped her eyes and pointed. "Look at that cheeky urchin."

Ginger glanced at the window. Khalib stood on the other side, face pressed against the glass, flashing a toothy smile. Relief went through her. If Khalib was nearby, so might be Noah.

She stood. Lucy looked at her with surprise. "I'll be right back." Ginger gave her a reassuring smile. "I thought I saw one of my former nursing friends out there."

Lucy wrinkled her nose, red from crying. "I'll stay right here, thank you. I don't want anyone to see me like this."

Thank goodness. Ginger hadn't been certain how she'd get away from Lucy otherwise. She clasped her handbag and moved around the café's crowded tables. Khalib disappeared from view.

Once outside, she followed in the direction he'd gone. Khalib sped ahead, turning into one of the shadowed streets of the Khan. Ginger kept a steady pace behind him. The place swarmed like a beehive.

She pushed past vendors, ignoring them as they gesticulated to tapestries and alabaster statues. Beggars and tourists brushed past her, the street so narrow she could hardly keep Khalib in sight.

Khalib turned into another, less crowded street. Descending deeper into the heart of the souk, Ginger stiffened. Where had Khalib gone? She no longer recognized her surroundings. She'd followed Khalib without paying attention.

How could she be so foolish? She was lost.

She dashed toward the direction she thought she'd come from. Each street vendor resembled the one before. She stopped by a man selling mango juice at a cart.

He lifted a glass eagerly. She shook her head. "No, no, thank you. Can you tell me where Fishawy's is?"

He pushed the cup toward her. Some of it splashed from the rim and dripped down his dark brown hand and elbow.

"No, thank you. Fishawy's. *Min fadlak.*"

The man's exasperation at her refusal increased. Her heart raced as she searched for an exit. He started jabbering. She scrambled away from his cart.

Another vendor grabbed her arm. He pressed a pendant bearing the eyelike symbol of the Wadjet close to her cheek as an onslaught of foul breath reached her. She escaped down a narrow path.

The turn led her to an alleyway. The call to prayer from one of the local mosques wailed and echoed off the walls. She slowed. Here and there, a few men sat in huddled groups, watching her. She tightened her grip on her handbag. She was an easy target.

Someone grabbed her arm. She screamed and tried to pull

free. A forceful shove pushed her against a wall. A hand covered her mouth.

Noah's dark-blue eyes stared into hers

She stiffened, relief flooding her. Thank goodness.

"Stop screaming." Noah lowered his hand, still pressing her into the wall.

Gone was the cold, indifferent man from the night before. The familiarity in his eyes made her heart ache.

"What are you doing here?" She lifted an unsteady hand to her forehead. The kiss he'd shared with Victoria on the dance floor still made her feel ill. The odor from the alleyway didn't help.

"I was going to ask you that." His eyes narrowed.

He wore civilian clothes, which gave him the odd look of a tourist. Funny, she'd never seen him outside of a uniform. Unless she counted the hotel room in Port Said. She pushed the thought away.

"I don't particularly trust that group of men over there." Noah tilted his head. "Shall we?" His hand found its way to the small of her back, protective and possessive at the same time. He kept her close as he led her out of the street.

"Where are you taking me?" She glanced at his profile.

"Somewhere we can talk." His gaze remained straight ahead. "Then back to Fishawy's."

They wouldn't have much time, with Lucy sitting in the café alone. "But my sister—"

"Jack's keeping her busy."

She faltered. "You sent Khalib to lead me here?"

"Not exactly. You ran from the café like a madwoman, and I had to catch up. You move fast. This isn't a place for a young English girl to be blundering alone."

His words goaded her. As though he purposely wanted to

make her feel ignorant in contrast to his vast superiority. As though nothing had ever happened between them.

She glared at him. "That was quite a display last night." They walked side by side. "Trying to show me my place?" Shame crept into her heart.

"How would you have preferred I acted?" Noah's voice was low.

"For one, you didn't need to imply that meeting me left no impression on you." She narrowed her gaze. "Considering you've seen me in far less than my nursing uniform, you bloody jackass."

Her words didn't have the intended effect. A smile touched his lips.

He navigated the souk with expertise. At last he stopped, gesturing toward a shop. She followed him in, ducking under a low weathered-wood door.

Noah spoke in hushed tones to the shopkeeper, a woman who studied Ginger with such intensity that she squirmed. The scent of incense burned her nose, but the store appeared little more than a trinket shop. The woman nodded and pointed to a darkened hallway in the back. She glowered at Ginger as she passed.

They reached the back of the hallway, and Noah opened a door. They stepped into another hallway, this one leading to several closed doors. A soft moaning reached her. Ginger whirled around. "What is this place?"

"There aren't many places in the Khan promising privacy." He opened a door and held it. She passed through to a bedroom with an ornate but clean bed occupying most of the space. A Moorish lamp with a red shade threw a warm glow, but most of the room remained shrouded by darkness.

He'd brought her to a brothel? She cringed. Hopefully this

wasn't a place he knew from frequenting it. She fidgeted with her handbag. "I didn't know they had this type of establishment in the Khan."

"The madam has the support of the protectorate. Gamila's girls have been effective in obtaining and relaying information from high-level sources who value an establishment offering absolute discretion, including its location." Noah closed the door. "Which is why she objected to me bringing you here. You're not hers."

She couldn't speak her mind. Not in a place like this. But she had no choice. She stared at her hands, her headache growing worse.

Noah frowned. "You're angry."

She gaped at him. "Of course." But it didn't matter. After she revealed the truth, he'd be out of her life forever. He would marry Victoria, and her dishonesty about murdering Ahmed would drive him further away.

"Jack said you wanted to speak to me." Noah stepped closer.

"I'm sorry I had to involve him. But you gave me no other method to contact you."

Noah's look softened. "What makes you think I haven't been keeping an eye on you the entire time you've been in Cairo?"

She swallowed, not wanting to feel the tenderness of his words. "Well, have you?"

"More than you know."

She crossed her arms. Was he afraid she'd expose him to Victoria? "I keep turning it over in my head. You had plenty of opportunity to mention Victoria in the desert." Thoughts of his silence now sullied the memories of their time together.

A shadow crossed his expression and he rolled his sleeves, as though the heat of the room suffocated him. "I should have. But, at first, I didn't think it relevant. And later I convinced myself it wasn't necessary, because I never dreamed anything would go further than a few stolen kisses."

Her chest tightened. "To be honest, that doesn't make me feel any better."

His fingers curled in loose fists at his sides. "I never meant to hurt you. What happened between us shouldn't have. I let the circumstances overwhelm my better judgement. And I owe you an apology. My engagement with Victoria is complicated, but it should have been enough to stop me."

The circumstances? As though that could soothe her heart. "You think I want an apology?" She glared at him. "What happened between us was my choice as much as yours. It wasn't something you did to me."

Noah tensed. "Then what? What do you want?"

She stepped closer. "I want you to stop acting as though you didn't feel everything I felt. It's insulting. You lied to me. You're lying to her. But I was there. I know the truth of who you are, no matter what you want me to believe now." She trailed her fingertips over his jawline. "No matter if you won't tell me the truth."

Noah caught her hand. "I never said I felt nothing." His fingers interlaced with hers, and he pulled her closer. He kissed her, his lips soft and warm against hers.

She tore her mouth from his and jumped back. "I can't. Not here. Not now that I know about Victoria." She didn't want to think of Victoria, or how happy she'd seemed the night before.

"I promise you. If I'm able to someday, I'll give you the answers you deserve." Noah released her. "But you deserve much more than I'd ever be able to give you. And I knew that a long time ago."

She deserved nothing. She was a murderer. Her fingers dragged against the gold brocade of the duvet cover as she sat, reminding her of the bed they'd shared in Port Said. "Do you love her?" She didn't want to know the answer. She'd seen them together.

Noah let out a frustrated breath. "Don't force me to hurt you, Ginger. I told you before, I can't end the engagement. I can't offer you anything."

The forcefulness with which he said it was enough of an answer. She nodded, trying to keep her poise. "We can discuss our situation later. I have something urgent to tell you."

Noah leaned against the wall opposite to her. "Jack said as much."

She swallowed. "You may be in grave danger."

Noah's expression didn't change. "How so?"

"After I arrived, my father and Henry questioned me." She cleared her throat. "And Henry joked that you needed to be killed. An accident, if possible. I don't know if they discussed it beyond that, but I know you consider him a friend, and I wanted you to be aware."

A look of surprise crossed Noah's face. "Henry? Not your father?"

She nodded.

Something dark and unreadable burned in his eyes. "I didn't expect that. Though I should have after the way he abandoned you in the desert. Did he say anything else?"

"Not that I heard." Her stomach felt as tightly bunched as a fist. Betraying Henry and her father had been logical, but now it felt so empty. How could he be safe with such sparse information?

The heady scent of sandalwood incense drifted from under the door. To break the silence, she added, "I'm sorry for not having more to share. I tried not to tell them much, but the truth is I don't know what's secret anymore. This isn't my world, and you're not confiding in me."

"You could have told Jack that, though, so I'm assuming there must be something else."

She had to tell him about Ahmed's death and the other document. Now. There wouldn't be another chance. "Actually, two things."

"I'm still listening."

She couldn't face him. "I'm the one who murdered Ahmed. I didn't do it on purpose. Henry spoke to him alone, and he must have told Henry something about what he knew. Henry fought him, and I overheard and tried to stop them. I thought I'd fire a warning shot, but I hit Ahmed by mistake." Her voice choked. "I-I wanted to save him. I swear it. I found him dying in a hut near a well in Belah, and I took him under my care. I never, ever intended to kill him. I wanted to help him."

Noah stared at her, and the seconds passed with her counting her breath like death knells.

Noah sat and took her hand. "If that's true, you didn't murder anyone. You could have as easily hit Henry."

Tears slipped down her cheeks. "But I fired the weapon. His death is on my hands."

"Did you fire it intending to kill Ahmed?"

"No—but it killed him all the same. I'm guilty."

Noah embraced her. "Actually, you're not. If there's anything I'm learning, it's your innocence in this. A little too insightful for your own good, but innocent." His arms tightened. "I don't know how I ever could have believed you'd participate in this treachery."

He was blurry to her gaze as he pressed a kiss to her forehead. How could he kiss her after what she'd confessed? She'd killed someone. "But he died—and it was my fault." She squeezed her eyes shut. "I can't forgive myself."

"You tried to save him. Forgive yourself." He kissed her lips. "And I treated you abominably—I'm sorry."

Her shoulders shook, and she pressed her forehead against his. "I'm sorry too, Noah. I am. I never wanted to be deceptive. I should have trusted you from the start."

"And I should have told you I was Thevshi the first time you asked." He pushed her hair away from her face and kissed her once more. "I'm the one who should beg for your forgiveness."

She let out a cry, desperate for the comfort he offered, and returned his kiss. Her arms slid around his neck, her heart beating wildly. It would be so easy. They had the benefit of privacy and a bed. And Victoria would never know.

If she kissed him for much longer, she wouldn't stop.

No. She wrenched herself away. "There's one more thing." She pressed her fingertips to her lips, her pulse still throbbing at her throat. "Ahmed had a bag on him when we first met. James hid it in his quarters. Actually, James was helping me with Ahmed's care. I said nothing because once I realized how dangerous it was, I didn't want anyone to know of James's involvement, nor did I want him to know the danger I'd put him in. I tried to tell you in Port Said, at lunch, but you wouldn't let me."

Noah stood, his expression grim. "You're saying James has the other clue to finding the documents? You never had them?"

She nodded. "It surprised me you didn't try harder to get them from me."

"That's because after we left Port Said, I was certain your father would wrest them from you and destroy them."

Destroy them? The weight of his statement couldn't be over-looked. He believed in her father's treachery, and he'd expected it. How deeply involved was her father with Stephen?

"Are you certain James still has them?"

"I think so. Though, when I arrived in Cairo, I sent a wire to my tentmate, Beatrice Thornton, and asked her to retrieve the bag and have it sent to me. Beatrice also knew about Ahmed. Neither she nor James ever knew what Ahmed entrusted me with, though."

Noah's gaze clouded. "I must leave for Gaza right away. Tonight, if possible. You need to be somewhere safe. Away from this. Is there anywhere safe you can go?"

"I want to help you." She reached for his hand. "I need to understand what my father and Henry are involved in, though. I'm frightened for my family."

Noah stared at the sliver of light coming in from under the door. "I can't tell you. And I can't risk seeing you again. I'll leave Khalib with you. For your protection and in case you need to send me a message. But, please—don't look for me." His hands tightened into fists. "Especially since I seem to lack the necessary self-control to keep my hands off you. Thank you for telling me all this."

She went to him. "I should have told you a long time ago." She touched his cheek. "One more thing."

He laughed, and the sound brought a teary smile to her eyes. "There's always one more thing with you, darling."

She nodded, tears pooling on the rims of her eyes and in her lashes. "If this has to be good-bye, I have to tell you. Because I waited my entire life for you, Noah Benson, and I didn't know it until after I found myself alone in my room in Cairo, kicking myself for not understanding what it was I felt." She swallowed. "I love you. And I know it won't change your mind. I know you're … hers. But I love you, despite —"

He silenced her with a kiss that spoke of the fever of their passion. His arms were tight around her, but his hands stayed firmly fixed on her back. He dragged his mouth from hers, his breath hot on her cheek. "Is there anything I can do to convince you to forget me? I want you safe."

She searched his eyes. In Port Said, she sensed he'd pushed her away on purpose. But something had changed. As though he could barely will himself to turn his back on her anymore. "Can you forget me?"

Noah wrapped her in a strong embrace. "Never. But I have to let you go."

CHAPTER TWENTY-SEVEN

When her father arrived home that evening, Ginger waited for him in his study. He opened the door, loosening the collar of his shirt as he walked. She stood from the high wing-backed chair in the corner.

"My errant daughter. Just whom I hoped to see." He lifted a pistol from the holster on his belt, then set it down with a dull thud on the mahogany desk.

"I hope you're not brandishing that at me." She tiptoed toward him.

"Don't be absurd." He glanced at the grandfather clock in the corner. "To what do I owe the honor of this lovely greeting?"

"You sold the house in London?" Ever since Lucy had told her about the news, it had nagged her.

He set his briefcase on the desktop. "You seem to be taking the news well."

She imagined what Lucy's reaction had been. Losing the London house had far greater implications to her. She had been looking forward to being a debutante after the war. "Why didn't anyone but Lucy tell me?"

"You could have gone to your mother with these questions."

"Mother doesn't manage the household finances." Ginger set her hands against the desk, leaning forward. "And I hear Penmore may be next. Why?" Selling the family home and estate in the country would be devastating.

Her father opened his briefcase and sifted through it. "The decisions I make for this family are none of your concern. But speaking of secrets ..." He tossed a telegram onto the desk. "What's the meaning of this?"

Ginger studied it—a copy of what she'd written to Beatrice. "You ... intercepted my wire?"

"Yes. Now"—he tapped his finger against the envelope—"tell me more about the 'personal effects' you're asking her to send to you."

She'd worded the message carefully, asking Beatrice to retrieve and pass along the personal effects of the patient they'd treated the day of the dispensary bombardment. She'd written enough information for Beatrice to understand she meant Ahmed. Had her father figured it out? "I had promised one of my patients who died in my care to forward his personal effects to his family. Nothing outside the realm of everyday duties for nurses."

"I see." He sat on the edge of the desk. "And if I were to ask her, would she give me the same response?"

She didn't move under his stare. "Yes." She squared the telegram neatly in the center of his desk. "I'm glad to see how much you trust me."

"After Port Said, should I trust you, Virginia? I've never been more disappointed in you in my life." His eyes bore into hers. "You're too clever to think I don't see right through your lies."

"What lies?"

Her father raised a decanter of whiskey and poured himself a glass. "I have it on good authority you've disobeyed me today at the Khan. It was a clever ruse, concealing your dalliance by pretending you were going on an outing with Lucy."

A shiver went up her spine. He knew she'd spoken to Noah. Did he know about the brothel? "You're spying on me now?"

Her father swallowed the contents of his glass. "You've left me no other choice. Your immoral, headstrong behavior will ruin us. And I mean to put a stop to it before you wind up carrying Benson's bastard child." He stared at the remnants of the liquid in his glass. "Stephen Fisher has asked for your hand once more. I've accepted his proposal on your behalf."

Ginger's hands clenched. "I'll be dead before I marry that man, Father."

"You may not believe it, but this is not my wish." The glass clinked against the decanter as her father poured himself another drink. "You should have married that doctor while you had a chance. Maybe then you could have tempered your base desires. But you've put me in a hopeless position. You're a sullied woman who insists on carrying on with that disgusting rake. After this, no one will have you. Your marriage to Stephen will solve many of our problems."

"Our problems?" She stared at him, mouth agape.

"Yes. Your behavior is threatening the union of your brother to the Fisher girl. Among other things. Now, you'll marry Stephen and that will be the end of it."

She ripped the glass from his hand before he could drink it and splashed the contents in his face. He barely flinched. "How dare you? How dare you treat me like a concubine you can sell to the highest bidder?" Whiskey dripped from her father's nose, but he stayed fixed in place, his breathing angry, like a bull about to gore her. She summoned her strength and stepped closer to him, despite her fear. "I'm not afraid of defying you. I won't marry him. Stephen is manipulating you, and you're turning a blind eye to it. And Henry too."

Her father fished out a handkerchief and wiped his face. "I told you to stay away from Noah Benson. I told you—"

"You told me a pack of lies," she said through clenched teeth. "You're clearly in over your head, Father. Is it the finances? Is that's what this is all about?" She slammed the whisky glass against the desk. "How much money do you owe Stephen Fisher?"

With a red face, her father stepped away. "Stop meddling, Virginia."

She'd struck a nerve. Of course, it had to be why her father protected Stephen. Stephen was his creditor. She dropped the level of her voice. "You must owe him a great deal if you're willing to betray your country and sell him your *daughter*."

Sagging into his chair, her father avoided her gaze. "My priority has always been keeping our family, and its name, intact. Unless you'd like to see your mother and sister penniless and disenfranchised, you would do well to remember your loyalties. You're risking everything we own."

The weight of his words battered against the bravado she'd managed during their conversation, and her legs went weak. This was worse than she'd imagined. She'd known Stephen was a miscreant and manipulator. But it was far more serious than that. Her pathetic, weak father had given Stephen the power to destroy them.

CHAPTER TWENTY-EIGHT

*G*inger sat at her vanity, pinning her hair. She sighed at her reflection. She couldn't hide the worry on her face or the exhaustion. Two cups of tea at breakfast hadn't been enough to clear her scattered thoughts.

A maid appeared in her doorway. "Lady Victoria Everill here to see you, my lady."

Ginger stiffened. What could Victoria possibly want with her? "Where is she?"

"In the foyer."

"I'll be down directly." She'd dressed plainly, in a simple lace blouse and long blue gored skirt. It would have to do.

Voices filtered from the bottom of the staircase. Lucy had apparently already received Victoria. Excitement resonated in her voice. "… you must stay for tea. Bahiti, please have tea set for us outside on the verandah. It's such a glorious morning."

When she neared the bottom of the stairs, Ginger cleared her throat.

Both Lucy and Victoria turned their heads. Victoria was dressed immaculately, her hat and gloves still on.

"Isn't it lovely that Victoria came to visit us?" Lucy grasped Victoria by the forearm. "Is that a yes to the tea?"

Victoria watched Ginger. "If you'll permit me."

"Of course." Ginger led Lucy and Victoria outside. The heat sweltered as they sat at a wicker table. A servant rushed out with a tea service.

"You have a charming house." Victoria's voice was soft.

"Thank you, it's so exotic—different from what we're used to, but I'm sure you understand." Lucy seemed oblivious. "I can't wait to return to England. The conditions here are barely tolerable. Ginny abandoned me yesterday at the Khan at the dingiest place. Fortunately, your friend Lieutenant Darby came along and kept me company until she returned. I'd never be afraid like that back home."

Victoria pulled her gloves off and set them on her lap. "And you, Lady Virginia? Are you as eager to go back?"

"Not at all. I'm afraid I'm not as attached to home as my sister is." A servant came to the table and poured them each a cup of steaming hot tea. "You seem to be content here in Egypt."

"Life abroad suits me." Victoria glanced at Lucy. "Lucy, you mentioned earlier a hat you'd purchased at the Khan yesterday. Would you be a dear and fetch it? I'd love to see it."

Delight filled Lucy's face. "Of course."

Ginger remembered the way her mother had sent Lucy on a mindless errand when she'd first arrived. Lucy had been aware but didn't make such a happy show of it. Her desire to please and impress Victoria went deep.

Victoria's eyes followed Lucy as she disappeared. "I haven't been entirely forthcoming about why I've called."

Ginger shifted in her seat. Lifting her teacup, she kept her hand steady. "To what do I owe the honor?"

A grimace came to Victoria's delicate mouth. "I'd call it an unwelcome chore." Victoria opened her handbag and pulled out a folded newspaper. She slid it toward Ginger. "Have you seen today's society pages?"

Ginger hesitated. Her eyes drifted to the garden. A pair of bare feet hung over the side of the gazebo. *Khalib.* Noah had sent him, after all. As glad as it made her, she looked away. Surely Victoria would know who Khalib was? What would she think if she saw him here?

Ginger unfolded the newspaper. Her heart lurched. A long gossip column bore her name. She scanned the article, which told a sordid account of her discharge from nursing and disappearance in the desert with Noah. It even mentioned Port Said. The blood drained from her face, and she forced her gaze over the edge of the paper to Victoria's awaiting stare.

It had to have been Stephen. Fury rippled through her.

Victoria reclined into her chair, the timbre of her voice dropping. "Is it true?"

Ginger couldn't keep the paper from fluttering with the shaking of her hand. She set it down. "Don't be ridiculous."

"Ridiculous?" Victoria's eyes flashed. "It's ridiculous to ask the woman who's accused of bedding my fiancé if the accusation has any merit? Wouldn't you want to know?"

"I suppose it would depend on how much I trusted my fiancé."

Victoria smirked. "He's a man, isn't he? Even an excellent one can be tempted to stray by a pretty face with dishonorable intentions." Victoria sat straighter. "We're women of the world, Lady Virginia—don't pretend otherwise. Neither of us has got where we want in life by holding on to virginal platitudes. You know as well as I our sex is our advantage in this world of men."

Ginger's face flushed, but Victoria's words brought her a strange sense of calm. It tempted Ginger to confess the truth. Victoria deserved the truth and wasn't afraid of it. She focused her attention on a bee balancing on a rose near them. "Speak for yourself. I'm a nurse. And a lady. What happened in the desert is top secret and I can't share any details. I suggest you take your questions to your fiancé. He's in a much better position to answer you than I am."

"If it were possible, I would have. But he's already left on an assignment." Victoria set her mouth to a thin line. Victoria leaned forward. "What would you expect a woman in my position to do? The man I know would never throw away his good name and risk scandal to me like this. Frankly, this seems absurd. Why would he vanish into the deserts of Palestine with you?"

The seconds crept by. Ginger's eyes darted to the door. She prayed for Lucy's return. "You're assuming it's true. The real truth is that someone is angry I won't marry him and attempting to retaliate."

"By besmirching you?" Victoria rested her chin on her hand. "Regardless, Noah pretended the other night he hardly recognized you, and that's a lie. And there was your behavior, ogling him at every glance. Drinking like a sodden fool."

Ginger pushed her chair back and stood. She would love to slap the smirk from Victoria's face. It wouldn't be worth it though.

"You're incorrect in what you think you observed. And if you think you can enter my house and insult me and I'll lie down and take it, you're sorely mistaken. No matter who your father is." Ginger smoothed her hands on her skirt. "Please leave."

"No, but you lay down and took it from him like a common whore, didn't you? Noah and I are engaged." Victoria banged her teacup against the table. A piece of porcelain chipped off the bottom and skidded against the tabletop. "And this isn't a private matter anymore. I'm humiliated by this gossip. My father is already working to undo what he can, but the truth is important to me."

What Ginger had done was horrible, but she could never admit it. "I owe you no further explanation. Good day, Lady Victoria."

Victoria rose with the grace and poise of a prima ballerina. "There's a dearth of women who advance the causes of our gender. It's a shame—I thought you were one who did." She set both hands on the table and leaned closer. The scent of her expensive perfume diffused from the smooth skin of her neck. "Stay away from my fiancé. You haven't the slightest idea what I'm willing to do to keep him from distractions."

Victoria stormed into the house, her heels clicking against the floor.

Shame filled Ginger. She had never intended the infidelity. But even the day before, she'd kissed Noah. Ginger pressed her hand against her chest. "Damn him."

Whatever the circumstances, she must forget him. Any dream she held on to needed extinguishing. No matter the hope Noah had given her. She couldn't live like this.

If someone had hammered a spike into her heart, it would have been less painful.

Lucy materialized beside her, a floral hat in her hands. Her face was pale. "What did you do?"

Ginger smirked. "I thought you were getting a hat?"

"How long do you think it takes to get a hat?" The paleness in her face transformed to an angry red. "Answer me!" She glanced at the opened paper and read the headline. "Is this true?"

She couldn't tell Lucy about why she'd vanished into the desert. The burden of that information was too much for her to bear. Ginger met her gaze squarely. "Yes."

Lucy buried her face in her hand. When she lowered it, tears brimmed. Lucy threw the hat at her. "You've ruined everything. Everything! Victoria will never be friends with me now."

"And you need her friendship?"

"Yes." Lucy's voice echoed against the high ceiling of the porch. She stamped her foot. "Don't you care? No, of course not. Oh, no, no, no. Everyone will know within a few hours." She grabbed the soiled serviette and threw it at Ginger.

Ginger peeled the serviette from the floor and folded it. "I do care."

"Stop." Lucy's voice came out in a screech. "You think you're so superior to me because you caught lice and bandaged wounds and ate hard biscuits. But you're not better than me. I have helped. We can't all be nurses, Ginny. Stop being so arrogant and pretending you're a saint." Lucy waved the newspaper at her. "This proves what a hypocrite you are You don't care about family loyalty."

Ginger took her sister's hands. "Lucy. Look at me. No, please, for a moment."

Lucy's watery brown eyes met hers.

"Loyalty for the sake of loyalty can be the most dishonest concept you ever encounter—"

Lucy let go of her hands. "Don't patronize me. You're an imbecile." She glowered down her pert nose at Ginger. "I'm proud of who I am. I'm happy with my life. I don't desire to be anything else."

"It's not about that. I don't begrudge the life our parents gave us or the world we were born into. But I want more from life."

"What? To be a tramp? Is this why Father has us chaperoning you everywhere?" Lucy gave her a sharp look.

Ginger couldn't find the words to speak, stunned at Lucy's ability to put on a façade. She wasn't as flighty as she frequently appeared. At last she said, "I don't want to pretend the family name is above all else. I won't be complicit."

Lucy stood and shrugged. "Don't be. If you're so tired of pretending, as you claim, stop. You're the only one who is."

The door to the house slammed in Lucy's wake.

Ginger sank into a chair and propped her elbows on the tabletop. Covering her face with her hands, she gulped for air.

She lifted her head at the echo of footsteps. Henry held a glass in his hand, a decanter in the other. After pouring himself a drink, he set the decanter by his well-polished shoes and sauntered toward Ginger, stumbling in his steps.

She stiffened and kept her gaze level with the garden beside her. How much had he overheard of the fiasco with Victoria and Lucy?

Henry stopped beside the table. After helping himself to a scone, he sat.

Ginger surveyed him. "Are you drunk?"

"A smidge." His eyes appeared red-rimmed. "You seem distressed."

She needed a good cry, but now wasn't the time. "It's not even noon."

His green eyes were unblinking. "Does it matter?" He finished his drink. "How would you proceed if you learned one of your dearest friends lied to you and betrayed your family … but defiled your sister, also?"

She recoiled. A lump rose in her throat. "Henry—"

Henry squinted. "You answered Lady Victoria's questions with care and intelligence. Impressively. But you can't fool me. I know where he took you yesterday. And when I told Father, he told me about Port Said."

Henry had followed her in the Khan? "That's not fair. I love him. And you owe him some loyalty rather than being so offended on my behalf. I would be dead if it weren't for him, and it would be on your shoulders."

Henry lifted the empty glass, stared at the inside, and plunked it down. "He's dead to me."

Ginger stood. "Don't you dare lecture me. You think I'm naïve enough to believe you haven't had indiscretions of your own?"

"I have never brought scandal and ruin to our family so publicly."

"It isn't me who has brought ruin to our family. This is Stephen's doing, I'm sure of it. Only he knew these details. Only he would want to use such a disgusting form of manipulation to force me into marrying him. As though I would ever agree to it."

Henry's lips curled in a snarl. "But you're every bit the whore you claim Stephen outed you to be. Don't be a fool. You should be on your knees thanking Stephen for being willing to offer you marriage knowing what he knows about you. You're fortunate he loves you as much as he does. And you'll marry him if I have to hold a gun to your head."

Fury twisted Ginger's stomach. "You're drunk, Henry. So I'll forgive the comment. But just this once. Don't dare ever threaten me again."

"Do you have any idea what you've done?" Henry's cheeks grew redder. "I received a letter from Angelica this morning. Her father has forbidden her to marry me!"

A maid hurried outside, toward Ginger.

"Captain James Clark is here to see you, my lady."

Ginger's brows furrowed. What on earth could James possibly be doing here? His timing couldn't be worse. "Have him await me in the parlor. I'll be there directly."

Whatever James had traveled so far for must be important, but she dreaded his visit right now. A stiff drink, maybe. A tête-à-tête with her former fiancé, no.

As the maid left, Ginger turned toward Henry. "You should

sleep. Before you say or do anything else that could harm our relationship."

Henry stood unsteadily. "I don't know what to believe about you anymore, little sister. But you're not the person I once thought."

She raised her chin. Gone was the confidant she'd always trusted. She should have known better when he'd left her to fend for herself with Ahmed. She'd given him the benefit of the doubt. No more.

"And neither are you."

Footsteps interrupted them once more. Angelica rushed outside. Her cheeks were tear-stained, her nose red. She fumbled, pausing when she saw Ginger. Her eyes narrowed, fury in her expression, then she turned her attention to Henry.

"Henry!" Angelica brushed past Ginger and embraced him, sobbing. "What are we going to do?"

Ginger backed away. She didn't want to feel responsible for this. Not when Stephen had caused it all. Yet the lengths he was willing to go to disturbed her. What wouldn't Stephen do to get what he wanted?

* * *

GINGER OPENED the door to the parlor, her composure shaken. After Victoria's inquiry, Lucy's fury, Henry's drunkenness, and Angelica's despair, a visit from James seemed fitting. She needed one more person to spit on her, surely.

James scrambled from his seat on the sofa.

Crossing the room with as much dignity as she could muster, she stopped several feet away. "James. How can I help you?"

James pulled his glasses from his face and rubbed the bridge of his nose. "Ginger, I—" He replaced his glasses and dropped his hands to his sides. "I had to come. I needed to see you." He bent and lifted a kitbag. "I brought that bag you requested Beatrice send to you, but she also told me the truth. You were sent away because of the aid we gave—"

Ginger held out her hand. "Don't speak of it," she hissed. Was it possible one thing had worked out the way it should? It seemed too easy to be true. She scanned the room. Her father was out of the house, at work, but it felt as though he was still watching her. A lump rose in her throat. "You haven't the slightest idea how thankful I am to you."

Redness crept into his cheeks. "I don't deserve your thanks. I owe you an apology. What I did to you was unforgivable. No matter how angry I was. I behaved abominably."

She hadn't expected this. Sitting on an armchair, she maintained her composure. "Would you like to sit?"

James nodded and took a seat at the armchair beside hers. For the first time, it occurred to Ginger what an odd, stiff arrangement these parlor rooms had. All the formality befitting the people who sat in them. Guests kept at arm's length, in uncomfortable furniture, meant for upright, tense postures—a world of difference from the way the Bedouins had received Noah and her in the desert.

"I—"

She put a hand on his wrist to stop him from humiliating himself. "You deserve to know the truth. If you don't hear it from me, you'll see it in the papers soon enough, regardless."

He clasped his hands. "I already saw the article in today's paper, actually."

And he'd still apologized? She blinked at him, stunned.

He offered an embarrassed, taut smile. "Once I had some distance from my hurt, I realized what an absolute ass I'd been. After you failed to return to the clearing station, I was in a panic and didn't allow myself to be rational. It occurred to me later several flaws existed in Captain Fisher's account, foremost being why he would have known about the supposed romantic rendezvous. If it had been true, you wouldn't have entrusted him with that information. And Benson wouldn't have been likely to tell him either."

Did that mean he didn't believe the account of Port Said from the paper? She drew her hand away from him. "Why didn't you give me a chance to explain myself to you?"

"Jealousy." He looked out the window of the parlor, where bright light trickled in, filling the room with the spring Egyptian heat. "I'd heard whispers of Benson's attentions to you. I'm accustomed to seeing other men admire you. But then I saw the way you looked at him."

"The way I looked at him?" A chortle left her.

He fidgeted with his glasses. "It's difficult to explain. But it's the way I always wished you'd look at me." James bowed his head. "The awful truth is I'd seen the light go out of your eyes whenever we spoke of our wedding. I blamed the war, thinking all would be well once we were away from the carnage of hospital work. But that wasn't it, was it?"

He asked for an honest response, his gaze earnest. She didn't want to hurt him, though, despite what he'd done to her. "It was complicated, James. But I had every intention of marrying you."

"You just weren't in love with me." He spoke in a soft, firm tone.

This wasn't the best conversation to have in her emotional state. But he'd acted with remarkable grace now and that counted for something. Her shoulders bunched. She didn't need to confess everything. But allowing him to think he'd been irrational wasn't fair either. "James, that story in the society pages—"

"It's my fault it got that far. If I had defended your honor when I should have, I could have put a stop to the gossip." He tapped the kitbag he'd given her. "And whatever Ahmed involved you in—I'm partially responsible too. We took a tremendous risk in helping him, and then I allowed you to endure the consequences alone. I have every intention of offering my confession about my role in the matter after this."

"Don't." She sat straighter, alarmed. "No one can know. Say nothing." The nervous feeling someone might overhear came over her again. "Everything he told us was true, I'm certain of it. But there are people who want to discredit him."

He searched her eyes. "Listen, I've been musing about it this morning. I don't deserve another chance, but I'd like to think of myself as more honorable than having left you in such an awful position. Especially now that I know Benson is engaged to someone else. I know you couldn't serve with the Queen Alexandra's if you married me, but the Red Cross doesn't care if you're married or not. I still want to marry you. If you'll have me. I love you. I'll transfer to the Red Cross, and we could serve together."

He was proposing? *Again?*

Ginger held her breath. James wasn't offering her marriage. He was offering her freedom.

But she didn't love him. Her heart belonged to Noah.

And he planned to marry Victoria, despite it.

She buried her face in her hands, her thoughts unclear.

James shifted. "You don't have to answer right now. I've done irreparable damage to you. But I would never forgive myself if I didn't ask. I need your forgiveness."

James wouldn't be saying any of this if he knew the truth about her relationship with Noah. Would he forgive her so easily if he knew? "I forgive you, but I must give it some thought."

He nodded. "I should have—"

She touched his arm. "We both made mistakes." She couldn't

allow him to torture himself over what had happened. Especially not after the way she'd behaved with Noah in the desert.

James produced Ahmed's bag from his kitbag. "Everything you asked for is here. It never left my tent." He turned it over in his hands. "I considered giving it to the authorities, but that was the one place my anger with you worked to the advantage—I didn't want to have to answer any questions about my involvement with the matter. Then Beatrice told me of your message."

Ginger took the bag and stared at the tan leather. Dark bloodstains streaked the cover—Ahmed's blood. The bag offered hope. Maybe she could finally bring justice to his death and atone for her actions.

But what to do with its contents? She needed to send Noah another message.

Khalib was in the garden. She could easily write a quick note to Noah and ask him to meet her. Sending Ahmed's bag would be too risky. But hopefully Noah would forgive her for asking for yet another meeting when he saw what she'd obtained.

Her optimism must have shown in her face. James smiled. "Did I do the right thing in bringing this to you?"

She nodded tearfully and hugged him, despite the awkwardness of the space between them. "Thank you."

James returned her embrace. "I hope you know I'll do anything to prove to you how much I care for you."

"I do." A heavy feeling weighed her down. Stephen had put her in an impossible situation. Here she was, three years later, faced with marriage proposals from the same two men. Fate had a funny way of bringing the situation full circle.

When she'd accepted James's offer last time, though, she hadn't been fully aware of what she'd agreed to. This time she knew. "And I will consider your offer," she added. How could she reject him when Noah offered her nothing?

Warmth shone in his gaze. "I can't stay long. But if you'd do me the honor of taking tea with me, I'd love to take you out to a café before I board the train to Palestine."

Going out right now could do further damage to her reputation—or prove to curious individuals she would face the scandal with the bravest face possible. She smiled.

"That would be lovely."

CHAPTER TWENTY-NINE

The steady clopping of horse hooves against cobblestones had almost lulled Ginger to sleep as the hired calishe driver pulled up in front of the Whitman home. She startled at the stop and glanced out of the carriage. Two men in waistcoats and hats stood near the front gate. She frowned. Newspapermen? They had that look about them.

She adjusted her hat and leaned toward the driver, directing him to drive to the back of the house. Whoever they were, she had no desire to talk to anyone. Apparently news traveled fast in Cairo high society. She'd had enough for the afternoon.

After paying the driver, she climbed out of the compartment and unlocked the gate. She hurried to the kitchen door. The smell of grease reached her as she let herself in. The servants, preparing supper, turned in surprise, straightening and bowing their heads. She greeted them with a smile, unable to remember the last time she'd come into the kitchens. She didn't even know their names.

The desperate feeling she'd fought to keep at bay reared its head, a lump forming in her throat.

She found refuge outside the kitchen, as the door closed behind her, and leaned into a wall of the dark hallway.

Where were those feelings of bold independence now?

As a publicly shamed unmarried woman, she couldn't expect to find work as a nurse—or in any other capacity. She could assume an alias, but she would live in the constant shadow of her past, a past that wouldn't be able to include her family.

Stephen had played the game of manipulation masterfully, and she felt like a lowly pawn being checked at every turn. No wonder her father and Henry had capitulated to him. He threatened everything they held most dear.

She touched her throat, feeling choked. Her hair was damp at her neck under her hat. She peeled it off and fanned her face with the brim. James's generous offer was made under the assumption of her innocence. Each moment she'd spent with him during the afternoon, the weight of her guilt grew stronger. She'd already used an engagement to him as an escape once, and it hadn't been fair to either of them. Could she truly be considering it? Had she learned nothing?

She composed herself and went up the back staircase toward the main level. She tiptoed through the house, not wanting to alert her family to her return. If the men outside the house were there because of her, her family would have an earful for her—and she still didn't know how to face her mother.

Hushed but emphatic voices came from her father's office as she passed. Her parents were arguing. She paused, her heart quickening.

"—and she won't. You know she won't. You can't do this, Edmund. You will drive her away from us forever," her mother said, her voice impassioned.

"What choice do I have? The man's boot is on my neck. And what he wants—what he's always wanted—is her."

"Well, you can't force this. What's the plan? Drug her and

drag her to the consulate? Invent some other scandal to control her? You saw what she did this afternoon. She went right through that door, behaving as though she couldn't care less. Ginger knows and follows her own mind."

Ginger's pulse pounded in her ears. She'd heard her parents argue about her before. But something about this felt different and more frantic.

"What would you have me do? What can I do?" A floorboard creaked as her father paced. "I've held him off as long as I can. But he's aware that I know Lawrence's location now—I had a meeting this morning with Sir Mark Sykes. Lawrence is heading out to the desert, and he'll be vulnerable. The timing couldn't be more perfect for Stephen's man."

Her mother's next words were inaudible as Ginger's mind raced. Captain T. E. Lawrence? What did he have to do with anything? And, more painfully, her mother appeared to know of her father's conflicted loyalties. Ginger strained to hear, edging closer to the door.

"... no assurances. You truly believe he won't go right back to his plans once he has what he wants? You're taking the word of a liar. A traitor." Her mother sounded tearful. "He's playing this to his advantage because he knows you'll do anything to stop it. Please, Edmund. You can't. Arabia will survive without T. E. Lawrence. He's such a minor part of the larger puzzle."

Ginger felt ill. Lawrence was in danger. It had to be the assassination Ahmed had mentioned. The Maslukha must have directed Stephen to discover Lawrence's location so he could kill him.

"... she's a loyal servant of the Crown. If she knows the truth, she's likely to go along with Stephen's demands to stop it," her father said, his voice sharper.

"She won't go along with it. She won't marry him even if you told her it was the key to winning the entire war—"

"—well, it might be the key to the war—"

"—please, Edmund. I'm begging you. Let me take her and Lucy to Alexandria, until this blows over."

As her parents' argument grew more heated, Ginger cautiously stepped back from the door. The last thing she wanted was for her parents to know she'd overheard them. When she'd put sufficient space between herself and the door, she turned toward the staircase.

Lucy stood at the top of the stairs, her arms crossed.

Ginger jumped and steadied herself on the rail. Lucy couldn't know what her mother and father were arguing about —or have heard it. She needed to remain calm. Ginger started up the stairs.

"Where were you?" Lucy demanded as Ginger drew closer.

Ginger narrowed her eyes. "I went out. The details aren't your concern."

Lucy's mouth puckered and she called out in a loud voice, "Mother!"

Gritting her teeth, Ginger pushed past Lucy and continued down the hallway toward her room. She'd been carrying around a haversack with Ahmed's bag inside it all afternoon, too afraid to leave it out of her sight. She didn't want her father to come upstairs and demand to see what she was carrying.

She entered her room, leaving the door open, and set the haversack and her hat down on her vanity. Footsteps approached and her mother streamed into the room, Lucy at her heels. "Oh, Ginger, thank goodness." Her mother's eyes were red, her fair cheeks blotchy. Her unhappy expression made Ginger's heart skip a beat.

Ginger turned her back to the vanity. "Mother."

Her mother stopped short and drew herself straighter. She glanced at Lucy. "You should go."

"But, Mother—" Lucy began.

"Go."

Lucy's eyes flashed with anger and she left, slamming the door behind her.

Her mother waited until Lucy's footsteps faded before she spoke. "I spoke to your father. Apparently he caught you with Major Benson in Port Said?" Hurt showed in her face. "Where have you been? With him?"

The humiliation of being caught in a hotel room with Noah might never fade. "I haven't been with him. James came by to see me. He renewed his offer of marriage."

Her mother blinked. "And did you accept?"

Ginger shook her head. "I have to consider my options."

Her mother's jaw dropped. "You have no options. Major Benson is engaged, I understand. He's handsome and charming, but what you're being accused of is unacceptable. He came here looking for you this afternoon. I sent him away."

Noah had been here? She stared at her mother, shocked. If he'd come so openly, it must have been because of the note she'd sent with Khalib. He wouldn't have dared to risk coming to her house otherwise.

"Did he say when he'd return?"

Her mother squared her shoulders. "I told him not to. Ever again. I've made arrangements. We will travel to Alexandria in the morning. From there, I'll book us a trip on a liner to England. I won't risk you bringing further scandal to this family." Her mother frowned. "I shouldn't have let you go without my guidance for so long."

"I'm not going with you. Let me speak to Father." Ginger started toward the door. She needed to find Noah and give him Ahmed's bag. Not to mention tell him about what she'd overheard from her parents.

Her mother blocked her path. "Don't you dare. You think I don't know you've been meddling in things you shouldn't?

You're endangering us." She gave Ginger a pleading look. "Let your father handle this. Your father will take care of us, as he's always done."

"Let me pass. I'm not a child. It's Father I want to speak to."

"You're my daughter." Her mother grabbed her. "I forbid you to go anywhere."

Ginger had never seen her mother behave like this before. "What do you know?"

Her mother shook her head. "Your father is doing his best to save this family. He may not be going about it correctly, but he loves us and will do anything to keep our family and Penmore intact."

A wave of nausea passed through her. "You know the truth. About everything."

Her mother stared her down. Her gaze softened. "Your father has always come to me for counsel when he's troubled. What did you expect him to do, Ginger? The estate was failing, and your father made some unfortunate, risky investments that fell apart because of the war. Now he's up to his neck in debt to Stephen Fisher."

Tears formed in her eyes. "And I will not sacrifice you to that man. No matter what he says now, he won't release your father from his debt once you're married. I know it in my heart. He likes the power it gives him too much."

Ah. Stephen must have attempted to use that as a trump card. "Stephen agreed to release Father from his debts if I married him?" The words came out thick, acid scorching her throat.

"Yes. And you and I both know he's lying. I've spent the last half hour begging your father to tell him no and allow me to take you to Alexandria, and he finally agreed. Don't you dare let your conscience get the better of you now and contradict me."

Ginger's gaze shot to the door. If her father had agreed to her mother's plan, it had to mean he intended to give Stephen the means to find Captain Lawrence. Her father's rank and status made him privy to Lawrence's whereabouts. "Mother, no." She reached for her mother's hand. "Let me find Noah. He can help us."

Her mother's eyes narrowed. "Noah? You mean Major Benson?" She gaped at Ginger in disbelief. "You can't be seriously suggesting to me I allow you to go and look for your lover? What does he have to do with any of this?"

Ginger pressed her lips together. If her mother didn't know about Noah's role in the matter, she might know less than Ginger had initially assumed. Maybe her father had been wise enough not to involve her in every detail. Ginger dropped her hand to her side, limply. "Noah is an honorable man, Mother. And a loyal British servant. He loves me, I know he does, and he—"

Her mother grabbed her by the shoulders. "That man does *not* love you, Ginger. He's dishonored you. He's nothing more than a charlatan and a social climber who has used you. Tell me —has he promised to marry you? When we saw him in Shepheard's, he was only too glad to feign disinterest in you. I've always believed you were sensible. What's got into you?"

Before Ginger could answer, a knock at the door interrupted them. A maid opened it. "My lady"—she curtsied toward her mother—"Stephen Fisher is in the parlor. He's requesting an audience with both you and Lady Virginia."

Ginger and her mother exchanged a look. Her mother checked her appearance in a full-length mirror by the armoire. "Tell Captain Fisher I cannot receive any visitors this evening," she said, her face pale.

The maid looked uncomfortable. "I'm sorry, my lady. He told me to say he insists."

His audacity knew no bounds. The maid left, and a heavy silence settled between the two Whitman women. At last, her mother scowled. "Henry and Angelica are devastated by all this. I finally had to send the poor girl home—she didn't want to leave your brother. What a wretch Stephen has grown up to be."

Ginger went over to the vanity. She tucked the haversack into a drawer and turned toward her mother. "And if he demands I marry him?"

Her mother drew a sharp breath. "We will think of a solution together." She approached Ginger and gripped her hand fiercely. "We are a family. Families stand by each other during the most grueling times. I may not support your relationship with the major, but I love you and I won't surrender you to Stephen Fisher's demands either."

Ginger's throat tightened as she stared at her mother's blazing, passionate eyes. How could she be disloyal to her?

They left Ginger's room together. Ginger walked down the staircase, her thoughts reeling. Whatever Stephen wanted, it couldn't be good. Not now. He'd been a step ahead throughout, carefully making plans before they were aware. A man who could murder children without a second thought was evil. No matter what it took for her to avoid it, she would never marry him.

The butler opened the door to the parlor for them, and Ginger lifted her head in surprise. Stephen wasn't alone in the parlor. Henry and her father stood by the desk, but Lucy had settled into a settee comfortably, and Stephen sat across from her in conversation. Angry as she'd been with Lucy earlier, a flare of sisterly protectiveness came over her. *Stay away from her.*

Stephen stood and bowed his head. "Lady Elizabeth. Ginny. So terribly sorry to interrupt your evening."

Ginger held her tongue, not wanting to give away her loathing of Stephen to Lucy. Despite what her mother knew, she was certain Lucy remained unaware of the underhanded situation at play.

Fortunately her mother compensated for her lack of a graceful response. She smiled with the easiness and affection of a friend. "Stephen, darling. You know you're always welcome in our home." She kissed his cheek before sitting beside Lucy.

The change in her mother's demeanor did her credit. Ginger came up behind the settee, fascinated by the comfortable façade her mother adopted. Her mother wouldn't want to give away what she knew. She was a better actress than Ginger had ever realized.

Stephen's eyes flickered toward Ginger. He didn't sit again, his long fingertips fiddling with the button of his officer's jacket. "I've come in friendship." He stared at her father and Henry. "I know this must have been a tiresome day for you given ..."

Stephen broke off and cleared his throat. "I'll be away for the next few weeks, as Lord Braddock is well aware. But I'd like to offer my home in Luxor and Angelica's hospitality as a refuge to the Whitman women." He stared directly at Ginger now. "You know what I've always wished for us, Ginny, but at least allow me to offer you shelter during this hard time."

Ginger dug her fingertips into the damask fabric of the settee. "Thank you." She wanted to grab a vase from the nearby end table and throw it at him. "But I think my mother has already planned for us to go to Alexandria."

"Alexandria's such a bore right now." Stephen's pale-blue eyes moved to Lucy's face, as though he understood where to appeal. "And Angelica could use some company. She'd be thrilled to have you ladies join her on a trip down the Nile in our boat. The weather right now is perfect for it. All four of you will need a break from the gossip."

Ginger doubted Angelica would want to be around her at all
—not after the way she'd looked at Ginger earlier that day.

Lucy turned toward her mother. "Oh, wouldn't it be a lovely
idea, Mother?"

"Indeed." Her mother smiled at her youngest daughter. "But
Ginger's right. The plans are in motion for us to go to
Alexandria."

"I'm certain Lord Braddock can rearrange those plans."
Stephen gave her father a firm look. "For the happiness of his
wife and daughters."

Ginger flinched, and watched her father and Henry.
Stephen's threat was obvious enough to her—they must have
understood it also. Stephen wasn't asking. He demanded the
Whitman women go with him.

"This is an uncertain, fearful time for your family, I'm sure. I
want to offer you ladies the safety of my household during these
next few weeks. Your every need will be attended to. I would
never dream of sending you on a journey without well-trained
escorts to protect you. And you can leave this evening."

Her father shifted and glanced at Henry, who paled.

This wasn't an invitation to a holiday but a kidnapping.

One more way to control her father.

Something had made Stephen determined to take control of
the situation. Given the tension in her father and Henry's
postures, they hadn't expected it. What had happened?

Her father and Henry's cowardice had never been so obvious
to her before. Ginger's knuckles turned white as she gripped the
settee. She'd seen Henry passionately defend his family before.
In fact, whatever Ahmed had told Henry had been enough for
Henry to prefer Ahmed dead than permit him to injure their
family.

But now? Both Henry and her father seemed weak,
frightened.

Ginger didn't hear the discussion between Lucy and her mother and Stephen. Her mother, God love her, continued to act with charm.

Ginger doubted Stephen would take no for an answer. If so, she wouldn't be able to get the information James had brought from Ahmed to Noah. She couldn't trust her father or Henry with it.

A strong gust of wind diverted her attention to the window outside the parlor, where a palm's fronds tossed and bent in the fading light of day.

If the documents in her possession would lead Noah to the Maslukha, maybe Stephen could be stopped. She didn't know if she was too late to do much about the plans the Maslukha had to kill T.E. Lawrence, but if the Maslukha was on the run, maybe he would tell Stephen to cancel the plan. And that was if Noah and the CID knew Lawrence was the target. They might not know. The information was too sensitive for her to trust anyone but Noah with it.

But her family was at Stephen's mercy.

She couldn't look at her father and Henry. Not now. They might read her expression and guess she understood what was happening.

She stared at Lucy. Despite her vanity and selfishness, Lucy wasn't what Ginger had expected upon her return from the front. Thank goodness she didn't know about any of this. Ignorance wasn't bliss, but in this case it was safety.

And her mother, at least, could keep pretending as long as necessary.

"I'll go." Ginger's voice cut into the conversation.

Stephen, who had been mid-sentence, stopped and stared at her.

"I think it would be good for us to go. If Mother and Lucy are so inclined." Ginger smiled tautly.

"Really?" Lucy's face brightened. "You want to go?"

"Of course, goose. I know how difficult this has been." Ginger ruffled her fingertips through the top of Lucy's hair. She wished she could apologize to her. To all of them. But she kept her gaze fixed on Lucy, feeling as though she might break if she didn't. "But I should go and pack my things, if we're to go tonight."

She smiled at Lucy and found her way out of the room. Though she didn't look back, she sensed Stephen's eyes on her. Goose bumps rose on her arms. She had to act. Now.

CHAPTER THIRTY

Once in her room, Ginger rushed to her vanity. She yanked the haversack out of the drawer. Her heart pounded as she checked for Ahmed's bag. At the sight of the bloodstained cover, she breathed a sigh of relief, her hands shaking.

She needed a way out. Slinging the haversack over her shoulder, she went to her nursing trunk and pulled out a few supplies. A change of clothes, a medical kit, a toothbrush, and some toiletries. She kicked off her dress shoes and traded them for more sensible desert boots.

She sped to the window and let herself outside onto the balcony. The warm, humid air of the evening made an instant sweat break out on her skin. She put her hands on the rail and hoisted herself up onto it. She swung her legs over to the other side and grasped the rail, the metal digging into her palms. Her feet found the narrow ledge of the balcony. She balanced her weight against the rail and squatted.

The time for thinking about action was over. She needed to leave, before anyone checked on her.

Two stories below her were the gardens, but she couldn't get down there. A fall from here could be deadly.

She couldn't make it to the next balcony, the one belonging to Lucy's room. Below her, the dining room windows gave no easy entrance.

Hands aching, she moved to the side of the balcony and grabbed the wall. A short ledge, a few inches in length, provided an architectural frame to the top of the dining room window. A palm tree on the other side of the window would be strong enough for Ginger to shimmy down, but crossing the ledge would be treacherous.

She had no choice.

Bracing herself against the wall, she climbed onto the ledge on the tips of her toes. One hand held the rail. She straightened and pushed her full weight against the wall.

Sliding her foot to the left, she reached her left arm out as far as she could before bringing her right foot to join the left one. She swayed, barely holding her balance. An ache in the palms of her hands increased as they broke out into a slick sweat.

Her arms and toes stung with each repetition as she wobbled her way across the ledge. She pressed her face against the stone façade. She couldn't look back. Any movement away from the wall could tip her over.

She gritted her teeth as an insect flitted by her face.

Sucking in short, shallow breaths, she moved across the ledge until the tree was within reach. Putting her weight on her right shoulder, she lifted her shaking left hand away from the wall. Her fingers stretched, trying to find a handhold.

Only centimeters from her goal, her feet slipped from the ledge. She threw her weight toward the tree. A sensation of panic zoomed through her as she fell toward it and her hand found a rough, jagged edge of the bark. She wedged herself against the tree and the wall, resting her forehead against the trunk.

Descending was difficult, but not as hard as crossing the ledge had been. Invigorated, she ignored the scratches on her arms and legs, thankful for her boots.

Finally, her feet landed in the grass with a dull thud. She made her way across the courtyard to the back of the house. She'd leave the way she'd come in—through the servants' gate. No doubt Stephen's motorcar waited in the front.

She opened the gate. She didn't know where she was going or how to find Noah, but she couldn't stay here. She prayed her family would forgive her. It might be the only way to save them from Stephen.

She stepped into the street and raced across the road.

A block down, a motorcar roared to life and careened from the curb. The motorcar barreled toward her.

Her mind slowly processed the vehicle's intentional direction. The howling clamor of the engine accelerating forced her into motion, at last. She sprang to the side, the car narrowly missing her. The driver stepped on the brakes, and the tires squealed as the car slowed.

Someone had tried to hit her with a motorcar.

Someone wanted to kill her.

Sweat broke out on the back of her neck, and her mouth went dry as her near brush with death became clearer. Had Stephen ordered an attack if she tried to flee?

Another car thundered across the street. It plowed into the driver's side door of the first car with a hideous screech of metal. Broken glass peppered the sidewalk like rain. Inside the car, the body of the man who had attacked her bounced like a rag doll against the windshield, blood splattering the spiderweb formation on the glass. She gasped in horror.

The second car backed away, then stopped beside her.

Jack Darby sat in the driver's seat. "Get in."

Ginger stared at the car that had nearly hit her. The driver sprawled against the steering wheel.

"If you'd prefer to take your chances with the fellow who tried to run you over, by all means." Jack motioned toward the wrecked car. Was he with British intelligence? He must be.

Her legs barely carried her as she edged toward his car, numb and shaking. She opened the passenger side door and climbed inside.

Jack started driving before she could shut the door. The quick movement threw her. She steadied herself on the dash. "Good Lord!"

"Sorry about that."

"Someone tried to kill me." Her trembling hands were icy with shock.

"I saw. Same car that brought Stephen Fisher to your door, coincidentally."

Then, Stephen had ordered it.

Her pulse didn't normalize, but she tried to slow her breathing. "What's going on, Jack? Where's Noah?" How was it Jack came by at the right moment?

"I'm taking you to him. He's had me watching your house all evening." Jack smiled at her. "That was an impressive escape you made from your balcony. Didn't want to use the old-fashioned front door?"

"If it had been that simple, I would have." She didn't intend to sound irritated, but the tone was there, regardless.

"Fair enough."

A few minutes later, the car slowed. A gated house loomed before them. "Whose house is this?"

"Lord Helton. He's been holding Noah here the last few hours."

He'd brought her to Victoria's house? She hadn't realized

how close Victoria lived to her, but many of the wealthy families in Cairo lived in the tight-knit European quarter. Much as she wanted to trust Jack, the last thing she wanted was to confront Victoria's anger again tonight. "Holding him?" Captive?

A servant opened the gate.

Jack avoided her gaze. "Noah's not himself. I'll let him explain."

His phrasing was ominous. Wouldn't Victoria object to her being here? Especially today, of all days. "But what about Victoria?"

"She's here too." Jack pulled in front of the main door to the house and stopped the car. "Don't worry. She's not as bad as you think."

Not as bad as she thought? She was the fiancée of the man she was in love with. That was bad enough without the backdrop of their confrontation earlier in the day. But a man's life was at stake. Her feelings about Victoria didn't matter in comparison. She had to focus.

Jack slid out of the driver's side and came around for her. He helped her stand and led her to the front door, which opened. A butler greeted Jack and stepped aside.

Ginger summoned her strength as she followed Jack into the dim foyer. Yellow lights threw a warm glow onto the black-and-white checkered tile. A taxidermic lion menaced them from the end of the hallway.

Voices echoed from a distant room. Footsteps approached. Ginger's heart lurched at the sight of Noah as he entered the hall. His pace quickened, and he came toward her.

Noah enveloped Ginger into his arms. "Thank God you're safe." His voice was a fierce whisper.

She wanted to melt into his embrace. But why would he hug her with such ease in this place, so close to Victoria? She stiffened at the sound of light footsteps. Victoria stood in the doorway. Ginger pulled away from Noah.

"Good evening, Lady Virginia." Victoria glided down the hall.

Ginger lifted her hand and smoothed a flyaway hair. "Good evening."

"Bixby, please prepare the Blue Room for Lady Virginia. I think she'll be joining us tonight," Victoria told the butler.

Joining them? How would Victoria possibly know Ginger had nowhere to go? Her frigid anger appeared well-restrained. What was going on?

The butler bowed and left them. Victoria gave Ginger a studious look. "Would you like a servant to draw a bath for you?"

"Much as I appreciate your hospitality, Lady Victoria, I need to talk to Major Benson right away."

"I'll have supper sent to your room." Victoria squeezed Noah's forearm. "Lieutenant Darby, can you have Carla take Lady Virginia to her room? Have her draw a bath. I'll send some clothes." She disappeared down the hallway.

Her words made Ginger squirm. Leave it to Victoria to make her feel dirty. Jack slipped away, leaving her alone with Noah.

"Noah, I need to tell you something urgently."

He pressed a kiss to her forehead. "I'll find you."

"No!" She grabbed his hand. "It's T. E. Lawrence. He's the target of the Maslukha's assassination plot. He's in danger."

Noah scanned her gaze, alarm in his face. "Are you certain?"

She nodded. "Please don't leave me. There's more I need to tell you." She braced herself against the wall beside her.

"I have to." Noah squeezed her hand. "You're safe here, I promise."

She'd escaped. Hopefully she'd done something good. But despite his assurances, guilt and fear clawed at her insides.

CHAPTER THIRTY-ONE

*T*he moon waxed brightly overhead while Ginger watched it from the window, sleep evading her. Two in the morning and no sign of Noah.

She shivered in her nightgown and pulled a shawl tighter around her shoulders. He wasn't coming tonight. With a sigh, she blew out the candle. She turned and startled, covering her mouth with a gasp. Noah's shadowed figure leaned against her bed.

"If you don't want me to get the wrong impression, you shouldn't stand in the moonlight dressed like that." Noah nodded toward the window. "Pull the curtain shut."

Her heart leapt at the sight of him, a warm flush spreading through her. She did as he instructed and lifted the candle. "When did you get here? You scared me." She fumbled with the matches. They spilled out of the matchbox, tumbling onto the rug.

Noah took the matchbox from her and lit one. "Only a moment ago. Ironically, I didn't want to startle you by coming up behind you."

"I need to talk to you." At his nearness, she stopped, frowned. The heady scent of whisky was on his breath, his neck was corded tightly. Lines creased his forehead. Much as everything she wanted to tell him made her head feel as if it would burst, she sensed his disquiet too strongly to say anything. "Are you all right?"

His eyes were red-rimmed.

"Khalib is in the hospital. Stephen Fisher beat and butchered him." The muscles in his arms flexed.

She stifled a cry. The note she'd given Khalib—oh no. *That* was what had happened with Stephen. It explained his sudden appearance and determination to gain control of the situation.

Noah's voice tightened as he wiped his eyes. "His left hand was so badly mangled the doctors had to amputate it."

She covered her mouth, feeling sick. The thought was horrific. Would he ever forgive her when she admitted her fault?

"After I got him to hospital, I tried to find you. I went to your home, and your mother asked me to leave." Noah caught her by the hand, moving closer to her. "I was sick with worry. I tried to go after Stephen, but Lord Helton stopped me."

Her lips brushed against the stubble of his cheek. She wanted so much to comfort him, to kiss him, but she didn't dare. Victoria was under this roof, for goodness' sake. His arms tightened around her until he lifted her off her feet. Setting her down again, he held her close. "I don't know what I would have done if something had happened to you."

Her conscience prickled. She stepped back from him and stared at the rug under her feet. "You need to know something. It's my fault Khalib is hurt."

"No, it's not." Noah gave her a firm look. "It's mine. I shouldn't have put him in the position I did. I knew better. He couldn't have known the danger. He's a child."

She needed physical space from him. Fighting against the desire to be at his side, she sat on a chair in front of the vanity, her body toward him, leaning her arms against the back of the chair. "James called on me today. He brought me Ahmed's belongings." She swallowed. "Khalib was in the garden and I wanted to give you Ahmed's bag, so I sent a note to you with him. Stephen must have caught him with it."

Noah moved toward the empty fireplace. He placed his hand on the mantel. "But you didn't give him the bag?"

"No. It's in my haversack. I brought it with me. But that's why I said it's my fault."

Was he angry with her? His posture hadn't changed. But he kept his back toward her. "Ginger, do you realize what you've done?" He turned, his expression a mix of admiration and wonder. "You saved everything. You recovered both pieces of intel from Ahmed—something I failed to do. Your bravery ..."

He paused, his voice dropping. He looked away. "Christ Almighty—I love you, Ginger. You're an incredible woman."

She stared at him in shock, his words threatening to undo her resolve to keep her distance. He'd probably had more to drink than he realized, and it lowered his inhibitions. "You aren't angry at me? For Khalib?"

"It's time I made you aware of what's going on," Noah said. "But what happened with Khalib is not your fault. You did as I instructed you to do."

"But if I hadn't—"

"Stephen hurt Khalib to get a reaction from me, Ginger. That's the sum of it. There was no reason to do what he did." Noah went over toward the table where the servant had left supper for Ginger earlier. A bottle of wine had come with the meal, but she'd ignored it. He poured himself a glass and offered her one.

She shook her head, thinking of how ill she'd felt the day

before from the alcohol she'd consumed at Shepheard's. She stood and went over to him. "Are you sure you should drink?" She placed a cautionary hand on his forearm.

"I'm sure." Noah swallowed a mouthful of the dark wine and handed her the glass. "And you might want some by the time we're done speaking."

Her stomach sank. She took it reluctantly and returned to the seat she'd vacated. She sipped it, set it on the vanity. The smooth, smoky flavor of the wine didn't appeal to her.

"A year ago, Lord Helton came to me about a smuggling ring involving high-level British officials. Mostly Egyptian artifacts, but weapons and hashish also. He suspected your father, but wanted me to gather evidence. I worked directly with your father for years, so I was in a natural position to observe."

She gripped the back of the chair. Her father? A smuggler? It sounded ludicrous. "So you work for Lord Helton?"

Noah nodded. "Yes, but because your father couldn't know, Lord Helton decided it would be best for me to use an engagement to his daughter as a cover, to make visits to his house less suspicious. Stephen had introduced me to Victoria a few years before, and it was a logical ruse."

An engagement to his daughter as a cover ...

She had the sensation of falling, which the darkness amplified. She squeezed her eyes shut, trying to make sense of what he'd said, her thoughts moving at a strange lag.

"Wait—" She stood. "Do you mean to tell me you aren't engaged?"

He shook his head.

A choked cry left her, her hand at her throat.

A thousand thoughts assailed her at once, her emotions equally jumbled. She blinked, her mouth open. Now she understood why he'd suggested the wine. She shut her mouth, swallowing back tears and the temptation to slap him. He wasn't engaged. He didn't love Victoria.

The engagement had been a part of his work, which is why he'd said he couldn't end it. And also why he hadn't been able to explain himself. It was a secret operation.

She lowered herself to the floor and covered her face with her hands, tears stinging.

Noah sat at her side. He pulled her hands down and kissed the backs of her fingers. "Ginger, I'm sorry. I know none of this has been easy for you. And it killed me to see the look on your face when your father told you I was engaged. It has tortured me thinking of how hurt you must be and how little I could do to ease your pain."

Ease her pain? He'd done worse than that. "So instead you pushed me away? You tried to make me believe you were every bit the traitor my father said."

An apologetic look crossed his face. "I thought you were safer believing the worst."

She fought to restrain her tears. "But you kissed her in front of me. You called her darling and—" Despite her best efforts, a few tears spilled over.

Noah wiped her tears away. "I had to convince everyone, especially Stephen, of my devotion to her. Particularly given what happened in Port Said between us. Lord Helton almost reassigned me when he heard it."

Lord Helton knew about Port Said? Did Victoria? A fresh wave of humiliation ascended through her. "But why couldn't you have told me this in Port Said? I wouldn't have said anything." She pulled her hands away from his, feeling justified in her anger. "You knew how hard it had been to earn my trust. Did you want me to hate you?"

"I wanted to tell you. You don't know how much. But I was

under orders." He rubbed the back of his neck. "If hating me had been an assurance of your safety, I would have accepted it."

His words did little to mollify her hurt. "And you didn't trust me."

"Lord Helton didn't trust you. Neither does Victoria. Given your father's history, you might understand why."

But nothing had changed about who her family was. "Why are you telling me now?"

Noah stared at her. "After Khalib was hurt, Lord Helton agreed it might work to our benefit to discover what you know by telling you some of this."

His revelations were part of a plan. "How convenient. Now that I'm deemed useful, my feelings matter."

He sighed and stood. "That's not it, Ginger. Your feelings have mattered to me all along. This information—any of it—in the wrong hands can cost lives. Lord Helton agreed you should know because I vouched for you." He held out a hand for her.

His words sobered her. She lifted her chin. "You can trust me." She rose from the floor and dusted herself off, ignoring his hand. She didn't want to be angry with him for the lie, especially when his excuse was reasonable. But she was. She went over to the vanity and grabbed the glass of wine. She took a few swallows, trying to regain her sense of calm. "What else do you want to tell me?"

He dropped his hand and went a few paces away. "In time, I realized your father was someone else's puppet. Someone whose plans far exceeded smuggling."

Ginger took another swallow of wine. "Stephen Fisher."

He nodded. "We think he's a German secret operative. As best I can tell, your father's involvement came about because of a financial issue."

"Yes, my father has incurred debts with Stephen."

Noah sat on the edge of the bed and continued. "At first, it was just the smuggling. After the treaty with the Senussi Bedouin revolt, whispers began about this unknown figure of the Maslukha. The Senussi leaders swore they knew of no one operating under that name."

Noah unbuttoned his jacket, removing and placing it at his side. "Within a month of the first reports of his existence, the newspapers recounted stories of his attacks, detailing the brutality of his men."

She shuddered, thinking of the crucified soldiers. "I can understand why. We saw it in person."

"Yes. But the interesting thing was, when I went to investigate the attacks, I found nothing to substantiate the reports. Villages, soldiers, outposts—they had surrendered to the raiders —but out of fear, not violence."

"Why would the newspapers report unsubstantiated rumors?"

Noah scowled. "The intelligence world focuses a lot of its work on the control of information. Whoever controls it controls the people. Stories are placed strategically or information twisted to make people believe what the government wants them to believe."

She thought of the misleading headlines and articles she'd seen when she returned from Belah. It was intentional. "Through brainwashing and propaganda?"

"Precisely. And that's something the Arab Bureau has been doing since its inception. Planting stories in the local newspapers of Egypt, to sway the masses into cooperation with the British."

She gasped. It all came full circle. No wonder her father had brushed off her questions about the newspaper reports. "My father. Stephen." She stared at Noah. "They've been planting stories for the Maslukha in the newspapers. To increase his notoriety?"

Noah lowered himself to the ground. His back rested against the foot of the bed. He pulled one knee up and rested his wrist on it. "That's what I suspected. Particularly after my capture in Aleppo. Shortly before I wired your father the information about Ahmed carrying intel about the Maslukha's identity, Stephen betrayed me. It was part of the reason Ahmed didn't bring the documents with him to meet me. Transporting the documents was too risky with Stephen on his trail. The cipher you uncovered—and hopefully whatever you brought tonight—will help us locate where he hid the intel and unmask the Maslukha's identity, which will allow us to put a bounty on him."

She drained her glass of wine. A flush of warmth already tingled at her fingertips from it. "But not all the stories are rumors. We saw the Bedouin refugees. And the three British scouts."

A pale sliver of moonlight illuminated part of Noah's face as he shifted. "Some attacks have been real. And vicious."

Given what the refugees had told her about the attack on their tribe, she could imagine. The terror on the girl's face as she screamed at the sight of Stephen indicated the horror she'd witnessed. She wrapped the shawl around her more tightly. "So the Maslukha desires infamy to stir the Egyptians and Arabs to revolution under his name." She frowned. "But why murder Lawrence?"

Noah shook his head. "We don't know. That's part of what was in Ahmed's documents. And the details of the plan. But my best guess is Lawrence ..." He drifted off. "It's a trifle complicated to explain. Lawrence made promises to the Arab leaders, and they believe in him. Implicitly. Promises of lands and support for their nationalist causes after the war." Noah cleared his throat. "With Lawrence gone, there's a chance they won't be so trusting of anyone else, especially when—"

She lifted her chin, thinking of Ahmed. "Especially when the Arabs hear the British now support the Zionist cause?"

Noah smiled appreciatively. "You are better at this than you think. It's all under the table, still. But it may become official soon enough."

Ginger stood and leaned against the wall. It felt cool to the touch against her burning skin. "But isn't that wrong, Noah? If the British promised the lands to the Arabs, promising to support the Zionist cause for a free Jewish state would be deceitful. Besides, the Yishuv pledged their support to the Turks."

He sighed. "There is a lot of deceit involved. And, yes, the official leadership of the Zionists in Jerusalem promised to support the Turks. But there have been some, like the group Ahmed worked for, who have given us intelligence and support, at great sacrifice."

Sacrifice like Ahmed's—the ultimate one. Ginger felt a stab of pain in her chest. "But still—if the land was promised to the Arabs, won't that lead to problems after the war?"

"I'm sure there will be problems. There are always problems with nationalist causes and division of the spoils of war. There's enough grey area in the negotiations that I'm certain all sides will feel deceived. But right now what matters is supporting the Allies. Because one thing is for certain: if we lose, the nationalist causes lose. The Turkish leadership has been busy stamping out the nationalists in the entire Levantine region from Aleppo to Palestine and Baghdad since before the war. They have no intention of relinquishing those lands should they win."

Then how would the Maslukha be able to tempt the Arabs into helping him? "So if the Arabs and Zionists have a better chance of freedom with us than with them, why support the Maslukha?"

"Because people who feel betrayed and mistreated have a

tendency to act irrationally. Which is why Lawrence makes sense as a target. If the Maslukha succeeds in his aims, it could be catastrophic for Arab-British relations. And the war."

Fear crawled from the dark shadows of the room, like grinning gargoyles, perched on the corner of the armoire, hiding in the invisibility of the dark hearth. Watching her. Waiting to pounce.

She wanted to take comfort in his strength, but she still had questions. "Can you stop the assassination?"

The sharp intake of breath Noah drew spoke of his tension. "I don't know. We're doing what we can."

She may not have done enough. What good did it do to transmit Ahmed's messages if they were too late to foil the Maslukha's plans? "And if you can't?"

"If we can't ... there may be enough evidence to charge your father with a crime. If we can prove it was an assassination. Only a handful of people know of Lawrence's location."

How much did her father owe Stephen that he would risk something of this magnitude? He risked arrest and execution. The shame on her family would be insurmountable. Her father must know this—was it possible he showed signs of hesitation? It could explain Stephen's sudden desire to hold her mother and Lucy hostage until he'd accomplished his aims. "And Henry?" she asked, lifting her head sharply. "How did he come to be involved in this?"

"Henry ..." Noah's face filled with regret. "Henry wasn't involved until he met Ahmed. Ahmed must have told him something to alert him to Stephen or your father. But you can't blame yourself."

His intuition wasn't wrong. How could she not blame herself? She'd been the one to get Henry involved. If she hadn't wired Henry, if she'd believed Noah and turned to him for help —Henry would be uninvolved. She didn't answer, the weight of the responsibility weighing on her heavily. At last, she asked, "Can you save my brother or father?" Her voice barely rose above a whisper.

"I can't save people from themselves. Henry and your father both know what they're doing. That's why I'm telling you not to blame yourself. Henry didn't have to go along with your father's betrayal."

"Stephen has my mother and sister. He arrived tonight to invite them to an extended holiday in Luxor. I was to go too, but I escaped at the first opportunity. I'm sure he intends to hold them as leverage."

"Is that why you climbed out of a window?" Noah raked his fingers through his hair. "Jack told me about your escape. I didn't know it was from Stephen himself."

"Yes. I knew if I went, I wouldn't have another chance to give you Ahmed's bag. I couldn't risk trusting anyone." Pressure built at her temples as she thought of the way she'd abandoned her mother and sister. Her palms grew slick with sweat. "And I'm still too late. Captain Lawrence could still die, and it would still be because I didn't give you Ahmed's message in time. Even after I turned my back on my family."

"You've done more than your share in this. I don't think your father will let any harm come to your mother and sister—not if he can avoid it. But I can talk to Lord Helton about committing someone to monitor them. I know it's not enough." Noah held out a hand to her. "Come here. Please. I know you're angry with me, but I can't stand this distance between us."

A haunted expression betrayed his cool exterior. She hesitated and grabbed the bottle of wine. She crossed the space between them and sank onto the floorboards beside him, maintaining a few inches between them.

Handing him the bottle, she asked, "But what now? You still must pretend to be engaged to Victoria—and how does that work? Does she know it's pretense? She came to me today, called me a whore, and told me to stay away from you." Ginger tensed. "It was one thing for me to tolerate her saying those things when I felt her anger justified—not that I liked it. I won't allow her to abuse me to maintain this charade."

"She went too far." Noah took a swig from the bottle and wiped his mouth with the back of his hand. "She's been working for the CID for years. When that story broke in the society pages, though, we knew she had to provide some reaction." He lifted her chin with his free hand. "But you're the only woman I want to be kissing. The only one occupying my mind."

His touch electrified her. She had to show some restraint. She leaned into him and kissed his cheek.

He pushed her hair behind her ear, his hand resting against the nape of her neck. His fingertips grazed her jawline. His thumb caressed her lips. "That's not the type of kiss I'm looking for." He pulled her closer, his lips meeting hers. He tasted of wine and whisky, and the glass she'd drunk made her feel weak.

She slid her arms around his neck, engulfed by a strange sense of devastation and joy. He crushed her against him. She pulled her head back. "Wait—what about the bag I have from Ahmed? Isn't it urgent?"

"It is urgent. But Lord Helton and Jack have gone out for an emergency meeting to act on the information you relayed about Lawrence. He ordered me to stay here and talk to you. As soon as they return, I'll discuss it with him." He kissed her neck, his lips trailing down toward her shoulder, pushing the edge of her nightgown over, exposing her bare skin.

"Do you have any idea how much I want you?" He kissed her shoulder, his fingertips trailing over her back. "I'm sorry for everything, my love—that you were caught in the middle of this. And that I didn't do a better job of staying away from you."

It would be so easy to listen to his soft, amorous words

now. She had to keep her focus. Ginger pulled away. "No, wait. You didn't answer my question." Her body felt traitorous, her own desire for him threatening to overtake her. "What happens next? Will you still have to pretend to be engaged to Victoria?"

Noah set the bottle of wine down. "For at least the length of the investigation."

How long would that be? She was afraid of the answer. "And beyond that?"

"There shouldn't be any need for the charade." Noah pulled her close.

She dodged his kiss. "But what if there is?" Twisting out of his arms, she moved away. "What if Lord Helton orders you to take another mission where you must pretend to be engaged to her? Will you have to?"

Noah's frustration showed. "I have to do whatever I'm ordered to do."

"And kissing her and holding her—" Ginger raked her fingers through her hair. She wished she'd never seen him kissing Victoria. She couldn't get the image out of her mind. "Have you been intimate with her?"

"That's a ridiculous question."

"You've been with other women. Your evasive answer makes me believe she must have been one of them."

"One of them? How many women do you imagine I have in my past, Ginger? I'm not a libertine." He shook his head and put out a hand. "Don't answer that. In fact, it would be better if you try not to think of my past, as I don't think of yours."

"My past does not include other men in my bed." She crossed her arms.

"No, but it includes your promise to marry someone else. A promise you seemed to be able to forget easily."

Her mouth opened in shock. "How dare you use the fact that

I fell in love with you against me?" Fury crept across every inch of her skin, her face growing hot.

Noah stood, his posture tense. He seemed taller somehow, more commanding in presence. "I'm not in the mood to argue with you, Ginger. I'm just pointing out the fact we both have things in our past I'm sure the other would prefer not to think of. But it doesn't matter now. We can sort these things out when the time comes."

"When the time comes?" She jumped up, glaring at him. "You know, even Stephen Fisher had the decency to offer me marriage. And James renewed his offer of marriage again today —both of them claiming to want to save my good name. You're the one who's dragging my name through the mud, and you don't dare mention the future because the time is inconvenient."

Noah's eyebrows snapped together. "Are you comparing me to Stephen Fisher and the man who humiliated you in front of the entire clearing station?"

"Better than humiliating me in front of the entire city of Cairo," she said, her hands in fists. "You have no idea the looks I received today in public."

"I can't marry you and pretend to be engaged to Victoria. If I could, I would marry you tonight. But I don't get to make those decisions. I swore an oath of—" Noah drew his hand back, his fingers curling into a fist, swallowing his words as though his annoyance was getting the better of him. "What did you tell James? When he proposed to you today?"

She shrank against a bedpost.

Noah chuckled sardonically. "So you didn't tell him no." He tilted his head. "I'm assuming you told Fisher to go to hell, and, please, lie to me if you didn't. You have a lot of gall condemning my actions when you throw a marriage proposal you're consid- ering in my face."

"Oh, for goodness' sake." Ginger crossed her arms, keeping

her voice to a low hiss. She didn't want to wake anyone with their arguing. "Why else would I be here if I didn't love you? Why would I walk into the house of the woman who called me a whore?"

Noah put his hands on her waist. "Because a man's life is at stake. You're too honorable to turn your back on that. It doesn't change the fact that you're considering another man's proposal."

She shoved him back. "I won't apologize. I don't have the luxury of throwing away my options, given my life circumstances at the moment. James himself wouldn't have me if he knew what transpired between us in Port Said. And given the way you've acted since, giving me no hope of a real future, and your behavior at Shepheard's, what was I to think? You told me you had to let me go."

He caught her wrists. "Well, I'm not letting go now, am I?" Dropping his mouth to hers, he gave her a bruising, hard kiss.

She slapped him. "Don't be so smug."

He kissed her and tossed her back onto the bed. He smiled, his eyes burning with fury and passion. "I am smug. And you're self-righteous. But I love you and I want you. All of you. And I won't share you with anyone."

His words broke through her anger. She loved him. She needed him. She choked back a sob. "You won't share me? You wouldn't step out in public with me if I asked it."

"My God, woman, will you stop arguing with me and kiss me?" Noah's voice had a ragged edge to it. "I need you." He caught her hand in both of his and brought her closer to him. "Kiss me and tell me again you don't want me just as much."

She leaned toward him and kissed him, intending to make a quick, perfunctory kiss. Before she could pull away, though, Noah lifted her and pulled her onto his lap. He tugged her nightgown over her head, and her eyes widened. "You're mad if you think I'm making love to you here."

Noah laid her on the bed and removed his shirt. "That's where you're wrong. I'm making love to you. If you'll have me. And maybe I am mad." He kissed her once more, his lips urgent and brutal. "Tell me yes."

"If you ever question my love again, I won't forgive you." She covered his mouth with a kiss. "I didn't abandon everything for you to have you question it."

Noah eyes locked with hers. "And you forgive me now?"

She trailed her kisses to his neck and whispered in his ear, "This time only. Because you're right. I need you, Noah."

CHAPTER THIRTY-TWO

*G*inger didn't sleep long. Even in Noah's arms, the darkness crept in, taking the shape of fears that clawed at her heart and a face with pale-blue eyes and Stephen's leer. Stephen reached for her, his fingers at her throat. She startled and gasped, trying to orient herself in the unfamiliar space. Noah breathed softly beside her, his eyes closed. She wouldn't wake him. He likely needed the sleep.

She counted the seconds ticking from the clock on the mantel, her thoughts returning to that awful, wretched smile. Stephen might not have been there, but he was still a threat, alive and as real as her nightmare.

The only way any of this would end was if he was dead.

She squeezed her eyes shut and pictured Ahmed's mouth open in surprise, the betrayal in his eyes as the light faded from them. She'd killed him, and it would weigh on her heart until the day she died. She wanted no part of ever killing anyone else again.

But Noah was right. There was murder in her heart. She

wanted Stephen dead. Noah had no problem with killing men he perceived as enemies in the war. Why not Stephen?

As the light of early morning filled the room, it did little to clear the webs spun in the darkness. She glanced at Noah again.

She loved him in a way she never would have believed possible. When logic told her to flee, she could do nothing but love him more, at the risk of breaking her own heart. One way or another, Noah would break her heart.

She woke him. He smiled as his eyes found hers. "Good morning."

She pulled the sheet over her shoulder. "I have a question."

"What's that?" He closed his eyes, still half asleep.

"Will you kill Stephen Fisher for me?"

Noah's eyes snapped open. "What?"

She wrapped herself tighter in the sheet and sat on the bed. "It's the perfect solution to everything. I know it's a lot to ask of you, but I can't see how it would be immoral to kill a man who—"

Noah rose and dressed, his movements surprisingly fluid for someone who hadn't slept for long. "There are rules, Ginger. And it won't save your father from criminal charges."

She suppressed an angry snort. "Maybe not, but it could save Henry. And my mother. And Lucy. And T. E. Lawrence, for that matter. Aren't their lives worth it?"

"It's not that simple." He sat on a chair, watching her with a sober expression as he pulled on his shoes. "I can't go rogue and kill someone without orders. That would result in my hanging. Believe me, the idea has crossed my mind. Especially after Aleppo. But we have to handle this situation with care, and not only because his father is a peer. Lord Helton feels strongly that once we have enough evidence to arrest him, Fisher will give up his contacts to save his own hide."

Stephen *would* turn on his allies. She lifted her chin. "I'll find someone else who will."

Noah strode toward the window and peeked outside the curtain. "You're not a spy, Ginger. Stop attempting to be one."

"Please tell me you'll consider it, at least."

"Lord Helton gives my orders." He interlaced his fingers with hers. "That's the reason I asked for Jack's help. I'm not entirely certain I trust my judgement with you."

What was that supposed to mean? She pulled her hands away. "Well, thank you very much."

"It's not meant as an insult. I'm supposed to be rational in my line of work. But love isn't rational. What happened in Port Said is one of the most irrational things I've ever done." Noah kissed her cheek. "I should go."

He led them to the door and opened it. Despite the darkness of the hallway, Ginger caught sight of Victoria standing at the rail overlooking the main staircase. Victoria's head snapped up at the sound of the door.

Ginger wished she could duck behind the wall beside the doorway. It was too late. Victoria stared at them, her face darkening. She stepped back from the rail and went down the stairs, her steps slow.

Noah grimaced. "I need to talk to Victoria. Stay here. I'll come back for you."

"But I thought you weren't—"

"I'm not engaged to her, but it doesn't mean we aren't friends. Or that she won't be hurt. I haven't been entirely forthcoming about the extent of our involvement to her, given the circumstances. But she deserves the truth."

Her eyes widened. "What exactly are you going to tell her?"

A ghost of a smile played at his lips. "Don't worry, I won't admit things that aren't her concern. She knows I needed to talk to you. She's not stupid, though."

Given Victoria's reaction and now Noah's words, it appeared Victoria's outburst the day before hadn't been entirely fabricated. She searched his eyes. "Did I get in the middle of something between the two of you?"

"Would it matter now if you had? Don't forget, darling. When we met, you were actually engaged." He kissed her and left.

Ginger closed the door to the room and leaned against it. Her heart felt strangely heavy, his question unsettling her. The implications of his words could be taken many ways, including that she wouldn't have cared about infidelity.

But, worse still, he'd evaded her question.

CHAPTER THIRTY-THREE

*F*ollowing a servant down the stairs of the Helton mansion, Ginger took in the details she'd been too distraught to notice the day before. Unlike her family's house in Cairo, the Heltons' home felt gloomy and brooding. Dark mahogany paneled the walls, and the bulbs from electric chandeliers threw a yellow glow into the spiral stairwell. A glass dome illuminated the landing directly below it, the rest of the staircase was shrouded. A crimson rug lining the stairs added to the moodiness of the space.

On the main floor, the servant led her to a set of closed double doors. The butler, Bixby, stood in front of them. At her approach, he opened the doors and announced her in.

An older gentleman approached her. Tall with silver-streaked black hair, he wore an immaculate suit and thin spectacles. Though he had a pleasant face, his lips were pressed into a line, his eyes dark.

"Lady Virginia Whitman." His baritone voice echoed from the walls.

Ginger straightened, her hand settling on the strap of her

haversack. She wished she'd slept more. She needed her poise and wits today. Had it only been a half hour since Noah had left her? It felt like hours had passed. "Yes, sir."

"I am Lord Helton. Please. Come in."

Victoria and Noah sat on a sofa together, by the fireplace, a comfortable distance between them. Noah stood when Ginger came in. Victoria lifted her chin, her eyes narrowing at Ginger.

Thankfully, Jack was also there, one foot propped up on an ottoman. He winked at Ginger.

"Please sit." Lord Helton directed Ginger to the armchair beside Jack, then made his way over to the fireplace. The air with which Lord Helton carried himself reminded Ginger of her father. He stood while everyone else sat.

Lord Helton settled his gaze on her. "Major Benson has informed us about your role in this whole nasty affair. While I can't say I'm pleased to hear of your involvement, we must deal with the situation as it is." He put his hands behind his back. "I understand you have recovered the operative Ahmed's personal effects."

Ginger met Noah's eyes. She wished she could read his expression better. She spoke to Lord Helton. "Yes, sir."

Lord Helton nodded but didn't thank her. "And who told you about Lawrence being the target of assassination?"

Despite everything her father had done, Ginger felt conflicted. She couldn't betray her mother. It might mean they'd drag her in for questioning, or worse, when the fault lay with her father. "I overheard my father."

Lord Helton and Victoria exchanged a glance. "An unverified claim isn't the best to go on, but, unfortunately, we can't afford to ignore it either." A look of annoyance darkened Lord Helton's face, and he crossed the room toward Ginger. "A few days ago, your brother, Henry, was spotted on a train to Palestine. We know he got as far as the clearing station at Belah. Do you know what he was doing?"

Ginger tensed. It was news to her. Her father had claimed Henry had gone to Alexandria. "Aren't you in a better position to find out than I am?"

Lord Helton moved toward the door. "If you have nothing else of use for us, I must go. My driver, Jahi, will take you to a safehouse later this morning."

"But what about Ahmed's bag—" Ginger began. Didn't he want to know what was in it?

"Major Benson will apprise me of its contents. I have other matters to attend to. If we recover the documents Ahmed left, you will be released accordingly."

Ginger stared in the direction he'd gone. The beginnings of a headache throbbed at the top of her skull. It sounded as if she was being detained against her will, despite the implication it was for her safety.

"I think," said Jack, stretching, "we could use some breakfast. I don't know about the rest of you, but I didn't get a chance to eat this morning."

"I'm not hungry," Ginger and Victoria said at the same time. The two women inspected each other.

Victoria stood. "I'll tell Bixby to have the servants bring something." She hurried from the room.

"Female drama is grand, isn't it?" Jack simpered.

Noah stood but didn't respond to Jack's comment.

Ginger wished Noah could be himself around her. The distance he maintained was appropriate but offered little comfort, given the situation. She met his eyes. "Why am I being held in a safehouse?"

Jack asked Noah, "Should I give you a minute?"

"No, Victoria will return any moment." Noah sat against the

arm of the sofa. "Lord Helton wants to keep you from being a liability to us. It's for your own safety, Ginger."

Ginger ignored Victoria as she breezed into the room. "Why would I be a liability?"

"Because"—Victoria stood beside Noah—"you've compromised Noah. They can use you against him."

Ginger met her gaze squarely. "How?"

"Don't pretend to be innocent now. You know how you've botched everything—up to and including hiding Ahmed for days. If this investigation fails, the blame ought to rest entirely on your shoulders," Victoria said.

Her words were a stark contrast to Noah's when he'd told her she had saved everything. Why didn't Noah defend her now?

"Maybe a little less vitriol, Tori," Jack muttered and gave an exaggerated yawn.

Noah approached Ginger and squatted beside her chair. "I didn't think you'd be happy about the arrangement." His expression grew darker. "But I won't allow your father or Stephen to use you against me."

Ginger frowned, irritated he'd let Victoria's attack go unanswered. "My father won't hurt me." Ginger peered at Jack. "What do you think?"

"Does it matter?" Jack laughed. "I'm not being paid for my opinion."

"It matters to me." Ginger ignored both Noah and Victoria. "You're more objective."

Jack shrugged. "I think they see you as Noah's weak spot. They'll want to use you to get to him either way, and we don't know what that will entail." He met Noah's gaze. "Everyone breaks. And they know how to break him. Just like Stephen's using your mom and sister against your father."

"Regardless, it's not up for discussion." Victoria lifted her hands and stood. "If you'll excuse me, there are a few details I need to discuss with my father before he leaves. Make yourselves comfortable." Victoria closed the door behind her.

"She's a joy." Ginger pursed her lips.

"I told you before, she doesn't trust you." Noah returned to the empty sofa.

"Loathes is more like it. And with her comments going unchecked by you, she feels she's earned the right to express that loathing."

Jack smirked. "I like this one, Noah. She's a keeper." Jack stood. "Coffee, anyone? I thought I'd go to the kitchen and grab a cup. The tea they'll bring is for the birds."

Noah nodded his response. Ginger smiled at Jack. "Make that three, thank you."

After he'd gone, she crossed her arms. "I take it your discussion with Victoria went poorly?"

Noah frowned. "She's fairly angry with me, as you can tell."

"She seems angrier at me than you. Though I'm surprised you didn't protest on my behalf at her rudeness."

Noah leaned back. "I've never known you not to speak your mind or defend yourself. I respect you too much to speak for you."

"I speak my mind with *you*. You seem to bring out both the best and the worst in me." She studied the door. "Is Victoria going to a safehouse? Don't they believe she's your fiancée?"

"That's different."

She bristled with irritation. "Why? Because she works for the CID? Or could it possibly be because they view me as a different sort of liability? One who might betray everyone here."

Noah looked away. "My feelings for you make the difference. Lord Helton even questioned my continued involvement on this. He thinks I'm no longer the right man for the job." He held his hand out toward her.

Shame burned within her. "I'm sorry," she murmured. She sat beside him. At least Victoria wouldn't be able to resume a place beside Noah now. It was a silly thought, but she couldn't avoid thinking it.

Noah met her gaze. "There'll be fallout from what your father has done. There may be others, like Stephen, who were working with him and feel threatened. I want you to be as far away from it as possible."

"When will I see you again?"

"As soon as I am able. I won't forget about you, if that's what you're worried about."

"That and the fact that I've spent my life dodging the orders of men who think they know better than I."

Noah lifted her hand to his lips. "Maybe, for once, you'll believe me when I tell you I know better than you in this. Not because you haven't shown tenacity and resilience both in this and as a nurse but because it's more dangerous than you could imagine."

His words sparked an idea. "Would you at least help me get my record cleared so I can go back to nursing? Surely I've proven my loyalty and been of service in some ways—shouldn't that count for something?"

"I'm sure Lord Helton could see to it." His expression said nothing about what he thought of the idea.

"And my mother and Lucy?"

Noah's brow furrowed. "What about them?"

"They're in Stephen's hands. Every time I've mentioned it to you, I feel as though you don't understand the weight of it. He was talking about sending them on a boat on the Nile with his sister to their home in Luxor—but I'm certain the intention was to make them hostages, even if they remain unaware of it. But their lives could be at stake."

Noah's fingers tightened around hers. "I understand. It's also why something like killing Stephen isn't wise right now. Who knows what he's told your father—if he's threatened harm against them should anything happen to him, we would be taking a risk. Lord Helton has promised to look into sending someone to monitor, but there aren't any guarantees."

The doorknob turned. Jack shouldered the door open, balancing two cups in one hand and a third cup in the other.

He handed over the steaming cups. "I put sugar and cream in yours," he told Ginger. "I should have asked, but I figured you looked like the type of girl who would want it."

What did that mean? "I'm not much of a coffee drinker." She took the cup and thanked him, then took a sip. Despite her dislike for the brew, Jack had put the right amount of sugar in it.

Jack sat in front of Ginger. He pulled out a flask and poured some amber liquid into his cup. At Ginger's curious stare, he lifted the flask. "Dewar's?"

Ginger chuckled. "Are all Americans like you?"

"You mean impolite, presumptuous, and arrogant?" Jack winked. "Sums us up well."

"That sums you up well," Noah said. "Though it's not a surprise you think you represent the entire country."

"The other Yanks wish they could be me." Jack lifted his drink in a mock toast. He settled into the armchair, his hands around his cup. He didn't wear a uniform of any kind, just loose khaki-colored trousers, a light tan jacket, and a white shirt. She remembered what he'd said about his archeology upbringing. She imagined him having a dusty pith helmet somewhere in his belongings.

"What did I miss?" Jack asked. "Other than necking."

Ginger blushed and Noah laughed, sitting forward.

"Ginger has promised to abandon her future as a spy for her future as a nurse." He stood.

"I don't know. She seems to have earned her stripes in both."

Jack smiled at Ginger. "Don't let him tell you otherwise. Those are the reasons he likes you."

What had Noah told Jack about their relationship? The ease with which Jack treated her helped her feel comfortable around him—but it also made her strangely happy. Noah confiding his love for her to someone else made it more real.

"You may as well get out Ahmed's bag." Noah rolled up his sleeves and glanced at Ginger. "We should see what's in there."

Ginger dug through the haversack. Her fingertips grazed across Ahmed's bag, and she thought of how she'd found him in the hut in Belah. Everything in her life had changed since that day. The time when she hadn't wholly trusted in Noah felt so distant now. A lump rose in her throat as she placed the bag on the table in front of the sofa.

Jack dumped out the contents without ceremony. He lifted the Bible and thumbed through it. "This must be where he left it."

"Can you be sure?" Ginger stared at the cigarette case and the lighter, a feeling of dismay rising in her.

Jack nodded. "Books tend to be easy places to leave clues."

Noah leaned over from his side of the table as Jack took out a pencil.

"What did the cipher say?" Jack asked Noah.

"Twenty-one at the dawn and thirty-one."

Ginger made no comment but remembered the gibberish line of code, fascinated Noah understood it.

"Let me have it." Jack reached a hand out toward Noah.

Noah pulled the cipher from his pocket and dropped it onto the table.

Jack lifted a pencil and tapped it against the Bible. He glanced at Ginger. "You sure Ahmed didn't say anything else to you?"

"I wish he had." Ginger looked at Noah. "How did you solve the cipher? Didn't you say you needed some key?"

Noah shook his head. "It took a while, but I figured it out."

She smiled slightly. "Impressive."

Jack twirled the pencil. "Give me a little silence. I need to concentrate, and I'll get nothing done with you two yammering on about the good old days."

Noah put his arm around Ginger's shoulder. "Ignore him. He'll stop making a spectacle eventually."

"You're wrong." Jack grinned. "I thrive on attention. Without it, I get louder."

She smiled and leaned against Noah, listening to the cry of a thrush outside the window.

The door opened once again and Victoria breezed in, followed by two servants carrying trays of food. She paused for a moment and glanced at Ginger and Noah. Her irritation at their proximity flashed in her eyes. She waited until the servants left and sat across from them. "Remember, Noah, even though we pay our servants handsomely, they still believe you're engaged to me." She nodded at a vase of gorgeous long-stemmed crimson roses on a table and added, "You've done a thorough job of convincing them."

She meant to stoke Ginger's jealousy. Ginger gritted her teeth, wishing she had thicker armor. She focused on her coffee instead and tried not to react when Noah removed his arm and leaned forward toward one of the breakfast trays.

For once, Jack didn't give a response, bent in concentration, his eyes darting between the cipher and a notepad he'd pulled out from his pocket. After a few minutes, his head snapped up. "I got it."

Noah sat straight. "And?"

Jack moved to the floor. His arm stretched over one bent knee. "It's simple. I'm embarrassed it took me as long as it did. I would have gotten it sooner, but you confused the words. It's not dawn. It's *beginning*."

Noah rubbed the back of his neck. "You didn't have to do everything without a key."

"I would have gotten it, anyway. You stick to espionage. I'll stick to puzzles." Jack drummed his fingers against the tabletop. He flipped through the first few pages and read out loud, "Genesis 21:31: 'So that place was called Beersheba, because the two men swore an oath there.'"

Noah lifted his head keenly. "Beersheba?"

Jack pushed the Bible toward him. "Not any place, either. Abraham's well. Which is a problem."

"Should we be discussing this in front of Lady Virginia?" Victoria frowned. "She has no reason to be here any longer."

Victoria would find a reason to get rid of her as soon as possible. "If you're locking me in a safehouse, whom could I tell?" Ginger glared at her and looked at Jack. "Is the well still there?"

Victoria rested against her chair, the corners of her mouth turning downward.

"Oh, it's there all right. At Tel el Saba. At least what they claim is Abraham's well, anyway. That's not the problem, is it, Noah?" Jack said.

"No." Noah cleared his throat and glanced at Ginger. "Beersheba is solidly in the hands of the Turks."

"Well, I know that. I was in Belah, for goodness' sake. It's about thirty miles from Gaza, isn't it?"

Jack chimed in. "Yes, but they're entrenched there. With their base of operations right at Tel el Saba because it's on a hill. General Kress von Kressenstein just added two divisions to the place."

"And Lieutenant General Chetwode gave orders to destroy the railway south of it," Noah added.

"And the columns are riding out today," Jack finished.

What did he mean? She didn't want to show her lack of experience with military movements and strategy, especially around Victoria. Would it make it more dangerous to go to Beersheba now than usual? "How do you know?" Ginger asked.

"Because the last couple of weeks," Noah said, "Jack's been working on scouting missions to determine the feasibility of demolishing the railway."

Ginger struggled for a safe question that wouldn't make her sound unintelligent. "Then this is not the time to go to Beersheba."

Jack laughed. "Going in there right now is like trying to sneak into a hornet's nest. Except these hornets are armed with machine guns."

Victoria stared at Noah. "You'll need a disguise to get to Tel el Saba. It's too bad you shaved the beard you grew last winter."

The corners of Noah's eyes squinted. "This is when it would have been useful to have Khalib with us."

Ginger's heart ached. Noah continued quietly in thought, loosening his collar.

"Rail is out. We'd have to go on the Hedjaz railway, and they're about to blast the tracks."

"You have plenty of friends in the Royal Flying Corps," Victoria said.

"That's what I was thinking."

Their comfortable banter reminded Ginger of how much longer they'd known each other. She, on the other hand, was useless. No wonder Victoria saw her as nothing more than an unnecessary distraction.

Still, she wanted to understand the situation as best she could. "Even if you get to Abraham's well, how are you going to find where Ahmed hid the documents?"

Jack flipped to one of the blank pages in the front of the

Bible. He lifted the book toward the window and separated the thin pages. Sunlight streamed through the paper, and a faint stain showed on the surface: a drawing.

"A map?" How had Jack seen it without the aid of the sunlight?

Jack tapped it. "Probably drawn with urine. It works well in a pinch."

Ginger grimaced.

Yawning, Jack put his hands on the table and stood. "Okay, it's settled. Now, if you three don't need my expertise anymore at the moment, I'm gonna catch a few winks." He moved to the armchair beside Victoria and put his feet on the ottoman.

Noah glanced at his wristwatch. "We need to be on the midday train to Ismailia."

Jack nodded. "I think the 408 runs at noon."

"Did you contact Alastair yet about the safehouse?" Victoria leaned forward and pulled a tin in the center of the coffee table toward her. She opened it and removed a slender cigarette holder and a cigarette. "There's no need for Jahi to take her. Alastair should send one of his men."

Noah moved to the window. "Your father insisted Jahi take her. He felt it was safer. I sent a note ahead, though."

"Good." Even smoking, Victoria oozed elegance. "It will be better for everyone when Lady Virginia is out of the picture."

The way she said it made it sound as though she wished Ginger's death. A myriad of biting remarks came to the tip of Ginger's tongue, but she suppressed the snark. "I want to do what's best for everyone."

Victoria smirked. "If true, you'd have the sense to leave Noah alone."

"Victoria, that's enough." Noah turned away from the window.

Blowing a puff of smoke, Victoria said, "She needs to understand: if it wasn't for you, she wouldn't be here." She looked at Ginger. "The reason you're here is Noah's reputation and his alone. And even that you've sullied. Don't be surprised if he's demoted for this egregious escapade with you."

"Enough." Noah's voice dropped so low it sent chills down Ginger's spine.

Jack jumped to his feet. "Tori, why don't we go see about buying some train tickets?"

Victoria shook her head. "I think the best thing would be for us to get on with it. I'll go and tell Jahi to ready the car."

Victoria left. Ginger remained seated, her shoulders stiff. The awkwardness in the room lingered, and she wished she could return to the bedroom and hide. "I should go." She glanced at Noah's profile. "I've made things worse for you."

"Victoria's bitter." Jack sat beside Ginger. "She doesn't want any other woman breaking into the men-only club she's fought so hard to be in."

"They won't demote me, don't worry. She's lashing out at me too." Noah gathered his duckbill cap from the sofa. "I'll be right back. I need to get something."

Noah left. Jack yawned again. "You know—and I'm not saying this to bring you any lower—but it makes perfect sense why Victoria wouldn't trust you."

Ginger's throat thickened. "She appears to be in love with him, doesn't she? I can't help feeling like an intruder."

Jack grinned. "I've seen the way you two look at each other. He's never looked at her that way." He put his hands behind his head. He watched the door. "I have no business telling you this, and Noah will be furious with me if he knows I said anything, but he's an overly sentimental person in private. He keeps two things with him at all times: his father's book of poetry and a picture of his mother. If that's not the mark of someone who has a heart, I don't know what is."

Ginger smiled sadly at the thought. She barely knew anything about Noah's family. He hid his wounds well. "Jack, what happened to Noah's parents?"

Jack frowned. "I shouldn't tell you." He wrinkled his nose. "As far as I know, I'm one of the few people he's ever told."

"I take it they didn't die of natural causes?"

"No. But ask him. If he's ready to share with you, he will. And if he doesn't, he'll come around, eventually. He's already done more to be with you than I've ever seen him ..." Jack broke off and grinned again. "You can't tell him any of this. Just because I've known him longer doesn't mean he won't kill me if he needs to."

The door opened. Noah strode in, holding a kitbag. He sat across from Ginger and put the bag on the table. He removed a handgun from a dark-brown leather holster and held it out to her. "This is for you. It's accurate and reliable. Have you fired a gun before?"

He knew the answer. Which meant he'd told no one she'd shot Ahmed. Including Jack. His eyes reflected it. Did he think she'd get in trouble for it? Maybe it was a risk he didn't want to take.

She nodded, her hands unsteady, and placed the gun on her lap. Holding any form of gun always made her nervous. "A shotgun, mostly. I've fired pistols, but usually when someone else loaded them for me. I'm a terrible shot."

She recognized this gun as the popular German Luger the British soldiers did their best to acquire. "Where did you get this?"

"Constantinople." Noah placed a box of ammunition on the seat beside him. He shut the kitbag and slid it onto the floor.

"Don't you think a revolver would be better?" Jack asked. "She could use my Colt."

"I think it may be too big for her hands. I'm not expecting her to be in a firefight anyway—I want her armed."

She frowned. "Against whom?"

"Anyone threatening you."

As much as Ginger hated the thought, she didn't want to show naïveté by questioning his judgement. She ran her fingers along the cool metal of the barrel. The last time she'd held a gun in her hands, she'd killed Ahmed by mistake. Could she ever fire another gun again? She never wanted to repeat that horror.

"I think you're scaring her." Jack crossed his arms.

Noah's fingers grasped hers. "Trust me when I tell you it doesn't make me feel any better about sending you away. After Khalib, I swore I wouldn't let you out of my sight."

"Hopefully my being in the safehouse helps." She did her best to sound confident, though a cold sweat broke out on her neck. "Don't forget about my mother and sister, Noah. If Stephen captured and hurt Khalib, I don't think he'd hesitate to do the same to innocent women."

"I know. That's what I'm afraid of." Noah kissed the back of her hand. "And why I want you to have a gun."

She stared at the metal object. For him, it represented a consolation. For her, a nightmare.

CHAPTER THIRTY-FOUR

From the backseat of the car, Ginger glanced out the window at the passing streets and buildings of Cairo. Noah had left her with a kiss and a promise to come for her as soon as he had the documents, but none of it made her feel any better. Sitting in a house in Cairo while he was out there, sneaking into a Turkish stronghold, terrified her.

Not that she could have done much to help. Her red hair made her stand out in Egypt.

Jahi didn't speak from the driver's seat, and she stared at the back of his head. An Egyptian, he wore the traditional skullcap or *taqiyah*. She would have preferred Noah drive her. He'd begged her to run away with him in Port Said and go to his friend's safehouse. Now she was being forced to go.

They turned down a street lined with houses and cafes. The scent of horse manure seeped into the car as it crawled, barely able to pass through the throngs of British soldiers and locals on the streets.

Ginger frowned. Why were there so many soldiers milling about?

On the balcony of a house, three women in flimsy gowns waved down at a group of passing soldiers. Ginger startled. The safehouse was in Wagh el Birket? She'd never visited the famous entertainment district of the Cairo. No respectable woman would.

Jahi turned the car down an alley and stopped. He came around to her door and opened it for her. She stepped onto the street carefully, avoiding the refuse coating the cobblestones. She followed Jahi to a door set into the side of a stone building.

Jahi knocked and stepped back. The door opened.

Stephen stood there.

Her heart hammered, and Ginger whirled around to flee. Jahi shoved her forward. Stephen caught her by the arms, his grip as unrelenting as iron. "Happy to see me, Ginny?"

Jahi slunk back. She stared at his blank expression, his lips unsmiling under a hooked nose. Had Lord Helton done this? Or Victoria?

"You bastard," Ginger said to Jahi.

Stephen held out a small coin-purse toward Jahi. "This is half. Stay here and wait for us to return. You'll get the rest of what I promised then." Stephen yanked her inside.

The door slammed shut behind her. She dug her nails into the palms of her hands, remembering what Stephen had done to Khalib. "Let me go."

Stephen dragged her down a dim hallway. "Walk. Don't worry, darling, your dear father is waiting for you upstairs." He pulled a pistol from the holster at his side. "Please."

Her father was here? She stiffened and walked forward, acutely aware of how simple it would be for Stephen to put a bullet in her back at any moment. "How dare you drag my family into your treachery?"

Stephen's footsteps followed behind her, echoing in the hall-way. "Treachery to whom? Jolly old England? My great-grandfather was German. Over half of my family still lives there. My ridiculous father has done his best to keep that inconvenient fact under cover, but he has no loyalty to our true bloodline."

For as long as she'd known him, she'd never heard him speak of Germany—but had she ever paid attention? Distant in her memory were conversations with Henry about Stephen visiting family for holidays. She may have assumed it was in South Africa, due to the family mines. Had Henry or her father known about the Fishers' connection to the Germans?

At the top of the stairs, Stephen reached around her and opened the closed door. Ginger blinked at the bright light.

"Come inside." Her father's voice sounded distant and tired.

Ginger moved further into the room. "Father!" She stopped a few yards in. She couldn't run to him for comfort. He was to blame for this.

Her father sat at a desk, his head bent over a ledger. His face showed the silver-and-brown stubble of a few days shadowing his jawline. A glass of spirits sat beside him on the desk, with the decanter open nearby. The neck of his white shirt hung open, unbuttoned.

Lord Braddock set his pencil down and closed the ledger. "Did you know, Virginia, in the wild, when a wolf chooses to leave its pack, it often has to travel hundreds of miles to eat? Life becomes infinitely more difficult for the creature."

She stood straighter, clasping her hands in front of her. "Am I the wolf in this scenario?"

"Are you?"

Her eyes narrowed. "Where's Mother?"

"She and Lucy are on their way to Luxor. Your mother wanted to wait for you, but I convinced her I'd send you along later."

Ginger raised her chin. "I'm not going to Luxor."

Her father came around and grabbed her by the arm. "I don't

care what you think you know, this ends now. Tell me what you've been up to."

Was his show of loyalty to Stephen a front? "Or what?"

Her father cracked his knuckles as he made a fist. "Don't underestimate me, Ginger. I'm not incapable of doing what's necessary to protect this family."

With Stephen right there, they lacked the ability to speak freely. Her diaphragm dropped low as she took a deep breath. "Old families and estates are failing all over England. There's no shame in it."

"Your mother deserves better. She deserves more than I've ever been able to give her. I've subjected myself to the most humiliating of posts, for her. With all my years of service, I deserved a post somewhere other than the most forgotten corner of the war. Filthy, stinking Egypt."

His words stunned her. Her father's various appointments throughout the British colonies had always been a source of pride for her. She'd thought nothing of the assignment to Cairo before the war or that her father had moved the family there from Penmore. He'd never hinted it had been out of necessity. In fact, she'd always believed him fond of the Egyptian people.

"Is that why you care nothing for what the Maslukha does to the people he terrorizes? I saw the damage inflicted by the Maslukha and his revolutionaries. Bedouin women and children, barefoot and bleeding. People who died because of your failure to turn in this traitor." She pointed to Stephen.

"I told you she knows a great deal." Henry's voice stunned her. He stood from an armchair facing the window.

She gasped at the sight of her beloved brother, who looked gaunt and dirty. She remembered what Noah had told her the night before. Henry was here because she'd involved him. "Henry, why are you involved in this? Why are you throwing everything away?"

"I won't allow the family's destruction, if I can help it."

A pang went through her heart. Faced with the same choice, what she'd chosen made her a traitor to her family.

"Whose side are you on, Ginny?" Henry asked.

She couldn't look at him, her stomach in knots. "Mine."

"Yours? Or Noah Benson's?" Stephen smirked as he came forward. He leaned against the desk. "Why not admit the truth?"

Her father and brother did nothing to come to her defense. She squeezed her hands. This was the way it was to be now? She couldn't accept it. She knew Henry. Henry loved her. She met his gaze, appealing to him. "Henry, you know the truth about Stephen. You know what he is. How could you choose him over me?"

"Ginny, you must understand—"

Her hands clenched as she stormed up to him. "I must understand you'd rather Stephen ruin our family, threaten our mother and sister, and betray England? You want me to accept you know the truth and you've done nothing about it? You're a good man, Henry. Don't let what Father has done ruin you."

Henry's eyes were veined with red. "It's much more complicated than you believe. Father has done nothing more dishonest than other British officials have. They lie to the French, to the Arabs, to the Zionists, telling each of them what they want to hear to accomplish their goals."

His justification was nauseating. "Even if the British are less than honest with their allies, how can you justify the murder of innocents? I saw it, Henry. I saw the Bedouin refugees who came to our clearing station, begging for help. Women, old men. Children"—her voice grew raw—"a girl, no older than five years old, burned alive in a lorry in front of my eyes. And an infant. How can you justify that?"

Henry grabbed her by the wrist, and his fingers dug into her skin. "Are you the arbiter of truth now, Ginny? The judge and the jury?"

She lifted her chin. Clearly, Henry was miserable with what he'd chosen. It explained why he'd been drinking, why he appeared not to be eating. Would it take much to bring him to her side? "I know you love England. I can see this is eating you alive. Don't turn your back on what's right."

"What makes you think Noah Benson can offer you salvation? You don't know him like I do. The man is the furthest thing imaginable from a saint. He's a cold and ruthless killer. It's what he's good at."

She narrowed her gaze at him. "At least he's not a traitor."

Henry sneered. "You think everything is so black and white, don't you? The traitor here is you."

The rowdy hollering of soldiers on the street filtered through the window. Ginger wished she could call out to them, to anyone, for help. She stared at Henry. "Noah has his flaws, but he's more honest than any of you."

Henry's face reddened. "Consider what he's doing with you, Ginny. You think he's never done it before? Never used a woman to get to someone else? Did you tell her about Constantinople?" he asked her father.

Her father gave a mirthless smile. "No. But maybe I should have."

Henry sneered, his gaze locking with Ginger's. "His assignment—assassinate a German officer. No one could get to him. But Noah found a way."

"Stop it, Henry." She didn't want to hear the story.

"The German officer had a wife. He had his fun with her—like he's doing with you, Ginny—even convinced her to let him into the house when her husband was away. All so he could lie in wait for his true target."

Goose bumps rose on Ginger's arms.

"And what happened to the woman, Father?" Henry's eyes darkened.

Her father said nothing. Henry answered for him. "The papers showed her body where he left her, her blood on the sheets of the bed he shared with her."

She remained calm despite the nausea rising in her throat. "Stop."

"He used her to betray her husband," Henry said. "And he's using you, Ginny. Against your father. And your brother. Your entire family. And when he's finished, he'll discard you without a backward glance too."

Was any of it true? She straightened. It didn't matter. "You made your choice, Henry, and I've made mine."

"That's all we need to hear, yes?" Stephen went around to the other side of the desk. He pulled a leather pouch from a drawer. "Have a seat, Ginny." He motioned toward a chair in front of the desk.

Her eyes shot toward her father, but he didn't look at her. She wanted to scream at him, demand he not be such a coward. Sinking into the seat, she watched as Stephen removed a series of tools from the pouch: a hammer, a knife, a steel awl, among others. She tore her gaze away, her heart pounding. "What—"

"Don't worry, they aren't for you." Stephen nodded at Henry.

Henry went to a closet and opened the door.

"Would you like to look inside, darling Ginny?" Stephen asked. "Henry brought me a present."

Ginger stiffened. A present? She didn't want to see what he had in there.

Stephen grabbed her by the chin and forced her to look.

There, gagged and bound, but eyes open, lay Beatrice.

Her head spun. What—how ...?

Henry had gone to Belah ...

Ginger cried out and bolted from the chair. Stephen shoved her down again.

"Father—" Ginger appealed to him, her eyes wide. "Father, please. I know you aren't like this. Don't let him hurt her."

Stephen left her side and dragged Beatrice out of the closet. The gag around Beatrice's mouth muffled her protests. Her uniform was dirty and spotted with dried blood. Tears shone in her eyes as Stephen set her down in a simple wooden chair in the middle of the room. Her gaze locked with Ginger's, her appeal for help written in her terror.

How could this be happening?

Her telegram to Beatrice. It implied she was involved. And how important she was to Ginger.

Oh, God . . .

Breathe. She needed to breathe.

"Virginia." Her father's voice was low. He stood in front of her. "You must tell us what you know. We have eyes everywhere —we know you were at Lord Helton's house. Fortunately, Stephen was able to convince Jahi to bring you here to us."

She could hardly think straight, but his words seemed to absolve Lord Helton of any involvement in her being here.

Stephen nodded to the desk. "Henry, grab me the awl. Speaking of eyes, I think they might be a superb place to start."

Ginger's horror grew as Henry lifted a long, sharp-pointed instrument. "No!" She thought of the gun strapped to her leg. But she couldn't risk using it—not with three men fully capable of stopping her. "Father, Henry . . . p-please! I know you're better than this. You can't allow this man to hurt an innocent woman. I don't believe you would."

The corners of Stephen's eyes crinkled. "You see, gentlemen? You hear? That's the problem. She doesn't believe you would." His hand shot out, grabbing Beatrice by the nape of her neck and hair. He tossed her down and Beatrice hit the floor with a thud. She moaned in pain.

"Stop it!" Ginger bolted toward Beatrice but Henry held her back, his arm gripped tightly across her chest.

Henry's breath was warm against her ear. "Just tell him what he wants, Ginny. Don't endanger Mother and Lucy."

She fought his grip. "Let me go."

Stephen delivered a fierce kick into Beatrice's abdomen with the toe of his boot. Beatrice cried out and rolled onto her side, her knees into her chest, her body shaking. Stephen placed his foot against her curled fingertips, withholding his weight. "Tell me or I will hurt her. And I will take my time doing so. This is your last chance."

Ginger pushed away from Henry. Could she risk telling them something untrue? She couldn't. Not with Beatrice's life on the line. If they found out or they discovered Ginger was lying, who knew what they would do? And she had no way of knowing what they already knew.

"Noah …" She drew a breath. Would Noah forgive her for this?

"Yes?" Stephen asked. He put more of his weight against Beatrice's hand and she whimpered.

She squeezed her eyes shut. She had to help Beatrice. "Noah knows where Ahmed hid the documents."

Her father and Stephen exchanged a look. "Damn it, I knew it—" her father started, worry crossing his face. His eyes darted around the room like a caged animal.

"Where?" Stephen demanded to Ginger. "Where are they?"

She couldn't tell him. If she did, she could endanger Noah's efforts to retrieve them.

Stephen extended his hand to Henry. "The awl, Henry."

"No!" Ginger held Henry's arm, refusing to let him go. "No, Henry, please listen to me. There's a way out of this still for all of us. If not for me, do it for Angelica. She loves you for the good man that you are. Doing this is the only sure way to lose her for good. Don't give Stephen any more power over you—"

Beatrice's scream and a sickening snap of bone filled the space. Stephen's eyes gleamed, the full weight of his boot against Beatrice's wrist. "A nurse with a mangled hand won't be too useful, will she now? What about both wrists?"

Was this what he had done to Khalib? Sickness threatened her. She had to tell him enough to satisfy him. Before he maimed Beatrice for life. "The documents are in Beersheba." She uttered the words so quietly she hardly heard them herself.

"What's that?" Stephen raised a brow.

"She said Beersheba, Stephen. Leave the girl be." Henry's shoulders bunched with tension.

Stephen straightened and spread his hands. "See? That wasn't so hard, was it?" His face gleamed as he quirked an eyebrow at Henry. "My methods work, dear friend. Now all we need to do is send a message to our friends in Beersheba. Let them know they'll have an intruder. More than likely dressed as a Bedouin."

"No—"

Stephen smiled cruelly. "I know our Major Benson. Once he finds out where those documents are, his first move will be retrieve them. He is rather adept at slipping in and out of Turkish camps—but not if the Turks know he's coming."

Ginger clutched her hands to her stomach. Noah and Jack were walking into a deadly situation. And it was her fault. "That's not true. He's not going for them. You've already given him enough rope to hang yourself, he doesn't need the documents."

Stephen smirked. "Don't be pathetic, darling. It's unbecoming."

Ginger covered her face with her hands. She didn't want

them to see her cry. But they had won, and she'd likely condemned the man she loved to death.

"Now," her father growled. "Enough of this. We had a deal, Fisher. She's done her part. Have your man take her to the boat with her mother and sister."

"And Beatrice?" Ginger lowered her hands. "Let her go. You can't hold an innocent woman." Her eyes darted to her friend, whose breathing remained panicked.

"No. We may yet need her. At a minimum to stop you from thinking you can warn your lover." Stephen's eyes narrowed. "She stays."

Ginger wrangled herself free from Henry and ran to Beatrice's side. Beatrice's eyebrows knitted, her body trembling. She moaned through the gag, trying to speak. Ginger reached for her wrist and Beatrice cried out.

Stephen yanked Ginger upright. "Leave her."

Ginger fought back, clawing against him. "I'm not leaving my friend. You broke her wrist. I need to help her."

"The bitch stays." Stephen's words were a harsh whisper. His fingers dug into her own wrist. Would he break her bone just as easily? Stephen lifted his head toward her father. "Change of plans. I'll see to it myself that Ginger is left at my house. She's too much of a risk to be out of my sight."

"You swore you would keep the women together." Her father's face colored.

Sweat ran down Ginger's back, the heat of the room too intense, the air stifling. She looked for a rubbish bin, but couldn't get away from Stephen's grasp before she vomited. Noah had praised her for saving everything. But Victoria had been right. The blame of every misstep lay on her shoulders.

Stephen held out a handkerchief. "Let's go, my dear."

She ignored the handkerchief, wiping her mouth with the back of her hand. Her gaze shot to Henry. She wouldn't have believed her brother capable of abducting an innocent woman, let alone her friend. "Henry, Henry—please. Don't allow him to hurt Beatrice. Promise me you'll—" Ginger flinched as Stephen grabbed her arm with a steel grip. He dragged her toward the door. "Please. You have to let her go."

Stephen shoved her out of the door and it slammed shut, the darkness of the hallway enclosing her. A sour taste permeated her mouth and she wrested her arm away from Stephen as he led her down the stairwell. "Don't touch me."

Stephen led her out into the alleyway. The scent of baked dust drifted past and she blinked in the sunlight. "Try not to look so miserable, darling. We're just taking a short drive."

Numb and raw, she glanced up at the building where she'd been as they stepped out into the street. The ground floor was a pub. British soldiers gathered both inside and outside, drinking and making a spectacle, even at this early hour. No wonder she'd heard them so close by.

If only Stephen had given her time to treat Beatrice. Somehow, she had to find a way to help Beatrice. She gripped her haversack, desperate to feel grounded to anything. "You have to release my friend. I gave you what you wanted."

"No." Stephen glanced at her. "You didn't. Don't you see? I gave you so many opportunities to make things right between us. I even promised your father I'd forgive his debts, in exchange for your hand."

She threw him the most satisfied look she could muster. "It must drive you mad to know you can have all the diamonds and money and power in the world—and I still won't marry you. You'll never have me."

Jahi waited for them in the motorcar he'd brought Ginger in. Stephen pushed her into the backseat and climbed in behind her. "Go. To my residence."

The motorcar sped out of the alleyway onto the main street.

Ginger recoiled as far as she could from Stephen, but he came closer. "You think I won't have you?" He held her face, his thumb and forefinger taut against her chin so that she couldn't turn her head away. His mouth descended on hers, with a hard and vicious kiss.

Her back pressed against the door, feeling for the handle. The cool metal slid past her fingertips and out of her grasp as she kicked Stephen to get away. He pushed her hand toward his crotch. "I'll have you when and how I want you, Ginny. And when I'm through with you, I can promise you even Noah Benson won't want you."

She searched his cold eyes, trying to think of a response. She felt for the gun at her leg. If he released her slightly, she might be able to pull it out.

Jahi slammed on the brake and they were forced to catch themselves as the motion propelled them forward.

"You idiot." Stephen spat at Jahi, the spittle running down the man's neck.

Jahi mumbled a low apology.

Ginger startled and caught her hand against the door handle. Jahi had been forced to stop because of traffic—in front of the train station.

What if she could catch up to Noah and Jack?

If she fled, Stephen might hurt Beatrice. But if she did nothing, the danger to Noah was assured. Noah was the only one who she knew she could trust. Noah might be her only hope for getting Beatrice back.

And if she stayed, Stephen would rape her.

She had only seconds to act. Kicking Stephen as hard as she could, she threw the door open as Jahi lurched forward once more. Tumbling out of the slow-moving car, she rolled onto the street. Stephen cursed behind her. She didn't look back as she dodged and wove her way across the street, past tumbling carriages and horses. A motorcar blared its horn and swerved as she escaped its bumper.

She had to find Noah. He would know what to do. Jack had said they planned on taking the number 408 to Ismailia at noon. Hopefully it would still be there.

Ginger fled into the train station. Her legs felt weak, her hands shaky as she passed through the ticket counters and the crowds in the main building and went toward the platforms.

She ran, praying the train hadn't left. One platform came into view with a sign indicating Ismailia as its destination. She tore through the throng and climbed into the first train car she reached.

She paused at the entrance to the car as passengers stared from their seats.

She hurried through a few train cars, scanning the seats for Noah or Jack. She didn't see them. A sway caused her to grip the seats as the train started forward.

She could no longer stop the tears. They spilled onto her cheeks as she slowed, blurring the faces of the people she passed.

Upon reaching the end of a train car, Ginger stopped. She lifted her hand to her head and wiped her eyes. Her shoulders shook. Someone grabbed her from behind. She screamed.

"Ginger." Noah turned her.

Her knees crumpled. He caught her by the shoulders, concern on his face.

The relief she felt at seeing him drained her last drop of energy. As he swept her into his arms, she said, "Stephen knows your plans. And he has Beatrice."

CHAPTER THIRTY-FIVE

$\mathcal{T}$ ilting her head back, Ginger stared into the electric bulb by the ceiling, counting between breaths. Noah squatted beside her. The squeal of the train's wheels against the tracks had dulled to such a consistent pitch that she found comfort in their cadence. From his seat on the bench across from them, Jack stared on in stony silence.

Noah offered her a flask of whiskey but she shook her head. "I don't want any more," she said. She squeezed her eyes shut. "Do you think …" She couldn't finish the thought. Had Stephen hurt Beatrice more by now? Or worse still, killed her?

"As soon as we get to Ismailia we'll send Lord Helton a message. If they can rescue her, they will." Noah held her hand in his, grazing his thumb over her knuckles.

She ground her teeth together. "Do you think you can trust Lord Helton? What if the reason he insisted on Jahi taking me is because he knew Stephen had made an arrangement with him?" Despite Noah's repeated assurances of Lord Helton's goodness, he'd left a bad impression.

"Lord Helton wouldn't betray the British to Stephen." Noah

glanced back at Jack, as though to get his support.

Jack didn't meet his eye.

Did his friendship with Victoria blind Noah to the possibility? Or was there something more? If she didn't know better, she'd suspect Jack agreed with her. Ginger almost pulled her hand from Noah's but stopped.The flash of her temper was displaced. She was angry at the situation, not at him.

She was angry at herself.

The train slowed as it arrived at a station. It was little more than a tumbledown shack, but British soldiers milled there.

For what must have been the hundredth time, she whispered, "I'm sorry, Noah—I didn't want to tell him anything."

Jack pulled his feet down from the bench and sat straight. "Red, you did the best you could. You don't need to keep apologizing."

Ginger lifted her brows at the moniker.

Jack winked and stood. "I'm going to see a man about a dog." He left their private compartment, closing the door behind him.

Noah sat beside her. "Jack's right. You can't keep tormenting yourself over it."

"But—what about the documents? You can't get them now." She wanted Noah to give her assurances he wouldn't dare continue with their plan to go into Beersheba. Yet, to her dismay, he hadn't.

"Lord Helton will decide that. It isn't for me to say." Noah slipped an arm around her shoulder and pulled her closer. He kissed her temple.

Did he sense her fear? She couldn't stop thinking about Beatrice. The snap of bone echoed in her mind, plaguing her thoughts.

She couldn't escape the guilt that came with the safety of Noah's presence. Had Stephen followed up on his threat to hurt her? Ginger prayed that Beatrice would be spared by her brother or father—her life depended on it. She'd never forgive herself for the telegram she'd sent her friend—or for getting away while she remained captured. How would she ever earn Beatrice's forgiveness?

She hoped she'd have the chance.

The wooden door to the compartment rattled as Jack pushed it open. He closed the door, the locked it. "I don't want to be the bearer of bad news, but we need to change."

Noah lifted his head sharply. "What is it?"

"A pair of lieutenants boarded at the last stop. They're looking for you, Noah." Jack didn't face them as he spoke, reaching to the overhead storage rack for their bags which he set on the bench.

Ginger felt Noah tense beside her. His reaction concerned her. "Did they say why?" she asked.

"I didn't talk to them—I just overheard them asking around." Jack dug into the bags and pulled out a set of robes. "They want to arrest him." He unbuttoned his jacket. "Apparently someone has sent out an urgent cable accusing him of espionage for the Ottomans and ordered it."

She searched Jack's face, her outrage muted by the dull reality of it all. It had to be her father. He was the only one with the authority and motivation to do so. How could she have arrived at a point where nothing vile he did seemed shocking?

Noah pulled away from Ginger and stood, calm but moving quickly as he reached for his own bag. "They're searching the train?" he asked Jack.

Jack pulled off his shirt, not waiting for Ginger to turn away. "One car away. And they're also looking for Ginger. If they get one glimpse of her hair, they'll suspect her at minimum—if she doesn't give us away outright."

"They want to arrest me, too?" Ginger stared at him, aghast.

"No." Jack pulled the robe over his head. "They want to

rescue you from your kidnapper." He jerked his head at Noah. "You don't happen to have a burqa in your bag of tricks, do you?"

"Unfortunately, no." Noah pulled out Bedouin clothing for himself—a white cotton, ankle-length robe, called a *thawb*. Over the *thawb*, he tied a cloth belt, a dark sleeveless coat, or *aba*, and on his head he placed a white *kufeya*, which resembled a loose turban tied with camel wool.

Despite the fact that she'd seen Noah disguise himself before, there was something in his transformation which impressed her. In uniform, he seemed as British as they came. But he was able to pass for a Turk and looked perfectly at ease in the Bedouin *thawb*, also. He really was a chameleon.

Given his proficiency with languages, it was no small wonder that he'd risen through the ranks.

Noah had just finished dressing when a knock came from the door. He grabbed Ginger by the wrist and guided her to the small wall right beside the door. He pressed her back to it.

Jack, wearing his own *thawb*, stuffed their clothing away in the bags. He sat on the bench, curling into the wall as though asleep, his face obscured.

"Get ready to shoot if necessary," Noah whispered back to Jack. He unlocked the door and opened it, the back of the door giving Ginger cover.

Noah greeted them with a gruff, Arabic phrase.

"Excuse us, sir, we've got to check every compartment. There's an Englishwoman been kidnapped," one of the soldiers said.

Ginger held still. If they found her here, would they attempt to take her back by force?

No. Noah wouldn't let that happen. But the consequences of that could be even more worrisome.

The irritation in Noah's voice was clear, despite her inability to understand his rapid speech. He gesticulated with wild hands, his movements broad. Noah spat at the soldiers and then slammed the door shut.

"Are you mad?" Ginger hissed at him, her eyes widening.

Jack chuckled from the corner as he sat straighter. His voice was low. "He knows what he's doing, Red. Those fellows aren't likely to try again quite yet." He stood. "In the meantime, we should get moving." He pulled another piece of linen cloth out of his bag and tossed it to Ginger. "Wrap this over your head, best you can."

Ginger fumbled with the cloth, tying it around her hair like a head scarf. "Where are we going?"

"Out of this car. In the opposite direction to those soldiers, in case they decide to come back to the one compartment they didn't get into." Jack slung his bag over his shoulder and then grabbed a pair of rifles from the luggage rack. He handed them to Noah.

And then what? Ginger hid her alarm and looked at Noah for answers.

Noah strapped the rifles across his back. He placed a steady hand on her shoulder. "We may need to get off the train in a hurry."

"You mean jump?" The compartment felt cramped with them standing in it.

"If necessary," Noah said.

Her eyes widened at Noah. *Jump from a moving train?*

"Don't look like that. It's not a real adventure until someone jumps from a train." Jack grinned.

Noah gave Jack an amused look. "If it comes to it, you need to stay on board. Ride the train to Ismailia and get a motorcar. We'll follow the tracks, but stay out of sight from them. You'll have to come back for us."

"And if there's no motorcar?" Jack rubbed the back of his

neck.

"Then get horses. Or camels. Whatever you can get. I can't imagine it would take you more than an hour to get back to us. We're nearly to Ismailia." Noah cracked open the door and peeked out. He held one finger up, watching. After a minute, he waved them forward. "Let's go."

They filed out of the compartment, Ginger between Jack and Noah. Jack led them as they hurried down the aisle of the train car.

Ginger's gaze fell to the path in front of her feet. As they went from one carriage to the next, they found themselves in an open-air passenger car. The warm wind pushed her hair in front of her face. She pulled it back, out of her eyes. The smell of smoke and cinders filled the air.

Passengers stared from their seats, including a British soldier sitting a few rows in. His chin jerked upward when he saw her.

Oh no. Her hair. It was the giveaway Jack had suggested it would be.

She glanced back at Noah. He focused his eyes forward but his pace increased.

They passed the soldier who was now standing. "You there!" He pointed at her. "Are you the woman those chaps were looking for? Are these men holding you against your will?"

"Keep going," Noah muttered behind her.

Ginger ignored the soldier, boring her eyes into Jack's back as they passed.

"Stop!" the soldier called after them.

Jack moved faster still. They hurried down the car until they reached the end. Ginger looked over her shoulder. The soldier had moved from his seat, but he didn't chase them. Instead, he headed in the direction they'd come from—and the direction the men who searched for her had gone.

They moved out of the train car into the small space between the cars, where the steps to the train car were located. Jack turned to face them. He cupped his hands around his mouth. "Give me your rifles. I'll toss them off after you jump." He held his hand out to Noah.

The landscape blurred past them, a rush of sand and stone. Noah lowered his head toward her ear. "We'll jump separately. I can go first if it helps."

Ginger nodded, jittery. Noah switched places with her. "Try not to overthink it," Jack shouted toward her, and put a comforting hand on her back. "Don't try too hard to do much but roll when you land."

Noah jumped. She watched, sick, as he stayed behind on the sand. Was he all right? Worry for him was replaced with fear, her palms slick. How could she jump?

Her hands gripped the rail by the steps, the metal hot from the sun. Jack tossed one rifle, then the next. "Your turn," Jack said.

What if she landed wrong? Or her legs got caught under the tracks? She shook her head, paralyzed with fear.

"You just climbed out a window last night!" Exasperation showed on Jack's features.

"The window wasn't moving," she shouted back.

"The longer you wait, the further you'll be from Noah. Think of it as jumping from a tree. Ready? One ... two ... three!"

She still held on. "I'm not ready!"

Jack's strong arms reached out. "Sorry, Red." With force, he shoved her forward.

Ginger's arms flailed as she tumbled from the train, getting her legs under her at the last moment. She was weightless for a flash and then the earth smacked her. The wind was knocked from her and she sprawled into the sand, her head spinning.

She groaned and rolled onto her back. "Damn that Jack

Darby," she muttered, spitting the grit from her lips. She tasted dirt in her mouth and spat again. Her eyes focused on the crystal blue sky and she sat, the train continuing past.

* * *

GINGER STOOD at the British airfield in Ismailia, leaning against a motorcar. Heat rose from the dusty airstrips, intensified by the black burqa she wore over her face. After Jack had rescued them from the heat of the desert, he'd given Ginger another gift: an outfit to hide her appearance and red hair.

She still hadn't forgiven him for pushing her from the train.

Noah sipped at a canteen. They didn't dare go any closer to the plane hangar—they'd spent their time in Ismailia with their profiles low.

Jack sauntered toward them, his Bedouin robes flowing around him.

"Well?" Noah capped the canteen, an impatient scowl on his lips.

"Ned says he'll take us. Just because it's you." Jack opened the motorcar door and sat in the passenger seat. "But if you insist on taking Ginger, it's going to take two trips ... which is a problem."

Insist on taking her? "Where else am I supposed to go?" Ginger glared at him. "Maybe to one of those safehouses you both swore by earlier this morning."

"Don't get your bloomers in a knot, Red. I'm not suggesting you shouldn't go, but the fact is that it's dangerous to take you to Beersheba."

"We don't have much of a choice." Noah drummed his thumbs against the steering wheel. "I don't trust that Stephen doesn't have men here in Ismailia—or that he couldn't buy some along the way."

"Well, and when Ned's the only one of our so-called friends willing to help us out—"

"I can't hold it against them. Not when the CID is telling them I'm a traitor on the run." Despite the evenness of his words, Ginger saw the ill humor in Noah's expression.

She grimaced. By discrediting Noah, her father had left them with nowhere to go.

"I don't see why you're still planning on going to Beersheba at all," Ginger said, pulling away from the motorcar and crossing her arms. "They know you're coming. They're going to capture you if you go there."

"Yes, but you didn't tell Stephen anything about the well, correct?" Noah searched her gaze. "They won't know where to look. Beersheba is a large stronghold."

"I only told them Beersheba." She uncrossed her arms again, conscious of appearing too Western in her mannerisms. She sat in the backseat. "But you said you were going to ask Lord Helton—"

"I can't ask him. I can't even go to an army post." Noah's frustration seeped into his tone. "I have to make the decision and I have to do it before we're out of time."

"And the documents are more important than your life?" She struggled to keep her volume down. They weren't close to any British soldiers, but it was better to be careful.

"Yes." Noah met her eyes. "They're more important than my life. Because they're not just about the Maslukha. They'll tell us the full plot against Lawrence. The plans the Ottomans have for this region—Ahmed sacrificed everything to get those documents as far as he did. He didn't leave them in Beersheba to be buried there for eternity. He left them there only because he couldn't risk letting the enemy get his hands on them. It's up to me to finish what he started."

Ginger clamped her mouth shut, chastened. Ahmed had

given his life for this. A lump rose in her throat. Rather ... she'd cost Ahmed his life for this.

Noah looked toward Jack. "Why are two trips a problem for Ned?"

"There's a *khamsin* headed the way we're going," Jack said. "He might be able to make one full trip, but no way he can make two full ones without getting caught in it on the way back. It'd be his death."

She'd endured many such sandstorms in Belah. Spring was *khamsin* season, and the particular nature of these sandstorms brought blistering temperatures with them. "And it's headed toward Beersheba?" She felt foolish repeating everything he'd said, but her mind raced. Both men nodded. "Isn't that perfect timing?"

Jack guffawed. "I'm not sure what your idea of perfect timing is. Maybe you can explain."

"Can't you use the sandstorm as cover to sneak in and out of Beersheba? The Turks won't be able to see, so there's less of a chance they'll capture you, even with Stephen's warning."

Noah shook his head. "And we won't be able to see anything either."

Jack held out his hand. "Now, hold on. That's not a half-bad idea."

"In what way?" Noah asked.

"I've done it before. Moved around in a sandstorm. It's difficult but doable." Jack's gaze wandered over the airfield as an airplane engine sounded in the distance. "But we'd want to have some camels to get away from there as soon as we've gotten the documents. We can't rely on the sandstorm for indefinite cover. We won't want to be found with our pants around our ankles standing in the middle of Tel el Saba when the thing blows over."

Noah pursed his lips. "General Chaytor has men out that

way. Maybe you could send a message to them about getting some camels?"

"That'd be the best option," Jack said.

"And you believe we can recover the documents in the sand-storm?" Noah asked.

"I'd say there's a fifty percent chance. Or we could get disoriented and fall down Abraham's well," Jack said.

Ginger held back a smile. Trust Jack to add humor to every situation.

"You know, the more we sit around talking about it, the less time we're giving Ned." Jack tapped his foot impatiently. "Ned can drop me off with Chaytor first, then put you as close to Beersheba as possible. I'll get the camels and meet you at a planned location. Red's plan to use the sandstorm is good."

Noah rubbed his eyes with his fingertips. "Lord Helton will be furious about her involvement in this. And there's no way I'm taking her into Tel el Saba, even in a sandstorm."

Jack lifted his chin. "She doesn't have to go in. She doesn't have to get anywhere near it. In fact, she can stay with the camels while we go for the documents."

"Let me help. Please." Ginger leaned forward to squeeze Noah's shoulder. "What choice do we have?"

"If anything happens to you, I'll never forgive myself." Noah's hands curled into fists. "What if we are seen during the *khamsin*? Or we leave you with the camels and you're seen?"

Ginger frowned. "Well then, would it be better to wait? Go tomorrow?"

"If we go tomorrow, Stephen will beat us to Beersheba," Jack countered.

Stephen? "Why would Stephen be going to Beersheba?"

Jack tore his gaze away. "I think it's a reasonable assumption."

It wasn't an *unreasonable* one. But it was the manner in which

Jack had said it that concerned her. "Yes but ... I get the feeling you aren't assuming." She stared at the back of Jack's neck. He didn't turn to look at her. "Jack? What is it?"

Jack turned his head, his eyes on Noah. "You should tell her."

"Jack ..." Noah's tone held a warning.

The exchange was enough for Ginger to understand Noah had kept something from her. "Tell me what?"

"Jack." Noah's voice hardened with anger.

Jack sighed with exasperation. "She has a right to know."

Ginger furrowed her brow. "Know what?"

"Your father is attempting to help us capture Stephen Fisher."

The news hit her like a thunderclap. Her jaw dropped and she stared at Noah and Jack, wide-eyed. "What?"

Noah glared fiercely at Jack. "The more she knows, the more danger she's in."

She leaned into the leather of the seat back. "No, I want to know. What does he mean?"

Noah glanced over the top of her head at Jack and shook his head. "Your father went to Lord Helton and offered himself, in exchange for a deal. He's heading toward Belah with Stephen, Henry, and your friend, Sister Thornton. He's convinced Stephen the goal is to capture Jack and me on the way back from Beersheba. Lord Helton was afraid Stephen would go into hiding and that we would lose the opportunity to bring him in if we didn't accept."

Her father had agreed to help? A surge of astonished hope moved through her. "When did my father do this?"

"This morning," Noah said. "It's why Lord Helton left in a rush."

She clutched her hand over her stomach. "Then you knew ..." The full weight of his words hit her. "You knew Jahi was taking me to my father." Fury built in her and she fisted her hands, wanting to punch him.

Noah turned in the seat to face her. "No, I didn't. I didn't learn about it until after you left."

Her lower lip trembled. "But Lord Helton knew, didn't he? That's why he sent me with Jahi? And you didn't tell me. He *let* Beatrice be tortured so that Stephen would find out where we were going. So that Stephen would think he had the upper hand."

"I didn't know, Ginger! I swear it. Lord Helton only said that you were being sent to your father, who had assured your safety. And even that, I was furious about."

She pounded his shoulder with her fist, tears pricking her eyes. "Furious? But resigned? Resigned to let Lord Helton send me back to the men I risked my life to escape? How dare you!" She leveled her gaze at Jack. "Did you know?"

Jack sank back, as though embarrassed to be caught. "No, neither of us did. He's telling the truth. Lord Helton told us after you left. And Noah tried to speak up against it—"

"Tried to? Stephen beat my friend! He threatened to rape me." Ginger's chest heaved as she fought to hold back the screams that threatened to explode from her chest. She narrowed her eyes back at Noah. "And you claim to love me? Yet you left me there. Do you know what would have happened if I hadn't escaped?"

Noah's face darkened. "Yes!" He swore and stormed from the motorcar, slamming the door behind him. He strode several paces away and stood there, facing the horizon.

"He wanted to go after you, Ginger," Jack said in a low voice. "He fought with Lord Helton about it. Threatened to resign. I haven't seen him that angry in a long time."

"But he still just left me there."

"I had to!" Noah turned and came back toward them. "I had

to. I didn't want to." His face was pain. "God knows it was torture for me. All I wanted to do was go after you. But Lord Helton swore your father had promised to keep you safe. And he threatened to call off the rescue of your sister and mother— which was part of the deal he made with your father—if I went after you. Even if I had managed to rescue you, I would have been risking their lives, and the life of T.E. Lawrence, and anyone else who is in danger while those documents remain out there." Noah pointed to the horizon.

Ginger focused her gaze at her feet, swallowing a calmer breath. He'd told her how inconvenient their love was. How it interfered with his work. Still, her disappointment in the choice he'd made was bitter. "And in exchange, what will happen to my father and Henry?"

"Your father and Henry will still be arrested, but it's likely they'll see time in prison as opposed to execution," Noah said.

Her father's redemptive act was more than she'd expected from him. He must have felt cornered, with no hope of escape. It wasn't heroic, just another act of cowardice. An inability to face the consequences of the disaster he had created, when he had no other choice left.

Jack spoke up from his seat, addressing them both. "I hate to interrupt, but we really have to get in the air if we're going to go."

A look of furious resignation burned in Noah's eyes. He glared at Jack. "If things go wrong, I'm blaming you entirely, Jack." He stalked away without a backward glance.

Ginger exchanged a look with Jack, and he gave her a comforting smile. "It's going to be all right. Just do me a favor?" Jack bent over, gathering their bags from the backseat.

"What's that?" Ginger asked.

"Don't die. Because that man will hate me for life if you do."

CHAPTER THIRTY-SIX

In the beautiful wilderness of the Negev, Ginger could almost forget the daunting task in front of them. The biplane ride that had brought them to the desert of rock and sand had felt surreal. As the shadows of the cliffs and canyon around them elongated with the sun's descent, she did her best not to think of the night to come. A sandstorm. A confrontation with Stephen.

She shuddered.

Resilient grass and reeds daring a life among the savage heat rustled in the breeze. She shifted on the blanket Noah had placed on the ground for their makeshift dinner. They would camp here alone tonight. Jack had already met them with the camels and gone on foot closer to Beersheba, to scout the best way into Tel el Saba.

The camels lay near them, their tails swishing occasionally. "They're such lazy beasts." She scowled as she pushed the burqa from her face, her neck and hair damp with sweat. Sipping from her canteen, she said, "I don't know how the Bedouin women manage with these things in their faces."

"As terrible as they may seem, they have some level of functionality." Noah removed supplies from his bag. "I've spent a lot of time in a Bedouin *thawb*. You come to appreciate them in the middle of the scorching desert sun. And it hides your red hair."

She grimaced. "Men do themselves the favor of wearing white. Black is a much more unforgiving color in the sun."

He smiled and held out a loaf of bread wrapped in a cloth. "Dinner?"

Her stomach gurgled in response. "Now I know why you'll eat anything. A few hours out here like this, and I think I'd eat dried locusts if offered."

"They're not a half-bad snack when you're hungry." He sat and opened tins of food.

He'd eaten dried locusts. His life experience dwarfed her own. She stretched and rolled her shoulders. "I have to admit, I never imagined doing any of this—and I thought I was adventurous."

"You are adventurous." Noah tore off a piece of bread. "Not many people will do half the things you do."

"And that's why you like me?" She laughed, chewing on the hard crust.

He paused. "It's part of why I love you, yes." He broke eye contact and cleared his throat. "When we find Jack tonight, after the sandstorm, I'll leave you with the camels. We'll go into Tel el Saba for the documents and return as soon as possible. Then we'll meet up with your father and wait for some of General Chaytor's men to rendezvous at the designated location and apprehend Stephen."

"And Beatrice?" In the hours that had passed since they'd been in the desert, they'd tiptoed around the subject.

Noah stretched his feet out in front of him. "Once we escape with the documents, we can offer to make a deal with your father—the documents for Sister Thornton's freedom."

"And you think everything will go according to plan?"

Noah fingers tightened. "I've seen many plans go astray. And I'm worried about the additional risks we're taking with you here."

She scooted closer to him. "I'm willing to take the risk. You can't let a desire to protect me get in the way of what may be our best option."

Noah was silent, a distant expression in his eyes. "For most of my life, I've been angry with my father. But, for the first time, I think I understand him better."

"In what sense?"

A muscle tightened in his jaw. "My parents were deeply in love. My mother kept a tapestry with their wedding vows in the dining room. The vows were in Irish, but they'd repeat those vows to each other every morning, right after prayers."

She'd imagined his parents were happy, even though she knew nothing about them. "Your mother knew Irish?"

"I think my father taught her. Chances are I got my linguistic abilities from her." Noah tore off another piece of bread. "Not that she had the chance to teach me much. She was murdered when I was quite young." Noah paused, the words hanging on his lips.

She shuddered at the horror of it and focused on Noah's face. "I'm so sorry." She put a hand on his shoulder.

"My father shot himself when he found her." He swallowed, the rims of his eyes red. In a low, guttural voice, he added, "The priest wouldn't give him a funeral, so some of my father's friends snuck his body into the casket with my mother. My father always said he didn't want to be without her."

No wonder he didn't speak of his tragic childhood.

He squeezed her hand. "I only ever saw what my father did as selfish. And it was. But the point is, I also never understood what it was like to love someone so much life without them seemed impossible."

Still, he must have spent most of his life wondering why his father hadn't thought more of his children. She'd had that thought one too many times in the last month herself.

"I'm sorry you had to go through that." She wrapped her arms around his neck.

"I wish I could save you from what lies ahead." He gathered a few pebbles in his hand and released them. "The coming days won't be easy. Even if we succeed, the case against your father is complicated."

"And Henry. He kidnapped Beatrice." Ginger laid her head against his shoulder. The idea of her brother doing such a horrible thing made her ill. "We'll get through it together."

He appeared lost in thought for a moment, his shoulders tense. "We should finish eating. We'll need some sleep before the *khamsin* rolls in."

After their meal, Noah unrolled a sleeping bag. She crawled in beside him, nestling against his arm as they watched the stars overhead. Shooting stars streaked through the sky. Ginger interlocked her fingers with his. Even in his arms, fear gripped her in the darkness.

Her heart weighed heavy with foreboding.

Noah kissed her, his lips gentle, tenuous.

"I won't break, Noah." She pulled the *thawb* off, feeling as though she'd drown in the fabric otherwise.

"I don't think you're broken." Noah slipped his hand behind her neck, dipping her head down toward his. "But you've been battered. And I don't know if—"

"Did I treat you as though you'd been battered when you showed me your scars?" She tugged at his robes, driven both by lust and a desperation she couldn't identify. She didn't want anything to be different between them because of Stephen.

His attempts to be gentle with her only made her kisses more fierce, her touch more aggressive. Both in Port Said and at the Heltons' house, she'd felt the restraint of the surroundings. But here in the Arabian wilds, with the man she loved, she wanted to melt her body into his, without concern or care. This was where she'd fallen in love with him, under this endless sky.

His fingers dug into her skin, his arms locking tightly around her, and she communicated every need through her body. Their lovemaking had an intensity it hadn't before. The stars seemed to pulse with them, the winds wrapping them in an embrace while the heat of the night climbed higher with the approaching *khamsin*.

When they'd settled against each other again, Ginger didn't move away, remaining connected to him. She listened to the pounding of his heart, its strong, steady rhythm the comfort she needed.

"When did you know you loved me?" she asked in a soft voice.

Noah opened his eyes. "You want to talk right now?"

"Mm-hmm." She pushed the sleeping bag off her shoulders so their torsos were exposed to the open air of the desert night, moonlight on their skin.

"I think you have the most perfect breasts imaginable."

She laughed. "Thank you. But that's not what I asked."

He touched her cheek. "I may have fallen in love with you when I saw you standing in the hut that first night."

"At first sight? How romantic." She teased a kiss on his earlobe. "I'm serious. When did you know?"

"Probably after I saw you running toward a burning lorry."

She'd thought about that moment so many times—both the explosion and the way he'd held her afterward. "I think that's when I knew too." She kissed down his neck, not wanting to let the sadness of the memory invade their current calm. "I like making love with you here in the open. We should take advantage of being alone tonight."

"*Rohi*, you are becoming insatiable."

"*Rohi?*"

"It means soul mate in Arabic. Or *mo chuisle* if you prefer."

"What's that?" She kissed him once again. "Or are you showing off?"

"My pulse. Irish." He met her eyes. "Maybe someday we can go there together. It's the only place in the world I own anything."

Her own pulse beat faster now. "Ireland?"

He nodded. "In Kinsale. County Cork." He played with a strand of her hair. "You'd fit in well there, my Ginger." He kissed her temple and released her. "We need to be more careful."

Content in her bliss, she closed her eyes, and lay against his chest. "Tonight's not about being careful. We're staring down a sandstorm."

"True." He kissed the top of her head. "But I love you too much to—"

"Then marry me." Her heart beat faster still.

His hand tightened on hers. "I will. Someday."

She rolled over and faced him, feeling impulsive. "I, Ginger, take thee Noah, to be my wedded husband. To have and to hold, for better or worse, for richer or poorer, in sickness and health, till death do us part. According to God's holy ordinance, and thereto I plight thee my troth." She smiled, half teasing. "There. I've said my vow. Now you say yours and we're married."

He lifted a brow. "What about witnesses?"

"Well, there's the Almighty. And the camels." She kissed his cheek. "Don't worry, darling, I know we won't actually be married."

"But we would be. At least in our hearts." Noah grew more serious. "I love you. And I will marry you, I promise. But if I say those words, they'll mean what I say, forever. Even if it's just until I can get a priest to make it official."

Something in the earnestness of his expression made her stomach flutter. "Do you want me to take back my vow?"

He pulled her closer. "You can't take it back. You're mine, *rohi*."

A locust buzzed from a nearby patch of grass.

"Noah, when this started, you intended it to be for that morning in Port Said. And"—she looked away—"my brother told me about Constantinople. And the woman you were involved with there."

Noah's shoulders dropped. "I'm not proud of the things I've had to do, but they were assignments. People far above me deemed them necessary."

"Then it's true?"

"I'm not sure what your brother told you. But I did ..." He cleared his throat. "I allowed a woman to take me on as her lover in order for me to assassinate her husband." Noah pulled her close. "But I won't let anything happen to you."

Noah's expression grew more somber. "I can't promise I'll be alive at the end of this war. Or even tonight. I'm not free. I made a vow to serve and obey the orders given to me. Sometimes they've included things like the pretense of an engagement. Either way, there's not a lot of room for what I want. Not right now. Not with the war going on. And if we continue as we have, we're risking a lot, especially if we aren't careful. We could end up with a child."

The wind brought a fine dust with it and she closed her eyes. "Are you suggesting we finish things?"

"Never. But I don't have the answers either."

Her eyes misted over. "We don't need to solve this now. We have enough to worry about with my father and Stephen."

"I know I want you to be my wife. And it doesn't matter to

me whether I say the vow in front of a priest or a thousand people." Noah kissed her temple. "But I should probably worry about surviving this war first."

His words make her heart ache. Surviving the war was optimistic. Her immediate concern was surviving the coming night.

CHAPTER THIRTY-SEVEN

*G*inger woke to eerie silence. She shuddered. Her cheek brushed against Noah's chest. Nighttime had come quickly, and the desolate wilderness of the Negev enclosed them. The howls of jackals echoed in the canyons.

Now they were silent. Ginger shivered at a powerful gust of wind. Nearby, the camels stamped their feet.

She shook Noah. "Wake up." She lifted her head at a low, distant rumble. "Something's wrong."

Noah rubbed his eyes. He yawned. His arms tightened around her, reflexively, and a soft fluttery feeling curled in her chest at the protective gesture. The wind blew her veil. "What is it?"

He stiffened and sat, flipping on a torch. After letting her go, he pulled out the goggles they'd used while on the airplane. "Here, put these on." His tone was calm, but his actions suggested urgency.

She took the goggles from him, her fingers sluggish.

"The *khamsin* is upon us."

"How do you know?" She saw nothing.

"I can tell." Noah pulled his goggles on. "The wind is stirring, and the temperatures have risen. We need to get on the camels. They'll be able to guide us through this. Have you been through a *khamsin* before?"

She nodded. "But never outside. They always made us take shelter indoors until they were over."

"All right. The goggles will protect your eyes, but it's important for you to keep your mouth covered with that burqa, and another cloth if you can tolerate it. It'll be hard to breathe. You won't be able to see anything, but I'll be right in front of you. You don't want to get lost and go off alone."

"Why would I go anywhere else?"

He helped her with her goggles. "Because sandstorms are disorienting. You'll feel you're suffocating and want to escape. But there's nowhere to go. Stay on the camel. They can see and breathe in these storms. They'll be much more surefooted than either of us." He pulled the *kufeya* from his head and tied it over his mouth and nose like a bandana.

"Can you keep the torch on so I can see you?"

Noah handed it to her. "You can try. You won't be able to see much, though. And these storms are so charged they can short a torch, so use it only if you need to. And keep your gun covered."

"Why?" His urgency struck fear into her, despite his calmness.

He packed his kitbag. "The dust. We want to keep the guns as clean as possible. Drink some water now. It might be awhile before you can again. You'll be parched by then."

She unscrewed the top of the canteen and drank. In the moonlight, a wall of sand and dirt approached down the length of the canyon. The winds grew louder. Noah led her to the camels. He brought one animal to its knees and helped Ginger mount. As the camel stood, Ginger held on to the riser handle in front of her, feeling as though she would topple over. The animal swayed.

The wind pushed through her burqa. She patted the camel's hump. As Noah tethered the camels together, a fine mist of sand and dust rolled on top of them. The howls of the wind intensified as the sand pelted them.

Ginger turned her cheek, to see what she could. She winced as the sand brushed a section of exposed skin near her eye. She lifted the neckline of her *thawb* over her nose, burying her face behind the extra fabric. The warm air became trapped between her lips, and the fabric over her mouth instantly grew stale.

Dust and sand collected in every crevice, weighing down her clothing. The camel started forward. Ginger peeked out. She could barely see Noah's form on the camel in front of her. The sand gathered in her ears. Could they be buried alive?

A crack of thunder startled her. She gripped the camel's fur. Blue sparks of electric current skipped between her fingers as she moved her hands up the short coarse hair of its hump. Lightning flashed in strange patterns in the distance, giving her glimpses of the surroundings.

Unlike other sandstorms she'd encountered in Cairo, the *khamsin*'s wind gusts were unbearably hot. She felt as though they scorched the surrounding earth.

As minutes passed, she futilely attempted to steel her mind to calm. She thought of Jack, surrounded by Turkish soldiers, trying to sneak into Tel el Saba. This storm would be his refuge.

The sandstorm battered them. Alone in the forsaken wasteland, her heart grew heavier. In her mind's eye, she saw Ahmed's dead body, the horse she'd stolen, the Turkish soldiers Noah had killed in the desert, the refugees, the crucified soldiers.

So many lives lost. What carnage would the next few days bring?

She put her feet up on the camel. She'd always hated their smell and the oddness of their rotary stride, but those traits brought her peace now. The animal moved forward, without hesitation or delay, undisturbed by the sand whirling around them. Her camel exuded a strange confidence that tied it to this land and this world. A gentle, wonderful beast with a beating heart.

Consumed by her thoughts, she hardly noticed the passage of time. Finally, the camel stopped. Her reverie broken, she pulled herself upright. The sand still scraped against her goggles. She lifted her hands to her ears, wiping the sand out of them with her fingertips as best she could.

Noah materialized from the darkness with a lit torch. He put his hand on hers. "How are you?" His voice barely carried over the noise.

"Alive." Had she spoken loudly enough?

Noah moved closer to her, the scarf over his mouth brushing against her ear. "I need you to stay here with the camels. We're close to the spot where Jack wanted us to meet him, but I can't see well enough to know what I'm heading into. I won't risk taking you further."

She squinted through the goggles, trying to see his face. How did he even know they were close? How could he see? The lightning came in flashes, and, even then, all she saw was sand. The plan to retrieve the documents in the storm now felt ill conceived.

His mouth grazed her ear again. "If Jack or I don't return before the storm is over, take the camels and head southwest." He pressed a compass into her hand. The dials glowed in the dark.

Trembling, she threw her arms around his neck. He embraced her. Then he was gone.

Ginger dug her hands into the fur of her camel, feeling for

the rope tethering it to the others. Tugging on one side and then the other, she pulled the camels closer.

She patted her camel. She tried to remember the connection she felt to the beast on the journey here, but even that couldn't settle her. The more time passed, the more she wanted to tear the cover from her mouth, but a lick to her lips revealed the sand's fine mist had found its way in despite her efforts. She spat, gritting her teeth. Sweat dripped from her upper lip.

Minutes later, the muted popping of gunfire drew her attention. Could it be Noah? She whispered a prayer for him. She strained, listening for any other sign he might be near.

The desolate howling of the wind greeted her.

Then, more pops. An eternity seemed to pass before someone ran straight into her camel. The creature swayed. She screamed. A hand found hers before a torch flipped on.

Jack. A bandana covered his nose and mouth. He pulled a camel down to mount it.

"We have to go," he shouted.

Where was Noah? She squinted into the swirling dark behind him and ripped the *thawb* from her nose. Instead of relief, it brought further suffocation. "What about Noah?"

Jack shook his head. "He doesn't want us to wait for him." His torch clicked off.

"No." Ginger's throat hurt from shouting. This wasn't the plan. Something must have gone wrong. "I'm not leaving without him. What happened to him?"

"He's trapped. We stumbled into a platoon. He made a diversion to get me through, but he's still back there."

She pressed her hands over the goggles. Why did he always have to be the sacrificial one? She couldn't leave him. Not like this. "We have to wait for him."

"He'll find a way out. We have to get out of here. Now." Jack started his camel forward. Her camel lurched.

She dug her heels against the creature's side, trying to stop it. "No, Jack. We can't leave without Noah." If they could give him a few more minutes, he might make it. She yanked on the rope tethering their camels, desperate to stop Jack before they put too much distance between themselves and Noah.

The action startled her camel, who broke into a run. Ginger clung to the saddle, her body unable to grasp the rhythm of the camel's movement. She braced herself as she slid down the camel's side. Her ankle rolled painfully as it hit the ground. Her knees followed, and she tumbled onto her hands. The torch rolled and disappeared into the dust.

She squinted, but Jack and the camels raced away, into the swirling sands.

"Ginger!" Jack's voice barely carried through the storm. She tripped on the edge of her *thawb*. As the cloth fell from her nose, she pushed forward. The flimsy material of the burqa flapped over her face, allowing sand to seep in. The winds pummeled her.

She whirled around trying to find Jack but couldn't see him. "Jack!" The wind drowned her scream. She ran, hoping she'd gone in the same direction as him, but there was no one there.

Collapsing onto her knees, she drew her *thawb* over her nose again. Would it be better for her to wait for Jack to find her? Would he?

She huddled on the ground, and time slipped away. When enough time had passed and there was no sight of Jack, she crawled to her hands and knees and fumbled in her pocket for the compass. It glowed brightly. She nearly kissed it. Crawling forward, she moved southwest. She needed to get as far away from Tel el Saba as possible, before the *khamsin* ended.

She wanted to stand and run. But she couldn't see and didn't know the terrain. For all she knew, she could run right off the edge of a cliff. Crawling felt more secure.

"God help me." The words tumbled from her lips. She repeated them over and over as she made her way across the desert. As she crawled over rocks and plants, her knees and fingers grew bruised and torn, and her arms burned from the effort of crawling.

She had to keep going, had to get away.

At last, she stumbled against an enormous boulder. She ran her hands up the side of it and noted it jutted at an angle from the earth. She sputtered, a half-mad laugh of relief, and crawled into the space between the earth and the boulder. She didn't know how far she'd traveled, but she could go no further. This was as close to a shelter as she would find.

And Noah? Would he find shelter? He was in a Turkish stronghold, surrounded by the enemy. Despair and exhaustion engulfed her as she curled her knees into her chest, wrapping her arms over her face. Here the wind and sand didn't batter her. Her eyes closed. Her heart slowed, her breath was less choked at last.

* * *

DAYLIGHT BLINDED GINGER. Something had woken her—a hand on her shoulder.

"Well. What do we have here?"

The voice woke her with its familiarity. She tried to sit. The back of her head smacked against hard rock, and she winced.

A pair of dusty boots met her eyes. She squinted and pulled the goggles from her face.

Stephen squatted beside her.

Still groggy and disoriented, she jerked upright. Her heart raced. How had he found her so easily?

Stephen seemed to sense her thoughts. "Black *thawb*? Red

hair? I could have spotted you a mile away with good binoculars. You practically sent up a flare to your location, darling."

She reached for her gun. Before she found it, his hand slapped the side of her face. She fell, white spots swimming in her vision.

Stephen's hands roamed over her clothing. Ginger pushed away.

He stepped back from her, holding her Luger. He unloaded the clip and put it in his belt. "Did you miss me? I hadn't finished with you when you ran away." Stephen glared at Ginger.

She shielded her eyes, trying to take in her surroundings. They were in the open, though partially hidden from the hill of Tel el Saba by the boulder where she'd slept. The surrounding terrain was rough, uneven, a mixture of rock, sand, and pebbles. Clumps of brush and grass appeared half dead. Hills and gullies cracked into the landscape.

Stephen grabbed her by the jaw, to focus her attention on him, and she spat at him.

"Where does it end for you? At what point is your bloodlust satisfied?"

"Maybe you ought to fear me more."

She pulled free from him. "I'm not afraid of you." Her heart pounded.

"Good show. Almost convincing." With a smirk, he pulled a knife out from a sheath. He grazed his finger over the blade. Blood dripped from a cut on his fingertip. He wiped it on her sleeve.

"Stay away—"

His arm rose roughly as he covered her mouth with his hand. Ginger dug her fingernails into his forearm, her screams muffled. She bared her teeth and bit the fleshy part of his hand until she tasted blood. He yanked it away and struck her across the face, knocking her to the ground.

Ginger lay against the sand, reeling from the blow. She rolled over and screamed as he descended on her. He straddled her waist, pinning her. Her arms flailed. She raised her hands and he caught them.

"You knew this wouldn't be painless. But don't worry—I won't kill you." Blood dripped from his palm onto the handle of his knife as he leaned over her. "Quiet." He pressed the blade against her throat.

The memory of her capture by the Turks came into her mind. Noah wouldn't rescue her this time. "If you touch me," she said, between labored gasps, "my father will kill you himself."

Stephen eyes gleamed. "I want to leave my mark. Let anyone who goes near you know you're mine."

She cried out as he dragged the knife toward the neckline of the *thawb*. He cut the fabric open a few inches, exposing the skin below her collarbone.

"Did it hurt Benson to see the filthy orphan? I would have paid in diamonds to see the look on his face." Stephen brought his face close to her ear. His breath, acidic from smoking, sickened her. She turned her face away.

Stephen raised the knife.

A few tears escaped, despite her best effort.

"You're mine and you always have been." Stephen pierced the tip of the blade into the flesh above her left breast. With a yowl of pain, she bit her lip, not wanting to give him the satisfaction of her agonized cries.

The excruciating pain was more than she could bear. She clenched her teeth, her screams throaty. The knife remained inches from her heart. A quick downward stroke and he'd easily kill her.

When he finished tracing her skin with the blade, Stephen leaned down and ran his lips over the wound he'd inflicted. His wet tongue slid over the cut, which burned like liquid fire. When he pulled away, blood tinged his mouth.

"Now"—Stephen stood—"with my initials carved over your heart, maybe you'll remember who owns you and your family."

Fighting tears and dizziness, Ginger sat. The wound in her chest throbbed.

A memory crested in the top of her skull. Three British soldiers, hanging from a cross, the Maslukha's symbol carved into their chests, like this. She couldn't restrain the gasp. "You ... you don't work for the Maslukha," she whispered, her eyes wide, "you *are* the Maslukha."

Stephen's eyes lit, ever so slightly, the admission written in his pride. He pulled her upright. She glanced down toward the crude cuts in her flesh, her head woozy as she caught sight of her own blood soaking the dark fabric below it.

Clasping the torn fabric shut, she clenched her teeth. She wouldn't give him the satisfaction of her tears.

Stephen dragged her forward. She hurried to keep up, the pain in her chest too overwhelming to put much effort into resisting. As they crested a hill, Jack's familiar voice called out, "Fisher, you son of a bitch. What did you do to her?"

Hope surged in her, but then she saw him. Jack sat on a camel, the other two still tethered to it. His hands were bound, a streak of blood oozing from a cut below his temple. When had he been captured?

And where was Noah?

A tremor passed through her and her legs wobbled. Stephen shoved her in front of him, a pistol at her back as she trudged toward Jack. Had Noah escaped?

What was the plan now?

A panicked feeling grew in her.

Jack's gaze fell on her wound as they approached him, his face darkening. "Are you all right?"

Stephen's mark on her burned. She likely needed stitches. Her fingernails dug into the skin over the wound and she nodded unsteadily. Her tongue felt dry as the sand.

Stephen fumbled with the rope as he bound her hands together.

From his perched position on the camel, Jack snickered. "Great job," he said, as Stephen finished tying her wrists. "You know what they say. Can't tie a knot, tie a lot."

Stephen scowled. "You stupid Yankee." He raised the pistol toward Jack and slammed it against his head. Jack slumped forward in the saddle. "Maybe you'll finally shut up for a few minutes." He tied Jack's torso to the camel and turned back toward her.

Acid burned in her throat. "I need water," Ginger said, tasting the blood from her cracked lips. "I won't make it ten minutes if I don't get some."

Stephen smirked and pulled the rope tighter until it dug into Ginger's wrists. He unhooked his canteen. "Open your mouth."

He meant to humiliate her, but her thirst was far more demanding. She did as he asked, and he took a swig, then capped it. She recoiled, furious with herself for allowing him yet another opportunity to feel powerful.

Stephen looked out over the hill at Tel el Saba. "The Turks are scouring every corner looking for Benson. If he's there, they'll find him soon enough. I told my friends in Beersheba I'd take care of you myself."

The thought of Noah hiding somewhere in Tel el Saba, needing an escape, terrified her. He had no supplies she knew of and only the ammunition and weapons he'd taken with him. How would he ever get out of there alive?

Stephen led Ginger toward the other camel. "Let's go. Get on a camel."

"Where are we going?" She didn't know how long she could last without water. Not long.

"Your father set up a camp about ten miles from here," Stephen said.

Did her father still plan to betray Stephen? An inkling of hope rose in her. How ironic, to pin her hope on the man who condemned her to this.

Beads of sweat gathered on her forehead. She'd lost her burqa in the sandstorm. Her eyes burned and grew watery. "I need water."

Stephen handed her a leather bag of water. Ginger fumbled with her tied wrists and pulled the bag to her lips. The water was warm and musty, but it was wonderful as it hit her tongue and the dry roof of her mouth.

When she finished drinking, Stephen helped her climb onto a camel and then mounted the last one.

An open plain stretched before them. The canyons she and Noah had come from lay to the left, the hills of Beersheba to the right.

Ginger squinted into the bright blue sky of the horizon. Sweat trickled down her neck. In the distance, dust devils swirled in the Negev. The Egyptians called the cyclones of dust and sand *fasset el 'afreet*, or 'ghost winds,' and considered them evil. She shuddered. Evil winds, come to sweep away her fading hopes.

CHAPTER THIRTY-EIGHT

Ginger trekked across the desert with Jack and Stephen, dust rising from the steps of the camels. Rocks and tufts of grass dotted the cracked earth. Ginger swatted a fly away as it landed on her forehead. The swarm of insects worsened with the heat.

Jack had come to after some time. A large contusion protruded from where Stephen had hit him.

They passed an animal's skeleton. The gaping holes of the skull stared at her. Ginger shivered.

Anyone who forgot the desert was as deadly as it was beautiful paid the price. She surveyed the vast expanse of flat earth. Was it possible Noah followed them? She doubted it. He'd be visible. And yet they appeared to be heading in the same southwesterly direction Noah had directed her to go.

What if the Ottoman troops in Tel el Saba found him? She tried not to imagine the horrors he would go through if captured. This time Khalib wouldn't be there to help.

A plume of smoke rose into the air from a distant campfire.

As they drew closer to the source of the smoke, she saw an oasis, ringed with scrub brush and a smattering of palm trees. It was a logical place for her father to have set up a camp, given the arid conditions.

She spotted her father, tending the fire, which was outside the patch of green. And Beatrice sat nearby on a flat rock. Ginger's heart flooded with relief. Beatrice's mangled wrist was in a makeshift sling, but she was still alive.

As they stopped in front of the oasis, Beatrice met Ginger's gaze, a haunted expression in her eyes. Ginger wanted to run to her side and comfort her, but she was acutely aware of Stephen's hands still resting on his rifle.

But where were the British soldiers Noah had mentioned would be here to trap Stephen? And where was Henry?

Her father lifted his head at their approach. His tired gaze fixed on Ginger. He wore his uniform and despite the money he'd lavished on it, it looked ill-fitting, as though he didn't belong in it. She wondered if he'd worn his British uniform as one last attempt to show solidarity to the cause he'd brought so much harm to. She huffed. As though he deserved the privilege of wearing it. Far better men had died in that uniform, under her care. Each with a thousand times the decency her father ever had, despite their lack of pedigree.

Her father strode up to Ginger. He brought the camel low to the ground and helped her stand. With his hands on her shoulders, he scanned her face. "Are you hurt?"

Ginger could barely form words. Her knees and legs bore scratches from crawling. Dirt caked her battered skin. She nodded, fury burning within her as she peeled her hand back to reveal the wound Stephen had given her, which still oozed.

Her father paled and he stepped back, hands shaking. "Fisher—"

Before her father could say more, Stephen came over and yanked her away with a sharp tug on the rope encircling her wrists. "She's not your concern." Stephen dragged her toward Beatrice and deposited her beside her friend. He moved back toward Jack, who remained on the camel.

The snort of a horse drew Ginger's attention to the horses tied nearby. She scooted closer to Beatrice, whose eyes brooded dark and angry. "Are you all right?" Ginger asked her in a low voice. She wanted to ask if Stephen had hurt her after she'd escaped, but her shame held her back. If Beatrice knew she'd chosen to save Noah instead of trying to help her, would she be able to ever forgive her?

Beatrice gestured to the black bruising and swelling by her wrist. "How can you even ask?"

What comfort could she offer her friend? Ginger stared into the limitless blue sky on the horizon, her heart aching. "Do you remember when we thought the worst thing imaginable were those first nights on Lemnos?"

Beatrice chortled, seemingly despite herself. "I remember." Her voice sounded strained. After a moment, she added, "I don't blame you for this, you know. I'm angry, because I never thought helping Ahmed was the right decision. I should have listened to my own instincts."

"You should blame me. I deserve it."

"Well." Beatrice kicked a pebble by her foot. "I don't." Her gaze fixed on the wound on Ginger's chest. "That looks painful. We need to treat that. It's going to scar even worse if it gets infected."

Beatrice's words almost made Ginger choke with emotion. Beatrice still clung to hope they'd get through this. Her resilience and grit had always been a source of strength.

"Beatrice, I-I owe you so much more than an apology. I put you at risk. Selfishly. And more than once."

Beatrice's eyes were flat. "Your punishment is great enough without my anger, to boot."

"But I have to apologize—"

"Will an apology help?" Beatrice's voice was strained, her features tight. "Will it make a difference? Neither of us can change what happened. Neither of us would have wished this for the other, though. I'm sure of that." Her eyes softened. "I can't give you the solace you need, I'm sorry. I have none left just at the moment."

Stephen's approach with Jack prevented a response. He prodded Jack with his rifle and had him sit. Her father drew closer, pacing. "Where was Benson planning on going?" her father asked Jack.

Jack turned his palms upward. "You expect me to know? We were in the middle of a *khamsin*. Who knows what the hell happened."

She doubted that was the truth, but she had to appreciate Jack's blasé approach. Something about it made it clear they wouldn't be able to get to him, no matter how hard they tried— a quality Stephen hadn't encountered often.

Her father turned to Stephen. "If he recovered the documents, he took them to safety. He would make that his priority."

Stephen retrieved an apple from his haversack. He polished it on the sleeve of his jacket and bit into it, eyeing Ginger. "He won't leave her. I'm confident."

"You can't say that with any—"

Stephen stepped closer to her father, his face hard. "I'm confident." He took another loud bite into the fruit, the crunch nauseating. "He brought her, didn't he? Ask her why. A serious breach in protocol."

Her father stepped back from Stephen, agitated. He looked at Ginger. "Why did Benson bring you?"

If her father's plan to turn Stephen in was still in place, she had to do her part to act as though she didn't know about it. "Because he loves me, Father. He wouldn't risk having Stephen use me against him. Stephen is the Maslukha. He has to be stopped. You can still stop him."

Her father's shoulders sagged. The proud face she'd always known seemed worn, as though defeated. "The Maslukha isn't a person, Virginia. It's an operation. An operation I conceived of and put into action at Stephen's direction. Yes, he's taken the name and morphed it into something more. But it's so much more than a name."

Ginger blinked at her father, the revelation a dull light on her numb mind.

Of course.

Stephen had infiltrated and found the perfect target: a senior officer in Cairo Intelligence who would have the knowledge, the means, and the know-how to develop a strategy identifying the weaknesses in the British plans in the Middle East.

It was why her father was so panicked about the documents being found. Ahmed must have learned of her father's involvement. Because her father was as much a part of the Maslukha plan as Stephen.

"That's why Henry wanted Ahmed dead. He named you." It explained Henry's confusion and why he'd fled.

Just where was Henry now, though? His absence bothered her, some part of the puzzle missing that she couldn't understand.

Hoofbeats approached in the distance.

Stephen reached for Beatrice, who was closest to him, and pulled her from the ground. He held a gun to her head. Beatrice cried out, struggling.

Noah galloped on horseback toward them.

He was safe. She guffawed at her relief. Safe from the Turks.

Nothing about what he rode toward seemed well-planned or under control.

Noah slowed his horse. His robes were disheveled. The *kufeya* had disappeared. Sand caked his hair and eyebrows. His eyes met Ginger's. He lifted his hands toward Stephen. "I'm coming to make a deal," he said, his tone clipped.

Stephen's eyes narrowed. "No." He gripped Beatrice tighter. "You're not in any position to make a deal."

"Stephen, please," Ginger's voice shook. Beatrice held her chin high, her face brave. "Beatrice has nothing to do with this."

"Stay where you are," her father told Noah as he brought the horse closer.

Noah pulled the horse to a halt. His eyes didn't waver from Stephen.

"Take any weapons you have and toss them a few feet in front of you," Stephen said.

Noah dropped his rifles on the ground, then pulled out his sidearm from under his robe and tossed it on top.

Why would Noah get rid of his weapons if the plan was to capture Stephen? Her agitation grew.

"Now dismount."

Noah slid from the saddle and stood. He held his hands up. "I won't try anything."

Stephen's grip on Beatrice loosened, but he did not lower his gun.

Her father moved toward Noah. "I made you. I snatched you from lowly ranks and gave you a name. And this is what you choose? How long have you been working against me?"

"I work for the Crown. That's where my loyalties lie. Unlike you." Noah stepped toward them calmly, his hands in the air.

"Don't come any closer." Stephen glared. "Enough of this. Where are the documents?"

"I have them. And your man in Wedj was caught before he

could do anything to T. E. Lawrence." Noah seemed calm. "You'll never set foot in Cairo, or any British territory, without being a wanted man, Fisher."

Relief flooded Ginger. She'd done something right. They had warned Lawrence in time. She looked to Jack, who had been silent the whole time. He offered a tight smile. The bindings on his wrists seemed looser. He winked, and her heart raced. Maybe it meant their plan was still in play.

A buzzard screeched, and goose bumps rose on her arms. Every sight and sound intensified.

Stephen shook his head. "It isn't possible. You didn't obtain the documents until last night. There's no way you got a wire off since then." His face hardened. "You're bluffing."

"Am I?" Noah stepped forward. "Are you willing to go back to Cairo to find out?"

A bead of sweat trickled down Stephen's temple. "You seem to think you have the advantage. And yet we're holding all the guns."

"But I've come to make a deal." Noah's ability to stay cool was his advantage. Noah freed a slender metal tube from his robe. "One document is in here. I buried the rest."

Anxiety pressed in on her chest. This had to be part of the plan. And Noah wouldn't move to arrest Stephen until Beatrice was safe. Could she help convince Stephen? "Noah, don't. Don't give them to him."

Her father spoke to Noah. "What do you propose?"

"Untie Ginger and Sister Thornton. Let them and Jack get on those camels. You give them an hour to ride away, and then I'll tell you the location of the rest of the documents," Noah said. "The plan against Lawrence is over—but the case against you will be more difficult without the documents."

"And you'll stay here?" Her father's eyes narrowed.

"I'll stay here." Noah glanced at Ginger.

The earth swayed beneath her feet. This had to be part of a plan. But she didn't see soldiers anywhere. How did they intend to capture Stephen?

But if something had gone wrong, Stephen wouldn't hesitate to kill Noah.

Jack acted alarmed. "Noah, they'll kill you."

Stephen pulled Beatrice even tighter. "What aren't you telling me? Something isn't right." His eyes shifted to her father. "Benson would never surrender those documents so easily."

Her father appeared agitated. "Let's take the deal, Fisher. This is the only chance we have. Let the nurse go." His eyes darted to Noah.

That had to be it. Her father was waiting, like Noah, for Beatrice to be safe before he betrayed Stephen.

The echoing of distant hoofbeats diverted Stephen's attention. A cloud of dust approached, along with it, a small group of riders. Though they were still far away, their jaunty hats and khaki uniforms were a familiar sight. Joy shot through her. British soldiers. At last.

But Stephen still had Beatrice.

She took advantage of his distraction to act.

With a quick motion, she rushed up behind Stephen and kicked him in the groin. "Beatrice, run," she cried. She reached for Stephen's rifle as he doubled over. Beatrice's fingertips managed to swipe the Luger Stephen had stolen from her, sending it clattering it the ground.

"Ginger, no." Noah dove for one of the guns he'd discarded.

Beatrice scrambled toward the Luger, but Stephen got to her first. With the butt of his pistol, he whacked Beatrice on the back of the head. She stumbled and fell on the ground, where she lay unmoving.

Stephen's face reddened as he slammed his shoulder into Ginger's chest, tackling her. The back of her head hit the ground, Stephen's weight crushing the air from her lungs. She gasped and clawed at his throat.

Stephen pressed a pistol to her forehead. "Stop."

Tears of pain slipped from the corners of her eyes, down the sides of her face toward her ears.

Stephen made a weak attempt to stand, drawing one knee up. His other knee pressed into her belly. With the pistol still pointed at her, he glowered at her father.

"Who's coming toward us, Braddock?" Stephen demanded, his sweat dripping on her.

"Release my daughter," her father growled.

"Shoot him," Ginger begged. "Even if he hurts me. Just kill him."

Stephen pulled her upright by her hair, and she cried out at the searing pain. "Do that and you'll be attending the funerals of all the women in your family." Stephen's eyes narrowed as he dug the pistol into Ginger's temple.

Her father's eyes widened. "No!" He leapt forward, his arms outstretched as he collided against Stephen.

Stephen's hand dropped away from Ginger as he turned the weapon toward her father instead. His pistol discharged three times, the shots piercing her ear drums.

"Father!" Ginger cried. Noah yanked her away, shielding her from Stephen with his body.

Her hands shook as she lunged for her father, but Noah held her back.

Her father fell and Jack caught him, bracing his body against his. With a gasp, her father's head lolled to the side as he collapsed.

Ginger screamed as Stephen fled for a horse. Jack set her father's body down onto the ground and lifted his rifle. Stephen leapt onto the horse and took off at a gallop. Jack fired, the shot splintering the bark of a palm tree, just inches from Stephen's head.

Jack scrambled to his feet. "You got this?" he called to Noah.

"Go on," Noah said.

Jack mounted one of the camels. With a flick of a whip, he took off after Stephen.

Noah pulled away from her. He inspected her chest, searching for injuries. She sucked air back in and rasped, "He shot my father. Let me go."

Ginger pulled away. She crawled toward her father. Tears formed in her eyes as she reached him. His face was pale, his lips blue. He gasped for breath, but the bullet had torn through his lungs.

"Father." She grabbed his hands, leaning over him.

"Virg—"

"Don't speak." Ginger's face twisted with grief.

He wouldn't last more than a minute, at most. Her eyes locked on her father's dark-brown eyes struggling to remain open. "I'm sorry." Ginger sobbed. Blood seeped from the corner of his mouth.

A last puff of air moved past his lips as his eyes went still.

Ginger lifted her hand to her mouth. Her fingers curled into a shaking fist.

She was dimly aware of the British soldiers arriving at the oasis, of Noah shouting at them. "Fisher's on the run," Noah called out. "Follow Lieutenant Darby." She couldn't tear her eyes from her father as the horses continued at a gallop, away from them.

"Father …" She wanted to hate him, for everything he'd done. But the emotions she wanted wouldn't come. Noah pulled her against his chest, and she pushed back. The sounds of galloping hooves grew softer. "Go after Stephen. Go and help Jack and the others."

"I'm not leaving you," Noah said in a firm tone.

"Father! Father, no!"

Henry. He must have stayed while the other riders kept going.

Ginger blinked through her tears as Henry threw himself toward their father. Fury flushed his face as he turned toward Noah and Ginger. "You! You did this!"

Henry fired his gun.

CHAPTER THIRTY-NINE

*H*enry's figure swam in her vision, a pistol in his hands. Noah slumped into her. Blood pooled onto the earth below him, his face twisted in agony.

Henry, scowling with fury, pulled the hammer back on the pistol once again. She sprang to her feet and threw herself between them. "Henry. No! What are you doing?"

"Stand aside, Ginny," he seethed.

Ginger shook her head. "You'll have to shoot me too."

Noah tried to sit. He held his right shoulder with his left hand, blood seeping between his fingers.

"My sister is too good for you, you bastard." Henry's voice showed a familiarity between them that still seemed like camaraderie. "How dare you turn her against me? Against my family? You used her!"

Noah swore. He let out another painful grunt as he shifted his weight, straightening.

Henry frowned. "It's too bad Stephen failed to kill you in Aleppo. You deserved it." He glowered at Ginger. "And you. What a heartless little bitch you've turned out to be."

Heartless bitch? The comment stung like a slap. "Stephen killed Father! And destroyed us, Henry. And you all just went along with his treason. You and Father betrayed our family and our country."

Henry's face grew purple as he seemed to lose his ability to be rational. "Father's death is your fault."

She sprang up, standing between her brother and Noah. "Henry, what are you doing? We can return to Cairo. Jack and the others will catch Stephen, and then this will be over."

Henry squinted at her. "Over? I'll go to prison, Ginny. You know I will." He glanced at Beatrice's prone body. Ginger was desperate to check her injuries, but she couldn't leave Noah now.

She fought to keep her voice steady, aware of how Noah sagged behind her. "Stop being such a coward! You brought this upon yourself. You'll never be able to live with yourself if you do this. Please. I love him. I'm begging you, please." Her voice cracked.

Henry pointed the gun at Noah. "Step aside."

She shook her head, spreading her arms out. "I won't let you kill him. I love him."

"Like I love Angelica? And yet, I can never marry the woman I love. Because of him. Because of you. Get out of my way." Henry pushed her with his shoulder and aimed. Ginger gasped as he fired and barreled into him. Noah cried out again as he slumped onto the dirt.

She wrestled Henry for the gun, fighting with her nails and fists, fury driving her. Henry kept her at bay. "I'm sorry but you don't understand." He threw her to the ground, and she landed close to Beatrice.

The sunlight glinted from the Luger beside Beatrice's fingertips.

The Luger.

Her hands shook as she reached for it. Her heart pounded with such force it blocked all other noise from her ears. In mere seconds, either she or Henry would do something she'd never be able to forgive.

The pistol weighed like an anvil in her hands. Time stopped. She still felt Noah's kiss on her lips, the taste of blood from her father's wounds. Blood. The same that ran through Henry's veins.

Tears blocked her view as Henry extended his hands to shoot again.

She fired, a scream ripping from her throat. The pistol kicked back in her hands. It dropped to the sand at her feet as Henry fell to the ground, shot through the head.

The gunshot echoed into the void then faded into the blistering air. Then, silence.

CHAPTER FORTY

The ringing in Ginger's ears gave time an ethereal quality. The harsh rays of the sun pulsated against her tear-streaked face. Heat rose from the desert sands in waves, the distant horizon a wavering mirage.

Noah struggled, the air in his throat raspy and labored. His dark eyelashes, encrusted with fine sand, twitched over his closed eyes.

She cradled his head in her lap. "Stay with me." Her tears splashed against his face. She pressed her forehead to his and kissed his chapped lips. His mouth was still warm, his jaw clenched in pain.

"You can't leave me here, Noah. Please."

The second bullet had torn through his chest, and a blood-stain was spreading under where her hand pressed. His hand covered hers and clasped it before he blinked. Blood seeped through their fingers.

"Have I told you I love you?" He blinked again.

She fought for composure, a choked sob catching in her throat. "You're not dying here. I've lost enough today. I won't lose you." She kissed his forehead, the salty taste of sweat on her lips. "I need to apply pressure to your wounds, and then I'll help you sit. It will slow the blood flow."

He was losing blood rapidly. She pressed her knee into his shoulder wound, ripping the *thawb* from her body. She could use strips of cloth to bind the wound with as much pressure as possible. But the one in his chest worried her more. His lung could collapse. He needed immediate surgery.

Noah grabbed her hands. "You need to go." His words were stilted. "You can't stay here. These are Ottoman lands."

She squeezed his hands. "The only way I'm leaving is with you by my side. Now hush and save your energy for surviving."

Noah's gaze focused on the wound on her chest. His eyes squeezed shut. "What did that bastard—"

"Don't worry about that now." She kissed him. "I need you alive, Major Benson."

The camels and horses stood nearby. Her medical kit was in one of the camel's saddlebags. She ran for it and tore through the bags, her fingers slippery with blood. When she found it, she dug through her kit. She needed something rubber, something she could tape down on his chest wound to block the air escaping from it. One of the army-issued condoms caught her eye. If she cut it, it might work.

A quiet voice came from behind. "Ginger?"

She whirled around. "Beatrice." She'd forgotten about her friend in her desperation.

Beatrice sat on the ground, a wound in the side of her head bleeding. She appeared dazed. "What happened?"

Ginger rushed over to her and checked her wound. The gash might need some stitches, but it wasn't something she could do here. "Stephen hit you. You're bleeding, but I have to take care of Noah. My brother sh-shot him." The words soured her stomach.

A horrified expression crossed Beatrice's pale face as she looked over toward where Noah sat. "And your brother …?"

Don't think. Don't think about Henry. Ginger couldn't meet her eyes. "He's dead."

Beatrice scrambled to stand, hugging her bad wrist to her chest. "Let me help you with Noah."

Ginger brushed her tears away. "Beatrice—I'm so sorry."

Tears shimmered in Beatrice's eyes. "We'll get through this. We're sisters. Now, did you get some compression on Noah's wounds to slow the bleeding?"

Ginger held up her medical kit. "Yes, I'm trying to cover his chest wound."

"Give me a rifle." Noah leaned his head back on the boulder he rested against.

"Why?" Ginger asked.

"Just in case. One of us should be armed." He squinted as she cut the square of rubber and taped it to his chest. "What does that do?"

"It'll help keep you breathing." They needed to get him on a horse. If she could help Noah mount, they could ride west to Gaza, but she didn't know the way. Noah might not stay conscious long enough to help guide her.

She had to try.

She returned to the animals. She grabbed them by the reins and brought them over to Beatrice and Noah.

She knelt beside them. Beatrice raised her eyes at Ginger, her expression dark. She shook her head. Ginger's heart dropped. "We won't make it in time," Beatrice whispered. "And even if we get him to the clearing station, they'll pass him over. He's too injured."

Beatrice was as seasoned a nurse as she, even if she hadn't worked in surgery as often. But Ginger had to hold on to hope.

She brushed tears away. "Stop it. We'll make it. He'll live." She took Noah's hands. He opened his eyes but barely.

"Listen to me. Fight. For me. Because I'll be damned if I'm waiting for this war to end to marry you, Noah. You hear me? I've decided that's how this ends between us." She choked on her words. "You don't get to die yet. I don't want to live without you."

"Fuil de mo fuil ..." His slurred words became incomprehensible. His grip weakened.

"What's he saying?" Beatrice asked.

"I don't know." Ginger squeezed his hand. "Noah! Noah. Please. Don't go." She put her head to his chest. His heartbeat was faint. "We must go. Now. There's no time to waste. We're losing him. Help me get him to a horse."

She and Beatrice got on either side of him and dragged him to the closest horse, Beatrice struggling with only one good hand. As carefully as possible, they lifted him. Noah gained enough consciousness to help as much as he could, and Ginger mounted behind him, to hold on to him.

As they prepared to leave, Ginger glanced at the ground. She didn't have time to load the bodies of her father and her brother. They would remain here until they became one with the sands and the desert. The composure she'd fought for shattered, a sob wrenching from her.

She heard another horse in the distance. Ginger lifted her head. Jack was approaching them, alone.

A prayer of gratefulness left her lips, hope rising in her.

Jack stopped beside them. His eyes scanned the scene, his face darkening as he saw Noah. "What do you need me to do?" he asked Ginger.

"Can you get us to Belah?"

* * *

Bursting into the clearing station, Ginger barely noticed the standstill she brought the area to. She headed to the operating theater and stepped inside. The face she searched for lifted, light-blue eyes meeting hers with equal parts astonishment and curiosity.

"James." Ginger fell to her knees from exhaustion. "Save him. Save him, please."

CHAPTER FORTY-ONE

*G*inger stood on the beach, her hair a tangled mess of knots, barefoot and numb. She barely remembered taking off her boots. She should go back there, say her good-byes if the time had come for it. But as long as she stayed out here, she could pretend there was hope.

Her pacing throughout the day had probably driven Jack mad. He'd suggested she go rest at least ten times, promising to update her if he heard anything. In the end, it had been a sudden rush of medical personnel into the theater that drove her away. Another doctor, an additional nurse, and an orderly. She knew what it meant. The surgery wasn't going well—or something more dire had happened.

She sank to her knees and pressed her forehead to the sand. Her heart may never heal. She couldn't recover what she'd lost when she fired a gun—either time.

Henry.

The thought of him was enough to make her feel sick. She didn't need the passage of time to know her mind would be forever haunted by him.

Yet what more could she have done? For any of them? She'd fought and she'd failed.

Something moved across the back of her hand. A dragonfly rested there, its body gleaming in the sunlight, the wings shifting. It remained for a moment longer before it took flight, disappearing in the dimming sky of the approaching dusk.

Of all the creatures to come to her.

Her eyes burned, her tears spent. She remained in that position a while longer, listening to the steady rhythm of the waves lapping against the shore, the occasional call of a seabird. The sun beat against her forearms and neck. The sand might ruin the blue cotton dress one of the sisters had lent her. But she couldn't muster the will to lift her head.

The soft crunch of sand roused her.

"Were you sleeping?" James's familiar voice made her sit upright. He sat on the ground beside her.

She wiped the sand stuck on her forehead. Had she been? She didn't know. The sun had dipped even lower, hanging low above the horizon line. "James—" She searched his eyes, terrified to ask.

James drew his legs up and placed his lanky arms around his knees. "I didn't realize how much you loved him." His voice was quiet, low. "I thought—" He broke off and tugged his glasses away. He'd removed his operating jacket, but traces of blood remained on his clothes. Noah's.

"Is he alive?" She couldn't keep the desperation from her tone.

James nodded and rubbed the bridge of his nose. "Barely, Ginger. He went into shock, and we were about to lose him. I used that method the American doctor who joined us last month introduced me to—the transfusion of blood. It seems to have stabilized him." James hesitated and then took her hand.

"But I can't make any promises. It will be days, maybe longer, before we can have any confidence in his prognosis."

Ginger's throat tightened, and the tears she was certain she'd emptied started to flow down her cheeks. "I didn't get here fast enough—"

James embraced her. "He wouldn't be alive if it wasn't for the actions you took."

The actions ...

Bitterness gnawed at her soul. Stephen had still escaped, despite everything. He'd managed to get to Tel el Saba before the British soldiers could catch him. Even though Jack had promised they'd do everything to bring him to justice, if Noah died, it would be little consolation.

She sank against James, accepting his comfort. When at last she straightened, he offered her a handkerchief. She wiped her nose and eyes, her hands trembling. "Will he be evacuated tonight?"

"Not until morning. Then we'll put him on the first train to El Arish." James rested a steady hand on her shoulder. "If you'd like to keep him company, I can see to it."

Thank goodness she still had allies here. A stab of guilt went through her. "And Beatrice?"

"She's being treated for dehydration and her head injury. I believe the matron has decided to send her to Cairo for some time."

She took his hand from her shoulder. She squeezed it, and the contact released something else—the forgiving gratefulness she owed him.

She wouldn't be who she was without James. She'd abused his proposal and his love to gain the independence she wanted and remain working as a nurse throughout the war. She'd betrayed him and hadn't been forthright, and yet he'd offered her an opportunity to save her reputation when Stephen had sold the scandal to the society pages of the paper.

And he'd saved the life of the man she loved.

A lump in her throat, she managed, "I didn't deserve you. Or your love, James. I hope you find someone who appreciates the wonderful man you are. I'm sorry for—"

James squeezed her hand to silence her. "I'll settle for finding someone who looks at me the way you look at him." He inhaled sharply. "Let me walk you back." He lifted a pair of boots. "I'm assuming these are yours? I found them strewn about twenty yards from here."

She nodded. After shaking them free of sand, she donned them and stood with James's help.

They returned in silence. They reached the officers' ward and Ginger entered alone. She searched the tented ward for Noah. She saw Jack first. He stood at the foot of a bed, arms crossed.

Ginger approached. She stood side by side with Jack. Noah lay on the bed in front of them. Compared to many of the wounded who came through these units, he didn't look terrible. An increased bulk under his pajamas by his shoulder and chest gave away the presence of bandages, but he appeared to be sleeping.

"Has he been conscious?" Ginger whispered.

"Nope." Jack's posture stiffened. "Not yet."

She couldn't summon tears. She couldn't think of the future. "How do you go on?"

Jack smiled sadly. "You just start walking. Eventually your soul catches up." He jerked his chin toward Noah's bed. "Go on. I know you don't want to be standing here talking to me when you could be over there." He moved away.

Ginger went to Noah's bedside. She'd never thought he seemed frail before. Not until she saw him in a bed like this, like other strong young men with lithe bodies broken into pieces.

She sat at his bedside and took his hand. He didn't squeeze it back. Didn't stir. He wasn't asleep, either. He was ... suspended. Between life and death.

There wasn't a privacy curtain around Noah's bed. Nothing to separate a view of him from the other patients or the nurses who tended to them. But propriety be damned. She kicked her boots off and curled onto the bed, resting her head against his uninjured shoulder. She placed a hand over his beating heart, taking comfort in it.

"Don't leave me." She closed her eyes and deep sleep found her.

* * *

IN THE MIDDLE of the night, Noah's hand gripped hers.

Her mind laden with sleep, she whispered, "I'm scared, Noah. I don't know what to expect."

"I meant what I said in the desert," he mumbled.

"What did you say?"

"Vows. The same ones I heard every morning as a child. Blood of my blood." Noah held her hand and kissed the tips of her fingers. "Forever."

Goose bumps rose on her skin. Ginger brought her fingers to her lips and jolted upright. She rubbed her eyes.

From the way light appeared to be filtering through the tent panels, she guessed it was close to dawn. She turned toward Noah eagerly, expecting to find him looking at her, but his eyes were still closed.

His face was pale, almost waxen in appearance.

Had he stopped breathing?

She reached out to feel his pulse.

Her hand shook.

A surge of relief moved through her at the soft thump against her fingertips. He was still alive.

A sniff caught her attention.

Not ten feet away, Lord Helton stood by one of the thick posts that supported the middle of the tent. How had he gotten here so quickly? Then again, it had been more than a day since Noah had turned over the documents to his superiors. And the flight from Ismailia had shown her how quickly one could travel with the RAF at the ready.

He didn't have to utter a command. She could tell by his demeanor he wanted her to follow.

She combed her fingers through her hair and tossed it behind her back. Scrubbing her eyes, she sat straighter. Once she'd pulled her boots on, she stood and went to him. "Lord Helton."

He strode from the tent. She glanced at Noah, wishing she could take an ounce of courage from him, and followed.

Lord Helton didn't slow his stride, expecting her to keep up. He continued his quick pace until he reached a private tent for officers of the RAMC.

No one else was inside. He indicated she should sit at a chair in front of one of the four desks near the entrance. He sat across from her and removed his hat.

"On the one hand, Lady Virginia, I owe you a debt of gratitude. You helped bring a speedy resolution to a matter of tremendous importance. Due to your assistance, your father and brother stopped before they could harm anyone else and an assassination attempt on T. E. Lawrence was thwarted. You recovered vital documents and brought to light the treachery of the German operative, Stephen Fisher. With any luck, the manhunt for him will be successful, and we'll be able to bring him in for justice."

His tone was dry, anything but grateful. The 'but' to his statement hung in the air, and she tensed. When he said nothing else right away, she began, "I'm happy to have—"

"On the other hand."

There it was.

Lord Helton's lips tightened, and he let out an exaggerated sigh. "You endangered the time, effort, and energy put into this investigation. You nearly ruined everything, more than once. And, to top it off, you began a scandalous and illicit relationship with one of my best men, bringing harm not only to his better judgement but also to my daughter's good name. How you convinced Major Benson to bring you out from Cairo is beyond my comprehension. But to bring you to Beersheba—"

As though it had been her choice. Noah's shared responsibility in their relationship didn't seem to factor into his rebuke. She stood. "Lord Helton. While I understand your anger and censure—"

"No, you do not understand, young lady. And you will sit."

She did as he'd asked, wearily.

"If it comes to light what your father and brother did, it will disgrace your family beyond measure. I don't want to see three women of high society left without the support of the earldom and estate your father managed and put in a position where everyone shuns them, merely for bearing the loathsome name of Braddock."

Ginger couldn't help but interrupt him again. "Lord Helton, my mother and sister—were they rescued?"

He nodded. "Our men intercepted the boat to Luxor and escorted them safely to Cairo. Now, your mother and sister remain unaware of the circumstances—we told them private boats were not being permitted on holiday at the moment—but they will learn soon enough about the deaths of your father and brother. I would prefer them not have to learn of their treason."

A knot of tension unwound in her shoulders. Her mother and Lucy were safe. And her mother had deflected any suspicion about her knowledge of the situation. Much as she hadn't agreed with her mother's complicit silence, she admired her strength through it all. She knew how to survive.

Maybe she was more like her mother than she'd realized.

"Thank you, Lord Helton. For helping them. But I don't see how it's possible for them not to learn the truth."

"Lady Virginia, I'm a position to help you, your mother, and your sister. If the information about your father and brother's treachery remains a classified secret, the harm to your family will be mitigated. I feel as though it would be a just payment to you for your help. I understand you have a desire to continue to serve as a nurse in the war effort. I could clear your record, have the society pages in the newspaper issue an apology for the attack on your good name, and have you reinstated to serve for the Queen Alexandra's nurses."

Once again, the unsaid part of his statement hung in the air, weightily. She blinked at him. "But ...?"

"But you would have to agree to cease all communication with Major Noah Benson for the duration of the war. If he lives."

She gasped. How could he possibly dictate such a thing? She shook her head and stood again. "Absolutely not. I love him. I won't abandon him now, when he needs me."

"Sit." His sharp tone made it clear he would not ask a fourth time.

He leaned forward. "Love does not mean putting Major Benson in a position where he has to compromise his duty to the British government and people in order to best serve you. *If* Benson survives this, we will need him. His expertise is irreplaceable. Do you think it's possible for us to snap our fingers and produce another such man, who speaks several languages of this region with such proficiency, who can blend seamlessly, and who has the wherewithal to make the missions we send him on successful?"

She wanted to argue with him. She'd found love. She'd escaped everything for Noah. Turned her back on her family. And he needed her.

But had she learned nothing?

She sank against the wooden chair, fighting tears.

She could help her mother and sister. They'd still be deprived of most of the comforts they were used to, between her father's debts and the entailment of Penmore and property in Cairo to go to whoever the new Earl of Braddock would be. Probably some distant cousin none of them knew. Her modest salary as a nurse might help them get by during the war.

At what cost?

Not Noah. Anything but losing Noah.

"Decide here and now, Lady Virginia. If you decide against my offer, I'll still be sending Major Benson away for his convalescence to a secure location. With Stephen Fisher on the loose and as we unwind his network, it would be too dangerous for us to keep Benson in a normal hospital. If he does recover, he'll be put to work right away."

"So you intend to take him away, regardless." Noah's words about not being free and the obstacles to their relationship rang through her memory.

Lord Helton's gaze appeared mildly sympathetic. "Take my offer. You deserve the gratitude it comes with, truly."

You're too selfish. You can't do it. The taunt in her mind had Stephen's voice behind it.

She was. She had been.

"Will I be able to know how he is?" Ginger gave him a pleading look. "Or if he even survives?"

Lord Helton replaced his hat. "I'll weigh the risks and consider it."

Her breath shattered. Her expression must have given away her mental anguish for he added, "The risk is great. As I said, we'll have to put him in a secure location for now, while Stephen Fisher remains at large."

Ginger lowered her head. He meant the risk to Noah's life. "What about my family? Won't they continue to be in danger from Stephen also? Will the restriction on travel to England be lifted for my mother and sister now that my father is dead?" At least in England they might be safer—and take refuge at her grandmother's home.

"It's not safe for civilians to travel to England. Enemy submarines have been attacking ships with alarming regularity." He crossed one leg over the other and placed his hands on his knee. "I suppose I can offer your mother and sister the use of my home in Alexandria. It would come with my protection in the form of trusted servants."

Trusted servants. Like Jahi?

She'd been clenching her jaw and she released it, her teeth aching. Wouldn't accepting this offer make her no better than her father? Her father had sacrificed everything at the expense of the family name and their status.

Yet, this was different. It meant sacrificing for the survival of her family. And for her country. And Noah's safety.

Throughout this, she'd tried so hard to be certain she was making the right decision. Certain Ahmed wasn't an enemy. Certain Noah wasn't a traitor. Certain her father was a villain.

She hadn't trusted what her heart told her enough. She had been unwilling to let go of the security *certainty* offered and do what her heart declared was right.

Would Noah find his way back to her after the war?

If she refused Lord Helton, what would she gain? She could obstinately break herself against his might … all for what?

She had to let Noah go. She loved him too much not to.

She stood and met Lord Helton's level gaze. She could barely breathe, but she pushed through. She was certain of one thing: she would persevere.

EPILOGUE

NOVEMBER 7, 1917

The singing and merriment outside the hospital tent contrasted starkly with the moans of the wounded men inside, but Ginger couldn't begrudge the celebration. Days ago, wearied men had risen from their trenches in Gaza and made a final assault on the city on the hill. Today, they'd finally broken through.

The Ottomans were on the run.

Ginger finished working on a dressing and made her way outside. The sun was setting, and, with it, the gaiety increased. Whisky and rum from the rations were being toasted freely, even among the medical personnel. She approached the Mess and saw dinner had spilled outside, where nurses exhausted from working fourteen-hour shifts ignored the call to their beds and instead danced with the medical officers.

Matron bumped past her as she hurried to pull a nurse from a rowdy embrace. "Oh, Sister Whitman—" Miss Walsh shook her head, glancing at the celebration. "I'm glad to have you here, even if it's only for a couple of weeks. You sure you can't convince that matron in Alexandria to send you back to me for good?"

Ginger smiled. "I think my extended time in clearing stations is over, unfortunately." Her work at the hospital in Alexandria kept her fulfilled while also giving her time to visit her mother and Lucy.

Miss Walsh scrutinized her dirty uniform. "Not enjoying the celebration, dear?"

"My shift just ended. I think my bed is more appealing right now."

Miss Walsh patted her hand. "These new sisters—they can't live up to the standard you set. You're a good person. One who always does her best. You don't need to feel so burdened. There's a war on. And you've already done more than your bit. Now go and enjoy yourself."

A weight seemed to lift from Ginger's shoulders. She'd taken Miss Walsh's praise for granted before. But time had allowed the matron's words to take on a meaning she hadn't quite allowed herself to believe before. She had signed up for nursing. What she'd actually accomplished had been far greater, and at a high price.

Ginger opened her mouth to reply when hooting began. An orderly had kissed the dancing nurse.

Miss Walsh lifted her hand and rushed off toward the other sister.

Ginger watched the merry group. None of the sisters she'd known while working here remained, though during her last lunch with Beatrice in Cairo, her friend had mentioned requesting to come back to the front soon. With the offensive into Palestine at last continuing, there would be a need to establish new clearing stations further down the line.

"Jerusalem by Christmas!" A medic caught her hands, attempting to pull her in toward the group.

She turned him away politely. He continued toward another nurse, undeterred. She'd heard the slogan all day, even from the wounded. They were the new crusaders, their goal decided. The year had been disastrous for the British, but they'd held the line in the Middle East and France by the skin of their teeth. Taking Jerusalem would be a morale boost for the entire country until the Americans arrived at the front in the spring.

Her spirits lifted at the surrounding happiness, despite the death and injury she'd seen during the day. This was the normal now. Miss Walsh was right. And Ginger was proud of her countrymen. She should enjoy the celebration, now that it was here.

An orderly tapped on her shoulder. "Sister Whitman?"

She gave him a wary sidelong glance, expecting he wanted to ask her to dance. "Yes?"

"There's an irritable colonel asking for you over by triage." He lowered his voice. "He's accusing you of making a terrible decision with one of his men."

She groaned inwardly. Not again. For as long as the war continued, she would butt heads with the brass. She thought of the inquiry to the London School of Medicine for Women sitting in her desk at the hospital in Alexandria. She'd send it as soon as she got back.

She left the noise near the Mess behind her, following the orderly in silence. She did a mental scan of the various risky calls she'd made throughout the day. Nothing untoward came to mind.

As they passed the railhead, she caught sight of the plain in the valley where the troops had encamped for months. Fires and raucous noise came from those men who had stayed behind from the battle. She had no doubts they were also enjoying extra sips of liquor and cigarettes.

Up ahead, the well and stone huts where she'd first met Ahmed and Noah came into view. She looked away. Eight days of being out here, and she'd avoided a trip in this direction. She'd hesitated accepting the assignment to the clearing station for this reason.

Her pace slowed. *Don't think about him.* She could think of Ahmed with more ease than she did Noah. Ahmed only haunted her dreams sometimes. Noah invaded them nightly.

The orderly turned in front of the well. "This way."

She sighed with relief. At least she wouldn't have to pass in front of the hut.

As the terrain shifted from the hard-trodden path into the soft sand, she relaxed. By the palm trees near the well and the distant ocean, she could almost forget how much had happened here. She'd spent months doing her best to keep the memories at bay, and she was determined to continue.

The orderly halted.

She looked at him, confused. She didn't see the triage station, just a sole tent ahead.

An officer stepped out.

Noah.

Her breath caught, her knees went weak.

The pain of the last six months, the constant wondering if he was alive, if she'd see him again, threatened to dissolve her into a puddle in the desert sand.

He was here.

He was here?

How long had he been close by? When had he recovered?

A thousand questions assailed her as one thought rose to warn her. She'd promised Lord Helton to stay away.

In her dreams, he'd come to her this way, almost within reach, and she was ready for him to sweep her into his arms, to feel the warmth of his kiss, the intensity of his dark-blue gaze.

And now that he was here, she wasn't ready.

He stopped a foot away. He removed his hat and tucked it

between his elbow and torso. He appeared thinner than she remembered. She recognized the insignia of a colonel on his cuffs.

A breeze rustled the palm fronds above them, the humid warmth of the November evening enveloping them. A mist clouded his eyes, his expression gentle. He wiped his eyes with his fingertips. "I thought I could be clever. But seeing you … I've lost every line I rehearsed."

She laughed tearfully and drew a shaking breath. Sinking to her knees, she covered her mouth, unable to find her voice.

He knelt in front of her and embraced her. She wept, joy and sorrow exploding through every fiber of her body. He stroked her back, his arms sturdy.

When her cries subsided, he pressed a kiss to her forehead. "Then you didn't forget me?"

She smiled, wiping her eyes. "Why, did you forget me?"

He held her face in both his hands and kissed her forehead again, before dropping his lips to hers for a brief kiss. "Forget my darling wife? Not possible."

She scanned his eyes. Something in his tone sounded serious. "Your …?" Tears still clung to her lashes. The memory of the last night she'd lain beside him pushed through her heart. "The vows you said in the desert …"

"Of course we'll have to make it official. I don't want there to be any doubt in anyone's mind." Noah kissed her again. "You've had my heart since the moment we met. And now you have all of me. Body and soul, *rohi*."

It hadn't been a dream.

"If your goal is to have me sob again, you're nearly there." She slid her arms around his neck and kissed him as though six months hadn't passed between their parting. "I love you, Noah."

Noah stood and pulled her to her feet. "Come with me."

She glanced over her shoulder. The orderly who had led her

out here had vanished, and they appeared to be alone. She hesitated. "I promised Lord Helton I'd stay away from you. While the war was going on."

Noah gripped her hands and tugged her in his direction. "I made no such promise."

She wasn't about to argue with his logic. Clasping his hand, she let him lead her toward the beach. They strolled along the side of the water. She had so many things she wanted to ask him. "How long are you here for?"

"Just for the night. I'm passing through on my way to Kantara." His hand tightened. "I know it's not much time. I tried to send you a few messages before now, but Lord Helton intercepted them. So I recommended you to the RAMC for duty here during the battle."

He'd been the one to arrange for her transfer out here? The revelation made her wonder what other lengths he had gone to in an attempt to contact her. "I almost didn't accept the assignment." A path of bird footprints crisscrossed the sand in front of them. "This place holds so many memories—both good and bad."

"I know." He cleared his throat. "Ahmed would be proud. You gave his work meaning. And Foreign Secretary Lord Balfour has issued a mandate officially committing our government to the Zionist cause of a Jewish state. The news should break in the newspapers within the next couple of days."

She bit her lip. She'd often thought about the politics behind the intrigue from May. "I'm not certain that's good."

"Neither am I. Not in the manner that it's happened, at least. And we're hearing news of a Bolshevik coup on the provisional government in Russia today, so our fears about the Russians pulling out of the war will likely be realized." Noah stopped and drew her into his arms. "But today is a good day, at least for us."

He reached into his pocket and opened his hand. "I have

something for you." A silver ring, the Irish Claddagh, lay in his palm. "It was my mother's. One of the few things I have of hers."

The ring glinted in the fading light, reflecting the reds and oranges of the sunset. She blinked at it as he pushed it onto the ring finger of her left hand, where it fit snugly. She'd sold almost every other piece of jewelry she owned in June to give her mother the money. While her mother accepted the situation with resoluteness, Lucy was nearly inconsolable about the changes in their lives. "It's beautiful."

"You're beautiful. It's just a ring." Noah kissed her, this time his kiss more ardent than before.

She broke away and led him toward a rocky area of the beach, where several boulders projected into the sea like a natural jetty. Tide pools formed near the natural coves in the rock formations, filled with warm water from the sun's rays. When she'd come out here in March, she and Beatrice had combed through these tide pools, looking for clams near the rocks.

She led him toward a low, flat boulder and sat him down facing the sea. With a hint of a smile, she stood in front of him and pushed his jacket away. She unbuttoned his shirt deftly, but it took his help to remove the undershirt.

She didn't mean to gasp at the scars on his shoulder and chest, but she did. The whitened scar tissue still looked new and angry. She traced a finger over the one by his shoulder. "How did your arm heal?"

Goose bumps rose on his skin under her fingertip. "I still can't lift it over my head. But it's not much, compared to what it could have been." He grinned and turned her in his arms so they faced the same direction. "Because of you." He placed a kiss near her jaw, below her earlobe, and kissed down the length of her neck, sending shivers down her spine. "It's your turn." He tugged at the buttons on the back of her dress.

"My turn for what?" She teased him with a smile, which turned into a laugh as he peeled her dress away. An excited thrill coursed through her. It had been so long since they'd been together, she'd expected to feel shy. Yet there wasn't any self-consciousness at all, just the comfort that came so naturally to her when they were in each other's company.

"Why on earth do women wear so many layers of clothing?" His grumble sounded deep in his chest as his hands settled at her hips, smoothing over her curves.

She stepped away from him and finished the process herself. "To frustrate our lovers. Or enforce chastity." She looked over her shoulder at him.

His eyes roamed her body appreciatively before he gathered her into his arms, his hands settling on her firm breasts. "Is that what you want?"

"Not at all. But now you're the one who's overdressed." She tilted her face toward his as their lips met. She returned his kiss eagerly, her arm wrapping up and back around his neck as the rough palms of his hands grazed over her skin.

He paused and swung her into his arms, then tossed her into one of the deeper tide pools. She shrieked, landing with a splash, the warm water to her shoulders as she sat. "Hilarious. You're lucky you didn't throw me on top of a pinching crab."

He smiled and removed his trousers, before wading in beside her. "I'll be more than happy to pinch you myself if you'd like." His hands glided behind her back before settling on her hips. He pushed her knees apart, setting her feet on either side of him. A quick lift brought her onto his lap.

A soft moan escaped her, and she gripped his neck, her eyes locked with his. "Impatient?" She fitted her mouth over his, sinking into the familiarity of his touch, the smoothness of their lovemaking.

"Famished." His lips trailed over her shoulder. "But if we only have this one night, I intend to make the most of it."

The sun made one final burst of light, the sky reminding her of a watercolor painting, an explosion of color. Her body, flushed and tingling, seemed to forget the difficult days behind them, the challenges still before them, as they surrendered themselves entirely to each other.

When they climbed out of the water, he gave her his shirt to wear and put on his trousers once again. They settled against the sand. She nestled her head against his chest, watching as the stars emerged. "Where will you go after this?"

"The same places they've assigned me the last few months: Cairo, Jerusalem, Aleppo. The desert. Never Alexandria."

She shook her head. "It's as though someone doesn't want you there."

He chuckled, resting his chin on the top of her head. "It wasn't easy coordinating a way to see you. But between the battles, there hasn't been the time either."

Although it had become an unconscious habit, she felt for the scar on her chest. "And no word on Stephen?"

"He's disappeared for now." Noah interlaced the fingers of his hand with hers, staring for a moment at the ring he'd given her. "But Lord Helton never put me on the hunt for him. He wanted me to move on to other assignments." He shifted her onto the sand and looked at her. "I'm not sure when or how, but I fear he'll return at some point. The thought keeps me awake more often than I'd like to admit."

She nodded. "I have nightmares about it. I don't feel safe ever."

"Lord Helton has good men keeping your family safe. They're protected." He pressed his forehead against hers. "And I'll always find my way back to you, Ginger. I promise. I won't let him or anyone else ever get between us. As long as I'm breathing, I'll be thinking of a way to come home to you."

Come home.

She kissed him, his words ringing true. She'd thought of home as a house and a name. It wasn't. Home was in their interwoven hearts, in their love.

Ginger closed her eyes, her shoulders falling back. In the distance, gunfire popped. The war raged on, but the day had brought a tide of hope not only to a sea of tired soldiers but their country, and to her. Even in the darkest days, when betrayal and death had nearly swept her away, hope had persisted. What had been carried off in the Arabian winds had been replaced with a love she'd never expected. And with Noah by her side, the quiet promise of dawn awaited.

AUTHOR'S NOTE

Though set during the British Gaza Campaign in World War I, *Windswept* is a work of historical fiction. As such, I have occasionally taken artistic liberties with actual events for the sake of the narrative.

In writing historical fiction, one of the concepts that has often held my attention the most is that of "what if." It's known that a great deal of intrigue occurred in the Middle Eastern theater of the Great War. But for the historically minded, here are some notes:

Stephen's story is loosely based off the efforts of Max von Oppenheim. In the beginning of the war, Oppenheim attempted to stir the Arab world, especially in Egypt, against the British colonizers. He was considered a spy by the French and British. His efforts failed and he had largely abandoned those pursuits by 1917.

My thought in creating Stephen's background and role started with the question of "what if" someone else had taken up that leadership position and continued the efforts? There were many who still wanted to pursue those goals such as

Mohammad Farid, an Egyptian political leader exiled in Germany at the time. Thus the concept of the *Maslukha* was born.

T.E. Lawrence, while now the most famous political figure from the Arabian front, was not actually as well-known during the war itself. Much of what we now know about Lawrence's work came from the publication of his memoir, *The Seven Pillars of Wisdom* in 1926. I took the liberty of implying that people within Arabia (and specifically Cairo Intelligence and the Arab Bureau) would have known the importance of his work and his role as a figurehead. It's not too far of a stretch: King George V did attempt to knight Lawrence in 1918.

The Zionist organization that was used as inspiration for Ahmed's work was the NILI spy network. On the subject of spies for NILI, while I couldn't include Sarah Aaronsohn's fascinating tale, it's worth a read.

The khamsin Noah and Ginger go through is historically documented as are the aerial bombardments of the camp at Deir el Belah in May 1917. The dispensary tent destruction occurred in April 1917, as recorded in the diaries of Australian Ion Idriess published as *The Desert Column*. I combined the bombardments and shelling for the sake of the narrative.

In all my research, what I couldn't find was definitive proof of the presence of QA nurses at the CCS in Belah in May 1917. However, nurses were assigned throughout that region and made their way to Jerusalem by 1918. Because nursing units had become a part of the clearing stations by the time the novel opens, I made the choice to include nurses accordingly.

* * *

Thanks so much for reading *Windswept*! I hope you enjoyed reading it as much as I enjoyed writing it. I'm always grateful for your enthusiastic reviews and ratings if you're willing to take the time to post a quick one at the retailer where you bought this book. Your good review helps me able to keep writing more books!

If you'd like to keep in touch or find out the latest about my new releases, please sign up for my newsletter! I love hearing from readers and have some great offers and giveaways lined up for my subscribers.

The next book in the series, *Sands of Sirocco*, will be released 9/27/22 but you can pre-order it at your favorite retailer.

ACKNOWLEDGMENTS

In the 20 years that Ginger and Noah have been tugging at my daydreams, there have been many people who have humored me by talking about them, reading pages, and giving me their support. They include:

Bill Bernhardt, Susanne Lakin, and Robin Seavill, whose editorial notes and guidance were absolutely invaluable in bringing these pages to life.

To Patrick Knowles, thank you for making a brilliant cover design. Working with you was wonderful!

Phil Rosensteel, there's no one I would trust more to make my book trailer dreams come true. Thanks for being a wonderful friend and collaborating with me in so many creative projects throughout the years.

The Red Pen Crew: Jaclyn, Anne, Andie, Cory, and Bob. Your encouragement, critique, and support resurrected an old dream.

My amazing beta readers who took the time to not only read my book (sometimes more than once) but also gave me their thoughtful feedback.

My mother, who nurtured a love of reading in me, and whose inspirational story deserves a book of its own.

My sister, Christi, who had the guts to tell me when I was far off-track and helped bring out the best version of many, many drafts.

And, last, but not the least: my husband, Patrick. Your love and support has been everything to me. Thank you for being my home.

ABOUT THE AUTHOR

Annabelle McCormack writes to bring under-explored periods of history to life. She is a graduate of the Johns Hopkins University's M.A. in Writing Program. She lives in Maryland with her hilarious husband, where she serves as a snack bitch for her (lucky-they're-cute) five children.

Visit her at www.annabellemccormack.com or http://instagram.com/annabellemccormack to follow her daily adventures.

CPSIA information can be obtained
at www.ICGtesting.com
Printed in the USA
BVHW040736211022
649669BV00006B/94